Once Upon an Austin Night

Daniel Lance Wright

ISBN: 978-1-62420-414-2

Credits
Cover Artist: Designs by Ms G
Editor: Amanda Armstrong

Chapter One

"I can't believe that idiot judge set bail for Ortiz," Jimmy Fenn said. "I may not be the brightest bulb on the tree, but even I saw this jump coming." He glanced to his rearview mirror and cut across a lane of traffic, shearing onto the entrance ramp at high speed up onto the Interstate en route to their destination—approximately thirty minutes south of Austin, Texas. The big V-8 engine roared in response to Fenn's hard acceleration. He quickly assimilated, blending with heavy fast moving traffic, and began working his way to the inside against a concrete barrier separating southbound from northbound lanes. Once to the inside, he pushed his speed upward. He sped southward heading for Manuel Ortiz's suspected hideout in New Braunfels offered up by an informant, almost fifty miles down the highway. Once Jimmy did not have to watch traffic so intensely, he looked sideways at his partner on the passenger side, thirty-seven-year-old Carlee Cayne. "What's your take on it, Cayne?"

Carlee glanced at him. "Take? I'm not allowed a *take*. All my decisions on this situation, or any other for that matter, come in the field on how best to handle the decisions and orders of others above my pay grade," she replied, glancing again, seeing he must have noted her dour mood.

"Come on. It's just you and me here. Don't you have an opinion?" he asked.

"Of course I do. But what difference does it make? At the end of the day, the result should be that we found Ortiz, slapped the cuffs on him, and then took him in to be locked up. This is what we're paid to do as deputy marshals in the field, not second guessing a federal judge's decision on whether bail should have been denied or not."

Jimmy Fenn held a gaze on Carlee for an inordinate amount of time, considering the speed he drove in relatively heavy Interstate traffic, constantly weaving in and out of slower moving vehicles. "You seem a might touchy this morning."

Carlee sighed. "Sorry, Jimbo. Didn't mean to snap at you." She bobbled her head. "If you must know my opinion, I agree with you. That judge *was* an idiot for letting Ortiz post bond pending trial. The judge might as well have shouted, 'Fly! Be free!' from the bench. Once the judge discovered Ortiz's link to that drug cartel kingpin, he had to have known Ortiz was a flight risk. So, yeah. That makes the judge an idiot, in my opinion." Carlee paused and smiled warmly at Fenn. "You're a good partner, Jimbo, and have been for...what, six years now?"

"Thereabouts."

Carlee appreciated her long-time partner. Jimmy Fenn was an unencumbered thirty-five-year-old single guy. He was extremely good-looking, drawing stares from passers-by all the time. He had dark hair, always neatly trimmed to a professional length, slender, and quite tall at six-three. Unfortunately, he was also totally unavailable to date. Even thinking about that, today, was an irritant. He was her best friend, for God's sake. Why couldn't he be her boyfriend, too? "My pissy mood certainly has nothing to do with you, my friend. It's what Turner told me before he put us in charge of this operation."

"Eh, don't pay any attention to him. He just has a twisted sense of humor."

"To you it's a sense of humor. To me it's just twisted. He's sexist and that *twisted* sense of humor, as you call it, *always* seems to be directed at me, like I'm some ditz from a secretarial pool."

"Really? Is it that bad? What the heck did he tell you?"

"Just before we left headquarters a few minutes ago, he pulled me off to the side and whispered in my ear, 'Now, darlin', try not to shoot yourself or kill anyone today,'" she drawled sardonically, impersonating her supervisor's arrogant tone. "Jimbo, I do *not* like Supervising Deputy, George Turner, *at all*." She turned to look out the window and added, mumbling, "The sleazy bastard."

Fenn snapped a fast hard look sideways at her. "Are you serious? He said it just like that?"

"Yep. Just like that." She frowned at Fenn. "Get that slack-jawed look off your face. Surely, you can't be *that* surprised."

"I know he has hit on you a few times, but I had no idea that he impugns your job performance."

"He most certainly does, on a regular basis. I have a feeling his snarkiness is nothing more than cheap shots in retaliation for my refusals of his disgustingly frequent indecent proposals. I never give him satisfaction of a verbal response—just walk away, not smiling, not frowning, nothing. It pisses him off. I can tell. And, after shooting and wounding that guy in the spring and then that other one I had to kill last month, it has provided Turner with a wealth of material to use when sniping at me."

"Those were justified—both times. You had no choice in either case whatsoever, for Christ's sake. I was there. I witnessed both shootings. I know. Either one of those boys would have killed you, or me, if you had not put them down."

"I know," Carlee deadpanned. "But that doesn't stop Turner." She sighed. "I'm getting tired of this job...damn tired."

"Hey, don't talk like that," Fenn whined. "If you leave the Marshals Service, what'll happen to me? I don't want to break in a new partner."

Carlee laughed melodramatically. "Oh sure. Let's make this about you." She sighed. "Honestly though, I don't think you need to worry. This is all I know how to do. If I left the Service, all I could do is jump from one law enforcement job to another, if I could even find one. And, if I'm tired of this job, how could that be an improvement, not to mention the hassle of it all? In the beginning, I didn't think I'd be at this job for as long as I have. I really thought David and I would have had a couple of kids by now and I would be knee deep in soccer, softball, parties, school functions, and holidays...you know, living the housewife's dream."

"Thanks to Rylee, that sweet girl of yours, part of that dream will come true anyhow. That's something you need to hear spoken aloud, I think, especially now."

Carlee stared at her partner for a couple of seconds. She drew a sincere heartfelt smile. "I suppose you're right. Thank you for that."

"As for David, that good-for-nothing ex-husband of yours," Fenn continued, "was a dick and probably still is. I knew it before he walked out on you. But, it wasn't my place to convince you. It broke my heart watching you go through that divorce. It has taken you a long time to regain your footing after the breakup a couple of years ago."

"That sure is the truth. Poor Rylee has not gotten over it yet."

"Have you sat her down and explained it all to her in terms a ten-year-old girl can understand?"

"Jimmy Fenn," she said and then paused, staring at him incredulously, "don't tell me you think I'm a ditz, too. *Of course*, I've explained it to her. She and I have had marathon discussions about it. I have explained it to her forty ways from sundown. She understands it intellectually but not in her heart. To her, it's like having a limb suddenly removed. She can understand how—maybe even why it happened—but it doesn't make the pain of loss any less."

"Sorry. I didn't mean it to sound like a parenting critique." He said no more, clearly leaving the subject where it belonged, in the rearview mirror with everything else shrinking away behind them as they sped southward.

After a quiet minute, *"Three* years, actually," Carlee said.

"Excuse me?"

"I've been divorced three years, not two." Carlee sighed. "In hindsight, I wish you *would have* gotten in the middle of my business when you saw it coming. Clearly, I did not, but...oh well." She gazed at Fenn quietly, with a questioning face, for a moment.

Fenn looked across at her in flicking glances. "What? Why are looking at me like that?"

"I wish you weren't into guys."

"Oh, that. Not only am I gay, I don't want to get married, period—man or woman. I don't even want a dog, for Christ's sake. I'm happy with my single situation, approaching ecstatic, actually." He grinned smugly. "I don't want a relationship beyond a couple of months. If I want to climb on a jet and fly to Tahiti this afternoon, I can do it...with supervisory blessing, of course. I don't need to clear it with anyone outside the Service. Just do it. Now that, sweet friend, is livin' the dream."

"For you, maybe." She paused and thought about Fenn's situation for a second. She added, "I didn't know there were that many gay guys in Austin. I keep thinking you're going to run out of choices."

4

Fenn lifted an eyebrow and grinned. "Never happen."

Carlee stared down the highway, watching the intermittent dashed lane markings blur beneath the car. She realized if this conversation went any further, it might drive her into a funk that may create hesitation at the wrong time. She had to get her head in this game or suffer dangerously negative consequences. She unsnapped the keeper strap on the holster holding her Glock 40 sidearm, released the magazine, and popped it out of the handgrip, checking its load, making sure it held a full complement of ammunition. It was a habit, a ritual she went through before each operation of this nature. At a glance, all was as it should be. She snugged the magazine back into its handgrip cradle, slapping it with the heel of her hand. It clicked into place securely. She then returned it to the holster on her hip, strapping it and then snapping it down. "I think I had better table this conversation for another time, before it clouds my judgment. Where was it Ortiz found to hole up?"

"The Ortiz brothers have a cousin in New Braunfels, Daniel Vega. It's just luck we found out about it so quickly. Otherwise, Manuel would have been across the border into Mexico, right into the protective arms of his brother, the cartel king, before we could act to apprehend him. Vega rents a house in an older part of New Braunfels."

"I heard Turner talking about that cartel. According to what he was saying, Rogelio Ortiz is one bad dude," she said.

"Ruthless for sure," replied Fenn. "Then again," he added, "all those types have to be ruthless to build an illegal empire of such scope. Not only must they keep eyes open for law enforcement but, also, from rival factions looking to move in like hyenas over a carcass. It's a dangerous world they create for themselves." He paused. "I wonder what the average life span is of those guys."

"Don't know. But, it would not surprise me to learn surviving to their fiftieth year, for most of them, to be an extraordinary feat," she replied. "Did I hear right? It was Vega's neighbors who didn't like the idea of Manuel Ortiz possibly taking up residence on their street?"

"Uh-huh. Little did the neighbors know it was only temporary while Rogelio got resources to Manuel so he could skip the country. It worked out well for us, timing-wise."

"Incidentally," Carlee said, "you just answered your own question."

"Huh?"

"About bail not being denied," she said. "Rogelio's drug cartel is very prosperous, operating across the border from Del Rio in Ciudad Acuña. Rogelio secured a high-priced attorney from some firm in San Antonio, convincing the judge Manuel was no flight risk and managed to have bail set."

"That I didn't know," Fenn said. "But there's no way he's going to avoid prison time for that string of violent armed robberies."

"True enough. It's also the reason he jumped bail and we find ourselves chasing him down to take him back. Once we do, Manuel Ortiz will not see the light of day before, *or after*, the trial for many years. I have a feeling he will be a might testy about going back with us."

Fenn glanced at her. "Ya think?"

"Where is Vega's place?" Carlee asked.

"It's in a rundown neighborhood near the Guadalupe River, probably the oldest area of New Braunfels. I was briefed before you came in to work this morning." Fenn tilted his head thoughtfully. "In fact, you seem to be late to work quite often these days. Does that have anything to do with George Turner?"

"It has *everything* to do with the jerk. The less I'm around Turner, the happier I am."

"Ah. That explains that. Anyhow, Daniel Vega's place is an old shotgun style house. You know the type, a house with two front doors side by side."

"Just point it out to me when we get there. What about backup?"

"Local police, Texas Rangers, and State Troopers have been notified. They're ready to move in as we speak. We just have to meet up with them at a predesignated place, and close in together as a unit."

Fenn peeled off, exiting the Interstate in New Braunfels and met up with other law enforcement in the parking lot of an agreed upon convenience store. It only took a couple of minutes to coordinate the operation. "Follow me," announced a local police officer, as he dropped into the driver's seat of his city cruiser, the lead car. Jimmy Fenn and Carlee Cayne followed closely with two other cars behind them. They had not driven far when the lead officer eased over against the curb and stopped in the older residential neighborhood. Cottonwood, oak, and pecan trees were huge. Some were dead and obviously had been for years, standing like nightmarish behemoths—another indication of the age of this neighborhood. Several of the houses were abandoned and yards overgrown. The New Braunfels officer slid out of his cruiser. His movements slowed. He crouched and glided, pistol held down to his side, displaying cautious stealth. He stabbed the air with a firm, stiff finger pointing to one house three down from where he'd parked.

"Showtime," Fenn said, as he got out of the car. He closed the car door with a light hand.

Carlee got out and met up with him at the rear of the vehicle. He opened the trunk. Inside lay items necessary to such an operation. He handed Carlee a Kevlar vest and retrieved two short-barrel 12-guage pump shotguns. These were assault weapons—no fore-pieces. Instead, these weapons were fitted with perpendicular handgrips for maximum control to chamber shells quickly when needed. After strapping her vest on, Jimmy Fenn handed her the other shotgun. She jacked a shell into the chamber. "Let's go get this done," she said.

"I'll lead the breach, Cayne. You did last time," Fenn said. He quickly slid the pump on the shotgun back then forward, chambering a shell. "How about you go around back so we can keep Ortiz buttoned up in there?"

Carlee did not answer, simply responded, peeling away from the single-file string of heavily armed law enforcement personnel. Alone, she trotted to the side of the house and up an old, cracked, and heaved double ribbon concrete driveway nearly camouflaged by overgrown Bermuda grass and a variety of invasive creeping weeds. She stopped short of a dilapidated one-car detached garage, yawing to a severe angle. The structure set back and to the left of the house. Clearly, it had not been used to park cars in for decades and should have been demolished years ago. She backed up and leaned against the blistered and peeling white paint on the back corner of the old house. She drew a deep breath, releasing it slowly through rounded lips. She craned her head around the corner to scope possible egress points Manuel Ortiz might use. Windows lining her side of the house were all obviously sealed with multiple layers of paint slathered on over decades. None had been opened in many years. That was clear enough. Carlee assumed all the windows on the other side of the house had to be in the same condition. If so, the only other escape route for Ortiz narrowed quickly to the back door, centered at the rear of the house, or diving through one of those windows. There was no porch. A pumice construction block laying on its side served as a step down out of the higher-than-normal pier and beam house. Judging by a dense stand of unkempt crepe myrtle bushes, standing as tall as trees at the opposite corner of the house, and a back gate chained with a padlock binding it, it seemed the only reasonable escape route out of the yard would be directly toward her. That was a good thing, if Ortiz bolted.

This thought had scarcely completed when she heard a hard rap on the front door. Fenn shouted, "Daniel Vega—US Marshals—open up!"

She heard the front door open and a conversation ensued that she could not make out. But, then she heard fast moving footsteps pounding the old wooden floor toward the rear of the house. She shouted as loud as she could, "He's running! Back door! Back door!" Her warning was followed by thunderous pounding of many footsteps racing through the house toward the back door. She rolled around the corner and squared her stance, holding the gun high, ready for whoever appeared. She had a clear lateral view of whoever might come racing out that door. She didn't know if it would be Daniel Vega or Manuel Ortiz that would appear, but she figured it had to be Ortiz. He had the most to lose.

Fenn shouted from inside the house, "Stop, Ortiz! Freeze!"

At that instant, the rickety and tattered screen door at the rear of the house swung open and slammed against the house. Manuel Ortiz appeared, leaping to the ground right over that makeshift construction block step to the ground.

Carlee saw he brandished a semi-automatic handgun in one hand and a machete in the other. "Drop your weapons!" she ordered.

Ortiz spun to face her. He did not comply, snapping the pistol to firing height, aiming in her direction.

Fenn came flying out the back door at the same instant, clearly misjudging the drop. He stumbled and was falling.

Ortiz reacted, swinging the pistol toward Fenn.

In that brief flash of time, Fenn squeezed off a round from the shotgun. The shot went wild as he tumbled to the ground.

Ortiz fired almost simultaneously at Fenn.

Carlee followed by firing a twelve-gauge load of double-aught buckshot into Manuel Ortiz's midsection.

The unfolding scenario slipped into slow motion as Ortiz flew backwards, landing hard onto the grassless ground. He grimaced. His face could not get any tighter. He put both hands over the wound and pulled his knees up, squealing in pain. And then, after scant seconds, he stopped screaming. His face relaxed. His hands fell away from the bloody wound as his knees fell sideways. If he wasn't dead already, he would be shortly.

All the support personnel streamed out the back door, lowering their weapons as they stepped into the yard, spotting the body of Manuel Ortiz. One ran to him and kicked the gun a safe distance away, just in case.

Carlee ran over to where Jimmy Fenn lay on his back. "Jimbo, Jimbo," she shouted. "Are you hit?"

"The only thing that hit me was the ground. My pride is injured, but nothing else." Fenn rolled his head to meet her manic expression. "It's okay, really. He didn't hit me."

Carlee dropped to her knees beside him, placed her shotgun on the ground. Her head wilted forward appreciatively. "Thank God. I thought he hit you squarely."

"Nah. I just fell out the back door. If you had not put him down, he would have taken a second shot and, at that range, he would have put a bullet between my eyes." He came up to recline on his elbows. "I owe you my life, Cayne. Thanks."

Carlee straightened and sat back on her heels. Pent up tension left her as adrenaline drained away. She slumped her head forward, taking a few calming breaths, exhaling through rounded lips. She then looked over at the lifeless body of Manuel Ortiz. "Crap."

"What?" Fenn asked. "Are you upset he didn't take that second shot?"

"No, funny man, that's not it at all. That's the third man I've shot this year. Two are dead and one is still on crutches. Do you realize what this means in this politically correct environment we live in these days?"

"Don't think that way. You have all the testimony you need to justify this shooting." He pointed to the other law enforcement personnel. One was reading Daniel Vega his rights for aiding and abetting a known fugitive, his cousin, Manuel Ortiz. Another was cuffing him, while two of the other guys were talking on their phones. "All of those guys will testify on your behalf."

Daniel Vega seemed stupefied, staring at his dead cousin. No matter how they turned him, Vega's eyes remained fixed on the body of Ortiz. He mumbled almost continuously, "Manny, Manny. What have they done to you? Manny, Manny."

"It's great that I'll have all the supporting testimony needed," Carlee said, "but it's not entirely what I was talking about. One of the guys I had to use force against and died was a black man, the injured one is a Latino, and then, of course we have Ortiz over there. They're all minorities, Jimbo. Even if things go perfectly, I bet Turner won't hesitate to put me on desk duty for an indefinite period." She rolled her eyes. "And he would likely relish having me so near every day, all day long. I don't think I could stand him for a single week, much less a month or two."

"Come on, now," Fenn said, coming to his feet. "Don't talk like that. I've got your back. None of those shootings were about race. It was about criminals with extraordinarily bad attitudes and hate for law enforcement. We'll face it together, whatever they throw at you. You know that." He dusted his pants and stepped toward her.

Carlee relaxed somewhat on those encouraging words. She sighed, turning away to walk toward the car. Fenn hurried to her side. She smiled at him and nudged him with her shoulder. "You've always had my back," she said. "You're a good partner and a great friend, Jimmy Fenn."

"And you've always had *my* back. Case in point..." He gestured back toward Ortiz's body.

Carlee hinted a smile. "What would it take to make you un-gay?"

"I'll be your friend, no matter what," he replied.

"I realize that, but...well, you know," she said, bobbling her head.

Fenn laughed. "Yeah. I do." He nudged her back.

Chapter Two

Forty-two-year-old Lincoln Bridger sat with his chin in his hand, staring out the fifth-floor window across Lady Bird Lake on the Colorado River. His eyes traced the Austin, Texas downtown skyline. His mind was elsewhere, not what he gazed upon. He rhythmically drummed fingertips of his free hand on the desktop, thinking about the events of earlier. *There should be more to life than arguing with Jeannine until exhaustion drags me down at night. And then, wake up in the morning to pick up where we left off the night before.*

"I'd offer you a penny for your thoughts, but I'm afraid I would be disappointed, and out a penny. Would I be?" said friend and coworker, Ben Fitzsimmons, coming into his office.

Lincoln startled and sat straight. "Aw, hey, Fitz. Mornin'." He smirked. "My thoughts ain't worth your hard-earned penny."

"Whew! Good to know. I was almost out a perfectly good copper coin. What the heck would you be thinking so seriously about this early in the day? It couldn't have anything to do with the Monolith spark plug account, or would it? It's already in the bag. In fact, I thought old man Adler was going to give you a big wet kiss over that one."

"Nah, it's not about work at all. Jeannine and I have been fighting again."

"Good grief, man," Fitz said. "Is that all you two ever do?"

Lincoln shrugged his shoulders. "It sure seems that way. Our worlds grow farther apart with every passing day."

"Anything I can do to help?"

"I appreciate it, but I don't know what it would be, other than keep on being the friend I can talk to without chewing on my ear and drawing blood."

"That's no problem. In fact, any tree in the park can serve that purpose." Fitz laughed.

"Ha-ha. Real funny." Lincoln paused. "I should have realized when Jeannine and I got married nineteen years ago the lives we came from were too different, radically different actually. I think all we ever truly had was sexual heat. Even that, these days, is tepid. But in the beginning, as is usually the case, young, horny, and stupid won out. Our ways of looking at the world don't jive at all, never have. Her notions of *needs* versus *wants* are a world apart from the way I view things. Coming from a wealthy family, and all that sort of thing, you know."

"I certainly cannot disagree. How many discount shoe stores does the Rosen family own now?" Fitz took a seat on the corner of Lincoln's desk, one foot on the floor.

"Twenty-two, I think. Not sure. Jeannine's dad, Saul, had been discussing adding locations in north Texas. I've heard him mention Lubbock or Amarillo, maybe both. I don't know if he has followed through yet or not. One way or the other, Saul and Lidia Rosen have more money than entire treasuries of many third world countries."

"Don't knock it. Marrying into the Rosen family got you this job," Fitz said, as he twirled a ballpoint pen atop the highly polished surface of Lincoln's desk.

"Yeah. I'm not denying it. Have I ever told you the whole story?"

"No. Just that you brought to this agency all of Rosen's huge advertising budget."

"After Jeannine and I got married, Saul knew I was interested in the advertising agency business. He put his arm around me and told me I needed to apply for an account executive position with this firm, and I needed to do it in a face to face meeting with Stuart Adler. Stuart and Saul knew one another from the country club and Adler had propositioned him several times, attempting to get the Rosen ad budget away from a Houston advertising agency. Saul even told me exactly how to work it by saying, 'When Adler asks you about your experience in the advertising business, tell him with confidence, within one month you can bring Adler, Howard and Levy Advertising Agency seven to ten-million dollars in annual billing.' Adler gave me the job on a ninety-day trial basis on the weight of that boast."

"Old man Adler should not have been surprised when, two weeks later, you brought in the Rosen Family Footwear account, worth about eight and a half million in annual billing."

"The thing was, Fitz, Mister Adler had no idea Saul Rosen was my father-in-law back then. It doesn't matter now though, because I have worked my ass off to prove my value to the company in other ways and securing many other accounts over the past fifteen years."

"I know you have, buddy." Fitz looked through the glass wall fronting Lincoln's office into the common area.

Lincoln's eyes followed his. It was Betty Jaworski heading straight for them, holding two tall paper cups.

"Uh-oh. Here comes your favorite stalker," Fitz said. "I think this is a good time for me to go to my office and get some work done." He stepped toward the door.

"Don't you dare leave me alone with her," Lincoln whispered, hissing through clenched teeth.

"Good morning, Betty," Fitz said in sing-song fashion as he walked by her, stepping out of Lincoln's office. "Linc is all yours. I'm done with him."

As Fitz walked away, he looked back over his shoulder with a stupid grin on his face and bouncing his eyebrows at Lincoln.

Lincoln gave his friend the best go-to-hell expression he could muster.

"Got some coffee for you, sweetie." Betty leaned across Lincoln's desk and set the cup in front of him, all the while putting on a show, her ample cleavage stuffed inside a low cut pink sweater, too low cut and quite inappropriate for the work place.

"Thanks, Betty. That was thoughtful," he said, trying not to maintain eye contact beyond appreciative glances. It wouldn't take much for Betty to misconstrue it as sexual interest in her.

Still leaning across the desk, "My pleasure, sweetie. I stopped at that little sandwich shop and coffee bar down on the corner. Their coffee is so much better than the stuff brewed here in the break room."

Lincoln pulled the top off the cup and took a sip. "I can't argue with that. This is good. Thanks."

Betty was not a bad looking woman—tall, slender, fifty-something, and always with perfectly coiffed hair, appearing to have been sprayed stiff. It also changed colors about once a month. On this day it was copper red, like a new penny. Her bright red lipstick on her smooth pale face was, perhaps, too stark of a contrast. Lincoln did respect her ability as the company's chief accountant and bookkeeper. She managed a department of three.

"I hear you're having a little trouble at home?" she asked. "Anything you want to talk about? I'm a good listener." She stood straight and held her coffee cup high, appearing to nestle it between her breasts.

Every move Betty Jaworski made was in-your-face suggestive in a sexual way. His friend, Ben Fitzsimmons was not far off the mark when he quipped about her being a stalker. "Where did you hear that I'm having trouble at home?" he asked.

"Oh, here and there. Word gets around." She pushed her lip into a mock pout. "The point is, doll, I want to be your ear, your shoulder to cry on, your confidant, anything you need, sugar...*anything.*"

On that comment, Lincoln squirmed. He saw his boss, Stuart Adler approach. He called out before Adler had reached his door, "Come in, Mister Adler, please."

Betty took a sip of her coffee and whispered, "Think about it, hon." She winked at him. "See you later." She sashayed past Adler on her way out. "Good morning, Sir."

Adler nodded. "Betty..." He watched her walk away then turned back to Lincoln while lifting a thumb over his shoulder toward Betty. "What was that all about?"

Lincoln took a deep breath and huffed it away. "Nothing, Sir. Absolutely nothing. But, let me add, your timing is appreciated." He took a long pull from the coffee cup. "Ah, I'm better now. I'll just say Betty is great at what she does in accounting and leave it at that. What can I do for you, Sir?"

"I was thinking more in terms of what it is that I might do for you. You've appeared pensive the past couple of days, maybe even a bit sad. Anything I can help with?" Adler asked.

"Oh, thanks for caring enough to notice, but no. It's a personal problem. A little trouble at home. That's all. I'll try harder not to bring it to work with me. I had no idea it was so noticeable."

"Lincoln, you're the best account executive this firm has, even factoring out the Rosen Family Shoe account. Not only that, I like you as a person. So, I hate to see you stressing over...well, anything."

"Thank you, Sir. That alone makes me feel better."

Adler put a thoughtful finger to his lips. "Maybe I do have a suggestion. What type of physical exercise regimen are you on?"

"No regimen really. I jog around the neighborhood a couple of evenings a week. I'm sporadic about it though," Lincoln replied.

"Then why don't you take advantage of our corporate discount at Power House Fitness Center?" He pointed out Lincoln's office window. "It's right across the river and very convenient to this building. You could drop by after work every day and work off some of that stress. It works for me." Adler crossed his arms over his chest, as if to suggest he would not take *no* for an answer. Adler was a consummate deal-closer and knew the last one to speak was the loser of any negotiation. He obviously was not about to add anything to what he had already said until he received a reply from Lincoln.

"It's a great idea, Mister Adler, but I don't—"

"Tell you what, Lincoln, take your buddy Fitz right now, drive over there and fill out a membership application and the company will cover the sign-up fee and the entire membership for the first year. How could you possibly pass up an offer like that?" Adler asked.

"I can't." Lincoln lightly slapped the desktop and stood. "All right, I'll do it." He shielded his mouth with the back of his hand and whispered, "But let's do it mostly for Fitz. The boy is getting a might pudgy."

Adler pulled a half-grin and tapped the side of his nose with a knowing fingertip and winked.

Lincoln walked past his boss toward the door of his office. "I'll get Fitz. We'll be back in about an hour. Thanks, Boss."

~ * ~

"How the heck did I get myself into this?" Fitz asked.

Lincoln smiled at his friend and co-worker, but didn't take his eyes from his route, as he steered his dark blue BMW sedan into the parking lot of Austin's Power House Fitness Center on the downtown side of the Colorado River. "Don't look at it like a sweat-inducing chore that must be endured. It'll be fun. Promise. Look at it like a favor to me. You can help keep me focused on stress reduction. You may not think you need it, but I do. Besides, it'll be easier to be regular with a friend...subtle peer pressure, let's say."

"The problem is, Linc, you look fine in a tee and shorts. Me? Not so much. I need to be in better shape before I expose this body to public scrutiny."

Lincoln chortled. "Do you realize how silly that sounds? Would you rather go to a grubby little corner gym somewhere and get into shape before suiting up here?" He laughed. "Get serious, man. We're here specifically to feel better and, yes, look better in our t-shirts and shorts."

"What if there are good looking women in there? Hard bodies, potential dating material, that sort of thing."

"I'm fairly certain there will be." Lincoln noticed Fitz, as silly as his concern was, seemed to be taking it seriously. "Look, you need this as much as I do, but for your own reasons. In an odd way, you're telling me all the reasons you *should* begin a workout regimen. Enjoy it. Have fun. You don't have to kill yourself to impress anyone...other than yourself, of course." Lincoln pulled into a parking slot, stopped, and shoved the gear selector into the park position. "Here's something else to consider. Adler is paying the sign-up fee, plus, first year dues for both of us. That means there is no reason you couldn't afford the help of a personal trainer a couple of times a week." He opened the car door and got out.

Fitz got out and looked across the roof of the car at him. "Humph. You're beginning to make sense. I don't like it when you make sense. That usually turns into a problem for me. My preferred sport in high school was chasing girls. Later, I added weekend beer-chugging to my repertoire of sports during my college years."

Lincoln laughed.

Fitz offered a listless smile. "This is definitely *not* going to be easy for me, ya know."

"Nothing worth having ever is. Come on, let's check this place out." Lincoln took the shortest route, angling across the parking lot, zigzagging around parked cars to the main entrance and stepped through the parting automatic sliding glass doors but stopped just inside to scope the place.

It was early, just now approaching noon. Judging by the number of cars parked outside and a throng of people milling about the foyer, it appeared the lunch hour was a rush period for the gym. Lincoln glanced back through the sliding door to the street and the skyline beyond it. The sun had reached its daily zenith, now tipping over to the western side of the sky. Other than old Sol, wispy clouds were the only other adornment in the brilliant sky and, of course, that jet that had just taken off from the airport a few miles away. The first month of spring was almost over. Days were getting longer and warmer.

As Lincoln stood and scanned the goings-on inside Power House Fitness Center, a cool brush of air flowed down over him and the pleasant aroma of air freshener, something akin to an island breeze coming off the surf or, maybe, a spring morning after an overnight rain, nothing flowery, just clean and refreshing, a great first impression. His background in marketing told him it was an intentional tool to relax and welcome visitors upon entering. He believed it a good one. The area nearest the front door was dedicated to product, racks of men's and women's exercise apparel, shelves loaded with vitamins and supplements, plus various exercise aids such as arm and leg bands, arch supports, and half gloves for weightlifting, among other things. As he and Fitz moved through the large front area, they slowed their pace and changed direction toward a tall black counter topped with red Formica. Two young guys were busy inputting data into computer terminals atop the counter. But it was the attractive young Latina arranging stacks of brochures announcing various courses and classes on the back counter that captured and held Lincoln's attention. The three employees were all dressed the same, black T-shirts with red company logos and black workout shorts. Each was a walking billboard for their craft and company, lean and muscular. But, the fetching young Latina could easily boast the added allure of feminine beauty. It seemed only right to walk directly toward her. He assumed she would be the perfect choice to ask questions of.

Fitz's head was in constant motion, looking around the visible parts of the facility. "Nice place. Not sure I could have afforded this if I had to pay for it."

"Of course you could. You're single. What else would you spend your money on?"

"Uh...do I really need to go over that beer-chugging part of my preferred sport again?"

"What can I do for you, gentlemen?" the young Latina called out from behind the tall counter as she turned away from her chore of organizing brochures.

"For me? Stress reduction," Lincoln replied.

The young woman smiled so big it disappeared into lightly freckled dimples. "You came to the right place for that," she said, extending a friendly hand over and across the counter.

Lincoln took the proffered hand into his own. "Hi, I'm Lincoln Bridger," he flipped a thumb toward his pal, "and this is Ben Fitzsimmons." Lincoln smirked at his friend then returned his attention to the beautiful and fit young lady. She had sparkling dark eyes and a gorgeous smile with a smattering of faded freckles across a button nose. "My friend is still wondering what he's doing here."

"Shut up," Fitz muttered. He shoved Lincoln out of the way and took the girl's hand, sandwiching it between both of his. "Hi, call me Fitz," he said in a silly and syrupy way while grinning goofily. "No one has called me Ben or Benjamin since elementary school, and I slapped the last person that called me Benny."

A shrill laugh escaped before the young girl could get her hand over her mouth. Her eyes shifted quickly around at the stares she drew. "Seriously?" she whispered.

"Nah. But I really don't like the name Benny."

Lincoln watched Fitz's reaction to the girl closely. His friend went beyond cordial to leering in the time span of a single heartbeat. "Take a good look at her, Fitz. That's what healthy looks like."

"Hey, you didn't have to tell me. I'm admiring it...I mean *her*, right now."

"Uh-huh. Sort of difficult to miss."

The girl's cheeks colored, embarrassment ratcheting a notch higher. She tried pulling her hand from Fitz's grasp, but he refused to relinquish it. The young woman was now looking everywhere but at Fitz, mostly at the floor. "My name is Dixie...Dixie Vega. Have y'all ever been here before?" After two more rather persistent attempts, she finally pulled her hand from Fitz's grasp.

Once her hand slipped away, Fitz dropped an elbow on the countertop and cradled his chin on it, keeping an admiring gaze on Dixie with an idiotic dreamy look smeared across his face.

"Nope. First time in," Lincoln replied, giving the girl his own admiring appraisal. She was five-five perhaps but beautifully proportioned, with long raven's wing black hair that would put the gloss on the bird's wing to shame. He guessed her to be in her late twenties or early thirties. Her creamed coffee complexion was smooth, cheeks shiny. It certainly was not a joke when he told Fitz she was the picture of health and she had the natural beauty to make a perfect package of femininity, punctuated by a long shimmering French braid to the center of her back. She was outstanding. "This is the first time for both of us to be here," he added.

"In that case, let me show you around." Dixie came out from behind the counter. "Come on. Follow me."

They turned a corner down a short hall, making an immediate left turn through a wide arched entrance into an expansive room with six long rows of machines—elliptical treaders, recumbent peddling machines, upright stationary bikes, stair climbing machines, rowing machines, and treadmills, all facing the busy street outside through a wall made entirely of tinted glass offering a magnificent view of downtown Austin. The brilliance of the day was subdued to a comfortable level by the smoky coloring on the glass. Dixie made a sweeping gesture to everything in the room. "This is our cardio room, where cardio vascular fitness is king," she said, and then grinned. "Or, queen. As the case may be. Should you decide to join us here at Power House, I'd suggest you both begin every visit in this room for a minimum of half an hour."

"Half an hour?" Fitz mumbled. "Humph, I can handle that."

Dixie waggled a finger at him with a grin. "I said *begin* your visit with it."

Fitz slumped a bit. "Oh."

Dixie walked past them directly across the hall through a mirror duplicate of the door she had just exited. "Over here is the weight room. We have all types of resistance equipment in here." She pointed. "Along the back row beneath those mirrors is a broad selection of dumbbells from two-and-a-half pounds apiece, up to a hundred-fifty."

"Seriously?" Fitz asked. "Do those big ones get used much?"

Dixie chuckled. "Come back later this evening and see for yourself. We have some really big dudes that lift here, all muscle." She pointed out and explained everything else—free weights, Olympic bars, universal cable machines, many machines to isolate various body parts, and a series of hydraulic circuit equipment lined up against a sidewall. She then led Lincoln and Fitz away and down the hall, explaining all the various classes available. They came upon a row of floor to ceiling clear glass walls and doors offering full unobstructed views of brilliantly lit rooms that were deep and narrow. "These rooms are equipped for racquetball, handball, half-court basketball...and, as you can see, martial arts training." They stopped and followed her pointing finger as she gestured through the glass.

Lincoln saw a tall woman and was quite abruptly enchanted. This vision of loveliness had to have been five-eight, maybe taller, with short sandy brown hair of fine texture cut to leave the ends ragged and free— flipped out slightly at the tips. The glistening locks shimmered and swayed with every movement. The woman was lean but muscular. Striations in her bare upper arms, shoulders, and down her thighs defined exquisitely well-formed muscularity. The woman's face belied her athletically charged body. Her features were delicate with bright brown eyes and a nose slightly upturned set in an alabaster face. She was dressed in a snug-fitting black leotard and gray tank top tucked into the waist band. She faced a practice dummy, the upper torso likeness of a well-muscled man. She wore lightly padded gloves over clenched fists, clearly in attack mode, perspiring profusely. At blurring speed, she turned sideways and leaned so far to the side her head stopped mere inches from the floor. She drove her left heel into the chin of the dummy and then spun three-sixty backwards, slapping the side of its head with the bottom of her foot. Both maneuvers done in less than a single second. "Wow," Lincoln drawled slowly. "She's somethin' else..." He then added, mumbling, "...and extremely easy on the eyes."

"She's sure not someone I want to have angry at me," Fitz said, wide-eyed and staring through the glass wall.

"Let me say, if you ever do get on her bad side, you may be singing soprano for a while," Dixie said. "That's Carlee Cayne. She's the best martial arts student I've ever had."

"You teach that stuff?" Fitz asked.

"I'm certified and proficient in several disciplines. I teach Korean Hapkido, Japanese Judo, and Krav Maga."

Fitz's eyes brightened. "Can you teach me to do that stuff?"

"Sure," Dixie said, and then tipped her head forward as an eyebrow went up. "I warn you though, it's not something that can be taught in a month or two. It's long term training, and I demand commitment going in and then ongoing, or I won't even begin the training. The reason is simple, I don't want an arrogant student getting hurt because they learned just enough to be foolish and picking fights simply to see if the training worked." She looked at Fitz from head to feet and then back to his head. "For you, we'd have to work on and elevate general fitness before attempting any kind of moves."

As she took a moment to assess Fitz, he spent the same time ogling every inch of her. It made Lincoln smile to the point of stifling a snicker. He shook it off and asked, "Krav Maga? What's that?"

"Krav Maga is a hand to hand combat style developed for the Israeli army back in the forties. It's more offensive than other types, designed not only to take down but incapacitate quickly because of the military application. Other disciplines tend to be more defensive. Krav Maga can be very damaging to the opponent in scant seconds during all-out conflict." Dixie pointed to the woman, still attempting to injure the practice dummy. "Carlee is highly skilled in the art of Krav Maga."

"Why would a woman like her want to be so well versed in such a fighting technique?" Lincoln asked.

"Yeah. Why?" Fitz chimed in.

"Carlee is a deputy for the US Marshals Service. She's out in the field often, apprehending known criminals on the run from the law. Believe me, the woman you're looking at in there is just as deadly with a Glock 40. Over the past couple of years, Carlee and I have become close. She's a good person and a great friend, a person anyone would love to have on their side. Don't let her toughness fool you though. She's a gentle soul. Still, she can be a real badass when necessary. Pardon the language."

In a sing-song lilt, "I like your language," Fitz said.

Lincoln slapped him on the shoulder. Would you stop embarrassing the girl?"

"It's okay," Dixie blurted. She shielded her mouth with the back of her hand, and whispered to Lincoln, "I think he's kinda cute." She paused. "Besides, your friend should always remember, I taught that woman in there everything she knows."

Lincoln grinned and snickered as Fitz and Dixie Vega exchanged banter that carried the cadence of a man and woman having known one another for years, not minutes. But their jovial back and forth faded into the background. Lincoln stared at the woman he now knew as Carlee Cayne with deep admiration, but it was more than simple appreciation of skill. He was awed by the lithe beauty drenched in perspiration attempting with every kick and punch to remove the head of that dummy. "Does she always go at it that hard?"

"No, not really." Dixie said. "The first thing you told me was you were here for stress relief. Right?"

"Yeah."

Dixie's smile wilted away. "It's no different for Carlee. She had to kill a man yesterday. This is how she deals with it. Plus, she has been removed from active duty, administrative leave, until the Service does a routine investigation of the shooting. That adds its own stress for a single woman in the middle of a work week, especially Carlee. She's a woman who doesn't care for girlie things like shopping. So, the gym is her activity of choice in such situations. It makes sense for her on several levels."

"It makes my stress seem paltry in comparison," Lincoln said. "So...she's single, huh?"

Dixie's grin came right back. "Divorced."

"Down boy," Fitz said. "Jeannine. Remember that name?"

"Is that your wife?" Dixie asked.

Lincoln sighed. "Yeah."

Carlee turned to face the three of them, glancing briefly at Fitz, offering a friendly wave to Dixie, but when her eyes fell on Lincoln, her smile broadened and her gaze lingered. Lincoln noticed and was compelled to maintain a smile as long as she continued looking at him. She glanced down to her hand as she ripped open the Velcro strap from one of her gloves and removed it. When she looked back up, it was directly at Lincoln, smile fixed. The effect on Lincoln was palpable. He swallowed hard.

Chapter Three

Forty-one-year old Jeannine Bridger stormed out the front door of her fashionable two-story house in north Austin carrying an ample load of bad attitude. *How could Linc do this to me? He knows every Thursday night we have dinner with my parents. Joined a gym, my ass! He's crazy if he thinks I'm going to alter my plans to suit his dumbass juvenile ideas.*

She remotely started her Land Rover and unlocked the door while hurrying to the circular driveway fronting the home she and Lincoln shared. The landscaping was professionally done on a regular basis and looked it — above average, even for this upscale north Austin neighborhood. She felt as though she could not get away from the house fast enough. It was big. It was gorgeous. It had all the amenities of fine living in this upper middle-class neighborhood but, lately, it had begun to feel more like a prison than home. It even echoed loneliness when no one else was in the house with her.

Once seated behind the steering wheel, she jerked the vehicle into gear and over-accelerated. Tires screeching, she lurched forward, speeding up rapidly on her way to her parents' house, a short drive away in an even swankier north Austin neighborhood.

During the drive over, she mulled her marital situation, becoming angrier as each mile clicked off. It was simply asinine Lincoln could not, or refused to, assimilate into her preferred way of life. Wasn't that what husbands were supposed to do? Jeannine was convinced she was right and Lincoln should be dropping to his knees and begging for forgiveness. Joining a gym without talking to her about it first was an abhorrent way to treat a wife.

When they married, she had realized his lifestyle at the time was pedestrian, but she had been supremely confident, with her mother's help, Lincoln Bridger would eventually fit snugly, like a puzzle piece, into the

Rosen family way of life. Jeannine believed strongly there was no other style of living and refused to consider such a ridiculous thing. And she did consider most of Lincoln's lifestyle preferences absurd. Why couldn't he see her friends as his friends? Why couldn't he play tennis at the country club on Saturday mornings, like all her friends' husbands or her father's friends? Even when Lincoln explained it to her, it did not help. She remained confounded by his deeply ingrained cultural habits. When he played golf, it was at the public courses. Why? The country club course was better, prettier, and impeccably maintained. Jeannine could not understand her own husband. Lincoln should be putting more effort, much more, into understanding what she wanted and work harder at making her happy. *He is so damn selfish!* She growled and gripped the steering wheel tighter.

A short drive later, Jeannine turned off the street and braked to a stop before a black iron double gate. A large ornately swirled cursive "R" within a circle was formed from both sides of the gate when closed. She let down her window and punched in a number code on an electronic pad attached to the end of a metal conduit coming out of the ground. Both sides of the massive gate with spear-tipped iron pickets opened simultaneously. She drove through before the gates had completed the opening sequence. The driveway was long and meandering in deference to the native landscape, curving around massive and stately live oak and pecan trees — some, hundreds of years old. Although the trees were old and native, the neatly manicured flower beds around them were not, lending a perfectly planned appearance to new and old. After about a hundred yards, a sprawling one-story home appeared as she rounded a massive oak tree with many of its substantially long limbs having drooped and grown to the ground over the decades. The house was Spanish hacienda style, tan stucco, red clay tile barrel shingles on the roof, and a sturdy but weathered oak walk-through gate built in the old style of black wrought iron hinges, knobby bolts, and flat bracing straps, all rife with hammer marks. It was suspended beneath a stucco arch that had been built and shaped with the same roofline as the Alamo. It opened into a courtyard.

Jeannine stopped and shut off the engine. She got out and marched through the gate, situated between two areas of spiny desert succulents, into the courtyard. The house surrounded this open area on three sides. The first row of rooms around the inside perimeter of this seven-thousand-square-foot house opened separately and directly into this courtyard, giving every room its own access to an outdoor living area. There was a swimming pool centered, complete with statuary, concrete fish and cherub fountains spewing streams of water into it. It was built to appear as a naturally formed pool beneath a waterfall deep within a tropical rain forest surrounded by large plants befitting such a setting. Aquatic plants in pots had been sunk to the bottom of the pool in one corner, offering the wild appearance of a deep woods or jungle setting. Jeannine saw a pair of shiny tanned legs with freshly pedicured nails on a chaise lounge chair next to the pool, partially hidden beyond a large potted caladium. "Mother?"

"Hi, sweetie," came her mother's voice from the other side of the huge dark green elephant ear leaves. "Come on over and sit."

Jeannine never broke stride. She rounded the big plant to see her mother in a one-piece swimsuit, skin glossy and dark. "Working on that tan again, I see."

"I like the real thing much better than color from that stuff in a bottle." Lidia Rosen was pretty and could pass for a woman in her late forties, but she had just turned sixty-three earlier in the year. The only possible give-away was a long silver-streaked bang she kept swept to the side seductively, setting off the perfectly preserved face beautifully. She patted the cushion of the chaise lounge next to her. "Have a seat and visit with me." Lidia leaned forward for a view of the gate behind Jeannine. "Where's Linc?"

Jeannine growled. "That man makes me so mad, Mother!" Her anger, now in the presence of her biggest cheerleader, began to manifest in tears. "He joined a gym today and decided he'd rather be there this evening than joining me in our regular evening together. Not only that, I found out he had already been at the gym around lunchtime. Why should he feel the need to go back this evening? It's not fair, Mother! I'm devastated, simply devastated."

"That doesn't sound like Linc. Are you two having trouble?"

Jeannine noticed her father, Saul Rosen, approach. He clearly saw her and her mother conversing. It seemed like a good time to take this to the next level and build her case for sympathy. He approached her. Now, she would take her frustration with Lincoln's detestable behavior to the next level. Welling tears spilled down her cheeks on cue. She sobbed. "He doesn't love me. I don't think he ever did," she wailed.

"Well," her mother said, "we'll have to sit the boy down and have a talk with him about it. Won't we? He has a responsibility to you. He apparently needs to be reminded what exactly is expected of him." Lidia moved over and sat next to her daughter, pulling her into a coddling embrace. She ran a calming hand over her daughter's cheeks. "Shh, sweet baby, it'll be all right," she cooed into her daughter's ear, as if Jeannine were still a toddler.

Jeannine glanced up to see her father frown and roll his eyes. "It's true, Daddy. Don't look at me that way. Linc does not love me."

Saul sat on the other side, bookending her between parents. He stared down for a moment at his daughter's fidgeting hands in her lap. She nervously picked at a split thumb cuticle with the forefinger of the same hand. After a time, he drew a breath and released it in a measured way. "Your mother and I need to take some responsibility, because of the way you were raised."

Jeannine did not like where this conversation appeared to be going. She snapped a look at her mother. "What is Daddy talking about?"

"I don't know," her mother replied and then turned to Saul. "What are you talking about?"

"Well, if you two will let me get it said, you would not need to be asking that question." Saul stood and backed away a few feet to purposely take a dominant position over daughter and mother. Addressing Jeannine, "Honey, you have lived your entire life to this point believing *your* happiness, *your* entertainment, *your* well-being...everything you are, should be the responsibility of someone or something else to provide for you. Yet, oddly, you want to retain control of everything that happens. Honestly, hon, it's simply a means of avoiding responsibility for your own life. Not once have I ever seen you accept accountability for who you are. You've always attempted to make others accountable for whatever inadequacies you may be feeling or experiencing." Saul took his voice down to a soothing tone. "Sweetheart, please understand, I say this with love. *You* are and always have been in complete control of your own happiness and direction of your life, not your mother, not me, and certainly not Linc. You and Linc should be full partners in the relationship to your *mutual* benefit and happiness."

Lidia sprang to her feet. "That's not fair, Saul. Jeannine is—"

Saul put a hand up. "Stop right there. Now, please sit down," he said, low and unflinching. And then in no less authoritative tone, "You both need to hear this, because the daily collaboration between you two has always been to manipulate people around you, attempting the alignment of acquaintances, friends and, yes, even family members into minions. Now, I see these games you play are about to go too far. It's time I spoke up, because I cannot and will not allow it to spin out of control."

Lidia slumped forward and then sheepishly, "Do you really see it that way?" she asked.

"Sorry." He shrugged his shoulders. "It's obvious to me, both of you feel self-esteem should come at others' expense," he replied.

"I—I didn't realize you saw us that way." Lidia's head followed her slumping body as her chin wilted toward her chest. "If that's true, then we'll try harder to be more accepting of others for who they are, while recognizing our own faults...I suppose," she said, near a whisper.

Saul stepped over to his wife who still sat next to Jeannine, placed a hand on her shoulder. He pulled her into a sideways hug into his leg. "I'm sorry I was abrupt. I don't like raising my voice like that. I love you both very much."

Lidia looked up at him and smiled, a look conveying many decades of a solid relationship that, on many occasions, required no words.

Jeannine was shocked by her mother's lack of will to stand her ground on her only child's behalf. And, here she sat, tears still rolling down her cheeks. *What is it with them? Can't they see I'm heart broken and it's Linc's fault, all his fault.* She no longer saw advantage in being consoled like a little girl. Her mood mutated into very adult anger born of perceived abandonment. Her lip quivered with rage. She glared at her father, unblinking.

"Look," Saul said in gentle tone, "Lincoln is a good man. He's honest and hard working. I may have given him a leg up with his career in the beginning, but he did not ask for it. Since then, the boy has had integrity and developed the wherewithal to succeed on his own. Jeannine, sweetheart, you should be applauding that and not comparing him to younger guys who hang around the country club and, yes, may be wealthy, but they all got that way on their parents' dime. Linc is doing it the old-fashioned way. He's earning it."

Jeannine, still glaring at her father, began to rise from the chaise lounge. "So, you don't think your only daughter, your only child, has a right to be happy?"

Lidia grabbed her wrist and gently pulled her back down. "Hon, I don't think that's what your father is trying to tell you…I mean us."

"Your mother is right." Saul vigorously rubbed his face with both hands, clearly frustrated. "Of course we want you to be happy, but not separately and aside from that of your husband's happiness. We want you two to be happy together, always. But, what I'm hearing is, you want your husband to feed your happiness, giving nothing in return."

"Hogwash," Jeannine muttered.

"You think so, huh?" Saul asked. He put a finger to his lip and thought for a second. "I'll tell you what. Let me ask a few questions and you answer them quickly without trying to spin the answers. You game?"

Jeannine crossed her arms beneath her breasts defiantly. "Go for it," she replied crisply without consideration.

"Here we go," he said. "How often do you see me and your mother?"

"I see Mom almost every day. You? I see three or four times a week, I suppose."

"Okay. How many major holidays do you and Linc celebrate here?"

"Almost all of them."

"Now, when was the last time you two celebrated a holiday with Linc's parents in Lubbock?"

"Uh, not sure. I guess Thanksgiving a couple of years ago was the last time." Jeannine began fidgeting.

"When was the last time y'all drove up to visit Mister and Missus Bridger?"

"February, I think."

"So, about five months ago?"

Jeannine's eyes drifted down to her feet. "Yeah," she replied, her voice rapidly losing its edge.

"You love doing things with your friends and spending many hours a week at the club, right?"

Still staring at her feet, "Sure."

"Does Linc accompany you when you go to the club?"

"Most of the time."

"Okay. Now, what does Linc enjoy doing?"

She looked up at her father, searching the archives of her mind, realizing she couldn't be sure. "I think he enjoys going to movies."

"When was the last time the two of you went to a movie together?"

Her father might as well have doused her with cold water when he asked that question. Lincoln had asked her less than two weeks ago if she would like to go with him to see a new science fiction flick that had just come to Austin. She summarily blew off the invitation. He went with his friend, Ben Fitzsimmons, and she met her two best friends, Mary Lou Beecham and Beth Wharton, at the club that night. The question did not cause the introspection her father had plainly sought. Instead, it renewed her anger and sent it soaring. She sprang to her feet. "This little Q and A game has just become tiresome, and clearly meant only to embarrass me."

Saul sighed. "Oh, sweetie, if you think that, then you have missed the point by a wide margin."

Jeannine began walking toward the courtyard gate. "I think I can find somewhere I will be appreciated this evening. It sure won't be here or at home." Without offering a goodbye, she marched to her car. The last vestige of light was disappearing in the west. A few stars now twinkled in a very clear sky, but Jeannine scarcely noticed, never having been a fan of nature or its beauty. Her world and enjoyment were tightly scripted, and only she had access to that script. Once she had driven the meandering driveway down to and through the gate, she stopped and thought for a second. She then pulled a cell phone from her purse and dialed her friend, Mary Lou. *It's time for dinner. I'll see if Mary Lou and Beth would like to meet at the club, eat something, and then ogle cute guys swimming in the pool next to the restaurant while enjoying a few cocktails.*

Chapter Four

Lincoln felt good. He had told Jeannine he would be going to a gym for the first time and refused to be talked out of it. She certainly attempted forcing guilt on him, shoveling his ear full of how such a desire that pleased only him would harm their marriage. If not a threat, it sounded like one. Jeannine wanted him to follow her plan for the evening and not one of his own making—a plan that he was certain did not exist before she had answered the phone. Besides, her plans were usually narrow in scope, the country club or dinner with Saul and Lidia. Neither remotely interested him. Her effort to smear him with fault did not work. He refused to buy into it and did not cower. There was nothing to feel awkward about. He was comfortable with the decision, but with his marriage, not so much.

It was after he had hung up the phone from the contentious conversation with Jeannine he found out the Monolith Spark Plug marketing people were coming in for an unscheduled meeting. Stuart Adler, managing partner of Adler, Howard and Levy Advertising Agency, invited him to stay for an after-hours meeting. As was the case with all Adler's invitations, it was inferred the invitation was not optional but a respectfully delivered demand. Lincoln had no problem with it. After all, he was the agency representative to solicit and secure the account. He should be in attendance. It turned out to be a productive meeting. They hammered out budget allocations for various advertising mediums and set the account's course for the remainder of the year and a tentative framework for next year. But, it left Lincoln mentally drained to the point of impaired concentration. All he wanted to do now was turn his mind off, turn his body on, and sweat at Power House Fitness Center.

It was after eight o'clock. The western horizon had already swallowed the sun for the day, leaving a colorful, but diminishing, blaze in the west. Darkness approached but had not taken over yet, still several minutes away. As Lincoln stepped out of his office building, he was struck with residual daytime heat drenched in copious humidity. Nevertheless, it invigorated him. For no other reason than it was natural, not artificially conditioned air. It put a spring in his step, looking forward to the beginning of a new experience at the gym. He easily foresaw that fitness facility, Power House, becoming a needed respite from, not only work, but also from a deteriorating home life. He settled into his BMW and wasted no time driving there.

"Mister Bridger, welcome," Dixie Vega called out as Lincoln came through the parting sliding doors into the gym foyer.

A small duffel bag, stuffed tight with workout apparel in hand, Lincoln stepped lively to the counter she stood behind, noticing she still had her long lustrous black hair in that plait down to a point below the center of her back. Although obviously a necessity of a physically active lifestyle, it was a fetching look on the pretty young Latina, and must be her signature look. Her dark eyes sparkled with friendly exuberance.

"I'm sure happy to see you back," she said.

As he continued admiring her, "I can't think of a place I'd rather be right now." His admiration for Dixie went beyond her appearance. He was becoming enchanted by her unforced friendliness and easy-going manner. Always offering a smile, a wave, and a terrific sense of humor. He had already seen her give as good as she got in a humorous exchange with Fitz. She was certainly a credit to her profession and he hoped her bosses noticed and realized it as well.

She checked him in on the computer then handed him a locker key and a couple of towels. "Are you ready for this?" she asked in a high bubbly voice with a smile so wide it disappeared beneath shiny cheeks.

"You bet. This is a perfect night to start. I had a long, mind-numbing day at work." He laid his bag on the countertop.

She looked toward the door. "Where's your friend?"

"Fitz actually had a working dinner scheduled with a potential client at the country club on the other side of town. For all his goofiness, Fitz is very good at what he does for the agency, which is the same thing I do, solicit new business as an account executive," Lincoln explained, noticing a loss of luster in Dixie's bubbly demeanor. "Is that disappointment I see on your face?"

Plainly embarrassed that Lincoln noticed, she grinned sheepishly and bobbled her head. "Maybe a little. But, not entirely for the reason I'm sure you're referring to. Both y'all get three free one-hour training sessions. I was hoping to bundle them and train you together."

"Makes sense. Sorry I misinterpreted the look on your face. I thought you might have seen something in ol' Fitz you liked."

One of Dixie's eyebrows lifted. "Oh, don't misunderstand me. That was part of what I was thinking."

"You like him?"

"I don't know. Maybe. I'd like to find out more about him." She wrinkled her nose. "I think he's kind o' cute. And he's a funny guy who keeps me laughing. I like being around him."

As Lincoln listened to Dixie, he saw the woman that had been doing damage to a practice dummy yesterday afternoon come through the automatic sliding doors. He watched her with interest and a touch of wonder. She glided toward the two of them in a tank top tucked into a tight pair of jeans with the grace of a dancer, presumably heading for the locker room. Enchanted by what he saw, his eyes remained fixed on the woman as he responded to Dixie's comment, "All I can tell you at this point, is your first impression of Fitz is mutual." As he spoke, he simply could not tear his eyes away from the woman he now knew by the name, Carlee Cayne.

As she walked by, she said, "Hey, Dix" and simply smiled at Lincoln, never breaking stride.

Dixie must have noticed his interest. "This is the second time Carlee has been in today," she said.

"She's on some kind of administrative leave, right? Did she go back to work today?" he asked.

"She came in earlier and immediately went to work out, so I haven't spoken to her about it, but I don't think so. I believe she's still on paid suspension until the review of the shooting is complete," Dixie replied, concern evident in her tone. And then in crisper voice, "Why don't you go on to the locker room and change into your exercise gear and then meet me in the cardio room?"

"I'm on my way," he said, walking away down the long hall, past the glass-walled courts toward the locker room. He breathed deep the cool fresh smell purposely pumped into the facility continuously. It was an inviting scent he appreciated. Checking the number on his locker key, he hurried through the men's dressing room and found the assigned locker. He shucked his slacks and not-so-fresh white dress shirt then donned a floppy over-sized white t-shirt above a pair of satiny black workout pants with white stripes down the legs and his jogging shoes. When he returned to the cardio room, he stopped at the door and scanned all the occupied exercise machines. He was surprised at the number of people still working out. It was almost nine o'clock. He thought it was quite late, but apparently not for the many folks in this giant room working hard on sculpting bodies and preserving health. The expansive space hummed and whirred with exercise machines in use. His scanning eyes stopped at a hand held high. Dixie waved him over to an unoccupied stationary bike between two other peddlers.

"Want me to start here?" he asked.

"Yeah, this is as good a machine as any for a cardio vascular work. Let's see if we can get your heart rate up a little...not too much though. We'll take it slow for a while."

He adjusted the seat height and then climbed onto it. Only then did he notice Carlee Cayne was peddling furiously on the bike next to him on the right. Her skin glistened but her breathing was unforced. Her face was pleasantly expressive and calm. Judging by the look, she could have been strolling down a sidewalk, not peddling at a speed that made the stationary bike hum. She wore a tight-rolled red bandanna around her head and snug bike shorts. Striations on thin but muscular thighs told the tale of a woman who did this often and worked it hard every time. He assessed the number of vacant bikes of this sort in the room. There were four just like this one available. Yet, Dixie chose the one next to Carlee for him. He looked back at Dixie. She offered a sparkling smile. *I'll be darned. She chose this bike purposely.* He returned her smile along with a slight nod of appreciation, as an unspoken display of understanding.

"Go ahead and begin peddling. I think you're in good enough condition to go thirty minutes, if I don't adjust the drag too much," Dixie said. She then added, "Don't attempt to keep up with Carlee though. If you try," she pointed to a box suspended from the wall, "we might have to use those defibrillator paddles on you."

Carlee chuckled but kept her eyes focused forward toward the tinted glass wall facing the street in front of the building. A veil of darkness was in the process of descending over the hill country. Street lights had come on, dappling the street with pink haloes of illumination.

"Thanks for the tip, Dixie," he replied. "There's no need to worry though. I couldn't keep up with her if I wanted to."

Dixie began walking away. "I'll be back in fifteen to check your progress and fatigue level." She began to withdraw but suddenly stopped and added, "Oh, and be sure and check your pulse on occasion. It should peak at about one-fifty, but no higher. If it does go higher, slow down or stop altogether. I want you to enjoy your visit, working into a regimen slowly."

"Got it," he replied. Lincoln was already peddling, but at a leisurely pace, about seventy percent slower than the beauty on his right. He visually gobbled her up in flicking glances. Although tall and slender, Carlee Cayne was not without attractive curves. Shapeliness created from strength not softness. That sandy brown hair appeared to have been hastily arranged and left slightly flipped and ragged at its short ends. It was a look that would not work on every woman, appearing mussed, but it certainly worked for her, and quite well. Coupled with those gorgeous dark brown eyes, he had a difficult time taking his own eyes from her. Fearing he would be caught ogling, he finally did look away, turning and glancing the other direction. A lady who appeared old enough to be his mother peddled faster than him as well. Still, he wisely chose not to over exert himself—not the first time in.

There were only three places to focus his attention—the old lady on his left, the street beyond the window and at the lovely creature peddling fast on his right. Of course, he could not help but go back to watching Carlee. The choice seemed simple enough, but he only indulged in stolen glances. He wanted to strike up a conversation but was afraid to make the first move. He was married after all and did not want to leave the impression he was hitting on her. After about four minutes, he had begun to breathe heavier. He noticed, despite Dixie's warning, he had taken his peddling pace up a couple of notches, an automatic response to the women peddling on both sides of him, unconsciously accelerating to more closely match their speed.

"You really ought to back it off and slow down. I'd hate it if you made yourself so sore I didn't get to see you here anymore," Carlee said without looking at him.

Her sudden admonition shocked him, but the fact she cared enough to say anything pleased him. And, she could not have chosen to say it any better than she did. He quite suddenly forgot about his shortness of breath and no longer focused on his heavy breathing.

"If this is your first time in, work into it slowly," she added. "Take it from someone who knows. You don't want to wake up in the morning so stiff you're walking like you have boards in your britches." She chuckled. "Keep it fun. You'll get better and faster at it soon enough. If you look at it like work and get stiff and sore, it becomes easy to blow off coming to the gym altogether. I sure would hate to see that happen." For the first time, she faced him and smiled. Her gaze lingered for a couple of seconds. He saw her eyes quickly take in his face then a trailing glance down his body. She may not have intended it, but she checked him out. He noticed and hoped what she saw pleased her.

Even as perspiration trickled down her cheeks and dripped from her nose, Lincoln saw this woman needed no cosmetics. She was lean, muscular, and beautiful, naturally, with dark lashes and eyebrows. "Dixie told me your name is Carlee," he said between breaths."

"That's right. Carlee Cayne. And you?"

"I'm Lincoln Bridger. My friends call me Linc. I hope you will too."

"Linc it is."

Your friend, Dixie, told us a little about you yesterday while my friend, Fitz, and I watched you kick the plastic fecal matter out of that dummy." He drew a deep breath and rolled his shoulder high to catch a drop of sweat from his cheek before it headed for the floor. "You sure take your workouts seriously...or so it would seem from what I've witnessed so far."

"For me, it goes beyond health maintenance. There are many times my job performance with the US Marshals Service depends on me making sudden and, sometimes, extreme demands on my body that most people never need to worry about. Maintaining peak strength and speed are important and could be a lifesaver in certain instances."

"Do you like law enforcement?"

"I used to. Not so much anymore."

"Is it a burnout issue?"

"Interesting question and not easy to answer. It's complicated," she said. "I've never broken it down and analyzed it. I think I'll respond by saying that burnout is part of it, I suppose. But it goes beyond that. I have a supervisor I don't like at all, plus, I have a ten-year-old daughter, Rylee, that I sure would like to devote more time to. My mother takes care of her and Rylee spends more time with her than me. The hours at my job are often long and erratic. So, it's quite the convoluted issue for me. Even when I have time for Rylee, like tonight, my at-home time is so unpredictable, neither Mom nor Rylee plan for me being there. She already had a sleepover planned with a friend for tonight. So...here I am again."

Ten minutes had passed since beginning on the bike and Lincoln felt oxygen deprivation increasing. His legs felt heavy—the muscles a bit too tight. Under any other circumstance he would have given up on a conversation, but he wanted to know more about Carlee. "So, you have a daughter. That must mean you're married," he said.

"Not any more. Divorced. Three years and a couple months. You?"

"Married."

"Children?"

"No...unless you count my wife. She acts like one."

Carlee laughed loudly, drawing curious looks from nearby exercisers. "Oops, sorry. That just came out," she said. "Trouble in paradise, huh?"

"Trouble? If you think of that word in varying degrees, then I suppose it would make an appropriate answer. So, yes. But, I keep hangin' in there, thinking we can work things out." He paused to pull a couple of deep breaths, and then added, "It hasn't been paradise for a long, long...*long* time."

"Sorry to hear it," she said while pulling the end of the towel around her neck up and swiping it across her face. "I admire you though for not jumping up and leavin' when things went awry. I sure can't say the same about my ex. At the first sign of trouble, his answer was to run...which he did. He never looked back. I have sole custody of Rylee. We haven't seen, or even heard from, the jerk in over three years. Still, if he ever shows back up, I'll try to be civil for Rylee's sake. She needs a father. Last time I heard, he was in Amarillo working at a cottonseed oil mill. I heard from mutual friends that he has gotten off into using cocaine, and heavily, as I understand it."

Dixie returned as promised. "Hey, I was serious about not overdoing it on your first visit," she told him.

He looked down at his legs, just then realizing he was peddling as fast as Carlee. The difference was, he sucked wind and Carlee still did not breathe heavily at all, speaking with ease. Whereas every word he uttered came at the expense of needed oxygen intake. He slowed the revolution rate dramatically, wrapping his hand around the special electronic sensor pad on the handgrips. The display showed his pulse near Dixie's announced maximum of one-fifty.

"It would appear," Dixie said, "you probably are not going to make the full thirty."

"Probably not," he gasped.

"Tell you what, continue on at this slower rate for about three more minutes. That should be enough time for your heart rate and breathing to slowly return to normal. Afterwards, meet me across the hall in the weight room. We'll do some light lifting."

"I'll be over in a few minutes," he replied, as Dixie walked away.

Carlee stopped peddling and came off the bike. "Would you like to get coffee sometime?" she blurted.

The question took Lincoln by surprise. "Uh...I'd really like to, but...well, it might not be appropriate." He forced a grin through his exhaustion. "In fact, I might enjoy it too much."

Carlee offered a smile. "You seem like a good man, Lincoln Bridger, and that answer made me believe it more. Still, I'm offering you a raincheck for a future day that may or may not come." She took a step, about to walk away, but stopped and turned back to face him. "Will I see you here tomorrow?"

"Count on it," he said.

Carlee smiled warmly, hinting of invitation and walked away toweling off her face.

As he watched her walk away, stroking her face, neck, and shoulders with the towel, he realized his breathlessness was not entirely about the bike anymore.

Chapter Five

"Come on, Deputy Turner, I *have* to work," Carlee said, frustration moving beyond a simmer.

Supervising Deputy George Turner ambled around behind his desk and sat, the chair groaning under his substantial girth. "Calm down, darlin'. It'll only be a couple more days. You know how these shooting reviews go." He chortled in a disgustingly wet way. "Hell, ya ought to. You've been through two others just this year," he added, louder than necessary.

Carlee glanced back through Turner's open office door into the bullpen area. She saw his snide remarks had drawn attention from many personnel at their desks. It pleased her that not one of them smiled. She did notice a couple of the women flash a disgusted look. Everyone was aware of Turner's repugnant, and often, inappropriate sense of humor. *The bastard. If he's not propositioning me, he's toying with me. I don't know how much more of this I can take.* She wanted to get in his face and curse him and made a move to do it but thought better of it and stopped herself. With everything else going on, it would be career suicide. She closed her eyes, attempting to huff away anger that was in the process of pushing her precipitously close to the tipping point. "Look, isn't there anything you can do to speed up the review, so I can get back to my life?"

He pointed to a vacant desk beyond the big window of his office out into the bullpen. Its only purpose was a place to stack folders, documents, pictures, and sundry other papers. The stacks were tall, some tilting precariously, appearing set to slide off onto the floor at any moment. "You can come in and file all that crap, if you like." He grinned, clearly knowing what her answer would be.

"You know what I mean," she replied, "and it's not that."

"Look at it as a gift. It's paid leave. Take that little girl of yours and enjoy some downtime on the beach at Port Aransas or Galveston...or any other place you can think of."

"Can you give me some assurance this shooting review won't turn into a disciplinary action because of the other two shootings?"

"Sorry, darlin'. Can't do that. It's not for me to decide. Although, I did tell them how valuable you are to this office."

Carlee hesitated to reply but finally mumbled, "Well...thanks for that."

"It's true," he replied, but then ruined the moment by winking at her.

She ignored the seductive gesture, pursed her lips, and nodded. "Here's the problem. There's no way I could enjoy time off with this review pending and hanging over my head, not knowing which way it's going to go. And, it doesn't matter what the destination would be. I couldn't show Rylee a good time. So, no. There's no way I could possibly view this time off as a vacation. When this is all behind me, maybe *then* I'll take a few days off, but on my own terms."

Turner leaned back and laced his fingers together across his bulging belly. "Well...I suppose there is *something* I could do."

Carlee brightened and became excited. "Seriously? What? Tell me."

"I can keep you warm at night while you're waitin'." He again winked at her. "I know you have my phone number."

Carlee felt that final ounce of optimism cruelly snatched, whisked away like a curl of smoke in a sudden breeze. She rolled her eyes and turned to leave without showing or sounding any other response to Deputy Turner's lascivious invitation.

"I'll call as soon as I have word on the outcome of the review," Turner called out as she left his office, his tone more serious.

Carlee offered only a limp wave without looking back as her only confirmation she heard Turner's parting comment. She walked directly to Jimmy Fenn's desk across the large room. He was stationed against a window overlooking a busy downtown street. She stepped to the window and took in the brightening morning sky. She watched passing cars below, filling every lane. Drivers sped, nearly bumper-to-bumper, jockeying for position, getting another day underway in the capitol city of Texas. Her mood was sour. She wanted to talk to her partner and friend but questioned whether it was fair to dump her bad mood on Fenn or not.

Fenn dropped a pen onto a tablet he had been taking notes on. He turned his swivel chair to face her directly, as she stood gazing out the window. "How'd it go?" he asked.

She kept her eyes fixed on the traffic below and beyond the window. She considered telling him it wasn't important and change the subject. But then, she sighed. "Another day, another lewd proposition," she replied.

"Really? Damn. You do realize that you could file a sexual harassment claim against him, don't you?"

"My job is precarious enough, with this review crap. I don't think it would be a wise move to toss gasoline on a fire already blazing. Besides, Turner has never pressed the issue and has never touched me inappropriately." She snickered sardonically. "I sort of wish he *would* grab my ass then I could file a claim with a clear conscience." She sat on the near corner of Fenn's desk and looked back toward Turner's office door. "Karma is a bitch though. Someday, he *will* get what's coming to him whether it's me dishing it or someone else."

Jimmy Fenn's eyes widened and stabbed the air with a finger. "Hey, I have an idea. Why don't you and I go to dinner this evening and kick back. You know, giggle and grin for a while like we used to? Maybe that'll take your mind off all the crap going on here."

"That sounds amazing, Jimbo, but I sort of made a promise to someone to be at the gym this evening."

"Male or female?"

"Male."

"Why, you little minx," Fenn slowly replied, tilting his head sultrily forward and lifting his eyebrows. "You have a date."

"Not really. But, if I did, he would sure be the one. In fact, if circumstances were slightly different, I'd ask him for a date and not wait for him to get around to it. Whew! That man has been on my mind since the first time I saw him."

"I don't understand. Why aren't you calling it a date, if you're *that* into the guy?"

"He's married." She sighed heavily. "Like I've said many times, all the good men are gay or married."

Fenn smiled.

"Why don't you go with me to the gym this evening?" she asked.

"Sounds like a plan. I've been ordered to serve a couple of subpoenas and a warrant later. Can we do it afterwards, say...eight thirty?"

"Of course. I can meet you at whatever time you like. Rylee is spending the night again at Mom's house with a couple of her school friends. It's not like I have anything else to do."

"All right. Eight thirty it is," he said.

Carlee stood and gaveled the top of Fenn's desk with a flat palm. "See you there this evening. Now, I'm leaving so you can get some work done. Have a great day, my friend."

~ * ~

The sun hung low in the west, behind a wispy cloud veil on the horizon, throwing off colorful early evening vibrancy. Lincoln had finished his out-of-town business meeting and was now leaving San Antonio, speeding northward up the Interstate toward Austin. The client meeting in the Alamo City went smoothly, but he wouldn't know if he'd successfully secured the fast food account until after the client had interviewed several other potential ad agencies. It would take a couple of days before he would know for sure, but he was confident. Either way, the likelihood of bagging the account was certainly great enough to warrant a day trip south for the meeting. He set aside further thought on it.

He would be back in town about eight o'clock, a couple of hours earlier than he had told Jeannine, which should work out well. This way, he did not have to go through another contentious conversation on his plan to go the gym. He would still get home about the time he promised. Besides, he was certain she was either at her parents' house or at that damn country club with her minions and wouldn't be home until his originally planned arrival time anyhow. If he skipped the gym and went straight home, he would be there alone. Of that, he was quite certain. So, what would be the point of going straight home?

That new woman he had met last evening, Carlee Cayne, wafted in and out of his thoughts all day. Once again, she moved front and center. It was not appropriate, but the closer he came to Austin, the more excited he became about seeing her again this evening at Power House Fitness. Unfortunately, each time he dwelled on the image of that gorgeous creature, guilt shadowed it. It wasn't fair to Jeannine to have these thoughts. He could not seem to help himself. Carlee's image had a way of pushing guilty feelings to the distant fringes of concern. He knew well enough, thoughts became actions if left unfettered. He forced his thoughts into an exercise frame, wondering what type of regimen Dixie Vega had planned for him.

His cell phone sounded off. Glancing, he noticed Fitz's name appear on the car's dash screen and punched a hands-free button on the instrument panel. "Hey, Fitz, what's up? How were things in the office today?"

"It was an okay day," Fitz replied.

"I haven't talked to you since yesterday afternoon. How'd the client meeting at the country club go last night? Was it good? Bad? What? This inquiring mind wants to know."

There was an obvious pause. "That's sort of why I'm calling."

"Uh-oh. Went badly, huh?"

"Oh, no, that's not it all," he quickly replied. "It was a great meeting. It's what happened while I was there I want to talk to you about, but not over the phone. Are you going straight home?"

"I thought I'd spend an hour or so at the gym. Why don't you join me?"

Fitz paused. "Uh, I guess that's as good a place as any to meet."

"Hey, I can hear the I'd-rather-be-anyplace-but-a-gym in your voice." Lincoln laughed. "It won't hurt you to get a little exercise. Besides, Dixie will be there."

"Oh, yeah, Dixie," Fitz blurted, suddenly much brighter of voice. "Point made. In that case, you bet I'll see you there."

"Allow me about an hour. I'm still a few miles away, down the Interstate, but traffic is fairly light."

"You got it," Fitz replied and ended the call.

Lincoln did not miss his estimated arrival time by much. He pulled into the Power House Fitness Center parking lot at eight-twenty, less than five minutes later than what he had told Fitz it would take to get there. He searched the parking lot and spotted Fitz's red Camaro right away, sparkling clean as usual. There was an empty parking space next to it. He wheeled his BMW into it. He looked forward to this, snatching the small duffel from the back seat with his workout gear in it then bounding out of the car.

Lincoln enjoyed the ambience of the place—the clean aroma of air freshener again greeted him as he walked through the door. It worked quite well on him, lightening his mood and his step. He drew a deep breath of the calming fragrance. He glanced around, appreciating the brilliant cheerful lighting and the ultra-cool air stirred by rows of large fans mounted in the tall ceiling throughout. He spotted Fitz leaning against the check-in counter talking to Dixie.

"This is wonderful," Dixie called out, gushing. "I have both of you at the same time tonight."

"You sure do," Lincoln replied with a huge grin. He then noticed Carlee Cayne coming down the hall from the direction of the locker rooms. She walked shoulder to shoulder with a tall good-looking man. The guy was clean-cut, lean, and muscular with an unusually smooth complexion. His wavy dark hair was neatly combed and he appeared to be a straight-laced kind of guy. They were laughing. Carlee jabbed him in the ribs with her elbow. The guy winced and threw up his hands defensively. It was easy to see that it was all good-natured fun. Seeing them made it difficult for Lincoln to maintain a smile. His face relaxed into a bland expression. *What the hell am I thinking? Why should I feel jealous? Even a twinge is too much.* The man she obviously knew well was tall but only slightly taller than Carlee. Like her, a glance was all it took to see he, too, was physically fit.

Once Carlee saw him, her gaze on him lingered. She smiled. A simple act of recognition, but it was enough to cause Lincoln's breath to hitch and his heart to flutter. As inappropriate as his feelings were, it was an uncontrollable response to the smile directed at him. The guy with her was talking on and on about something. He had not noticed she might not be paying attention to whatever he was telling her. She took the guy by the arm and veered toward where he and Fitz stood at the counter. "Hi," Lincoln said as Carlee and the man closed the gap.

"Hello to you, too," she replied. "I'm glad you made it."

Lincoln put his hand on Fitz's shoulder. "Carlee Cayne, I'd like you to meet a friend. This is Ben Fitzsimmons."

"Call him Fitz," Dixie blurted, as Carlee extended a friendly hand toward him. "And I would suggest that you not call him Benny." She giggled.

Fitz smiled at Dixie then swung his attention to Carlee. "Yeah, call me Fitz." He took her hand and added, "I watched your fighting technique the other day. I want to say right now, if I *ever* piss you off or displease you in *any* way, please give me fair warning, so I can run."

Carlee smiled and looked to her feet modestly. "Deal," she replied. She looked to her companion while gesturing toward Lincoln and said, "Jimbo, I'd like you to meet a new friend. This is Lincoln Bridger. Linc, this is my *old* friend, Jimmy Fenn."

Jimmy Fenn frowned and reared his head. "You don't have to make it sound like you're trading me in for a newer model."

Carlee snickered. "You're right. You don't have that many miles on you."

Fenn slapped his hand into Lincoln's extended hand. Lincoln noted and appreciated Fenn's firm handshake. "It's good to meet you, Linc."

An awkward silence fell over the small gathering of new acquaintances. "Well, I guess Fenn and I need to get busy and get a workout done," Carlee said to break the silence. All the time she spoke, her eyes remained fixed on Lincoln. "Y'all have a good one too. Okay?"

Lincoln noticed Carlee blush. "I think Dixie will see to that," he replied. He watched them turn and walk away, but his eyes remained trained on Carlee. She walked with an alluring feminine dancer's glide, as if heading to center stage. It enamored him, considering how tough he was told she could be when necessary. "They make a really nice looking couple," he said as he turned his attention back to Dixie behind the counter.

"Couple?" Dixie laughed. "If you're calling them a couple in the romantic sense, you're a few miles off base, Linc."

"Huh? I don't understand."

"You sure don't." She laughed again. "Jimmy is her partner at work and he is so very...*gay*."

Fitz slapped him on the back and joined Dixie in a chorus of laughter.

Lincoln's shock transformed into a smile. "Oh." He suddenly felt lighter on that bit of good news.

Dixie clapped her hands. "Okay, guys, enough socializing. Head for the locker room and change." She came out from behind the counter. "I'll be waiting in the cardio room."

When they entered, Lincoln saw Dixie standing behind two vacant treadmills side-by-side. "Okay, boys. Climb on," she said. She then offered a fast tutorial in their use. Once he and Fitz had settled into a crisp gait, Dixie told them she would be back to check on them and walked away.

Following quiet seconds, getting into a comfortable rhythm, "Okay, Fitz, tell me about your client meeting at the country club last night and why you're being so secretive about it."

His friend's face turned to stone, no more happy-go-lucky Fitz. "After I ended the call to you earlier, I began to think about it. I'm not at all sure I want to tell you now."

"Why? Did you lose the account?"

"That's not it at all. It has nothing to do with the account or the agency. It's what I saw while I was there. I can tell you, it was distracting enough that it could have hurt my chances with the client, but I think I secured the account anyhow."

"Okay. If it's not about that, then what?"

Fitz glanced at him, then again. He heaved a sigh. "Jeannine. I saw Jeannine. She never noticed me."

"Is that all? She's always at that damn club. That's not news."

"In that case, maybe I should tell you the whole story after all."

"Wouldn't hurt. If you really want me to understand what you're driving at, that is."

"She was across the club restaurant from where I sat, but I had a good view of her table. She was with two other women and two men. After a few minutes, they all stood. The other two women and one of the men stood opposite Jeannine and the remaining guy. They exchanged pleasantries. Those three walked away, leaving Jeannine and that other guy behind. After the others left, Jeannine and the guy returned to the table, but this time the guy came around to her side. He pulled a chair close to her and sat. They carried on a quiet conversation for a few minutes and then got up together and walked outside by the pool. You know what it's like there. The wall separating the restaurant from the pool is all glass, so they remained in full view of the entire restaurant the whole time. It appeared to me, neither one of them cared who saw them. The guy pulled her into full body contact. From where I sat, it did not appear Jeannine resisted whatsoever. In fact, it looked as though she literally fell against him...and they kissed." His voice went up an octave, "Linc, it was no peck on the cheek. Those two were playing tonsil hockey, their bodies tight together."

As Lincoln listened to Fitz's story, the oddest feeling came over him. A strange mix of thoughts and emotions swarmed him, including lack of surprise, a touch of relief, and wondering who the guy was. The truly peculiar part was, he wasn't sure if he was jealous about it.

"Linc," Fitz continued, beginning to breathe deeper from the fast-paced walk on the treadmill, "now you know why I was hesitant to tell you. I am the messenger, ya know. I hear messengers get shot sometimes."

"Don't worry, buddy. You did the right thing. Only a true friend would share a hard truth without concern for the consequences. It's not something I wanted to hear, but it's sure something I need to think long and hard about."

Between Fitz's breathlessness and Lincoln's sudden contemplative frame of mind, there was no more conversation for a time. He had become so engrossed sorting what his next step should be with Jeannine and potential future paths, he had not noticed he was becoming winded as well. Now he did.

He looked around the room at all the people doing their chosen exercise routines. He needed the distraction to get his mind off growing physical discomfort complicated by dark thoughts. His roving eyes stopped when he spotted Carlee and that guy, Jimmy Fenn, on side by side elliptical striders working them fast, yet laughing and carrying on a conversation as if they were strolling through a park, telling jokes and listening to the birds sing. Sweat glistened and streamed in rivulets from beneath a towel around her neck, down her bare shoulders and arms. He suddenly remembered Carlee's invitation last night to join her for coffee sometime. *Why not?*

~ * ~

Dixie glanced at her watch. *Better check on my boys*. Approaching Lincoln and Fitz on the treadmills from behind, she noticed Fitz's level of fitness was somewhat less than okay—a lot less. Whereas Lincoln walked with zest, Fitz trudged flat-footed, slapping the moving tread with each footfall although moving at the same speed. She figured she had better intervene. "Linc, remember that shoulder routine I taught you last night in the weight room?" she asked as she came alongside him.

"Sure do."

"Why don't you go across the hall and get started on it while I stay and give Fitz here encouragement to go a while longer."

"Sounds like a plan," Lincoln replied. He punched a button to bring the treadmill to a stop.

"A plan? That's not a plan. It's an unspoken agreement to torture me," Fitz sputtered around heaving breaths, his lower lip bouncing with every step. "That means I have to keep going."

"Sorry, man," Lincoln said. He turned to Dixie. "He's all yours. Be gentle with him," he added, grinning. He stepped down and headed directly for the exit out of the cardio room, walking across the corridor to the weight room.

After watching Lincoln walk away, Dixie stepped onto the now vacant treadmill next to Fitz and put it in motion to walk with him. "Grab that silver plate on the handle. Let's check your pulse and see how fast that big ol' heart of yours is pumping." As she waited for his pulse to calculate and then register on the read-out panel, she glanced to Lincoln disappearing out the door. She noticed Carlee, on an elliptical strider some distance away, twisting her head to an unnatural degree to watch him walk out of the room. Even from where Dixie stood, it was clear Carlee was not merely glancing in Lincoln's direction. Her friend was drinking in the sight of the man and wanted to know exactly where he was going. That was plain enough. Her partner, Jimmy Fenn, working out on the machine next to her, slapped Carlee playfully on the arm and told her something. Dixie figured he said something like, "Don't be so obvious. A little subtlety will go a long way." Dixie thought it, because that's what she would have told Carlee.

"One...twenty...seven," Fitz said between breaths.

"Huh?" Dixie said, returning her attention to her charge.

"Pulse...one-twenty-seven. Good? Bad? What?"

"Two thoughts: number one, you've just been walking fast for ten minutes and you cannot put two words together without a breath between each one. Number two, the heart rate should not be more than ninety, or maybe, a hundred at the outside, no faster than you're moving and no longer than you've been at it. It looks like I'll be working with you for a *long* time."

Fitz held a sideways gaze on her, jaw loose, and lower lip bouncing. Still, he gave her the biggest, stupidest grin.

She loved it. She then stabbed the air his direction with a stiff index finger. "But, I'm not going to do it for free. You're going to come in three days a week, one hour per visit, and you're going to pay me for the sessions."

"I wish...I could...close deals...as fast as you closed this one," Fitz said, huffing for air.

"Less talking, more walking," she said while striding long on her own treadmill. She glanced sideways, liking what she saw. She looked sideways at him again, this time, holding the gaze for a second. There was something about this guy she was instantly comfortable with, as if she had known him for years, not mere hours. Now, it seemed she might have the chance after all to learn what made Ben Fitzsimmons tick.

Chapter Six

"I thought you were about to fall off your elliptical, twisting so far around to keep that longing eye of yours on Mister Bridger," Fenn told Carlee. They continued at an expert pace on their respective exercise machines, both streaming perspiration.

"Stop it. You're exaggerating," she replied. "I'm starting to think you enjoy embarrassing me."

"Maybe a little," Fenn said with a grin. "But, I'm sure it's not an exaggeration. You know, he'd be easier to keep an eye on if you'd join him in the weight room."

"I don't want to be *that* obvious," she said, and then added, "I'll go another couple of minutes here to round out twenty, and then I'll head over there."

"Oh sure. That's not obvious at all," Fenn quipped. His jovial manner melted away. He stared straight ahead.

Carlee had worked with Jimmy long enough to recognize when a worrisome thought shaded his mind. "Okay, where'd you go? What're you thinking about now?"

"A strange call came into headquarters today, asking to 'talk to that brave lady deputy, Carlee Cayne, who took out that evil man, Manuel Ortiz.' Whoever it was said he wanted to thank you personally for keeping us all a little safer."

"Oh?"

"Yeah. Supervising Deputy Turner took the call. As big of a dip-wad as Turner can be sometimes, even he thought the call was suspicious and quizzed the guy. The man quickly became evasive and hung up. Turner immediately dialed the number still on his phone console display. And, guess what?"

"Don't want to. Just tell me," Carlee replied.

"The call came from a land line in San Antonio and was answered by the same law office that represented Manuel Ortiz at his bail hearing. "

"That *is* unsettling. What do you think the truth of it was?"

"I don't know. I can't think of anything good. What if Rogelio Ortiz is looking to mete out retribution in one form or another for the death of his brother?" Fenn asked. "With the money that man is pulling in from his drug business, on both sides of the border, he can afford about anything he takes a notion to do...like pay a sleazy lawyer to make a phone call like that, as an example. I'm surprised he didn't use a burner phone. The guy obviously wasn't accustomed to making clandestine phone calls. I am getting a bad feeling Ortiz may try something."

"Maybe. But I can't live in fear of every family member, or friends, of criminals that feel wronged by my actions."

"I know. I wouldn't either. All I am saying is watch your back for a while until the stench wears off this thing. I'll keep a closer eye on you too."

"Thanks, Jimbo. I will. You're a pal," Carlee replied. She glanced at the timer on her elliptical machine. "Twenty-two minutes. Good enough." She stopped and wiped her face, neck, and shoulders with the towel around her neck. "If you won't think I've abandoned you, I'm walking across the hall to do some lifting."

Fenn's smile returned. "Lifting? Right. I do believe you may try picking up something though. Or, maybe, 'lifting' is a euphemism for stalking. Sweet Lord, the possibilities are endless." He laughed.

"Oh, shut up." Carlee's sardonic smile was the only additional response Fenn's quips deserved. She fluttered her fingers at her friend, dismissively waving goodbye as she walked away. On her way to the weight room, she thought briefly about what he had told her, but by the time she turned the corner into the room across the hall, she had already canned the notion Rogelio Ortiz might orchestrate something nefarious against her. She did not, could not, believe he would endanger the flow of drug money in that manner, even for family. That would be an impulsive act unbefitting a wealthy drug lord, not to mention totally unprofitable. The only reason people like Rogelio kill or have people killed is to protect the money and its source, not go after vengeance for a perceived wrong that had nothing to do with the inner workings of his cartel. She figured the guy saw deaths in his ranks, even family members, as collateral damage and would move on. Rogelio did not attain his wealth by delving into dangerously spontaneous acts like revenge. Only a cool head could prosper in the ruthless world in which he clearly thrived.

She stopped long enough to scan the expansive weight room and saw Lincoln sitting at a machine, chest against a pad and pulling on a resistance bar, elbows held high. She maneuvered around equipment and walked toward him, but did so slowly, timing the completion of his set, so she might arrive after he was finished. She crossed the room and stepped in beside him in time to hear him grunt out one final repetition. "Working rear delts?"

Lincoln startled. "Oh, hey." His surprise at her sudden appearance settled into a smile. "Sorry. My mind was far, far away. Rear delts, huh? Is that what I'm working?"

Carlee chuckled. "I apologize for breaking your concentration."

"What if I told you I really like the way you distract me?"

She smiled. "I assume you're doing that exercise because Dixie told you to, right?"

"Yeah. Dixie told me I'll be working everything in the back from the butt up." He paused and then slid backwards off the seat. "I'm glad you're here. That offer to have coffee, does it still stand?"

"Of course it does." Carlee frowned slightly. "Has something changed since yesterday?"

He sighed. "Let me answer by saying, I believe a process of change has definitely begun. I honestly cannot say, yet, if it's good or bad. For now, it's simply a feeling of developing transformation in the air, albeit a strong feeling."

Carlee could not prevent a deep-seated giddiness but did not allow it to show. "Then sure, let's have coffee."

"How about after our gym time this evening?" Lincoln asked.

"A little late for caffeine, isn't it?"

"How about a glass of wine then?"

"Perfect," she said.

Lincoln thought for a moment. "There's a nice bar I take clients to occasionally not far from here. It's off the lobby of that hotel next to the lake at the end of this street. How about I meet you there?"

"I know the bar. It's nice and quiet. I'll see you there."

Carlee left Lincoln to his workout and made a beeline to Dixie. She convinced her friend to make Lincoln's and Fitz's training session short. Dixie did not have a problem agreeing right away. After all, it was one of the gratis sessions. After about fifteen minutes of resistance training for both the guys, Dixie cut them loose and gestured to Carlee with a little slashing motion with her finger across at her throat. Carlee tipped her head to affirm the message was received. Carlee spun around on her heels and stepped lively to the locker room. She hurriedly shucked her workout clothing and left the garments lying in a heap in front of her locker. She hurried toward the shower.

As water cascaded down over her, she wondered how big of a change had taken place in Lincoln's marriage. A dogged and troublesome little thought was he saw a chance for an extra-marital fling and was taking advantage of her infatuation. She must find out what happened to his marriage, if anything. Confident if he lied to her, she could read it and back away before anything happened between them. Her attraction to the guy was undeniable from the first moment she saw him, becoming stronger fast. Still, she did not want to race headlong into an emotional blender where she became *the other woman* and broke up a marriage. Although, it did not stop her from wanting to follow through with this man to see where it might lead. *One step at a time. Take it one step at a time.*

She toweled off and put her jeans back on and pulled out a fresh tank top from her gym bag, next to her holstered Glock 40 and badge. She waited for Lincoln near the gym's front door. Moments later, he emerged from the locker room and joined her. "Ready?" she asked.

"Follow me in your car," he replied, walking through the automatic doors opening onto the parking lot, Carlee at his side.

Carlee brushed her shoulder across his chest as she crossed his path, heading for her car. She felt a miniscule, but tingling, charge of excitement from the simple inadvertent touch. Heat rose in her face, but there was no way he could know, or even suspect, the near-overpowering sexual attraction coursing through her right now. It took a force of will to keep her expression pleasant, more importantly, neutral. It had to remain that way, for now. It would be too easy to fall into bed with the guy and, for God's sake, she barely knew him. It had been too long. It would take every ounce of her willpower to prevent a headlong rush to a sexual encounter. The price might turn out to be too costly. But she was now on a path and determined to see what lay at the end of it.

She drew in the night air. Temperature had abated, leaving it comfortably cool. Perfect. "It's a beautiful evening," she said then noticed her partner, Jimmy Fenn, about to get into his car three parked cars over. She shouted, "See you tomorrow, Jimbo."

"You coming in to work tomorrow?" he shouted.

"Turner hasn't called, so no, I don't guess I am." She waved at him as he nodded and dropped in to the driver's seat of his car. She watched him back out and head for the exit that emptied onto the street. Fenn drove past a shiny new black Escalade SUV parked in the last row of the lot next to the street but crosswise to the parking slots, taking up three. *Some people can be so rude when it comes to their cars*. Lincoln had already gotten into his car, prompting her to hurry. She tossed her gym bag onto the passenger side seat of her own car and followed him.

Carlee found it difficult not to stare at him as they walked abreast through the lobby of the hotel toward the bar. She purposely slowed and walked a half-step behind him so she could continue admiring him without his knowledge. "I've only been to this bar once before," she said.

"It's a good choice when conversation is the goal," he replied. "It's quiet with a nice ambience."

It was after ten o'clock. The bar had only one other customer, but he was leaving as they entered. Now, it was only the two of them and the lone bartender. Lincoln pulled out a chair at a small round table for Carlee. The bartender called out from behind the bar, "What can I get you folks?"

Standing behind Carlee, Lincoln leaned over and whispered, "You said wine, right?"

She felt his breath on her neck, shivered, and flinched involuntarily. She smiled up and over her shoulder at him. "Chardonnay or any dry white will be fine."

Lincoln straightened and moved around the table, "A Chardonnay for the lady and I'm sure I'll enjoy whatever Merlot you have uncorked."

"Coming right up," the young bartender said, with a lingering smile at her. She fidgeted uncomfortably from the young man's persistent gaze. She wondered if he might already be pegging her as a mistress. Carlee's power of observation from her law enforcement training and years of application thought the young bartender's expression odd. She thought about it briefly but dismissed it as a guy thing. It did bring on a pang of guilt though, as her eyes picked up Lincoln coming around the table to seat himself.

Lincoln Bridger was handsome, devastatingly so in her opinion, to the point of total distraction. His dark hair was thick with a smattering of premature gray in the short sideburns, face lean, and sparkling brown eyes that picked up flickering light from candles burning on each table. *If I can make it through this evening without acting like a giddy school girl, or dragging him off to a room for my personal pleasure, I'll call it a success.*

"I probably don't need to tell you," he said, "but I should not be doing this."

"I am surprised by your acceptance of my invitation, which, by the way, you felt was inappropriate just last night because you were married. I was embarrassed the moment the invitation came out of my mouth. I knew it was highly inappropriate to have even asked."

Lincoln sighed. "Not your fault. Not my fault, but our collective responsibilities, or lack thereof, that brought us here. Fault or not, it still pleases me." He paused. "So, here we sit, a married man and a single mother in a hotel bar late at night in the middle of the week. And, we have only known one another for a total of less than a day, much less. Now what?"

"I can't tell you how happy that very uncertain comment has made me." The bartender set a white wine before her. "Thank you," she muttered.

"Why would my anxiety make you happy?" he asked her as his eyes followed the bartender setting a glass of red wine in front of him. Lincoln made glancing eye contact and simply nodded approval.

"Because your anxiety matches my own, and knowing that has, all by itself, relaxed me. I didn't want to be all alone in my nervousness. So, thank you." She stared at him while taking a sip from her glass. "Um, that's good." She set her glass on the table. "If nothing else, we can be friends." Then quickly added, "I *really* want that, at the very least." Carlee did not attempt to mask desire propelling the comment.

"I'd like that too. Somewhere in time down the road, regardless of the paths that our lives take, I can look back, fondly remembering that once upon an Austin night, I met a magnificent woman. What a wonderful story that would be."

Carlee visibly shuddered. "Wow. Nicely said." She sipped her wine. "Why don't you tell me the Lincoln Bridger story? I really am interested in learning more about you. Aside from the fact, of course, that you really know how to flatter a girl."

"Okay. But, only if I get to hear the story that brought Carlee Cayne to this point in her life. Deal?"

"Deal. So, Linc, who exactly are you?"

As Lincoln began detailing his childhood in Lubbock, it gave Carlee the excuse and opportunity to gaze at this handsome guy sitting across the small table from her. She held the wine glass to her lips and kept it dangling between her fingers close to her mouth. The sultry buttery voice of Diana Krall ended a soft jazz tune and, seconds later, the voice of Norah Jones seamlessly picked up the slack and continued. It was the perfect accompaniment to the conversation, piped into the bar via a speaker in the ceiling—an ideal soundtrack for Lincoln's recitation of growing up on the South Plains of Texas. He became charmingly animated as he told of the dumbest stunts he had pulled as a teenager while in high school.

She lowered her wine glass to the table. "It sounds as though you had a very normal childhood. Later, you came to Austin to attend U-T, right?"

"Yeah, I did." The smile that had become a fixture over the past few minutes faltered, while maintaining a pleasant manner. "As is usually the case with most folks, I guess, life became complicated fast when I moved from Lubbock to Austin. My sister, who is less than two years older than me, was already enrolled in Texas Tech, there in Lubbock..."

"Oh, so you have siblings," Carlee blurted.

"Just one. My sister, Beverly. After her college days, Bev moved back to Lubbock to help my parents with the small furniture store they bought in the early sixties. She has three kids, all of them grown, or nearly so. She and her husband, Ernie, took over the store several years ago. They seem happy enough with life, I suppose."

Carlee nodded. "Sounds like it." She loved listening to Lincoln talk. It did not matter what was coming out of his mouth, she simply wanted him to continue in that soft velvety baritone. "Okay, you're in the University. Then what?"

"Like I said, things got complicated. Mom and Dad struggled financially to get Bev and me through college, but they were committed to it and never complained...*much*." He snickered. "My grades never were what you would describe as stellar, or even adequate sometimes. That didn't help matters." He rolled his eyes, clearly uncomfortable by the admission. "My greatest feat in college was the innate ability to ferret out the best parties to crash. That was a perfected talent of mine and I used it often. It was at one of those parties, a highbrow sorority thing, I met Jeannine. We dated, got married, have no children, and now..." He sighed. The last vestige of pleasantness slipped from his face. "That's all I want to say about that. I have a problem that must be dealt with somehow...and soon." He put the wine glass to his lips and downed the remaining half glass in a single pull.

~ * ~

As Lincoln told his story to Carlee, he glanced beyond her to the only other person in the room, the bartender. The young man worked a towel, polishing and hanging multiple rows of stemware. It seemed he paid more attention to their conversation than to his task. Not surprising though. They were the only other living creatures within his field of vision. Still, it bothered Lincoln, feeling as though he and Carlee were being judged, as if they were doing something illicit. It was straight up guilt, but Lincoln could not ease the small knot in his gut that the assumption created. He noticed Carlee's glass had only a sip remaining in it. "Care for another?" he asked.

"I'm not sure I should. I don't drink often and almost any amount of alcohol goes straight to my head." She checked her watch. "And it is getting late." She smiled demurely. "I don't need my inhibitions tampered with—not tonight."

"Your choice," Lincoln said, "but you still owe me the Carlee Cayne story. I can't imagine you telling it with an empty glass in front of you."

"You have a point. Okay, but just one more."

Lincoln took advantage of the bartender's intrusive attention from behind the bar and tapped the top of his glass. The bartender held up two questioning fingers. Lincoln nodded. "Since it is getting late, why don't you confine your story to your job at the US Marshals Service? It sounds much more interesting than my job at the advertising agency as an account executive."

"Interesting? I suppose it was at one time, but now, that's certainly debatable." The bartender came out from behind the bar with two fresh glasses, one white, one red, and set them on the table. Carlee glanced up at the young man. "Thank you," she muttered as she surrounded her glass with both hands and returned her attention to Lincoln. "Maybe I've become jaded," she continued. "Not sure, but it's a grind and no longer holds the same appeal it did at one time for me. Or," she quickly added, "maybe it's a little burnout complicated by the greasy attention of a supervisor. The combination is probably the cause of my growing general intolerance." She shrugged her shoulders to emphasize the point she wasn't sure. She took a sip.

Lincoln chuckled. "Greasy attention? I've never heard that one before."

"Well...yeah. I'll stand by that. It's accurate. His unwanted attention leaves me feeling unclean." She sighed. "I'm working for a fat guy with more testosterone than sense. Plus, he doesn't have the looks to back it up. I honestly don't think he's even classy enough to undress me with his eyes. I think he imagines me stripped naked all the time and propositions me at least once a day, every day. And, God Almighty, his breath would make a buzzard cringe. I'm sure if I ever let him stand close enough, I'd find carrion smelling drool spots on my clothes. So, yeah, greasy attention is a good way to describe my feelings about the guy, who just so happens to be my supervisor."

Lincoln grinned. "Okay, okay." He chuckled again. "Seems as

though I may have slapped a hornets' nest, questioning such a colorful turn of phrase."

Carlee's frown softened. She smiled and joined him in a laugh. "I may be exaggerating, but only a little. And, now, I'm on suspension while they perform due diligence on a guy I had to put down a few days ago."

"'Put down?' Is that insider terminology for shot?"

"Yeah. Sorry. It's better than saying killed."

"He's dead?"

"Afraid so. I've shot three fugitives this year, two dead and one was sent to the hospital. It's really weighing on me and has only gotten worse since the last one. With my little one, Rylee, turning ten this year, I need to be spending more time with her, giving her assurance I'll be coming home after work each day. I know there are no guarantees in this life, but I could come much closer in a less-dangerous profession, I think."

"Where is Rylee now?"

Carlee raised a suspicious eyebrow. "Are you getting judgy on me?"

"Oh no. I was simply wondering. Since you have long, irregular hours, you must have a super baby sitter."

"The best. My mother. She lives here in Austin too." She drew deep and sighed long. "And, honestly, that sort of makes my point."

"How's that?" he asked.

"Mom spends more time with Rylee than I do. It's not right. Rylee is in her formative years and needs her mother now more than ever and will certainly need close parental guidance through her teen years. She's a sweet girl, but I don't want to burden Mom with the responsibility of corralling Rylee when the hormones of womanhood kick in. You know how wild teenagers can be sometimes."

He grinned. "Oh yeah. I remember it well."

"I need to be there for her much more. I don't know what I would have done if it had not been for my mother. Still, it should not be her burden to guide her granddaughter through the most trying times of Rylee's development. That's my job...or should be."

"Sounds like a great lady."

"She is. Her name is Beth and she looks like an older version of me."

"Which means that she's a beautiful lady."

"Thank you," Carlee replied, rimming her glass with a finger, her eyes drifting down to that action instead of on Lincoln. "There's that flattery again."

Lincoln paused, wondering if he should pursue the shooting story, but curiosity stole choice away. "That guy you had to *put down*, what happened?"

Carlee looked up from the mindless action of her hand and reconnected with him. She clearly thought for a second and then drew a not-so-dainty swallow of the Chardonnay. "Well...Fenn and I were tapped to lead a team to serve an arrest warrant and apprehend a bail-jumper by the name of Manuel Ortiz, accused of multiple armed robberies in central and south Texas. We received a tip he was in New Braunfels. He was holed up at his cousin's house there. A guy by the name of Daniel Vega."

"Vega? Any kin to Dixie?"

The question plainly took her by surprise. "Uh...I don't know. The name of Vega is a common Hispanic name. But I'm not sure. It never crossed my mind as a possibility. In fact, as close as we are, I know very little about her siblings or her family life in general. That's my failing. I'm always going on and on about my problems, and she listens patiently. I need to be a better friend. I'll make a point of asking Dixie if she and Daniel are related. Speaking of Daniel Vega, he's in a world of his own trouble now for criminal facilitation. He took Manuel in to his home, knowing his cousin was under indictment. He actively helped Manuel get in touch with his brother, Rogelio, in Acuña, Mexico, just across the border from Del Rio. Rogelio is a drug kingpin there. A plan was in the works to sneak Manuel back into Mexico. Daniel actively aided and abetted Ortiz in that effort."

"And you had to shoot Ortiz?"

"Afraid so. I was watching the back door of the house and he came running out, slamming the screen door against the house, wielding a machete in one hand and a semi-automatic pistol in the other. My partner, Jimmy Fenn, the guy you met earlier, chased him through the house and out the back door but stumbled, accidentally discharging his shotgun as he fell. Ortiz rounded on Fenn and squeezed off a shot. A heartbeat later, I shot Ortiz. Ortiz missed the first shot but Fenn lay so close to Ortiz's feet a second attempt would surely have killed Fenn. That's the whole story. If you don't mind though, let's not talk any more about that stuff."

"I let curiosity get the better of me."

"That's okay."

Lincoln drank the final swallow of his wine. He stared at Carlee for awkward seconds.

"What?" she asked with a shy smile.

"I am utterly in awe of you."

Carlee's cheeks reddened. "Thanks. I guess," she demurred.

It was unintentional but he had embarrassed her. "I'm serious," he added. "You are strong, courageous, but most importantly, a beautifully feminine lady. Yes, Carlee, I didn't choose the word *awe* haphazardly. It explains succinctly what I think of you. I am so grateful our paths crossed."

She reached for his hand and squeezed it. "Oh, Linc, so am I," she replied. She did not relinquish her grasp.

Lincoln broke his gaze on her eyes and looked to her hand as she rubbed a small circle on the back of his hand with her thumb. The touch was electric. It threatened to rob his breath. He suddenly blurted, "I guess we'd better call it an evening before I say, or ask, something inappropriate. And, honestly, I'm only seconds away from doing exactly that."

Carlee gave his hand a final squeeze. "I don't think it's possible to ask something inappropriate, Linc. Not as far as I'm concerned." She sighed. "But, yeah, I agree. Inhibitions are slipping away with every sip."

He rose, walked around the table and pulled her chair. "Would you mind if I called you my friend?"

"You don't need to ask," she replied.

Lincoln dropped a twenty and a ten on the table and they walked out of the bar and through the hotel lobby to the main entrance. As they exited the hotel through the automatic doors and stepped into the wonderfully cool Austin evening, Lincoln stopped walking. Carlee followed suit and faced him. He reached for her hand, wanting to feel the warmth of her body and kiss her. *Maybe I shouldn't. Not yet.* He returned the subtle gesture of rubbing the back of her hand with his thumb before releasing it. "I'd better just head out," he said. "Will I see you at the gym again soon?"

"I'm there almost every evening. While I endure this awful suspension, I'll be there around lunchtime as well." She smiled sweetly. "I'll be watching for you." Carlee made the first move and began walking toward her car.

Lincoln was already at his car with his keys out unlocking it. He saw Carlee abruptly stop beside her car, her eyes followed a dark colored SUV with blacked out windows driving into the hotel parking lot off the street very fast, screeching tires, driving directly for where Lincoln stood.

"Gun!" Carlee shouted as loud as she could. "Get down, Linc!"

Lincoln looked to the vehicle across the top of his car to see what she was yelling about. He saw a rear darkened window going down. The short barrel of a gun emerged into the illumination of the pinkish sodium vapor parking lot lights.

The rattling pops of automatic gunfire sounded off. Bullets ripped holes through the other side of his car.

His first panicked instinct was to run. He turned to do just that when he heard Carlee yell, "Damn it, Linc, get down!" He jerked his head around to see her sprinting high on her toes toward him.

Another staccato rant of gunfire came his direction.

He dropped to his stomach and looked across underneath his car. He saw Carlee carrying her gym bag, unzipping it on the run. She retrieved a pistol in a holster from it and dropped the bag on the fly. She then threw the holster off the pistol, racked the slide, chambering a shell, and fired three fast shots at the driver's side of the windshield on the SUV. "Stay down, Linc! Don't get up!"

The rattling trill of automatic gunfire again ripped through the night. This time, not at him, but from the opposite side of the offending vehicle toward Carlee. He saw her dive and roll out of the line of fire behind a parked car. Her head and gun arm emerged seconds later from behind the front end of another parked vehicle. She squeezed off three more quick shots. He heard a heavily accented voice from inside the SUV yell, "The bitch shot me! Let's get out of here! Drive! Drive!"

The vehicle smoked its rear tires on the way out of the parking lot.

Carlee sprang up from the safety of the vehicle she had crouched behind. She squeezed off three more parting shots, hitting the rear window with all three as the vehicle screamed off down the street at high speed. She immediately spun around and ran for where Lincoln lay beside his car.

"Linc, are you okay!" she was shouting as she rounded the rear of his car.

Lincoln pushed himself to a sitting position and scooted back to lean against the car. "I think so," he replied and then held both hands out. They were shaking. "But, I may need to change my underwear."

Carlee drew a breath and blew it out as her body slumped forward, adrenaline charge leaving her in a sudden rush. She stepped next to him, backed up to his car, and oozed down to sit beside him. She pulled a cell phone from the side pocket of her jeans and dialed 911.

As she offered as many details as she could to the dispatcher, Lincoln thought about what had just happened. It occurred to him, for better or worse, the two of them had quite suddenly become more than friends. The thought came heavily tinged with fear. They were now bound by circumstances, lives inexorably linked for the foreseeable future. It did not take Sherlock Holmes to see this was likely a retaliatory thing for the shooting of Manuel Ortiz. Lincoln wondered if they would soon make another attempt. It seemed likely. It also seemed obvious to him, whoever was in that black SUV was going after someone she cared for, and that happened to be him on this night. It spoke to the cartel's ruthlessness. They wanted her to see a friend or relative killed. Whoever they were had no way of knowing he and Carlee were mere acquaintances.

Another thought quickly moved in. It would now be impossible to keep Carlee a secret from Jeannine or her parents. It would be on every local news channel all day tomorrow and, possibly, a couple of network news sequences. There could be live bulletins going out tonight, due to the use of fully automatic weapons within the city limits. Television stations may determine it to be a public safety issue. It made him uneasy to think his wife and her parents would easily learn of the attack and that he and Carlee had been together. After a few seconds, his mind eased, when he considered Jeannine's likely tryst Fitz told him about. He became conflicted. Should he even care what they thought? He and Carlee escaped harm. That's what was important. He assumed Jeannine would be relieved that he was safe. *What the hell am I thinking? I can't assume that at all.*

Chapter Seven

Dixie's eyes drifted toward the clock on the wall of the fitness center's lobby with increasing frequency as the evening wore on. Every night about this time, clock watching was an unconscious compulsion as the waning work day wore her down. It was a few minutes after ten o'clock. The time of evening her mind wandered to things other than her job of fitness training or martial arts instructing. On this night, there happened to be an added layer of fidget and fret. She had difficulty concentrating on simple tasks of daily due diligence, like updating the computerized membership database. It required little concentration, yet she could not seem to put the tiniest amount of focus on the job. She saw Fitz step out of the locker room down the corridor parallel to where she stood. The sight of him lifted her mood.

He walked briskly toward her. "Have you seen Linc?" he asked, still approaching.

She looked at him, puzzled. "Your question indicates he didn't tell you what his plan was."

"Uh-uh. He showered like a man on fire, dressed, and bolted from the locker room."

"In that case, I'm not sure it's my place to divulge that information."

"Aw, come on Dix. You and I have become fast friends, soon to be old friends. You can tell me. Besides, I know everything there is to know about Linc...other than where he happens to be right now, of course."

She grinned and jacked an eyebrow. "We may be on a fairly solid path to friendship, but if you use the word *old* ever again when referring to me, our friendship may come to a grinding halt. In the future, confine it to a description of yourself and leave me out of it." She paused and then sighed. "I suppose it really wasn't meant to be a secret. Linc and Carlee left together to go have a glass of wine a few minutes ago."

His eyes moved toward the entrance, as if watching his pal walk out the door. "Wow. That *is* big news," Fitz drawled. His attention snapped back to Dixie. "How strong is the attraction between those two? You seem to know something about it."

"I really don't. I do know Carlee was smitten the first time she saw Linc watching her practice Krav Maga. She invited him out for coffee yesterday, but he declined, telling her he was married and it would not be appropriate. I have no idea what changed. Plus, that coffee date turned into a glass of wine in a quiet bar."

Fitz stood unspeaking for a couple of seconds staring at a point over her head. "I have a sinking feeling I may have had something to do with it."

"How's that?"

"I saw his wife, Jeannine, with another man last night. I'll spare you salacious details, but it didn't require a psychoanalyst to see there was more between his wife and that guy I saw her with than a glass of wine and conversation. I told Linc what I had seen. He's reacting to it. I'm sure of it." He tipped his head quizzically. "Although...it was a little strange. He barely reacted to the information and showed no anger or sadness over it."

"Well, all I can say now is, if there is any willpower put forth to prevent things from going too far, it must come from Linc. Carlee is a very lonely woman and Linc is, quite frankly, a hunk. Her job and lifestyle hinder romantic relationships. Her love life is nil, and I mean that in the most literal sense. The poor girl comes in here, works herself to exhaustion, then goes home, kisses her daughter good night, and falls into bed alone every night. That's an everyday thing with her."

"Can I assume, by inference, you have a bevy of men awaiting your dating choice at any given time?"

"Say what? Are you crazy?"

"As a matter of pure fact...yes, I am. Be that as it may, you didn't answer the question. "Do you date a lot?"

"Heavens no."

"You say that with a detectable level of disgust in your voice," Fitz said.

"I didn't mean to. Guys who have asked me out recently are all pompous jerks. That was the reason for the tone and abruptness. Sorry."

"How in the world could you have determined that, if you didn't go out with any of them?"

"I have excellent radar for such things."

Fitz's eyes widened. "You're scaring me. How come I get the feeling your radar is sweeping me right now?"

"Because it is."

"Should I be concerned?"

"Let's put it this way, I'm still talking to you, aren't I?"

"Does that mean I passed your test?"

"Not yet. For all I know, you may be the Stealth Bomber of all jerks, capable of evading my radar."

"Sometimes, I wish I *was* a player of that caliber. There is no more to me than what you've already seen—so sad and, unfortunately, so disgustingly true. Now that I've said it aloud..." He forced his body into a melodramatic slump, complete with puppy dog eyes and quivering lip.

"So, you're shallow *and* a pretty good actor, you say," Dixie deadpanned.

"Now, hold on a second. I—"

Dixie burst into a boisterous peal of laughter. "Oh, stop it. I was kidding." She had been so into her conversation with Fitz, she had not paid attention to the numerous members now exiting the gym for the evening. The sudden eruption of laughter drew stares. Near a whisper, she quickly added, "Tell you what, I don't get off for another twenty minutes. Why don't you come around behind the counter and keep me company? There's more to you than you're telling. I can feel it. That sad and abused little-boy thing you have going on can't be all there is to you. The last half hour of my work day is boring. It would make the time go faster. That is, if you don't have anything better to do."

Fitz smiled and appeared appreciative. "I'd like that. We can explore my shallowness in depth."

Dixie stabbed the air with a stiff finger. "Word of warning, when I get off work, I'm going straight home and straight to bed...*alone*. Got it?"

"Whew! I'm *so* glad you said that."

"You don't have to sound relieved," Dixie replied.

"Oh yes, I do. Let me set up the scenario had you not said it. I would have spent our twenty minutes together hearing about half of what you say, all the while trying to think of a way to continue the evening outside this place and where it might lead. Thanks to you, all I have to do now is concentrate on getting to know as much about you as I can in less than half an hour, without searching for the correct words for...well, something more."

She smiled. "Gee whiz! Great answer. My pomposity detection apparatus dropped back into the green zone." She watched Fitz come around the counter, considering his attributes as he did. Although it's what she did for a living, her assessment of this man went beyond a physical training frame of reference. He had a good personality and a great sense of humor, capable of making her laugh and feel happy. His smile was infectious. Fitz had a manner about him that made up for physical deficiencies. A little pudgy maybe, but he displayed the glow of health a brief regimen in the gym would fix. Slowing his beer consumption would go a long way to that end. She made a mental note to work on it, should things progress with this guy. He was over six feet tall and well-tanned, with thick and course sandy colored blond hair that hung straight—no body to those follicles whatsoever. It laid there, like a Congolese thatched roof draping the top of his head. He clearly tried keeping it parted and combed but, just as obviously, it did not stay that way past the first half hour each morning. Still, on him it looked right. The upside to hair like that was that, although it would not stay combed, it would not stay mussed either. Once the wind stopped blowing, it would always drop back into place as it was.

She rolled two desk chairs close together. *Our names would make a great title for a movie. Yeah, a romantic comedy, "Fitz and Vega". It could also be the name of a degenerative disease.* She snickered.

"Why are you looking at me and stifling a laugh?" he asked. "It doesn't exactly inspire confidence."

"It's nothing. Just a flight of fantasy."

"It must have been a short, funny flight."

"It was." She sat and gestured him to the chair she had positioned next to her. Suddenly an apprehensive veil drifted down over her. Her darkening mood had nothing to do with Fitz. It was what she was worrying about when he appeared and lightened her disposition. He had almost succeeded in wiping the concern from her mind. Regrettably, it came back on her without warning when the banter ceased momentarily. She would rather be thinking about this guy sitting next to her, or, frankly, anything else. The invasive problem she contemplated was an unwelcome intrusion.

Once seated, Fitz turned to her, examined her face. He inquisitively reared his head. "In two seconds flat, you have gone from giddy to...this." He waved a finger in front of her face and added, "Whatever *this* is. Now, what's on your mind?" he asked.

"Sorry. I'm worried about my brother."

Fitz swiveled around to square with her. "Talk to me."

"His name is Daniel. I told him last year that hanging out with his cousin, Manuel Ortiz would come to no good. Well, as expected, that day came." She sighed. "Manuel held up a convenience store at gunpoint a few years back. Over the following months he became bolder and bolder but finally was caught, arrested, and indicted. Thanks to a sleazy high-priced attorney provided by his brother and my other cousin, the Mexican drug lord, Rogelio, Manuel made bail.

That's where Daniel comes in. My brother had *nothing* to do with the robberies, but the idiot took Manuel into his house after he had jumped bail and hid him while Rogelio worked at getting Manuel out of the country and back into Mexico. Daniel was arrested and charged with criminal facilitation by aiding and abetting a known fugitive on the run. Rogelio's attorney managed to have bail set for Daniel, and Rogelio put up the cash to post the bond. Now, Daniel is out of jail awaiting trial. To make things worse, Daniel is indebted to our cousin, Rogelio, a cold-blooded drug cartel kingpin.

I had just ended a phone call from Daniel before you came out of the locker room. He wants to stay in my apartment until his trial. I told him no." Dixie's voice shifted into a higher octave. "In fact, I told him *hell* no. I wouldn't even let him tell me where he was. That's how badly I want his life of crap to remain all his. I don't want any of that smell on me. Daniel need not say it. It's clear, he owes that drug lord cousin of ours a debt and *will* get mixed up in that sleazy underbelly of existence even deeper now, probably part of a dangerous drug smuggling operation from Acuña into

Texas. Rogelio Ortiz has hooked a figurative ring in Daniel's nose, meaning my idiot brother will have no choice but do whatever Rogelio wants him to do, illegal or not."

"For what it's worth, I think you did the right thing," Fitz whispered.

She nodded affirmation. "Thanks for saying it. It was a difficult thing to say to my only sibling. I still wonder if there may be something I can do for him, short of allowing him to live with me. He is the last of my immediate family, after all." Her eyes drifted away from Fitz to the floor. When she looked back up, a wave of emotion swarmed her. The view she had of Fitz blurred through watery eyes.

"I'm sorry you're having this trouble," he said in hushed tone as he watched a man and a woman walk by the check-in counter, heading toward the main entrance. It was clear at a glance, Fitz was trying hard to keep a potentially embarrassing conversation strictly between the two of them.

"Oh, Fitz, this whole story only sets up my real dilemma. The trouble Daniel is having is *his* problem. I have a bigger concern. I'm worried more about Carlee's problem."

"Carlee? What does she have to do with it?"

"Everything."

Fitz ran a palm over his face. "Sorry. You just lost me."

"Carlee shot and killed Manuel during an arrest gone bad, and Daniel told me Rogelio is going after her and her family. At the time, Daniel didn't know Carlee is such a close friend. Otherwise, he may not have told me about it. I'm certain Daniel knows by now, if he has communicated at all with our cousin recently. Rogelio certainly has the money and influence to do the worst."

"You have to tell her."

"I know. That's why I'm twisted in knots. I don't think Carlee knows Manuel was my cousin and Daniel is my brother. That woman is more of a sibling to me than Daniel ever was or ever will be. She is my *Hermana* that I have come to love very much. Carlee has not only accepted me but has insisted that I be part of her family, sharing holidays and special occasions, like...well, like all families are supposed to do. I'm scared it may screw her head up to know it's a relative of mine she had to kill, and another relative that may try to kill her. But you're right. I do have to tell her. She must take precautions to protect herself, Rylee, and her mother. I've just been hesitating because I didn't want to mess up her evening. She hasn't been out in so long."

Fitz nodded, retrieving a cell phone from his pants pocket. "Call her." He handed her his phone. "An evening interrupted by bad news is better than the alternative."

Dixie stared at the phone for only a second. She snatched it from Fitz's hand and punched in Carlee's number.

"Carlee Cayne."

"Carlee, I apologize for interrupting your evening." She heard an exaggerated sigh. "Oh, geez. I did mess up your evening. Didn't I?"

"No, no, Dix. That's not it at all. I'm still coming down from riding an adrenaline high. Some people in a big black SUV took shots at Linc. When I fired back at them, they turned automatic gunfire on me."

"Oh my God. Is Linc okay?" Dixie blurted.

Fitz suddenly became extremely interested and wheeled his chair closer, trying to hear what Carlee was saying.

"He's fine," Carlee told her, "just shaken up, but no more so than I am. How Linc and I managed to survive without taking a single bullet is a miracle. My hands are shaking so badly I can barely keep this phone to my ear, and the reason I still don't have control of my breathing."

"Have the police been called?"

"The hotel parking lot is filled with Austin PD cruisers and Department of Public Safety vehicles right now. It's a kaleidoscope of red, white, and blue strobing lights. They're cordoning off the scene. I've already told them everything I know. It didn't take long. I'm worried, Dix—very worried."

"You're at that tall hotel by the river, aren't you?"

"Yeah, why?"

"I'll be there in a couple of minutes. I have something to tell you that can't wait—not anymore." Dixie ended the call, not allowing Carlee to respond. She was out of her chair and on her feet before she had finished talking.

"Where are you going?" Fitz asked, springing to his feet.

"You were right, Fitz. I was a fool for not telling Carlee sooner. She must know it all, and she has to know it now. I can truthfully say, it is now a matter of life and death."

Fitz took the lead out the front door. "Come on, we'll take my Camaro."

Dixie trailed him, shouting over her shoulder at a young man with a Power House T-shirt on, "Bobby, I have an emergency. Would you take over the desk for me till closing?"

"Not a problem. Go on and take care of things," the boy called out as she exited the building.

It did not matter what the young man's reply had been, she was leaving to meet Carlee. Friends like her are rare, and Dixie would do anything necessary to prevent harm from coming to her.

She dropped into the passenger seat of Fitz's car an instant after he'd unlocked it. As he slid in beneath the steering wheel, she realized he had not asked if there was anything he could do to help. He had taken the lead. Her heart swelled, appreciating that Fitz was a man she could count on—the first one in a long, long time.

Chapter Eight

After driving around Austin in a daze for two hours, it was almost one o'clock in the morning when Lincoln finally had the key in the lock to the front door of his home. Even now, the fear had not entirely settled from the attempt on his life. But fatigue was beginning to replace it. He was coming down fast, comparable to crashing after one of those drug-induced highs he remembered so well from his college days. Utter exhaustion weighted his body as he entered his home. He gazed up the stairs toward his bedroom, not looking forward to what should have been the simple task of climbing them. He briefly considered collapsing on the sofa in the media room. *No, I want to be in my own bed*. He drew a breath and soldiered on, trudging up the stairs. All he wanted was to lie prone and let sleep overtake him. His thoughts narrowed to that bed and only that bed, certain he would be asleep by the time his head touched the pillow.

He reached for the bedroom door knob clumsily, misjudging its location. Not so delicately, he poked the doorknob with his knuckles, rattling it. He opened the door. Through the fog of exhaustion, it abruptly occurred to him it was late and he had not called Jeannine to tell her where he was.

The noise startled her awake. Remaining rolled in a tight fetal ball on her side wrapped around a pillow, head turned away, she moaned lightly. "So, you saw fit to come home. I should feel blessed," she mumbled.

Lincoln did not want to argue, or talk at all. Nonetheless, a conversation was plainly begun. What he wanted wasn't even on the table as a topic of discussion. Then again, what he wanted never mattered to Jeannine anyhow. *Damn. I could have been comfortably drifting off to sleep in the media room by now*. He sat on the edge of the bed. "This is where I live. Where else would I go?" he asked as he kicked off his shoes.

It was reasonable to assume she already knew where he had been, if she watched any news reports or someone had called to tell her about the shooting. For God's sake, the hotel parking lot was full of television news vans with antennae masts run up, broadcasting live. A row of reporters with microphones in hand stood in brilliant haloes of white light in front of rolling cameras, all doing live broadcast feeds. He and Carlee's faces were on every channel. There was no way Jeannine did not know where he had been.

As he stood to take off his shirt, Jeannine asked, "Who was the woman you were standing next to in the hotel parking lot? And, why were you at a hotel?" She rolled onto her back and slid up to lean back against the headboard of the bed. She yawned.

"Her name is Carlee Cayne, a deputy for the US Marshals Service. She saved my life tonight, literally."

"Okay. What about the second part of the question? What were you doing at a hotel so late on a weeknight?"

"When I left the gym, I drove over there for a glass of wine at a small bar just off the lobby."

"Alone?"

The conversation spiraled into territory Lincoln did not want to travel to, not yet anyhow. Although, there was much that needed to be discussed, he wanted to put it off for another time. He began to unbuckle his belt, but suddenly thought leaving his pants on was the better choice for now, uncertain how far down this rabbit hole he would have to travel. "No, Jeannine, I was not alone. I was with Miss Cayne."

Jeannine flailed her arms. "Well, ain't that just great! I'm here alone and you're out with another woman! Tell me, and don't you dare lie to me, when you walked out into that parking lot together, had you two come straight from the bar or down from a room?"

Lincoln stared at her with cold, hard eyes. "Jeannine, I've always had a rule when negotiating with clients. If he or she is extremely worried about *me* cheating *them,* doing something illegal—gouging, lying, or any other nefarious thing—it only means they would cheat me in a heartbeat if given the chance. They're, frankly, wanting the upper hand, unfairly as a rule. All the while accusing me of the same thing."

"What are you talking about? What does that little story have to do with what we're talking about?"

He took a deep breath. "Nothing happened, Jeannine. We came straight from the bar to go our separate ways. Oh, and by the way, I didn't get shot, in case you were interested at all in my health."

She crossed her arms and pouted. "Maybe you should have been."

Exhaustion drove billowing anger. He was in no mood for this. "Yeah, maybe you're right. I should have been shot. I would, at least, be in a hospital bed getting some good drug-induced sleep right now."

"I should get out of bed this very minute and head straight to Mama and Daddy's house and not come back."

"Yeah, right. No use doing anything new or different at this stage of the game."

Jeannine's jaw fell slack. "You're having late night liaisons with a woman, and you have the gall to talk to me in that tone? You should be begging me for forgiveness." she said, face reddening and tightening.

The thread holding Lincoln's emotions in check snapped. "Damn it, Jeannine! It was not anything illicit. It was a goddamn drink with a friend! Okay?"

Not to be outdone, "Are you tellin' me nothing happened and nothing ever will?" she countered even louder.

"No. I'm saying nothing happened, but I will not guarantee you nothing ever will," he fired back without a blink of hesitation. "Your questions are making my point, if you think *I'm* guilty of cheating."

The abrupt frankness plainly shocked her. Her face relaxed. "I, uh, you and me..." She shook off confusion, angry face quickly returning. "Why would you say such a thing to me?"

The desire for sleep left him. He was wide awake and not happily so, red and burning eyes bulging. This was as good a time as any. He sat on the end of the bed, refusing to make eye contact, no less angry but more in control. "Who was that man you were with at the club last night?"

She did not answer, but he felt the bed move as she abruptly shifted her weight.

He glanced back over his shoulder. She squirmed. "I need an answer, Jeannine. It's a simple question."

"Were you at the club last night?" she asked.

"That's not an answer," he replied. "Judging by your hesitance, it's not something you wanted me to find out about."

"Are you having me followed?" she asked, apprehension building.

"No. Now answer my question."

"It was Arthur Brooks," she replied in a whisper.

Lincoln turned his head slowly, deliberately. "Are you talking about Artie, the manager of the Rosen shoe store in the mall?"

Her head slumped forward as she nodded affirmation.

"Are you having an affair?"

She sat unmoving, head downturned. She did not reply and appeared as though there was no intention to say anything at all.

That was answer enough. He sighed. "Jeannine, our marriage has been floundering for a long time, years actually. You've had your parents, your north side friends, and that country club. Regardless how I've tried, I never fit into that world—your world. There's simply no room for me in it. And, you never lifted a finger to join me in mine. Our entire marriage has been nothing shared. It has always been a situation where you do your thing, I do my thing, and then we meet at home in the evenings and never talk about either one."

Although Jeannine was not openly weeping, tears poured freely as she sat up in bed uncharacteristically quiet, knees drawn up, arms encircling them. Desire to argue, or speak at all, had vanished.

There was no need to ask. He saw it on her face. She knew where this conversation was going and what the inevitable end of it would be. "Look," Lincoln said softly as he put a hand on her leg below the knee and rubbed it tenderly, "you and I deserve happiness, both of us. *Surely* you can see we're not finding it together, or we would have long ago." He preferred she respond, although unnecessary. His mind was set. Although, he had no desire to hurt her any more than he had to, to get it said. Lincoln was determined to make his peace one way or the other, and to get it done right now.

"I'll move out and find an apartment on the south side of town, closer to the agency. If you want the Rosen family attorney to draft divorce papers, that's fine. All I require, or want, is my job and a car. You can have everything else. In the next few days, I'll have a talk with your father. Saul and Lidia have always been good to me. I don't want to disappear without your father knowing how much I appreciate everything he's done for me—for us. He's a good man, and your mother is a wonderful lady." He paused. Awkward silence filled the room.

Lincoln rose, intending that to be the final word. As he came to his feet, the weight of his decision doubled the effect of gravity upon his body. He picked up his shirt and shoes and plodded toward the bedroom door. Emotion tugged backwards at him, like a surging tide, back toward the bed, toward a life he struggled to break free of and leave behind.

"Linc?" Jeannine asked, sounding more mature than usual. "Regardless what I've said or done, or what has gone on between us, I do love you. You need to know that."

He hesitated, but now incapable of facing her. If he did, he might not leave. He fought the force, putting one heavy foot in front of the other toward the door. Lincoln said the only thing he should say—nothing.

As he walked out of the bedroom, he heard Jeannine finally break. She sobbed.

Once outside the house, he sat on the front steps and put his shoes on. He rose and shuffled toward his car parked in the circular driveway in front of the house. He took a moment to look at the stripe of evenly placed bullet holes down the side below the windows. He then walked around the driver's side and looked back over the top of his car at the upscale two-story house he and Jeannine had called home for over fifteen years. His eyes traced the lines of it, envisioning a chapter of his life coming to an end. *What a night this has been? My whole life has suddenly flipped upside down.* He hesitatingly slid into the driver's seat, fatigue back on him with a vengeance.

Following the semi-circle driveway out to the street, he glanced at the house in his rearview mirror. A view of it, he thought, may well be his last.

Chapter Nine

"Turner called while I was at the gym," Fenn said as he and Carlee sat side by side in her car in the hotel parking lot. "Apparently, he had been trying to contact you and couldn't get through to you. I was his second choice. Is your phone turned off?"

"It was but not now." She bounced a shoulder shrug. "I didn't want to be disturbed."

Fenn cut a smile short. "Remember me telling you about that strange call Turner received?"

"Yeah. So?"

"The thing is, the guy wanted to thank you *personally* for keeping a dangerous criminal element off the streets. That brings me to my point."

"Which is what?"

"Whoever it was seemed a little too eager to know where you were. When questioned, the caller became evasive and hung up. That's when Turner immediately checked the last number that called and dialed it — finding out it came from the same shady law office in San Antonio that represents Rogelio and Manuel Ortiz. Turner wanted to warn you to watch your back. He's convinced the cartel is on the hunt...*for you*."

Carlee noticed Lincoln's BMW pulling out onto the street, presumably heading home. Sadness coursed through her, afraid he might not want to be around her any longer. All the media had left and most law enforcement as well. She apparently had become a lightning rod to herself and anyone standing too close to her. She assumed it had something to do with her job, but did not know what specifically prompted the attack. But, why did they open fire on Linc? As Linc disappeared down the street, a red Camaro turned off the street and stopped behind her car. In the rearview mirror, she saw Dixie and Lincoln's friend, Fitz, bound out of the car. Carlee let down her window as Dixie trotted up.

Dixie reached through the open window and embraced Carlee around the neck, going cheek to cheek. "Are you okay, sweetie?"

Carlee patted her friend's arms encircling her neck. "I'm fine." She gazed into unbelieving eyes. "Really, Dix. I'm fine. Not a scratch. Just shaken up. That's all."

"There's something I need to tell you, Carlee, and it pains me more than you know," Dixie said as she was getting into the back seat of Carlee's four door company sedan. Fitz got in the other side.

"About what?" Carlee asked, turning sideways in the seat.

"About all this stuff you're going through."

"I don't understand. What would you know about any of it, other than what I've told you?"

Carlee's partner, Fenn, suddenly became interested in the conversation and turned to face Dixie in the back seat. "I need to hear this, too," he said.

Dixie abruptly seemed unable to maintain eye contact and began watching her fidgeting hands lying in her lap. After a couple of seconds, in low tones, she began, "First, I want to apologize for my family. Daniel Vega is my brother, the one y'all arrested for aiding and abetting Manuel Ortiz, our cousin. Manuel was as crooked as they come. I'm afraid Daniel has launched himself down the same road. I've never had anything to do with Manuel or Rogelio. Less than an hour ago, I told Daniel I wanted nothing more to do with him either, *if* he chose to side with our cousin, Rogelio."

Carlee looked to Fenn as his eyes came around to lock onto hers. She returned her attention to Dixie. "That would mean the drug lord of Acuña, Rogelio Ortiz, is also your cousin. Do you have information that would be pertinent to what happened here this evening?"

Dixie nodded. "Daniel told me Rogelio is out for revenge. His plan is to kill those closest to you. He wants you to watch him or his cronies gun down someone dear to you. I'm not sure, but I think he plans on coming after you next. At the time he was telling me this, Daniel was not aware you are my friend. Otherwise, he would not have told me about it. I'm sure of it."

Carlee snapped a hard look at Fenn. "That's why they opened fire on Linc. He was with *me*, and the only reason. Oh my God. Mom and Rylee..." She squared her body with the steering wheel and cranked the engine. "I've got to get to Mom's house. Dixie, you and Fitz get out. Hurry."

Fenn was already on the phone, calling Austin Police, detailing as much of the situation as he could.

Dixie and Fitz threw open their doors and exited. With tears in her eyes, Dixie leaned over and looked back through the window at Carlee. "I'm so sorry. I hope someday you can forgive me."

Carlee forced her manner to slow. She reached through the window and grabbed Dixie's arm. "You have *nothing* to apologize for," she said slowly, deliberately. "You are my friend and it took great courage to tell me what you did. It puts you in their cross-hairs, too, you know."

"You can't go back to your apartment. Get your mom and Rylee and come to my place," Dixie said.

"Not a good idea," Fenn blurted as he ended his call. "Even if they don't know yet where Carlee lives, they certainly know where your apartment is located, Dixie. That would provide no more security. I actually believe it would be less safe. Rogelio has probably made the relationship connection between you and Carlee by now. It's a necessary assumption that they already know where you both live. You'll need a safe place to stay for a while too. Hopefully, they don't have Beth Cayne's address yet. Carlee and I will pick up her and Rylee and take them to my house. I live alone in a roomy three-bedroom house." He jotted his address on a small notepad and ripped off the sheet, handing it to Fitz. "Y'all meet us there, at this address."

"We'll be there when you get there," Fitz replied, already turning to jog back to his car.

Carlee slammed the shifter into the drive position and accelerated hard—tires squealing, leaving Dixie standing. She bounced out onto the street fronting the hotel. "Do you think Rogelio is personally spearheading this revenge quest?" she asked her partner.

"I don't know," Fenn replied, "but, since it concerns his brother, he may be throwing caution to the wind in this case, to make sure it all comes off the way he wants."

"I hope he *does* get careless," Carlee muttered as she hit the on-ramp of the interstate heading north. "I've never hated anyone more than Rogelio Ortiz, an arrogant jerk I've never met. I don't even know what he looks like. I'll deny it, if you repeat this, but if we can be so lucky as to trap him on this side of the border, I'm going to put the bastard down. And, what happened tonight will be the only provocation I'll need to do it. I don't care if he sees it coming or not."

Chapter Ten

Without stating intention, Fitz committed to helping Dixie protect Carlee and her family. He was coming to admire Dixie Vega in the deepest way. Every look, every glance, and every new thing he learned about her strengthened the notion. A bond tightened between them. He felt her loyalty, not only toward him but to all the people she held dear. Unfortunately, Dixie's own brother, Daniel, had fallen out of favor, and thusly, out of her life. She identified with Carlee Cayne and her family as her own. He wondered, though, how far Dixie would go to protect them. Fitz's feeling was, this cute *Latina* would march through hell itself for her friends.

Slowing his Camaro, Fitz, cruised at a snail's pace, checking house numbers on Jimmy Fenn's street, searching for the number jotted on the note he held. He counted down the houses in this middle-class Austin neighborhood until he saw a number matching the note. He veered toward the curb and eased forward, stopping in front of it. "This must be the place," he said. He turned off the headlights and the engine.

"That's the house number Mister Fenn gave us. It must be this one." Dixie was clearly anxious, but neither of them could do anything until Carlee returned with her family. "Fitz," she said, "I have no clue how dangerous this will become, but it's not your fight. When Carlee gets here, I want you to go home."

The words cut deep, as if she ground salt into an open wound. "Aw, hell no! It may not have been my fight a day ago, or even a few hours ago, but it is now. I refuse to allow an inflated sense of responsibility on your part crush you under its weight."

Dixie's lips parted. Her mouth hung loosely open. She stared.

Realizing that his response was no less abrasive, he drew a breath and sighed long. "Dixie, you have a big heart," he said, then paused. He smiled. "I would have to be blind, deaf, and exceedingly ignorant not to notice."

Dixie's eyes grew ever larger and glossed over, shimmering in the moonlight.

Fitz reached for her hand and held it. "If nothing else," he said, "I can share the burden with you, and I want to. So, don't insult me like that again." He kissed the back of her hand. "Pretty please?"

Dixie swiped a leaking tear with the fingertips of her free hand. She pulled their locked hands from his lips to her own, kissing the back of his hand. "Would you be my friend, Ben Fitzsimmons?"

"I thought we already were friends."

The little girl look was replaced by an expression more adult, but still demure. "We were acquaintances. Some people confuse that for friendship." She kissed his hand again. "But, it sure would be nice to have a stable male influence in my life. As you may be figuring out, I've never had one."

Dixie's answer was like honey to his ears. He tipped his head. His smile grew larger. "I would be honored to call you my friend, Miss Vega." He noticed her eyes move away from his face to a point ahead of the car before he added, "I will add, I expect this to be only the beginning." Suddenly realizing he had lost her attention, his eyes followed hers and saw an SUV pull up and stop against the curb of a side street half a block ahead, perpendicular to the street they were parked on. The vehicle's headlights shone at a right angle across the intersection. The headlights went out. Fitz scanned all within view in the neighborhood. It was almost midnight. *There is no other traffic, yet a vehicle stops at the end of a street and parks like that. If they live around here, why not park in front of a house or in a driveway?* It seemed and looked suspicious, especially on this night. "That doesn't look right...*at all*," he said.

"I know what you mean. And, look, no one is getting out of the vehicle," she replied, turning her attention to him. "Do you think Rogelio or his crew could have found this place so quickly?"

"I don't know. But let's be logical about this. It's a given they know where *you* live, the family connection and all. It also means they have definitely discovered your close friendship with Carlee. If their plan is to harm Carlee and her family, then they know where she lives and, I'm sure, they looked up her mother's address. That would not be difficult for someone, even without money and resources. The fact Jimmy Fenn is Carlee's friend and partner would put him squarely in their sights as well. The final point is if the people in that vehicle up there are up to no good. That means they've already been to Carlee's apartment and her mother's house and found no one home at either place." He shot Dixie a hard look. "That can only mean Jimmy Fenn's house is next on the list. Crap! How long do you think it will take Carlee to drive back here?" he asked.

"Beth Cayne doesn't live far from here. If they didn't encounter some unexpected delay, they should be here any minute," Dixie replied.

Fitz snatched his phone from a cup holder in the console. His hand was shaking. "Carlee's number? What's Carlee's number?"

She took the phone from him. "I can dial it faster than tell you what it is." By the time it started ringing, a pair of headlights turned onto the street behind them and shone directly through Fitz's car.

"Quick, get down," Fitz ordered as he fell over onto his side with his head near her lap at the same time she slid down in the seat. "Those lights will silhouette us perfectly to whoever is in that SUV up there."

Carlee answered the phone. "We're right behind you. What's up?"

"Stay in your car," Dixie blurted. "I think we're about to be in the middle of an ambush."

"I've got you on speaker, so Fenn can hear this. Why do you think that?"

"Look straight ahead to that side street intersecting with this one. See that SUV?"

"Yeah."

"It pulled up and parked a few minutes ago. No one has gotten out of it."

"Thanks, Miss Vega," Fenn said. "You and Mister Fitzsimmons stay down. I'm calling for backup. Carlee and I will act at the appropriate time, hopefully after backup gets here. You two stay out of sight. Got it?"

"Understood," Dixie replied.

"It may become imperative that we know exactly where you are at all times, in case it becomes confusing in the dark," Fenn added in a quick clipped manner.

~ * ~

Once Fenn ended the call, Carlee turned to the backseat. "Mom, no matter what happens, hang on to Rylee and keep both your heads down. Fenn and I will be fine, if we know y'all are safe and where you are at all times. Understand?"

"Yes, dear, I do understand. *Please* be careful," her mother implored.

Rylee whimpered. "Don't go, Mama," the youngster whined as she reached for Carlee. "I'm scared."

Carlee gently removed Rylee's hand from her shoulder. "I'll be fine, baby, if I know you are too. Now put your head on your Grandma's lap and stay there. Don't look out the window for any reason. Okay?"

As Rylee fell over onto Beth Cayne's lap, "I won't. I promise," came the child's nervously halting response.

Carlee pulled her Glock 40 from the holster on her hip. She popped the magazine from its handgrip clip, checked the load, and then slammed it home with a decisive click. She racked the slide, jacking a shell into the chamber.

"Carlee, look," Fenn said tentatively. "There's no doubt now. They saw your headlights come to a stop and then go off."

Carlee looked ahead the half block to the residential intersection and, by the light of the moon and nearby streetlights, she saw the back door of the SUV ease open and a leg drop out, placing a foot on the curb. A figure exited the vehicle. "We don't have the luxury of waiting for backup," she said. "We have to lead those guys away from these cars."

"I know," he replied and then pointed to a specific location. "Get out and head straight for that fence gate as fast as you can run. It opens into the backyard. We already know they have automatic weapons. We can't win a heads-up shootout. If it does happen, we don't want hell unleashed near these two cars," Fenn said. He paused a beat before continuing, "There're bushes around back that I'm glad now I never trimmed. Maybe we can lure them back there, hide, and turn the ambush on them. There is no outdoor lighting back there and no nearby streetlights, so we should have the advantage *if* we beat them back there and drop behind those shaggy bushes."

"Copy that. I see another guy coming around the front of the vehicle to meet up with the first one. They'll be upon us in a few seconds." Carlee put her hand on the door handle but hesitated, knowing as soon as the interior dome light of her car came on, all hell was going to break loose. She glanced into the backseat and saw her mother gawking. "Damn it, Mom! Get down and stay down." She looked to Fenn. "Let's go."

~ * ~

Dixie heard a commotion coming from Carlee's car parked behind Fitz's Camaro. She lifted her head far enough to see both their front car doors had been flung open. She watched Carlee sprint toward the house. Since Fenn had to run around the car, he trailed Carlee by about twenty feet as they angled toward the right side of the house running flat-out.

Automatic gunfire erupted. Dixie saw fire spitting from the weapons of two men chasing after them. She heard shouted Spanish in a quick exchange by the two gunmen. Translated, they were simply formulating a plan of attack on the fly. A symphony of distant sirens caught her attention.

Fitz grabbed her loose-fitting windbreaker sleeve and pulled. "Get down, Dixie!"

She wrenched her arm from his grasp. "They're not shooting at us," she scolded. Dixie could barely make out Fenn in the darkened shadows at the end of the house. He appeared to be fumbling with the gate latch. Carlee was at his back facing the opposite direction, gun drawn.

One of the attackers stopped. He began raising the automatic weapon at his side when Dixie heard pop, pop, pop. She saw accompanying muzzle flashes from the other direction. Carlee had fired three quick shots and apparently hit the guy.

As he fell, another riff of bullets flew in Carlee's direction from his fully automatic weapon. Carlee spun sideways and Fenn grabbed for the back of his thigh just as the gate swung open. They both had been hit.

Carlee stumbled past Fenn through the gate. He followed her through. Dixie fidgeted, reaching for the car door handle. "Oh my God. They're hurt. I've got to do something."

"Stop," Fitz hissed. "Think, girl, think. You're unarmed. You'd be going up against two guys with more fire power than the cops'll have, who are racing this direction right now. What is it that you think you can do?"

Dixie looked toward the house, trying to make out details in the dim light. She glanced back to the other car. Beth Cayne and Rylee, grandmother and granddaughter, were keeping their heads down. It was a small measure of comfort, but very small. She continued scanning the vicinity for fast clues, something from which to fashion a plan. As her eyes settled on the SUV, she saw a third man exit the vehicle. He began trotting down the sidewalk. He was holding something, presumably another automatic weapon. He angled away from the sidewalk toward that backyard gate at the end of Jimmy Fenn's house.

"Sorry, Fitz, but by the hands of my own family, Carlee and Fenn are in deep trouble and it's about to get worse. They think they're only dealing with two. That guy running this way, they're not expecting him at all. Being unaware of a third man could get them killed. No time. Must act." She threw open the car door.

"Dixie! Wait!"

By the time Fitz's words reached her ears, Dixie was already running as fast as she could toward the man, the long single plait of hair flagging as she sprinted high on her toes. She raced directly for the third intruder, trying to catch him before he reached the wooden picket privacy gate that matched the fence standing six feet tall. Judging by the height of the fence, the man was short, not much taller than herself. On the fly, his short stature spawned a plan, if she could get to him before he saw her coming at him. So far, she retained the advantage. Slim as it was. The man remained focused on the gate and had not looked back.

He slowed his advance, becoming cautious, as he approached the open gate.

She was running across an open stretch of lawn devoid of cover— no shrubs, no trees, no place to take refuge should he turn that gun on her before she could get to him.

Dixie opted for a quieter approach as she came near the man. She slowed. Noise had become an additional nemesis. It was going well until, about ten feet from the guy, she stepped on a pecan. It crunched under her foot.

The man flinched and spun, raising his weapon at the same time.

Time had run out for options.

Before the gun made it to an appropriate firing angle, Dixie took three quick steps and went airborne, going prone five and a half feet in the air. She had thrown her body into a spinning motion as she left the ground. She sandwiched the man's head between her thighs as she rolled over the top of his head.

The thug inadvertently squeezed and held the trigger. A staccato spray of bullets struck in a random arc across the end of the house, blowing brick chips back at them, stinging Dixie's face.

Still, the momentum of her move had the guy's body uncontrollably following the twisting motion of his head between her thighs. He hit the ground so hard it forced the entire capacity of his lungs to explosively exit his body, leaving him gasping for air.

Dixie had to get control of the gun before he regained his wind and strength. She would not be able to match him in a straight up tug-of-war for control of it. He had landed on his side. She unclenched her thighs, releasing his head. In a smooth and exceedingly fast move, she rolled around his prone body to a position behind him, dropping a knee onto his neck.

But, at five-foot-five and a hundred-ten pounds, this brute would toss her like a bean bag in another second, maybe less. She could not stop, needing to complete the planned maneuver in a single fast action.

As she moved to immobilize him from using the gun on her, the thug didn't even try to get up. Instead, he switched the gun to his free hand, attempting to shoot her off him.

As the gun arm came up, Dixie twined her arm around it and immobilized his arm by locking his elbow. The gun rattled off another wild spritz of bullets, this time into the air.

Dixie suddenly became aware that a fire fight had erupted in the back yard.

Lights were coming on all over the neighborhood.

The first Austin Police cruiser turned onto the street.

Sirens wailed.

The guy attempted, once again, to point the gun at her.

Dixie came up off her knee against the guy's neck and replaced it with the side of her foot using it for leverage. She then twisted the thug's locked gun arm until she felt the shoulder joint pop, followed by a grinding as she twisted the arm from its socket. He howled in pain but now had no choice but to drop the gun.

Two police officers ran up and kicked the gun away from the man, while the other replaced Dixie by flipping the guy over onto his belly. The man screamed in pain as the officer unceremoniously grabbed the injured arm, showing it no more consideration than the healthy one. He pulled the thug's hands together in the back and cuffed him.

Exchanged gunfire continued in the back yard.

As the officer stood with his back to the fence, gun drawn, elbows tight to his side with his service pistol held ready for action, "The back yard, what's the story?" he asked as quickly as his mouth could form the words.

"Two deputy marshals are trapped by two of this yahoo's buddies," Dixie answered in kind. "The bad guys are the ones with fully automatic weapons."

By the time she finished the explanation, four more law enforcement officers arrived. The one by the gate yelled, "Austin PD! Cease firing and drop your weapons!"

The shooting stopped and Dixie heard one of the assailants shout, "*Vamonos! Andale! Andale!*" The punks were bolting due to the convergence of law enforcement.

Officers ran through the gate into the back yard.

Dixie trotted over and eased her face around the edge of the opening in the fence in time to see one of the shooters swing his gun around, but he never had a chance to fire. Three police officers opened fire and dropped him. The other one kept running. Two of the officers gave chase over the fence while a third attended the one they had just shot.

Dixie stepped through the gate into the back yard. "Carlee, Mister

Fenn...where are y'all? Are you okay?"

"Yeah. I think so," came Carlee's fatigued response, buried within a sigh.

Dixie looked to the cluster of unruly bushes and saw a small light flash on. She followed it, pushing aside gangling limbs. Jimmy Fenn and Carlee sat side by side with their backs against the foundation of the house. Jimmy Fenn was looking at Carlee's wound with a small flashlight. Dixie drew a deep relieved breath. "Well, aren't you two a raggedy pair?" she said and then noticed the blood. "I heard one of the officers call for an ambulance. You'll have help in a couple of minutes. Can you move?"

"I can," Carlee said. "A bullet caught me low on the side. Stings like hell, but I'm all right. How about you, Jimbo? Did that bullet catch the bone or femoral artery?"

"Nah, I'm okay, I think. But I may need an assist getting to my feet. The bullet is playing havoc with my thigh muscles."

Carlee rolled over and crawled out from under the bush.

Dixie replaced her and gave Fenn a hand, helping him out.

Carlee stepped out through the gate. An officer was having to forcefully restrain Rylee and, to a lesser extent, Beth Cayne as well near the street. "It's okay, officer. The area has been secured," she called out.

"Mama! Mama!" Rylee sobbed. The youngster came running and flew into her mother's arms. Carlee winced but did not attempt to pull the girl's arms away, happy just to be holding her daughter. She let Rylee cry while stroking the youngster's hair. Beth joined her daughter and granddaughter in a thankful group embrace.

Fitz followed Beth and wrapped Dixie up in his arms. "Damn it, girl, don't ever pull a stunt like that again."

She pulled her head back and smiled up at him. "You sure are demanding for a guy I've only known a couple of days."

He smirked. "Well, if it's okay with you, princess, I'd like to know you for a couple more."

Dixie pressed the side of her head onto his chest. "I have just two things to say to you. Number one...you are such a wiseass," she said and then added, whispering, "and, number two...thank you."

"For what?"

She pulled her head away from his chest and looked up at him. "If I have to explain it to you, forget it."

"You don't. I just wanted to hear you say it."

She grinned and made a point to look him straight in the eyes. "Shut up."

Fenn hobbled to where Dixie and Fitz stood. "Miss Vega, do you recognize either one of the guys that attacked us?"

"Sorry. No. But I never got a look at the one that went over the fence."

Emergency Medical Techs raced into the back yard. "We're okay," Carlee said, "but you had better check that guy over there. I don't think he's long for this world if left unattended, and may not make it anyhow. He took a couple of bullets to the chest."

As Carlee and Fenn helped one another across the front yard to get treatment at the ambulance, grandmother and granddaughter followed close behind. "Come on," Fitz said. "Let's leave the scene of the crime," he quipped.

Dixie nodded, yet did not make a move to follow. "Go on. I'll be along in a second," she replied.

As Fitz followed the others, Dixie returned to the backyard and stood over the dying gunman lying on a stretcher in the grass near the back fence. Two emergency medical techs worked on him, trying to stanch the bleeding. She looked down at him, her heart growing cold and her eyes hard. "Where is Rogelio, you son of a bitch?" she hissed through tightly clenched teeth. "Was he the one that went over the fence?"

The man's mouth moved but no words came out.

"Answer me, damn you!"

Dixie thought she detected an affirming nod. She had the strongest desire to spit in the man's face. At the gate, she stopped and looked toward the street, seeing Carlee sitting with her feet dangling out the back of the ambulance, talking to Jimmy Fenn who lay on a gurney inside. Beth, Rylee, and Fitz surrounded her. A sudden chill coursed her body. Those people meant everything to her. They were more than friends. She had always considered Carlee, Rylee, and Beth her family but now, quite suddenly, Fitz, Lincoln, and Jimmy Fenn had been thrown into the mix. To her way of thinking, they were all her only family now.

Chapter Eleven

By the time Carlee and Fenn had been treated at the emergency room and Carlee had taken Fenn home, dawn was breaking across Austin. The city was coming to life and traffic on the rise, right along with the sun to begin a new day. The smell of diesel fumes, the sound of car horns, and fast moving vehicles of all sorts filled the air. At the end of the cross-town trip, which she believed took far too long, she was exhausted as she pulled into her mother's driveway. The morning sun, uncomfortably bright, shone at a sharp angle through the car. The vehicle cast a long shadow across the front lawn. She glanced over at Rylee in the front passenger seat. The girl slept. She turned to her mother in the back seat. "Mom, if it's okay with you, I'll sleep here for a while. I'm so beat I don't want to make another trip across town to my apartment. In fact, I might fall asleep at the wheel if I tried."

"Heavens yes, sweetheart. Take the guest room. The sheets are clean."

Carlee smiled wanly. *As if clean sheets really matter right now. I think I could sleep on a dung heap, if it were soft enough.* She leaned across and whispered, "Rylee, honey, let's go in Grandma's house and get some sleep. Sorry to wake you. I wish I could still carry you, but you're a big girl now."

Rylee sat straight and wallowed balled fists into closed eyes. "It's okay, Mama," she slurred, not fully awake.

Once in the house, Beth stopped at her own bedroom door. "I'll cook a big lunch in a few hours." She yawned. "For now, let's all get some sleep. I'm exhausted too." She peeled off into her room.

As Beth was closing her bedroom door, "Believe me," Carlee said to her, "sleep is all I want right now." Walking behind her, with both hands on the girl's shoulders, Carlee guided Rylee to the guest bedroom. She turned down the covers and helped the youngster out of her jeans. Rylee remained more asleep than awake. The child limply fell over onto the bed. Immediately, the youngster sank into a sound sleep, drawing deep even breaths. Carlee kissed her on the cheek and pulled the covers over the child's shoulders as the central air conditioning system cycled on and welcome coolness settled over them both.

Finally, alone. The night had been long and arduous. She headed for the bathroom looking forward to washing away filth that went beyond grime. Every time she engaged criminals violently, the underbelly of society, it left her feeling unclean. She swore it also left a stench on her. She knew it was all in her head. Regardless, it was real enough. She worked her tight jeans to the floor and then skinned off her tank top. Carlee stared back through the open bathroom door to her daughter, wondering once again if there was anything else she could do to make a living to support Rylee. She held up her shirt, blood soaked at the bottom. She poked her finger through the bullet hole at the center of the stain. *I have to explore other career options before Rylee ends up without a mother.*

Her eyebrows drew down as the thought took her to a place she didn't want to be. She grunted and shook her head, attempting to sling thoughts of death and dying out of her mind. She scratched her head and yawned. *Or, I wind up in prison for shooting Supervising Deputy George Turner.* She tossed the shirt into the wastebasket. As she removed her bra in front of the mirror, she checked her face and hair. The face looking back was smudge streaked from crouching and wallowing on the damp ground in the bushes behind Fenn's house. Her short light brown hair was matted. She picked a couple of leaf bits from it. Those things could be cleaned, but the dark circles under her eyes could not be washed away. She sighed while reaching inside the shower to turn the water on. She allowed it time to warm while she stepped out of her panties. She flicked the undergarment with the point of her toe onto her grimy jeans that lay crumpled on the floor.

Stepping into the steam-filled shower stall, she closed the door and adjusted the shower head to hit her directly in the face. The sensation was sublime. It was at that point she decided to stand, moving little as possible, until every drop of hot water had been drained onto her aching body.

Leaning against the wall with extended hands, water cascading down over her hair and face, an image of Lincoln Bridger floated in to her thoughts and stayed. It was definitely a welcome imagining, considering the thoughts she was having a couple of minutes ago. She allowed herself to visualize snapshots of them as a couple—traveling, dining, and doing yard work together. Beyond the mundane, Carlee envisioned the two of them in the throes of lovemaking. She had no intention of breaking up his marriage, but by his own admission, things were not solid with his wife. Should she dare to hope his marriage would break up? That question played in her mind until she finally deemed her thoughts cruel. *What the hell am I thinking? I don't know his wife. I've never even seen her. She may be the sweetest human being on the planet and here I stand, hoping she loses her husband.* Carlee determined the best thing to do was to sleep and stop allowing her imagination to run wild, although, wonderful. Things would be much clearer after a few hours of sleep.

After several minutes of a long self-indulgent hot shower, she dried off and stepped out of the stall. While vigorously drying her hair with the towel, she walked out of the bathroom to the closet. She saw a few of her deceased father's flannel shirts hanging in a back corner of the closet and put one of them on, taking a moment to inhale the aroma of the shirt, stroking the soft fabric, thinking she could almost smell him. It was impossible though. Her father had been gone for nearly a decade—a victim of heart disease before hitting his sixtieth year. Quietly and gently she slid into bed next to Rylee, careful not to wake the child. Her head sank into a soft pillow. *Sleep—no more thoughts—just sleep.*

It took her quickly.

A buzzing sound pricked her awakening ears. After a second or so, it stopped. But Carlee remained within slumber's clutches and did not recognize the source. The buzzing sounded off again. This time, startling her. Her eyes popped open to see her cell phone vibrating atop the nightstand. The alarm clock on the opposite corner of the same table showed nine-thirty-six in annoyingly bright LED numerals. She thought it might be Fenn or someone else from the Service trying to contact her. Maybe they were calling to put her back on active duty today. Better yet, maybe it was Fenn calling to say they picked up Rogelio Ortiz. She snatched the phone up. "Hello."

"Carlee?"

"Speaking."

"Lincoln Bridger," he said tentatively.

She relaxed back down onto the pillow. "Oh, hey, Linc." She yawned.

"I didn't know if I should be calling or not. But I wanted to make sure you're okay after our ordeal last night in the hotel parking lot."

Carlee moved her head around, searching for that lost sweet spot of comfort on the pillow. "I'm the one that should be asking you that question. Are *you* okay?" She yawned again.

"I'm fine. Did I wake you?"

"Yes. But don't worry about it...*although*, I could sure use another couple of hours sleep. I didn't get home until just before sunup this morning."

"I—I'm sorry," he babbled. "I'll hang up and let you get back to sleep."

Carlee jerked her head off the pillow. "No, wait. Sure, I'm sleepy, but I'd rather talk to you than sleep." The blurted admission surprised even her.

Lincoln was slow to reply. Finally, "Okay, but only if you're sure."

Carlee smiled and pushed her head back onto the pillow. "I'm sure...very sure," she said and then swirled her tongue around in her dry mouth.

"Why did it take you so long to get home?" he asked.

"Without putting too fine a point on it, all hell broke loose at Jimmy Fenn's house last night."

"Same guys?" Lincoln asked.

"Not sure. But, if not, I am certain they were sent by the same guy. In fact, Rogelio Ortiz may have been the one that got away. Can't be sure though. The goal was clearly the same. One is dead and one was wounded and arrested. The third one jumped a fence and disappeared. There's a manhunt underway as we speak."

"That suddenly makes my first question more important now. Are you okay?"

Carlee danced fingers lightly over the patch bandage on the lower right side of her abdomen. "Wounded slightly, but I'm fine." She turned to face Rylee, still sleeping. "Linc, I think the time has come for me to put my daughter first and find another line of work outside law enforcement. My ex may be her father, but he's immature and undependable to a ridiculous degree. If anything should happen to me, Rylee's care would fall entirely on my mother. She's wonderful. But it would be unfair of me to burden her that way at this stage of her life, should the worst happen."

Lincoln didn't respond.

"Linc? You still there?"

"Uh, yeah. I was just thinking."

"Care to share?"

"What would you think about becoming a media buyer for Adler, Howard and Levy Advertising Agency?"

"Why? Is a position open?"

"No. But I think I have enough influence to create one."

"That's sweet of you, but everything I know about that business could fit on the head of a pin with room to spare." She sighed. "Unfortunately, the job I have is all I know." She chuckled lazily. "Unless, I consider my time at that hamburger joint while I was going to college. And, frankly, I don't want that on my résumé."

"Look, media buying is nothing more than researching demographics and statistics for the best way to spend a client's advertising dollars. You'd learn how to read and apply Nielsen demographic numbers plus other forms of statistical research data to find the best deals on television, radio, billboards, social media, and myriads of emerging advertising mediums, depending on the client's needs. Getting more eyeballs and ears for the client's dollar is what it's all about. It's certainly not as exciting as what you do. In fact, it might be boring for you, but a heck of a lot safer."

"Safe usually is boring." She sighed. "It's what I need though for Rylee's sake."

"I would be more than happy to be your teacher," he quickly added.

"It sounds wonderful." She paused. "If you are my trainer, wouldn't we have to work closely together for a time?"

"Of course."

"Would your wife have a problem with it, if she found out? I think you realize I'm seeing you as something more than an acquaintance."

"I'm glad you brought that up."

"I don't understand."

"I left Jeannine last night."

Carlee was quite suddenly no longer sleepy but wide awake and speechless.

"Can I assume by your silence I've surprised you?"

"That's putting it mildly." She dropped her feet onto the floor and sat on the edge of the bed. She pulled down the tail of the oversized flannel shirt to cover her nudity. "I—I hope it wasn't *because* of me."

"The drink we shared in the bar was no secret after what happened to us afterwards in the hotel parking lot, but it only shined a spotlight on problems that needed addressing *long* before I met you," he replied.

Carlee heard a strong tone of resoluteness in his response. "Okay. Go on," she said while getting out of bed. She shuffled slowly to the bedroom window, blankly scanning the view of her mother's back yard, waiting for Lincoln to get his thoughts together. Shadows cast by the midmorning sun were shrinking as the solar orb rose higher in the sky. A breeze swayed leaves of the live oak tree shading almost the entire backyard. Her eyes followed two squirrels playing chase through its branches.

"Right now," Lincoln continued, "I'm sitting on the end of a bed in a cheap motel on the Interstate. When it occurred to me to call you, I was on my way out the door to drive over to Jeannine's parents' house to talk to them. I'm nervous about it. Or, to be more specific, scared as hell. It won't be a pleasant conversation, but necessary. Saul and Lidia Rosen have been very good to me over the years. I've already called my boss, Mister Adler, and told him I wouldn't be in to work today and explained to him why."

While surveying her mother's backyard, Carlee abruptly narrowed her focus on the reflection of her own face in the window glass. She had not realized how big her smile had grown until she saw it grinning back at her. "Linc?"

"Yeah."

"I know this is where I should tell you I'm sorry about your marriage but, somehow, I can't make myself say it."

"Don't give it a second thought. I'm not going to. It essentially has been over between us for years. I'm simply going to make it official. That's all," Lincoln said.

"How about letting Rylee and I cook dinner for you at our apartment this evening? You and I can talk about advertising. I'll spring for a pay-per-view movie we can watch afterwards. What do you think of that idea?"

"Nothing in this whole wide world could possibly please me more."

Chapter Twelve

Lincoln's mood was buoyed, frown transforming into a relaxed smile, as he ended the call with Carlee, thinking how wonderful an evening with her would be. To be a guest in her home—her environment—her world. What would that be like? The thought was nice. A twinge of excitement coursed through him.

Unfortunately, a quick deflation of mood weaseled in. He, first, must endure what might turn out to be an unpleasant visit with Saul and Lidia Rosen. After a distasteful day, dinner with Carlee may prove as necessary as delightful. Being without companionship in the evening could weaken his resolve to follow through with the separation and ultimate divorce from Jeannine. He had to keep pressing forward. Even a single look back at the good times with Jeannine could bring his better judgment to a grinding halt.

Time to quit thinking and start doing. He sighed heavily, slapped his knees, and rose from the motel bed. Resolutely, he clenched his jaws and headed out the door.

On the drive to the Rosen's home, he attempted to gauge Lidia's mood by the tone of the short conversation he'd had with her right before he called Carlee. He had asked her if she and Saul would be home for the next couple of hours. She said they would be and then prodded him for a reason for his visit. Lincoln successfully thwarted her attempts to get an answer. He had to do it in person, face to face. Giving Lidia time to formulate a red-faced diatribe would be a mistake. Although he loved Lidia and knew her to be a good person, he was equally certain her loyalty to her daughter would trump any explanation he might come up with. Better to hit Lidia, and Saul as well, cold with news of the separation and the impending divorce from their only child. He hoped not, but it might become a contentious conversation. Since Jeannine's actions contributed heavily to the break up, he figured it would take his soon-to-be ex-wife some time to confront them with her version of events. It was his intention to announce the divorce but did not want to do any finger-pointing at Jeannine. Lincoln knew his wife well enough to realize she would not talk to her parents until she could control the narrative. And that would take a while to devise the perfect explanation, spinning events to her favor. Lincoln was confident this would be news to Saul and Lidia, and he would be the first one breaking it to them. That thought alone was somewhat unnerving. He feared an emotional meltdown.

He steered off the meandering upscale residential street, through the open black-iron gate onto the Rosen's driveway ascending to their stately home—a short drive he had taken hundreds of times over the past nineteen years of marriage to Jeannine Lucille Rosen. This time, it was different.

Lincoln rolled to a stop in front of the sprawling one-story white stucco hacienda-style home worthy of the wealthiest Mexican *patrón.* He sat for a moment, mustering courage, taking in the view of the house, which could be the last time he would ever be inside it. It might also be the last time he ever saw this place. It occurred to him he was beginning to see all things relating to Jeannine shifting to past tense.

Although Saul was a second generation Jewish-American by birthright, his grandparents emigrated out of Lithuania in the mid-nineteenth century to escape the conflict between The Eastern Orthodox Church of Russia and the Roman Catholic Church known as the Crimean War. Although raised in the New York area, Saul and Lidia came to love the culture of the southwest, thus the choice in architecture.

It was time. Lincoln got out of the car and stepped through the heavy oaken walk-through gate into the walled courtyard where a large swimming pool was centered and landscaped to appear as a clear, heavily shaded jungle pond. He saw no one. He did not break stride, walking briskly for the door he knew to be the kitchen at the back corner of this open courtyard. He was afraid that if his approach became hesitating, or slowed in the slightest, steadfastness might crumble. Every room facing the courtyard was constructed to offer a view and egress to the pool, including the kitchen. He rounded a mass of huge caladiums. The kitchen came into view. He saw Saul and Lidia sitting on tall stools drinking coffee at a handsomely tiled bar facing an unobstructed view of the pool and courtyard. Saul noticed, smiled, and waved him in.

"Hi, Lincoln," Lidia said. She seemed to be in a jovial mood. "Care for a cup of coffee?" she asked as he walked through the open sliding glass door.

"Thanks, but I don't think I'll be staying long enough to drink it."

"You look serious. What's on your mind?" Saul asked.

Lincoln pursed his lips and stared at the floor for a couple of seconds. *I knew this was going to be tough, but I had no idea that I'd totally lose my voice.*

Lidia's smile faded. She pulled back a stool the other side of Saul. "At least sit down for a minute."

Lincoln nodded rapidly without even a glance toward Lidia, realizing he could not look her in the eyes. He sat on the proffered stool but on the absolute edge, as if ready to run should it become necessary. He drew a deep breath and began, "Saul...Lidia..." Their names hung in his throat.

"If there's a problem you're dealing with, Linc, maybe Lidia and I can help you with it," Saul said, putting a fatherly hand on his shoulder.

"Saul, you and Lidia have been really good to me over the years. From the first time I met y'all while dating Jeannine, I was made to feel welcome in your home. I've never felt any other way around both of you. But..." He drew a breath. "...something will soon happen that will alter our relationship forever, I'm afraid. It pains me to say it, but Jeannine and I are going to get a divorce."

Lidia gasped. Her face hardened. "What the hell have you done, Lincoln Bridger?" she snapped.

Lincoln kept his eyes lowered, attempting, the only way he knew how, to show respect and humility. "It's not what I have done, but what *we* have done as husband and wife, and that's drift apart until our differences became too great to ignore any longer and...things happened that should not have, if the marriage had been strong."

Lidia slapped the countertop. "I knew it! I damn well knew it! You cheated on our baby, didn't you? And Jeannine found out. Isn't that right?"

A touch of anger bubbled in his gut. He raised his eyes to connect with Lidia's angry stare. "I'm going to let Jeannine answer that question. It's her story to tell."

Saul rose from the stool and took Lincoln's arm, gently tugging him to his feet. He was calm, eerily so. He led Lincoln away from Jeannine's mother to a distance he could not be overheard and whispered in Lincoln's ear. "Son, you don't need to say a thing. Just nod if it's true. I've heard scuttlebutt at the club that Jeannine has been carrying on a dalliance with one of my employees and not even trying to hide it. To your knowledge, is it true?"

Lincoln slowly pulled his head away from Saul's whisper and looked him directly in the eyes. He nodded once.

Saul stepped back over to Lidia and whispered into her ear.

Tears exploded from her eyes. "No! It can't be true! He's lying!"

Saul offered only a simple negative headshake with a neutral expression as a response to her assertion.

Lidia ran from the room, crying.

Saul waited for the bedroom door to close behind her. He turned his attention back to Lincoln. "Linc, you will always be welcome in this house. It took a helluva man to have enough courage to come here and face us with this news and do it without maligning our daughter. Although, in my opinion, you had every right to do so."

Lincoln became emotional. "I love both of you. I really do...always will." He stepped toward Mister Rosen extending his hand.

Saul not only took Lincoln's hand, he pulled him into a full embrace. "If you ever need *anything*, anything at all, call me." He pushed Lincoln back and gave him a warm smile. "Now, my boy, I have to go to my store in the mall and fire the manager."

Chapter Thirteen

As Carlee busied herself in the kitchen, she flicked glances at Lincoln. He sat at the dining table the other side of the bar, separating kitchen from dining where she was preparing dinner. Her apartment was small but comfortable for a mother and daughter. It crossed her mind it might not be roomy enough for a father, mother, and daughter. She smiled that she would even have the thought. Such a fantasy felt good and right, leaving her with a peaceful warmth deep inside. *I wonder if this anxious state of mind I've fallen into lately and sudden lonely feelings is the ticking of my biological clock.* She snickered. *It just might be.*

Lincoln seemed engrossed in a conversation with her daughter, Rylee. Carlee was awed and deeply enchanted by what she saw. He was not talking down to the child as might be expected from an adult. He was exchanging ideas with a ten-year-old girl as her equal, but on her intellectual level. He listened to the problems Rylee was having in school with grades and other things but did not dictate arbitrary answers and rules she should follow. Instead, he asked questions about each problem until Rylee devised her own well-thought-out plans. In less than a half-hour, Lincoln took a shy little girl and turned her into a confident seeker of truth and solutions.

"Are you two getting hungry?" Carlee asked.

Rylee rolled her eyes. "Well, it *is* supper time."

"How about you, Linc? Am I moving too slowly over here to suit you? Rylee seems to think so. Of course, the girl has the metabolism of a humming bird." She flashed a grin. "I expect comments like that from her."

"I'll only say I haven't thought about it," he replied. He smiled and winked at the youngster sitting across the table. "Rylee is such a fascinating conversationalist she has kept me enthralled."

Rylee wrinkled her nose. "What does that word mean?"

"It means Linc has been interested in what you had to tell him," Carlee said.

"You do know what the word enchanting means, don't you, Rylee?" he asked.

"Sure."

"Well, as far as I'm concerned you own that word too." He gave her another wink and shoved his chair back, coming to his feet. He turned his attention to Carlee. "For the young Miss Cayne's benefit, I'll come around and help, if you like. Working together, I bet we can speed up the process."

"Sure." Carlee retrieved a large chef's knife from a drawer and placed it on a cutting board next to a grouping of raw vegetables. "You can make the salad. How about that?"

By the time she had finished asking the question, Lincoln had the knife in hand. He cut two slices from a whole peeled purple onion.

Carlee stepped up behind him and watched over his shoulder for a moment—her chin only an inch above it. He was separating the slices into attractive rings. She whispered, "If you like, you can go easy on the onion. Your choice." She then brushed her cheek against his.

Onion slice in one hand and onion ring in the other, the work of his hands abruptly stopped. He gazed sideways at Carlee's facial profile, her chin now resting on his shoulder.

His smile broadened, as he shoved the onion to the back of the cutting board with the knife. He offered a knowing smile and placed a carrot under the blade. Regardless of the quiet subtlety, the inference of his action was equally obvious as her suggestion had been. Still at his ear, she added, whispering, "Thank you for how you're treating Rylee. You're an instant hit. I can tell. Usually when adults are around, she can't get far enough away from them. That's certainly not what she's doing with you."

"Rylee is a wonderful kid...smart, too. I'm not saying it to garner points from you either. It's true. The girl's a peach."

Carlee kissed him lightly on the cheek. "You may not have wanted points from me, but you've got 'em, mister. I'll leave you alone now so you can get the salad cut up. I'm starting to get hungry too." She gave him another quick smooch on the cheek.

Carlee was pleased how the meal turned out. It was simple but good—wine, baked marinated chicken breasts, sauce, salad, and toasted French bread. For the duration of the meal, Rylee concentrated only on her plate, ravenous appetite on display and certainly worth a smile. Lincoln, on the other hand, could not keep quiet, complimentary after nearly every bite. Carlee ate little. Her appetite was growing for the man sitting at the other end of the small dining table. She spent more time looking at Lincoln than at her plate. Each time their eyes connected, her breath quickened. And, each time that happened, she followed it by glancing at her daughter, hoping her own deepening desires for Lincoln were not showing up in her expression in a lusty way that a ten-year-old girl could pick up on.

Work and career suddenly interrupted the infinitely more pleasant thoughts of sexual heat and passion. She did not want this night to be about that or cast a cloud of any kind over this special evening. But, a sudden intrusive stinging pain from the gunshot wound in her lower right side refocused her attention abruptly. The pain pushed her attention over to Rylee. She stared at the child who continued eating as if it were her last meal. Eyes remaining locked on the youngster, "Linc, that advertising job you mentioned. Were you serious about it?" she asked.

"Absolutely." He whisked a napkin across his mouth and shoved his plate back. At the same time, he pulled his nearly empty wine glass in closer. "The pay won't equal what you've been making. I can say that with confidence without knowing what your salary is, but the benefits are excellent. I believe even better than what you have now. The company principals pay what they can but make sure all employees remain happy in other ways. Hardly anyone ever leaves the agency for greener pastures." He shielded his mouth with a flattened hand as if telling a secret. "I think they offer hefty benefits packages because they don't like training newbies all the time."

"It's an enticing thing to consider." She put a hand on Rylee's arm. "Not only for my peace of mind but hers as well. Rylee needs a mother at home every evening, not occasionally. She also needs a mother that shows up for recitals, soccer games, and other school functions…like normal mothers do." She emptied her wine glass and retrieved the bottle from the corner of the table, refilling his glass, and then hers.

"It's okay, Mama," Rylee said. "I know you're doing the best you can."

"You're a special girl," Lincoln told the youngster.

Carlee smiled warmly. "She sure is."

"At this point," Lincoln said, turning his attention back to Carlee, "I cannot make any firm promises, save one. I guarantee you right now I will speak to Stuart Adler first thing tomorrow morning and see if he would be amenable to the idea of bringing you on board and beefing up our media buying department."

Carlee held her wine glass up. "Here's to your powers of persuasion," she said, smiling. She held his gaze and relished the sparkle in those beautiful brown eyes of his.

Smiling, Lincoln lightly clinked her glass with his. "Here's to success." It became clear he was not going to look away until she did.

"Okay, that's enough of that stuff, Mama," Rylee said. "Let's watch that movie you promised."

The spell developing between them fizzled. "Uh, sure," Carlee stammered. "Turn the television on and find the correct pay-per-view channel while I put the dishes in the washer."

Lincoln sprang to his feet. "I'll help. Together, we can make quick work of it."

It was after ten o'clock when the movie ended. Rylee had fallen asleep thirty minutes before, head in her mother's lap, legs resting on Lincoln's knees. Carlee stroked the child's hair and looked across her small prone body to Lincoln. "I hope you didn't mind a romantic comedy as a movie choice," she said.

"It was great. The whole evening was great. Thank you for allowing me to live a few blissful hours in your wonderful world."

Wonderful? She thought about that word a moment. The warmth of his comment swelled her heart.

Lincoln gently set Rylee's legs aside and came up off the sofa to his feet. "Let me carry her to bed, so you don't have to wake her."

"That's sweet. Thanks." She grinned, adding, "Rylee would think so, too, I'm sure."

Lincoln snickered softly as he scooped the child into his arms.

Carlee studied the beautiful sight of Rylee in Lincoln's arms, the child's little arms wrapped around his neck. She followed them into the bedroom. *He may have no children of his own, but Linc is a father in every way imaginable*. She pulled the bed covers down. Lincoln gently placed the girl on her back. Carlee covered the child and kissed her on the forehead.

"I wasn't kidding earlier. Rylee is a wonderful little girl," he whispered.

Carlee straightened and faced him, unable to hold her feelings inside any longer. "Oh, Linc, you're the one that's wonderful." She pressed her mouth to his and explored his lips. Although this was the first time for such a kiss, she knew from the moment of her first conversation with Lincoln Bridger at Power House Fitness Center he was everything she never had. And, tonight, she would know him completely.

Chapter Fourteen

Lincoln walked through the glass door to the reception area of Adler, Howard and Levy Advertising Agency. He breathed in the, not unpleasant, smells of the workplace. He had never truly taken note of the little things about this place—the aroma of various colognes and perfumes, toner and paper, among other things—all familiar but usually ignored, until this morning. Also, he had not appreciated his co-workers as he should have. He stood motionless, taking a moment to watch people beginning the day, going about the daily due diligence of advancing client businesses through advertising. The advertising agencies that prospered, like this one, understood nuances of attracting hearts and minds to products and services. The people in this building were a dedicated group under capable and benevolent leadership. It was a great place to work. Carlee Cayne, suddenly appearing in his life, was responsible for making him feel renewed. After his time blissfully spent with her last night, there was nothing that could bring him down today.

He suddenly felt a hand thread between his arm and body from behind and then another hand coming into play, holding his arm firmly. "You sure look like a happy boy this morning," said Betty Jaworski, looking up at him with a big dimpled smile as she held tight to his arm.

Lincoln's first instinct was to put non-invasive space between them. He noticed that either she blushed or she had rouged her cheeks. It amused him. He smiled. Instead of his usual avoidance of his ardent admirer, he patted her hand upon his arm and said, "I am happy. Thanks for noticing, Betty."

His jaunty response obviously took her by surprise, but the shock he saw on her face transformed into a come-hither look. Betty was once again a woman on the prowl. She was dressed as she nearly always was— a form fitting skirt, high heel patent leather shoes and a button-up white blouse with the top two buttons unfastened, allowing ample freckled cleavage to see more than an appropriate amount of daylight, and clearly had frequently, judging by the tan lines. "That's not all I notice about you, big boy." She released his arm and began walking back toward her office. She waggled a finger at him. "Someday, Lincoln Bridger...someday..." she cooed, allowing the words to trail her like the heavy scent of whatever that perfume was she wore, which lingered around him even after Betty had disappeared through her office door.

A chuckle snared his attention. Lincoln turned to see the receptionist at her front desk post with a broad knowing grin. The young woman snickered and shook her head over Betty's antics. His responses may have appeared comical too. "Good morning, Linc." Pamela Hernandez was the youngest member of the ad agency team, in her early twenties. She worked full-time but took college classes in the evening. Stuart Adler thought enough of the young lady that he offered her a limited scholarship if she attended all scheduled classes and maintained her grades. She always had a smile and a cheery welcome for everyone. She was a great receptionist.

"Good morning to you, too, Pamela. Is Mister Adler in this morning?"

"He sure is. He came in a few minutes before you did. Want me to call back for you?"

"Thanks, but that won't be necessary. I'll walk on back to his office," he replied. "Have a wonderful day."

"I sure will." She shielded her mouth and whispered, "It sure looks like you made Betty's whole day too." She snickered again.

He walked on through the next full-view glass door beside Pamela's desk into the back offices. Almost all the walls of the central part of this complex of offices were glass. A view of the lake across the street was visible even from the reception area. He walked past all the glass-walled offices to a perpendicular corridor and made a left turn to walk toward the private offices at the end of the suite. He approached Jenny Stockton, Stuart Adler's personal secretary. "Mornin', Jenny. Would you ask Mister Adler if he can spare a few minutes to visit with me?"

"Sure thing, Linc," she quickly replied and hit a call button on her phone console.

"Yes, Jenny," came the familiar disembodied voice.

"Linc was wondering if you had a few minutes to visit with him."

"Sure. Tell him to come on in."

She looked up at Lincoln. "You heard the man."

"Thanks, Jenny," he said. As he was passing her desk, he suddenly stopped and turned back. "By the way, have a wonderful day." Jenny had been Stuart Adler's secretary for eleven years. She was married with two teenage boys. Her powers of observation were phenomenal. She had saved her boss on many occasions from costly or embarrassing mistakes. Her job was secure.

Jenny blinked surprise at his exuberance but then smiled. "Well, you sure are a happy camper this morning. I hope you have a great day too."

He continued past Jenny's desk and opened the heavy hardwood door. As soon as he stepped into the private office, the last one in this far end of the complex, Adler said, "Mornin', Linc." He flipped a finger toward a coffee maker on a low buffet table at the end of the long narrow office, "Grab a cup of coffee. It's a particularly good Colombian dark roast. I usually reserve this time each morning to swill coffee and think." He laughed. "But I always have time for my top account executive. What can I do for you?"

Lincoln walked toward the coffee maker, while directing his attention to the opposite end of the office where Adler sat behind his desk. "I have a friend, a lady friend, who is currently a deputy, a field agent, for the US Marshals Service. It can be a dangerous job. She's the single mom of a beautiful ten-year-old girl and is beginning to worry about the possibility of leaving the child without a parent. Lately, the job has taken an even more dangerous turn."

Adler's smile faded to pensive. "It doesn't sound like a job I'd want," Adler said, leaning back in his costly high-backed button-tufted chair, the rich oxblood leather squeaking as he did.

Lincoln sipped his freshly poured cup of coffee. "Um. Good. I wouldn't want the job either. That brings me to my point," he said. "Do you think the agency could swing an additional full-time media buyer on staff?"

Adler did not answer. He sat, stroking his chin thoughtfully for a moment. "Interesting notion. Ann Harvey and Joan Massey do put in long brutal hours, especially prior to the beginning of each new quarter. It might actually make us money to get them help and keep them happy while, at the same time, help out your friend." He paused. "Is she the one that was with you the other night in the hotel parking lot?"

Heat rose in Lincoln's face, as embarrassment bloomed. He eased down into a chair fronting Adler's desk hesitatingly, like a school boy in the principal's office. "So...you heard about that, huh?"

"All of Austin, the state of Texas, and most of the nation know about it. Her name is Cayne, I think. Am I right?"

"Yeah," Lincoln replied, "Carlee Cayne." He chuckled nervously. "And one thing I can tell you right now, she won't be letting media sales reps intimidate her. She's a tough lady. I've witnessed it first-hand. Still, she's one of the nicest people you'll ever meet. I'm certain you'd like her."

"That's quite a recommendation," Adler said. He paused. "Speaking of first-hand knowledge, how are you doing? This is the first time I've talked to you since that night."

"It was a wild night, for sure. Other than peeing my pants a little during the attack, I'm fine. If it had not been for Carlee, though, it would have turned out totally different. I am certain I would not be in any condition to be telling this story right now. That's for sure."

"You really care for this woman, don't you?"

"Yes sir. I do. She's quite a woman and, frankly, a good person. I will certainly vouch for her character. And I'm perfectly willing to put it in writing for you and sign it, if you wish."

"No, no. That's not necessary. You've never steered me wrong before. Your word is good enough. Tell you what I'll do. I'll get with the partners. We'll put a pencil to your proposition and see if we can come to a consensus on whether it makes good business sense. I'm thinking it might." He stabbed the air with a warning finger. "But no guarantees mind you, not at this point."

"You're a good man." Lincoln rose and turned to leave. "Thanks for the coffee, Sir. And, you're right. It *is* a particularly good dark roast."

"It may take a couple of days," Adler said as Lincoln opened the office door to step out, "but I'll let you know soon."

~ * ~

"I know you can take care of yourself, Dixie," Fitz said as he held his office phone to his ear, pacing to and fro to the extent the cord allowed. "I was there. Remember? The courage and daring that you displayed was...well, hell, the only way to describe it, is to say that what I saw you do was jaw-dropping *awesome*, girl." He noticed Lincoln walking by his door. He put a silencing hand on the receiver while Dixie was responding. "Hey, Linc, ya busy?" As Lincoln walked into his office, Fitz returned to his phone conversation with Dixie. "Would you let me take you to dinner this evening?"

Dixie was quiet for a moment and then replied, "Have you forgotten that I don't get off until ten-thirty?"

"I know."

"Are you sure you can stay up that late?"

"For you I will."

"Good answer. That would be nice." She then added in pointed tone, "*But* we must talk about something other than my, so-called, family. I want only to laugh and smile tonight. So, that topic will have no place in the conversational mix."

"I'll agree to that, with a caveat or two."

Dixie sighed melodramatically. "Oh...all right. Meet me in the foyer at the gym at ten thirty. Where are you taking me?"

"I don't know. How about Whataburger?"

There was a moment of silence. "You sure know how to treat a girl," Dixie finally replied.

"Do I detect sarcasm?"

"Well, aren't you the genius?" she asked. "I thought your job required learning what clients are thinking. It sounds as though you might not be terribly adept at profiling. I'm surprised you had to ask." She chuckled sardonically and ended the call.

"What was that all about?" Linc asked as Fitz returned the receiver to its console cradle.

Fitz sighed. "I was trying to explain to Dixie that whatever family loyalties she may have enjoyed in the past probably went right out the window when she helped thwart the attempt on Carlee and Jimmy Fenn, night before last."

"Make any headway?"

"Of course not," Fitz replied, coming around to sit on the front of his desk. "She's shouldering responsibility for Rogelio Ortiz coming after Carlee. That's just wrong. The girl is about as stubborn and headstrong as they come." His face softened and he blew a breathy whistle. "That said, she is the sweetest, most beautiful woman I've ever met. She gives the impression of a shy young *Latina* but, let me tell ya, Linc...wow, that girl can be a dangerous fighting dynamo when necessary. You should have seen her. It was the most extraordinary martial arts display I've ever witnessed, and it was not in a controlled atmosphere like the gym. It was real world danger. Unarmed, she engaged a stocky guy holding a machine gun. That little girl leaped high, going prone in mid-air, clamping her legs around the thug's head, spinning him to the ground in a single move, driving the idiot's face into the grass. She then put a foot in the side of his head, holding it to the ground while she wrenched his arm until he dropped the gun. It all happened so fast, I could barely keep up with it in the dim light next to Jimmy Fenn's house."

"Damn," Linc muttered.

"I think I used that same word in the same inflection when I saw it. It happened so quickly I didn't have time to become frightened for her." Fitz stood and stepped over to the window overlooking Ladybird Lake, created by a low-water damn in the river. "Dixie's fighting skills aside, Linc, I believe she is in as much danger as Carlee, but she doesn't think so. In fact, she may be in more danger and too stubborn to realize it." He again faced Lincoln. "Or, she may know the danger and doesn't care about it. Either way, I believe she's running headlong into a life-threatening situation. Although, she's quick and a fighting little dynamo, bullets are faster. At least Carlee is armed, *aware*, and fully *understanding* that they are after her."

"You might be right," Lincoln said. "Carlee was called back in to work today. Her supervisor decided she would be safer there in the office where people would have her back. I'm told he's checking with the Feds. They maintain a couple of safe houses at secret locations in the area, hoping to secure availability to protect Carlee's daughter and mother until Ortiz can be neutralized. Carlee told me the forensics team found traces of blood on the fence where the third assailant went over and disappeared. It was a familial match to his brother, Manuel. The one Carlee killed."

"So, it was Rogelio himself?" Fitz asked.

"Looks like it. Texas Rangers have gotten in on the act, trying to locate and capture him before he can make it back to safer haven, across the border in Mexico where it's much easier for him to buy off cops and hole up in a well-guarded fortress-like setting. If he makes it down there, he will *certainly* regroup and come back at a time of his choosing. He'll try it all over again. In fact, I believe he'll keep coming back until he succeeds, regardless how many return trips it takes. I'm sure of it."

Fitz took a step toward Lincoln. "Damn. I wish there was something I could do besides argue with Dixie over the danger."

"I know what you mean. I feel the same way about Carlee. But, I've concluded the best way to help her is simply be there for her, be her confidant, be her friend, and let Rylee, that sweet girl of hers, in on all of it. Think about it, Fitz. The simple fact you're willing to take Dixie to dinner so late in the evening probably means more to her than you know. Just be there for her too. That's all I'm saying. I can't think of a way that you could do more for her than that. Also, it's the fastest way to rack up points in your favor. That is, of course, if you really like the girl."

It was clear that he successfully steered Fitz into a more pleasant frame of mind. His friend's grin grew to such proportion, clenched lips disappeared into his cheeks. "Oh, I like her all right. Although, for the time being, just having her as a friend is enough. She's a hoot to hang-out with."

~ * ~

The evening could not have been more beautiful. The moon was rising, washing out stars as it went. Pink sodium vapor lights cast warm haloes at regular intervals along the street. Traffic was light in downtown

Austin. Night life mostly moved to other areas of the city as evening progressed. Fitz rolled into the Power House Fitness Center parking lot at nine-thirty. Since he had so much time after work to wait for his date with Dixie, he figured the best way to work off anxieties was to go for a jog on the gym's outdoor track fenced in at the rear of the facility. He scanned the sky opposite the rising moon. The stars on that side of the sky were so bright Austin's skyline lights masked only the faintest—a beautiful night of tremendous clarity, lacking the familiar humid haze normally hanging in the air on most evenings in the Texas Hill Country.

Having already changed into his workout clothes before leaving work, Fitz carried a change of clothes in a small duffel bag and bypassed the locker room altogether. He walked through the foyer, heading straight for the back door of Power House, which also happened to be the only accessible egress to the fenced-in outdoor track. As he walked past the full-view glass-walled series of courts, he saw Dixie in one, busy with a martial arts class. He stopped and smiled big, waving enthusiastically when she noticed him. She returned the greeting with a brilliant smile but immediately turned her attention back to her class of four. Fitz chose not to interrupt her.

As he exited the back of the building, he tossed his duffel bag onto a bench, took a breath, and patted himself on the stomach. *I can tell myself I'm going for a jog to ease anxieties, but I'd sure like to be in better shape for Dixie. She's so pretty and fit and I look like...well, like this.* Fitz grabbed a pinch of his belly next to his navel and shook it. *If this isn't a blubbery handful of anxiety, I don't know what is.* He started to take off but stuttered to a stop. *Should I consider giving up the beer?* He again began to jog. *Nah.*

Coming to the completion of his fourth lap around the eighth-of-a-mile track, he decided if he tried to make another lap his heart would explode. He noticed Dixie coming out the door onto the track just ahead. *Thank God. A reason to quit.* He slowed and stopped. Bending at the waist, he grabbed his aching side, drawing deep the night air, unable to get enough. He supported his upper body with hands on knees.

"Hi, Fitz," Dixie drawled in buttery tone.

He drew a large quantity of air to get out a short greeting. "Hey to you too."

"I'm glad to see you out here. I'm impressed. I didn't have to goad you into it."

Remaining bent at the waist, he lifted his head slightly and squinted up at her. Still having trouble getting his wind back, he managed, "Not...in very good...shape. Am I?"

She chuckled. "We'll work on it. Don't worry about it. It'll come. Just persevere."

"No choice," he wheezed. "*Must* take it gently for a while."

"Breathe deep and exhale slowly and completely," she said. "You'll recuperate much quicker."

He huffed. "Okay."

Dixie checked her watch. "Go ahead and shower. Maybe I can sneak out a few minutes early."

"Too tired to shower." He straightened slowly and dropped his hands on his hips. "What's the matter? I thought you'd appreciate a musky manly stench?"

"Of course, I appreciate it," she cooed. "Like now and, maybe, later tonight. But not in the hours between."

Realizing Dixie's inference, his aversion to taking a shower took an abrupt turn. Driven by her tone and word choice, he suddenly had a strong desire to head for the showers. "That's all I needed to hear," he replied. "I'm on my way to shower right now, Miss Vega." Energized, he stepped lively and began to walk by her toward the door that opened into the building.

"I'll be waiting at the front desk, Mister Fitzsimmons," she said, putting an encouraging hand on his arm as he passed her. "By the way..." she added.

He stopped and took a thoughtful look at her hand on his arm.

She winked at him and nodded. "...Good workout."

Her touch warmed him. The feel of her hand sliding down his arm lingered. Thoughts for what the remainder of the evening may hold swirled through Fitz's head in a dizzying montage of possibilities. *I should do better than a quick trip to Whataburger. Dixie is worth more, possibly much more.*

Chapter Fifteen

Dixie caught herself glancing often down the hall toward the men's locker room while waiting for Fitz to appear. As excitement amplified in anticipation of a late dinner with such a good looking and fun guy as Ben Fitzsimmons, so did apprehension. Her thoughts took on a life of their own. Questions that, as yet, remained unanswerable rolled out with the alarming regularity of a drumbeat. *What if a relationship develops? Do I even want to consider such a thing? Do I dare consider it? If a relationship did develop, how could it possibly work? Our backgrounds and lives are different, radically different. He drinks. I don't. He doesn't include physical fitness as a lifestyle. I do. Our eating habits are diametrically opposed.* Dixie abruptly realized something else. *I've only known the man a few days and these differences may only be the beginning, the tip of the iceberg. Aside from animal attraction we clearly share, what do we have in common?* Although concerns flit back and forth, she continued coming full circle back to allowing the infatuation to play out and see where it went. Although, there was no getting around it, a serious conversation with Fitz would have to take place at some point in this budding friendship but long before romantic seriousness developed. Still, she enjoyed getting to know Fitz. He was a man with an amazing sense of humor. More importantly, a guy that had proven himself a friend she could count on. But, for now, maybe he should be held to arm's length. The stream of people exiting the fitness center indicated the remainder of the evening would be slow and, possibly, easier to walk away from a few minutes early.

After what seemed like a long wait, Dixie noticed Fitz, walking briskly toward the front desk where she did the mind-numbing busy work of filling in blanks on a computer database. "Finally," she called out with a roll of the eyes. "I was beginning to wonder if I should send in the assistant manager, Bobby Dunwoody, to check on you. I thought you might have slipped in the shower and whacked your noggin."

"I'll have you know, milady, I am scrubbed so clean my skin squeaks. Besides, it took a few minutes to come down off my runner's high."

"'Runner's high?' Ha! That was not a runner's high I saw. It was exhaustion," she said, coming around the counter to join him.

"You're not going to allow me to maintain a shred of ego, are ya?"

She came to stand next to him and circled his arm with her own. She looked up at him and wrinkled her nose. "Well, maybe a shred." She pulled him in tow toward the main entrance.

He followed a few steps and then stopped. "It's not quite ten-thirty yet. Is it okay for you to be walking out the door?"

"Bobby told me he would keep an eye on things for me. He's a good guy. I'll return the favor." She yanked his arm. "Now, come on. I'm hungry."

Dixie was duly impressed with Fitz's selection of eateries. He escorted her through the door of a bistro bookended by tall downtown buildings about halfway between the gym and the capitol building in the heart of Austin. "Wow, this place is nice," she said. "When you told me that you were taking me to Whataburger, I thought you were serious." She looked down at herself, dressed in her work clothes—an unzipped black nylon warmup top over matching pants, a white tank top, plus the obligatory sneakers. She pushed errant hair strands from her face and ran a hand over the top of her head to the single plait of hair down her back, extending almost to her waist. "I'm terribly under-dressed for a restaurant of this caliber," she whispered. "It's embarrassing."

"Embarrassing? What in the world would you have to be self-conscious of?" He then put his lips to her ear and whispered, "Look around. *You* are the loveliest creature in this place. Every woman you see glancing our way is jealous...of *you*. And, every man envies me. They're not judging. They're admiring," he said and then added, "I'll gladly add, if jealousy *is* involved, it's because you look as good as you do, dressed as you are." He pulled away and added a firm nod of punctuation accompanied by a smile.

Fitz's flattering comments gave her a tingling rush of emotion. "I...I've never had anyone say something like that to me. Thank you."

Fitz held up two fingers to an approaching waiter who responded by saying, "Please follow me." The waiter threaded his way between closely arranged tables, followed by Dixie. Fitz trailed her. It was an odd shaped restaurant of modest size, narrow but deep. Considering the hour was late, about ten-thirty, the place still had a full complement of diners. The waiter stopped at the only free table in the restaurant, near the back corner just off the double doors to the kitchen. "I hope this will suffice," the young man said. "It's all I have available at the moment. It is an unusually busy night, considering the hour."

Fitz said nothing, simply deferred the question to Dixie. "Oh sure," she quickly replied, noticing the question in his expression. "When we have to eat this late, just finding an open table is a treat. Besides, I have no right to complain. It's because of me that we're so late."

The waiter smiled at her answer. While seating her, he said, "This table, although not the best in the house, does come with a perk. Your first glass of wine is on the house for allowing us to seat you next to the kitchen door."

"White or red?" Fitz asked her.

"Sorry. I don't drink."

"Oh. I didn't know that," Fitz replied.

"How about an ice-cold glass of raspberry tea," the waiter suggested.

"That sounds nice," she said.

"I think I'll have a glass of Merlot," Fitz told the waiter but immediately turned to Dixie. "If that's okay with you."

"Of course it is, silly."

The waiter took the order and left. "I'm sorry. That's something I should have realized about you," Fitz said.

"That's what this dinner is about, getting to know one another. I'm eager to find out more about what past adventures have molded Ben Fitzsimmons into the person I see before me."

"Oh, my God. The pressure is on to come across as interesting. I don't know if I'm up to the challenge." In melodramatic fashion, he widened his eyes and swallowed hard.

Dixie laughed.

"Unfortunately, life has not been terribly adventuresome. I'm sorry to admit. Just think of me as a sailboat, going whichever way the wind blows. And, it just so happens, it blew me to you." He chuckled. "I have to give Linc credit. If he had not forced me to join Power House Fitness, I would have never met you. I guess that makes Linc the wind." He paused. "There is something I've been wondering about you."

"Oh?"

"Is Dixie your real name or a nickname?"

"Nickname. My birth name is Ramona Louise Vega. Growing up in San Antonio, my friends called me Mona." Her eyes drifted away for a moment. She muttered, "That seems like a lifetime ago." She paused and sighed, thinking about that for a moment and then abruptly re-animated. "Oh well. Now, if someone should shout that name at me from across a crowded room, it probably wouldn't even get my attention, because I wouldn't recognize it as mine."

"Who gave you the name Dixie?"

"My entire political science class in college."

"Don't stop there. It sounds as though this might be a good story."

"Actually, it is. As part of our class everyone knew what all the students' political affiliations were. I was a Democrat at the time. I've since learned colleges and universities tend to push students left. Back then, I didn't notice the subtle persuasion in that direction by professors, staff, and the general culture of dependency within our higher educational system. Anyhow, when I heard a mouthy right-winger start spouting off about the origin of the Democratic Party being the Dixiecrats and how abhorrent the party had been, I was compelled to shout him down with glaring differences in the modern party and those earlier southern extremists."

"Humph! That's all it took to get a nickname that became permanent?"

"Oh no. That merely sets up the story. You see, our professor decided that for the class to gain political perspective through another person's eyes and belief system, every student was assigned political parties they were adamantly opposed to and then give a five-minute speech *favoring* it, with supporting evidence why. And, yes, I was assigned the Dixiecrats. It so happens I was awarded a certificate for Speaker of the

Week for my short verbal dissertation in favor of the Dixiecrats. I've been called Dixie since that day. It was even the name typed on the Speaker of the Week certificate I was awarded. I still have it...somewhere. Now, I get to ask a question," she continued. "What's your middle name?"

He cocked his head belligerently. "I don't want to tell you." He sipped his wine.

"Why not?"

"I don't like it."

"Come on, Fitz," she drawled in a lazy southern way. "I shared. Now you share."

He sighed. "Okay," he said, mimicking her drawl by overemphasizing but then hesitated. "It's...Aloysius. Thanks to my maternal grandfather. It's of Germanic origin, meaning *fame in war*. A masculine definition for a feminine sounding name."

"There's nothing wrong with that name," she said, and then took a sip of raspberry tea. "Although, I do prefer Fitz or Ben," she added. "Do you have siblings?"

"'Do I have siblings'?" he repeated, rolling his eyes. "Mom and Dad had three boys and a girl in rapid succession over a five-year period and then took a break. When those siblings were in their teens, or nearly so, our parents suddenly decided they wanted more kids and started over. I was born twelve years after my older sister, and then two younger sisters were born in the two years following my world debut."

"If I kept up, that's seven children."

"Yep."

"Wow." She chuckled. "I bet your mother stayed exhausted."

"She did. But she loved being a mother. Still does."

"So, you were literally in the middle of a big family."

"Yeah. It was easy to get lost in the wrapping paper Christmas morning at our house when we all still lived at home."

She laughed. "That could be a nice euphemism for having a bad case of middle-child-syndrome."

"You could be right about that. It's probably the reason I was always in trouble in school for being the class clown and practical joker, for the attention. And, hey, it worked." He sipped his wine. "How about you? Do you have siblings...other than Daniel, I mean?"

Dixie's smile wilted away. She had not thought of her family troubles this entire conversation until now. "No. It's just Daniel and me," she said, inflection descending. "Being raised in a Catholic environment, our family would have likely been as large as yours, maybe larger, had my mom not died in childbirth with what would have been my second brother. He didn't make it either. As for Daniel, I'm having a hard time calling him family since he got himself mixed up with our cousins, the Ortiz brothers. They may be blood, but they're not good people, no sense of morality whatsoever." She quickly put the tea glass to her lips and looked up and over his head and focused on a slowly turning ceiling fan suspended from a vintage tin-tiled ceiling on a long pipe extension, wanting Fitz to end this line of questioning.

"I'm sorry," he said. "I didn't intend to put sad things on your mind."

"I know. Still, let's change the subject."

The remainder of dinner was wonderful. Fitz did as she asked and avoided any reference to her family. He rattled on and on about his past. All the shenanigans and antics he had been involved with over the years, one story after the other. She did little talking, but she enjoyed saying enough to keep him going. Listening to his ramblings was more fun than talking about herself. It became easy to smile as Fitz's humorous side kicked in. He did a marvelous job of keeping her entertained for the rest of their time in the restaurant. He had a wonderful knack for making her smile and laugh.

Dixie noticed a small huddled group of wait staff eyeing them. She glanced around, only then noticing that she and Fitz were the last patrons in the place. It quickly became clear the small group of employees wanted them to leave so they could close. "Fitz," she whispered while surreptitiously pointing to the small group of employees, "I think it's time to leave."

Fitz drove her back to Power House Fitness Center to her car. He pulled into the empty parking lot slowly. He seemed not to want the evening to end. "I had a wonderful time," she said as he eased into the space next to her aging Toyota and stopped. "You seem to be a good guy." She bounced a quick smile and nervously glanced at him. "Nice guys are hard to find these days."

He reached across and placed two fingers beneath her chin, gently lifting and coaxing her head around to look at him. He studied her face for a moment.

Dixie watched him as his eyes sketched the details of her face.

He stared into her eyes. "You really are beautiful," Fitz whispered. He leaned across the console and kissed her softly on the lips. He studied her again at extremely close range and leaned in to kiss her again.

Dixie pulled away. "I'm sorry, Fitz. At the beginning of this evening, I saw this *date* as a casual thing with a new friend. I even had fantasies I should not have had about where this evening might lead. I never thought I would begin seeing you through the eyes I do now. I like you. I like you a lot. And that makes me very nervous. It's too soon to lose myself. It would be a dangerously easy thing to do. If I allowed this to go any further, I would not be able to control my feelings and would not be able to walk away, calling it a casual fling." She dropped her eyes and stared at her lap. "You truly are wonderful. Will you forgive me for this sudden change in attitude? I really am sorry, if I led you on, but I now see that I need to ease into this, not dive in."

After a moment of obvious contemplation, Fitz smiled. "Of course."

Dixie smiled sheepishly. "Tell ya what...we can say the wind changed and we need a slight course correction. How about that?" She studied his face in nervous glances, searching for hurt feelings, wondering if she, indeed, had made him feel as though he had been led down a path that she suddenly did not want to travel yet.

"Take it slowly? Is that what you're suggesting?" he whispered and leaned back to sit straight.

Dixie opened her mouth to respond but was suddenly afraid whatever came out might be the wrong thing and drive him away. So, she simply nodded affirmation. She had begun to imagine the two of them as a couple. She didn't want to do or say anything that might jeopardize a future possibility, if it was indeed possible. She had to be certain where all this was going. She had been hurt too many times by too many people, having developed a strong skepticism of people's intentions toward her. She had her family to thank for that. If people were nice to her or sought to be near her, it almost always ended with them wanting something from her, usually something she was not willing to give. She refused to allow her feelings to ever be trampled on again.

Fitz smiled. "To keep on with the sailing metaphors, I don't mind tacking into the wind until the direction of it changes. If it eases your mind, I cannot think of anyone I'd rather take it slow with. Although, I do hope we might still hang out together."

Once again, she felt a sudden rush of heat and a full-body tingle. "Oh, Fitz..." She leaned across, kissed him again. "You're proving yourself to be a true friend. Thank you. Thank you, so much." She then quickly got out of his Camaro, turning away so he had no clear view of her face as she walked towards her car. She was falling for the guy and afraid he might be able to read uneasiness on her face, possibly even a look of apprehension. She could not show him any face that hinted she had no growing affection for him, because she did. Although, to the opposite extreme, she certainly could not show him a love-struck face either, not yet. Walk away without looking back was her only option at the moment, with her jubilant words of thanks still hanging in the air. She smiled.

Chapter Sixteen

"I hope I'm not bothering you, Linc," Carlee said. She held the phone tight against her ear as she paced in a tight circle inside her apartment.

"Of course not. There's no way talking to you would ever be a bother, under any circumstances."

"I hope you believe me when I say calling you at work goes totally against my character. I don't do this sort of thing. Frankly, I don't want personal calls coming to me at the Service. God knows, I don't want you thinking I'm some kind of psycho stalker."

Although Lincoln did not laugh aloud, Carlee distinctly felt the smile in his voice. "Stalker? Maybe. But if you leave off the psycho part, I think I'd be okay with it."

"Seriously, am I keeping you or, maybe, catching you in the middle of something important?"

"Same-old, same-old. Besides, I always have time for you."

Carlee sighed relief, stopped pacing, and sank down to sit on the sofa. "I didn't want too much time to pass before I let you know how I treasured our evening together the other night at my place."

"It *was* special. Wasn't it?" he replied in a whispery lilt.

"Oh yes. And, it's not only me. Rylee won't shut up about it." She chuckled. "Want it or not, you have a new best friend and, if you don't mind me saying so, I put myself in there at a close second."

Lincoln did not respond.

"Linc? Are you still there?"

"Sorry. I was thinking how much I wish all my problems with Jeannine were behind me. I'm hoping she won't be opposed to fast-tracking the divorce. If I can keep my car, I'm not contesting anything. There shouldn't be a problem, but...you never know."

"The last thing I want to do is add to your burden. I won't be pressuring you for your time. Although, I'll never let a call from you go to voice mail, if I can help it. Deal?" she asked.

"Deal."

"I really do want to be a friend to you and then let everything else take its course."

"In that case, *friend*, I think I'll have good news for you before this day is over."

Enthusiasm shot through her. She sprang off the sofa and stood. "The job at your agency? Is it about the job? Please say yes," she rattled quickly.

"As we speak, Mister Adler is with Betty Jaworski, our head of accounting. They're working out an employment package the agency is planning on offering you to gauge your level of interest. I don't know what it is yet, but it's in the works."

Carlee could not prevent a squeal of pleasure accompanied by a quick pirouette. The news was sweeter than music. "Oh, Linc, that's wonderful!"

"It'll be presented to you formally here at the agency in Adler's office in the next day or so, but how about I meet you at the gym this evening after work. I'll tell you everything I know, so you don't have to walk in blind to the offer?"

"Perfect," she replied. "I'll see you at Power House at seven."

Lincoln ended the call.

Now, with an excited spring in her step, she helped Rylee get her things together and hurried the child to dress and get ready to leave. After a few minutes, she and her daughter walked to her car. It was the daily workday ritual of taking the youngster to her grandmother's house, now that the school year had ended, and then on to work.

At work, she poured a cup of coffee and sat at her desk in the bullpen, but could not, and didn't want to, concentrate on paperwork. Carlee stared across the clustered desks in the large open area within the US Marshal's office. Her eyes may have followed her co-workers scurrying about, but it was only movement that drew her in. Her thoughts were elsewhere. She paid the goings-on in the office no conscious mind. She considered many wonderful possibilities should she leave the Service for the more sedate life of an ad agency media buyer. *Linc, you waltzed into my life at the perfect time.* Her smile broadened further but then faded. Negativity suddenly shaded contentment as downsides wriggled in. What if things did not work out with Linc? What if he decided not to divorce Jeannine? And, there she'd be, working day in and day out in very close quarters with the man, a guy that would be so very easy to fall in love with. It might turn into a heart-shattering situation. She would be trapped with no way out. Things must work out perfectly for this arrangement to have a chance. Finally, what if she could not handle a job that required remaining office-bound forty-plus hours a week? A mind's-eye image of Rylee suddenly appeared and Carlee's smile eased back. *Oh, for heaven's sake, I need to stop creating things to worry about and stop thinking selfishly. After all, the whole idea of a job change was for Rylee's sake.*

"Hey, Cayne," Jimmy Fenn said, rushing by her desk, "let's roll."

Carlee fell in behind and followed him. "What's up?"

"Austin PD followed Daniel Vega to a low-end motel on the Interstate. It's thought they may have identified Rogelio Ortiz inside one of the rooms when Vega opened the door. Police called for backup. Thought you might want to be in on this."

She noted his heavy limp. "Wait a minute. You're in no condition to be backing up anyone. You took a bullet in the leg. Remember?"

He didn't break his impaired stride but glanced back. "I won't be chasing bad guys today, but neither will you. Turner told me that we could go but only as second-tier back up."

"Meaning what exactly?"

"We have to stay with the car and observe."

"Aw, hell no. I want to be in on the breach. I want to see Ortiz subdued for myself. I want to look him in the eyes when they put the cuffs on him, if they don't kill him first. I want to see with my own eyes what the certifiably ruthless psychopath looks like."

Fenn abruptly stopped and clumsily danced a one-eighty turn on his good leg to face her but looked first over her shoulder toward Supervising Deputy George Turner's office across the expansive bullpen area to the glass wall where his office was located. "Keep your voice down. If you do that, Turner will take your badge and gun. So, if you want to tag-along at all, don't let that kind of talk hit Turner's ears. Besides, if just seeing what Rogelio Ortiz looks like is your goal, Turner had a photograph of him in a folder sent to us by the field office of the FBI. It's a few years old but, hey, you'll know what he looks, if that's what you want."

"Not really. But I sure would like to see him on the floor with a knee in his back while they cuff him. Also, what's Turner going to do, fire me? Ha!"

"The safer bet is that he'll ask for a sexual favor to keep your job." Fenn pulled a half grin and jacked one eyebrow.

Carlee pulled her mouth into a tight straight line and backhanded Fenn hard on the stomach.

"Ow!"

"That's not funny, Jimbo, not in the slightest." She took a quick breath and huffed it away. "Besides, by this time tomorrow, keeping this job with the Service may be a non-issue, especially if Ortiz is in custody or dead."

"Why? That advertising job?

"Yeah."

"So, it's going to happen, is it?"

"Not an absolute yet, but it is more promising today than yesterday."

Okay," he said, suddenly becoming serious. He draped his hands over her shoulders, "Then do it for me. Hang back with me at the car. Please. I personally promised Turner that we would hold back and observe and only engage if Ortiz gets through a wall of law enforcement which, of course, is highly unlikely...unless he is carrying some major weaponry, like grenades. And, here's the important part, I don't have an advertising job to go to. I need to wake up in the morning, knowing I still have this job."

Carlee deflated, feeling ashamed over her selfish behavior. "I'm sorry. I didn't consider that."

"Still want to go? I mean, if you have to follow the rules of non-engagement?"

She pursed her lips and forced air between tight lips. "Sure. Why not? Let's go."

On their way to the low-end motel, the radio scanner in the car virtually buzzed with chatter across several bands. Austin Police, Texas Rangers, and Department of Public Safety were in constant communication as they converged on the motel just off the Interstate where Rogelio Ortiz was purportedly spotted, along with Dixie's brother, Daniel. Carlee had no qualms about wishing harm to Ortiz but was conflicted about Dixie's brother, should a confrontation take a violent turn. It was an upsetting contradiction of desires.

By the time Fenn and Carlee made it to the scene, a half-dozen cars had already created an arc, blockading the street-level motel room door. Five officers in riot gear—helmets, Kevlar vests, and assault rifles hurried toward the suspected room Ortiz was holed up in. They ran crouched and cautious. One man carried a battering ram. Four others carried assault rifles held in the ready position to fire.

Standing beside the door, an officer motioned for the helmeted man with the battering ram to force the door.

One mighty thrust with the heavy two-handled iron tube was all it took.

The door crashed open and the other four helmeted men rushed inside the room, shouting demands as they did.

Seconds later, an Austin police officer exited the small motel room, gun lowered and relaxed. "It's empty," he shouted to all the backup officers.

"What the...?" Carlee muttered as she came away from the car heading toward the motel room. Fenn limped along behind her. She approached the officers coming out, asking as she neared, "What happened?"

One of the men skinned the helmet from his head. "It appears the Austin Police cruiser that spotted Vega and then Ortiz had been noticed the minute Vega entered the room. There's a frosted vertical crank window in the bathroom left open. They're gone, probably long enough to have found a hiding place a mile or two away. They're on foot though." He pointed to two vehicles. "That's their cars parked over there."

"Damn," Carlee hissed through clenched teeth. "He could be anywhere in Austin by now, maybe another freakin' town altogether, for that matter."

"It's okay, Cayne. Calm down," Fenn said low and soothingly. "They'll get him. He can't hide forever. Too many cops looking for him."

"I know. It's just that as long as he's on the loose, my family and all my friends are in danger. It's not just me I'm worried about." She pointed to Fenn's leg. "Case in point," she added.

"Hey, kiddo, in this job caca happens. You can't blame yourself for my injury. No way."

She nodded. "Yeah. Okay." She fell into the driver's seat of the car. "Come on. Nothing left to see here."

~ * ~

"No, Daniel! Absolutely not!" Dixie shouted into the phone at her brother.

"Come on, Dixie. You're my blood, my *Hermana*, my sweet little Mona. Are you forgetting that I took care of you after Mama died?"

Dixie looked to the ceiling of her apartment and pinched the bridge of her nose, aggravated into silence that Daniel chose to take his appeal in this direction. It wasn't fair. She wondered if disallowing her brother to play the family card would take a larger force of will than she could pull in. She held her eyes tightly shut and slammed her teeth together with an audible clack, jaw muscles flexing. She ground her teeth, fighting an urge to allow him such emotional latitude and refused to respond. Her silence resulted from a mixture of anger with a touch of fear that she might break and give in to him.

"Surely you haven't forgotten all I did for you back then," he added. "Don't you realize that if they catch me, they'll revoke my bail."

The dam on her struggle to remain silent was suddenly breached by the asinine comment. "You idiot! Bail revocation is the least of your worries. You're directly linked to the attempted murder of Lincoln Bridger, Carlee Cayne, and Jimmy Fenn. You're complicit. Are you even capable of understanding what that means? You were not only seen but followed by the cops to that motel. You were identified. Rogelio was identified. Every cop in town is looking for you both. And you have the audacity to ask for my help at the expense of *my own* reputation and freedom? Bullshit, *Hermano*! Bull...shit!"

The phone line was quiet momentarily. In a softer pleading tone, "All I want is for you to pick me up and take me to New Braunfels. Please, sweet Mona. I need you. I need this favor," he said. "I have friends there. They can get me across the border into Mexico. If I can just make it across the border, I'll be safe. Come on. I'm begging you. Please?"

"Where is Rogelio?"

"I don't know. Once we climbed out the motel window, he went one way and I went the other. We ran on foot because the cops had our cars surrounded. Rogelio probably stole a car somewhere. He may be a hundred miles down the highway by now. I'm still without wheels."

"Are you armed?"

"Well, yeah," came his quick surprised reply. "It's kind of dangerous out here right now. I need a weapon."

Dixie paused as a possible solution came to her.

"Well," he repeated, "are you going to help me or not?"

"Where are you right now?"

"I don't want to answer that question until I get a promise from you to help me. Are you going to pick me up and get me out of Austin?"

Dixie nibbled on the inside of her cheek. She sighed heavily. "You are my brother. It's hard to deny a family member, no matter if that member *is* an idiot."

"Is that a yes?"

"I suppose. But we have to get it done right now. Where are you?"

"Do you know that Target store off Ben White Boulevard where it merges with Capitol of Texas Highway?"

"Sure."

"There's an abandoned construction area grown up in weeds and grass next to Ben White. I'll be crouching in the weeds and waiting."

"Give me thirty, maybe forty, minutes." She ended the call and dropped to sit on the sofa in her apartment, feeling as though she had been slammed in the chest by a wrecking ball. It was hard to breathe, knowing what must be done to save Daniel from himself. She snatched her phone up and dialed Carlee's number.

"Carlee Cayne."

"Carlee, this is Dix. I...I need a huge favor."

"What's going on?"

"I just hung up from talking to Daniel."

"I'm sorry, but that boy is in a world of trouble and there is nothing I can do about it."

"I know what you're saying," Dixie said. "But, I think there *is* something you might be able to do."

"What's that?"

"Keep the idiot from getting himself killed. I keep trying to walk away and forget him, but I can't get past the fact he's the last of my immediate family."

"I feel horrible for you, but I don't know what it is I can do."

"You can arrest him. I know where he is."

"You do?"

"Afraid so. Rogelio is not with him but Daniel is armed. I'm afraid if a large group of law enforcement types surround him, he'll use that gun and get himself killed. He may be family, but I've never given him credit for an overabundance of forethought. He'll just react. What I'm asking is you and I go together, *just* you and me, and talk him out of that gun, and then you take him into custody. I promised him I would get him out of Austin to New Braunfels to where waiting friends would help him get across the border at Del Rio. He'll hate me for betraying him, but he'll be alive."

"You at home?"

"Yeah. I'm here in my apartment."

"I'll be there in about ten minutes," Carlee said.

"Hurry. I told Daniel I would meet him in about thirty minutes and that was five minutes ago."

"I'm walking out right now." Carlee ended the call.

Dixie agonized over the decision. There was no other way and this might keep him alive. The only other plan of action would turn her into a fugitive as well. She refused to be sucked down that hole.

~ * ~

Carlee steered into the parking area fronting the apartments and saw her waiting. Dixie stood by her car parked near her apartment. When this unsanctioned operation to go after and arrest her brother came to light, how would it affect her job? Did she care? She didn't know Daniel Vega's degree of inclination toward violence. How dangerous was he? Questions that would eventually have answers, but not at the moment. Carlee braked to a hard stop. The front of her company car dipped before settling back. Dixie flung the door open and got in. Carlee gave her friend a gentle squeeze on the knee and said, "Let's go see if, together, we can talk some sense into your brother."

"God, I hope so."

Carlee glanced sideways at her friend. "I have to say though, this is a helluva way to meet him, and certainly not ideal."

Dixie sat wringing her hands. "I know. It's horrible and shameful."

Carlee reached across and, again, put a hand on her friend's leg. "Dix, believe it...or not, if you prefer, but you *are* being a good sister to Daniel, the best. I'll be as gentle and non-threatening as I can. Okay?"

Dixie affirmed with a quick nod and weak smile.

"Dix, can you give me some insight into your brother? What do you think his reaction will be when the two of us approach him when he's expecting only you?"

"I'm thinking he'll turn and run. He has always hated confrontation. That's the reason he never won an argument with me." She paused. "That tendency worries me since he has a gun. If, by chance, he has nowhere to run to and feels cornered then...I don't know."

That was a worrisome comment. Carlee frowned. Dixie was honest about it. Carlee was sure of that. It left her with little to go on, other than make a quick assessment of the terrain where Daniel was hiding.

"Look," Dixie said, "I think it's best I approach him first and tell him what's about to happen and then attempt to calm him. He doesn't know you're such a close friend. When he sees you coming, all he's going to notice is a badge and a gun. If that's the case, all hell may break loose."

"Good point. What if he bolts and runs?"

"Don't worry about that. He runs like a girl. Even I can outrun him.

I'm more concerned about the gun he's carrying. Neither one of us can outrun that, if he panics and starts shooting."

"If he's hiding in a place with an unobstructed view from the car, I'll stay in it and wait for your signal to approach. How's that?"

"I think that's best."

Carlee stole glances at her friend, admiring her. What Dixie was doing had to be monumentally difficult. This lovable little Latina, standing five-five and barely over a hundred pounds was a mountain of unadulterated fortitude. She was proud to call Dixie her friend and confidant, her best friend.

The radio in her car suddenly broke squelch. "Cayne, what's your twenty?" came the static-laced voice of partner, Jimmy Fenn, through the speaker."

Carlee and Dixie exchanged glances. Carlee lifted the microphone and thought briefly how to frame her response. "Just running an errand. On Ben White Boulevard right now. I'll be back to HQ shortly."

"I have good news that can't wait."

"Oh? What might that be?"

"State Troopers spotted a stolen car speeding through San Marcos. They gave chase. It flipped over a guard rail and guess who popped out firing an automatic assault rifle at them?"

"Rogelio Ortiz?" Carlee blurted abruptly.

"Yep."

"Outcome?"

"Shot, and now deceased. They assume he was trying to make it back across the border at Del Rio into Ciudad Acuña. Personally, I think he was only going back to regroup, reload, round up a few more thugs, and come back up here to take another run at you."

"Yeah. I agree," Carlee replied, becoming giddy as all the tension of the past few days left her. Suddenly, she remembered Rogelio and his brother Manuel were Dixie's cousins. She looked to Dixie who sat expressionless and quiet, staring down at her lap. "Fenn, would you call back on my cell phone? There's a personal favor I'd like to ask of you."

"Sure. Standby."

Carlee looked at her friend. "I know Rogelio was family. I'm so sorry it had to end this way."

"All I have to say is *vaya con Dios*, Cousin. He deserved it. Rogelio died the way he lived," she muttered, staring down at her lap. She then faced Carlee. "It scares me that my idiot brother may try the same thing." Her eyes now had a teary shine.

"You have my solemn promise that I will do everything possible to prevent that type of situation."

Dixie nodded rapidly and swiped a trickling tear from her cheek. "You really are more than a friend. You're my sister."

Carlee swallowed a lump in her throat. "Hang in there, sweetie."

Carlee's ringtone sounded off. "Jimbo?"

"How can I help you, Carlee?"

"I need help running an off-book op."

"Sounds dicey. What is it?"

Carlee spent a couple of minutes detailing what was about to go down and asked that he back her up from a distance. Once he understood her reasoning, Fenn was quick to offer help and now only a few minutes behind her.

Carlee exited Ben White Boulevard and saw the vacant lot Daniel detailed to Dixie. Waist high Johnson grass, even taller broad-leafed sunflower plants in full foliage, and a variety of other weeds choked an area covering approximately three acres. It was a place where highway construction had been underway but, for unknown reasons, suspended. Bridge abutments stood like unadorned Greek pillars with no caps, only bare concrete cylinders reaching twenty-five feet into the air. It was an ideal place, located near major thoroughfares at a right angle for choice of directions to flee, if necessary. Plus, Daniel could not be seen unless he chose to be.

"Pull over here," Dixie said, pointing. Dirt had been piled to create a temporary incline over the curb to allow trucks onto the lot joltless.

Carlee eased up and over the curb. She parked parallel to the street but out of traffic. She made a cursory scan of all that lay before them. "Over there," Carlee said. "That bridge abutment at the far left in a row of three. I saw a head poke out from behind it. The presence of this car is apparently enough to make him antsy. You had better get a move on, Dix, and quickly establish that it's you."

"Right," was Dixie's only reply as she flung the door open, leaped out and shouted, "Daniel, it's me."

He again craned his head out and around the concrete monolith. "Who's that with you?" came his shouted reply.

"Just a friend that offered to help." Dixie began to approach her brother, still about fifty feet away. "She has promised to help me make sure you're not harmed."

"She? Who are you talking about?"

Dixie was silent for a second, but then said, "Carlee Cayne. She's a deputy US Marshal, but—"

Daniel did not wait for further explanation. He took off loping awkwardly through the tangled mass of grass and weeds.

"Daniel! Wait! Here me out!" Dixie shouted, with increasing urgency, trying one last time to make him think about the danger he was in.

Carlee saw that a tall, steep, and elongated scree pile forced Daniel to angle his escape toward her car, not away from it, but was putting too much distance between him and his sister. At five-five, Dixie was too short to navigate the tall weeds as quickly as her taller brother could. They were like thousands of grabbing hands impeding her speed. It didn't matter that she could run faster than her brother on a track. There was no possibility of her catching up to him in these conditions.

Hurriedly exiting the car, Carlee gave chase. Dixie was right, the boy was not a runner. Catching him was not the issue. It was that semi-automatic pistol Carlee spotted tucked into the waistband of his grimy jeans. If this had been an officially sanctioned operation, she should have been shouting commands while identifying herself as law enforcement. She did not, and would not, not yet. She let Dixie be the one to give voice to the chase.

"Damn it, Daniel, stop!" Dixie yelled. "Don't be a fool. You're going to get yourself killed."

Daniel raced for the end of the mounded gravel that had been in place so long ago that Johnson grass and lanky sunflowers were growing through it in many places. It was clear at a glance Daniel was hoping to get through the heavy traffic on the service road behind it, allowing precious seconds to extend his lead and facilitate a get-away. It was also obvious he knew it was becoming hopeless to get away from Carlee on foot. Although continuing to run, he clumsily pulled the pistol from the waistband of his jeans.

Dixie waved wildly with both hands over her head, sprinting best she could through the ground cover. "No, Daniel! Drop the gun! Don't be stupid!"

Daniel gave up trying to run. He stopped, sweating profusely, searching for one good breath. He squared his body to Carlee.

Carlee slowed to a jog, then down to a walk, but continued advancing. Although the heel of her hand was on the pistol grip, she left it holstered. In an almost conversational tone, she said, "Daniel Vega, my name is Carlee Cayne and, yes, I am with the office of the US Marshals Service—"

Daniel's gun-wielding arm stiffened straight toward Carlee but shaking violently. He was scared, possibly beyond rationality.

Carlee raised a defensive palm. "Hang on, Daniel. Calm down. Let me finish," she said in a slow, monotonous way. "I was going to say I am first and foremost your sister's friend. Dixie is like my own sister would be, if I had one. Through it all, she loves you and does not, I repeat, *does not* want to see you harmed." She inched to within a few feet of the barrel of his gun, held at firing height. His gun hand was shaking to an unnerving degree. Daniel was holding his breath—not a good sign. His face reddened, nearing some form of explosive outburst.

Dixie ran to within a few feet of her brother. She stopped and stood her ground. "It's true Daniel. I'll do whatever it takes to keep you from getting yourself killed."

He finally expelled that held breath in a huff. "You gave me up!" he shouted.

"For once in your life, *please* think about what you're doing. If I did take you to New Braunfels to your friends, that's not going to stop the statewide capture order on you. You will run into other situations where you'll be pulling that gun out some other time at some other place and you *will* get shot. Can't you understand that?" she questioned, pleadingly.

"They'll be looking for Rogelio before me."

"Rogelio is dead."

Suddenly, Daniel's rigid posture eased. "What?"

"Rogelio did exactly what you will do when they come for you. He tried shooting his way out of the country. He failed. And, so will you," Dixie said, voice trailing.

Unfortunately, rage over this situation overrode the temporary jolt Daniel received by the news. His adrenalin-charged anger rebounded quickly.

Defensive palm still toward him, Carlee nodded agreement. "It's true, Daniel. Rogelio, Manuel and those two working for him. They're all dead. You are the last one, but you have a chance to survive, if you will take what is being offered to you right now. I won't lie to you. There will be jail time but you're not as deeply involved in the more serious charges of attempted murder. *Please*, let me peacefully take you into custody and your safety will be assured."

Daniel abruptly turned his resentment on Dixie. "You bitch! You did this to me! My own blood!" He supported his gun hand with the other and swung the pistol around, drawing down on his sister.

Carlee spun a quarter turn to stand perpendicular to Daniel. She leaped high into the air and planted the heel of her booted foot squarely into the wrist of Daniel's gun hand. His fingers sprang open and the pistol went spinning through the air. She landed as gracefully as a cat and then seamlessly spun backwards, slapping his face with the sole of that same booted foot, sending him reeling to the ground onto his stomach.

He lay dazed.

Dixie dropped to her knees beside him and pushed him over onto his back. His nose bled.

Daniel's eyes fluttered open. He looked up at his sister. He moaned "I hope you're happy."

Dixie look down on him with kind eyes. She thumbed away a drop of blood below his nose. "Happy? No, *Hermano*. I'm not happy, not at all. Look at where we are and what I'm having to do to my only living family to prevent him from being killed. Happy is not the word."

Carlee pulled handcuffs from a clip on her belt. "Daniel Vega, you are under arrest for violating the rules and regulations established by your bond."

The women helped him to his feet. Carlee cuffed and Mirandized him. She then pulled her cell phone from her pocket and hit Fenn's quick dial number, turning away from Dixie. "Hey, Jimbo, no need to hold back. Come on in. It's over."

"Over? Really? That was fast," Fenn replied. "See you in less than a minute."

"I'd appreciate help in taking Daniel in for booking."

"You got it."

Carlee ended the call. She felt bad for Dixie until she turned and saw her friend quietly smiling at her for how this hastily arranged operation turned out. Suddenly, tension and anxiety drained away, leaving behind a distinct feeling of peace.

Chapter Seventeen

Lincoln Bridger stared out the large window fronting Power House Fitness Center as he walked on the treadmill. His gait was slow, almost ambling, certainly not up to healthy cardio-vascular speed. Everyone around him worked hard and perspired copiously, but not him. He was in his own world of mental meanderings, hopes, and worries—another dimension of mind altogether. Thoughts spun out randomly, occasionally jumbling to a nonsensical mix. His wife, Jeannine, had called as he was walking out the door of his office at the agency to end another work day. She begged him not to divorce her, apologizing profusely, promising to do better, to be better. As immature as he knew her to be, there was something different in her voice. Within contrition, he heard the adult he always knew she could be, if she wanted to be. *Is it possible Jeannine is serious? Or, is she playing an angle, some kind of game?* The questions were simple enough. The answers were not.

"Mind if I join you?"

The question surprised him. His step stuttered as he jerked his head around to see Carlee. His deer-in-the-headlights expression settled into a smile. "I was so deep into that odd world I call a brain, I forgot where I was. You startled me." He snickered. "Of course you can join me. You might be the peer pressure I need to get out of my own head and get on with a serious workout."

Carlee stepped up onto the treadmill next to him and set the controls. "Been here long?"

Lincoln shook his head. "Nah. About ten minutes, I'd say. How was your day?"

"It was a wild one." She engaged the machine and began walking, punching up the speed. "I had to arrest Dixie's brother. It was tense for a few seconds but, fortunately, it ended peacefully."

As she explained, he took the opportunity to admire her all over again. The simple act of seeing her again, and the opportunity to watch her, was exactly where he needed to focus his mind, and his heart. She was such a magnificent creature—of mind, body, spirit, and courage. Those tight black Spandex athletic pants topped with a beige tank top hugged a near-perfect form. Short light brown hair, left a bit ragged and flipped out at the ends looked so right on her. She had the profile and appearance of a physically fit runway model. "I hate it for Dixie's sake but I'm sure glad it turned out well...for *your* sake, of course. Now, if only they can take the final step and capture his cousin," he said.

Carlee glanced sideways. "Rogelio Ortiz is dead, shot to death in a gun battle with law enforcement this afternoon near San Marcos."

"I'm hesitant to say that's a good thing, since a death was involved, but...doesn't that end your problem?"

Carlee smiled and faced him. "If there aren't other Ortiz brothers out there I don't know about, then yeah, it certainly does put the kibosh on it."

It crossed Lincoln's mind how easily Jeannine had vacated his thoughts when Carlee showed up. That alone was worth consideration. "Now that your life will be settling down, I assume you want to go full bore on a job change."

"That would have been true anyhow. Do you have new information for me?" she asked.

His smile widened. "Basically, the job is yours if you like the terms of employment."

Carlee changed her pace so abruptly, she almost shot off the treadmill backwards. "Just like that?"

"Just like that. It's pretty much what I figured. The pay will be about two-thirds what you are making, but the benefits Adler agreed to, I believe, are better than what you have now. He bumped up the benefits a bit more than he would have for any other new hire. That should make up the shortfall."

Carlee's excitement forced her to abandon the moving tread and straddle it. "Oh, Linc. That's wonderful!" She leaped down from the treadmill and joined him on his, forcing him to stop the machine. She grabbed a double fistful of his T-shirt and pulled him into an exuberant kiss, unconcerned by staring people.

An older lady on the treadmill next to Lincoln channeled the iconic movie line, "I'll have some of what she's having."

Lincoln and Carlee laughed. She threw her arms around him and hugged him.

Since others within earshot also laughed, the older lady followed up by asking, "Is he included in the membership here?" After a few more laughs were elicited, the woman ended by saying, "God, I hope so."

"I love your enthusiasm," Lincoln told Carlee, "But, first, you need to hear the offer directly from Mister Adler. After he explains the job, you might not be interested. I told him you'd probably be able to join us for lunch tomorrow. Can you? Or did I lie to him?"

"Sure, I can. Call me tomorrow with details and I'll make it happen." She quickly kissed him again, on the cheek this time, and climbed down from the treadmill. "I suddenly lost my desire to exercise. I think I'll go home and tell Mom and Rylee the good news." She walked away but hesitated and turned to blow him one more kiss. Then she left, almost skipping out the door and out of sight.

Lincoln stepped back onto the moving tread and continued walking. *I cannot imagine a scenario that would prevent Carlee and me from becoming closer now. In fact, I don't want to even think about such a possibility.* He suddenly felt livelier. The spring in his step returned. He punched up the speed and began to jog. After a few minutes, he was breathing hard, but neither that, nor streaming perspiration, could erase the smile from his face or the warmth in his hammering heart.

~ * ~

Carlee sat waiting in the restaurant alone, eyes trained on the entrance. She had shown up a few minutes before the appointed time, waiting for Stuart Adler and Lincoln. She checked her wristwatch repeatedly, so looking forward to this meeting. Excitement and anticipation robbed her of a good night's sleep, but it didn't matter. She was running on adrenalin.

It was a work day for her. She had delivered a couple of court summons earlier and picked up a small-time crook for failing to check in with his parole officer. Getting home to change into something more appropriate for a job interview pressed her for time. Still, she arrived first. She fished in her purse and pulled out a small compact mirror and checked her makeup one last time. She did not often wear much makeup, if any at all. It simply was not necessary for her job as a deputy marshal. This was different. She had to put on the best face possible, even if it was not entirely her own. She pressed her lips together and puckered them for the mirror. She snapped the small compact shut and dropped it back into her purse. She perched her chin upon steepled fingertips, but it certainly was not a restful pose. She looked down at the conservative white button-up blouse she wore over a red skirt, wondering if it was the appropriate choice, smoothing every wrinkle from it, and then again. Finally deciding it was the best of what she had in her closet for its businesslike modesty, she chose not to worry about it further.

Although, she wished she'd had a pretty pair of high heels to wear with the outfit, instead of sandals. She did not own a single pair of high-heeled shoes. Her choices ranged from sneakers to boots to other utilitarian forms of footwear. The sandals were the most feminine thing she owned. *No doubt about it. Shopping for clothes has to be made a priority. Jeans and shirts won't hack it at an ad agency.* She grimaced. *I hate clothes shopping.* She realized it was odd of almost any woman to think that way. She held firm to the notion it was the type of body inside the clothes, not what wrapped it, that was most important. Still, a closet full of jeans, plain pull-over tops, denim jackets, and other similar apparel would not, at all, be appropriate in the professional setting of Adler, Howard and Levy Advertising. *Oh, God,* she thought. *It's going to take more than one shopping trip, maybe many more.* She grunted displeasure at such an unappealing notion and, to her, not a joyful endeavor, just a necessary chore, like scrubbing out the toilet. Again, she checked her wristwatch.

Carlee looked up to see Lincoln walking ahead of the man she assumed to be Stuart Adler. They both trailed an approaching waitress. Carlee made a move to stand to greet them.

"Please, keep your seat," the distinguished appearing man said jovially, as he closed on the table, waving her back down onto her chair. He reached across and took her extended hand with a very large smile on his face. "I'm Stuart Adler. So very glad to finally meet you, Miss Cayne." Adler was shorter than Lincoln with thinning, solid silver hair. He was of average build but walked with an air of calm authority. He made a wonderful first impression. Adler's smile persisted. "I must tell you," he said, flipping a waggling thumb toward Lincoln, "you have a real fan here in this guy."

Carlee smiled when she noticed how Lincoln's cheeks and ears reddened. "It's mutual admiration, Mister Adler. I assure you," she replied.

Lincoln bobbled his head, almost like a shy pre-pubescent boy and grinned. "Thanks." He pulled his chair out and sat. As did Adler.

Adler exuded sincerity and warmth with an easy unforced smile. Anyone would enjoy being in his aura. "Linc has told me a little about the job," she said. "I cannot express enough how much I appreciate being thought of for the position."

"Honestly, Miss Cayne—"

"Please call me Carlee."

"Thank you. I will. Linc's idea of bringing you on board at the agency kick-started an idea that had been tossed around previously among the three principle owners of the agency for some time. When Linc, coincidentally, proffered your name, that was all it took to push us off the fence on the issue and we proceeded to make it happen. It aided and expedited the decision-making process when he volunteered to train you as well. The two buyers we have in-house now, Ann Massey and Joan Harvey, are wonderful employees and both are very busy ladies, but feel free to lean on their expertise when you have questions, or when Linc's not around. I'm sure they'll appreciate the help and will do everything in their power to help out whenever and wherever possible. They're very good at what they do."

All the while Adler spoke, Carlee flicked continual glances at Linc. Whereas, he was free to gaze at her nonstop. It was not fair he was afforded such latitude and she wasn't. Adler did most of the talking, interrupting himself occasionally with questions about her background, education, interests, and abilities. Oddly, it did not feel like an interrogation or any job interview she had ever been on before. It felt more like a genuine conversation between friends-becoming. He encouraged her to ask any questions she might have about the agency or about him personally. As lunch progressed and talk subsided, she looked up from her salad to again see Lincoln staring at her. He glanced at Adler who was busy cutting his filet mignon. Lincoln quickly cut his gaze back to Carlee. He mouthed, "You're beautiful."

She returned the compliment with a silent, "Thank you."

As lunch came to an end, Adler vigorously swiped the linen napkin across his mouth. "And, now, I must ask you, Carlee, did you learn anything objectionable about the job from our conversation today?"

"Absolutely not," she replied. "Quite the opposite. I want the job even more now. That is, of course, if you are so inclined, Mister Adler."

"Let me put it this way, I prefer you call me Stuart. We do not stand on formality at Adler, Howard and Levy. How about that for an answer?"

"Hey, wait a second," Lincoln blurted. "How come I still have to call you Mister Adler?"

Adler laughed. "You don't. Never did, actually. I just never formalized an invitation. Besides," he added, returning his attention to Carlee, "that's the least I can do for Carlee as her first perk of her new job. Was my answer to your question a bit too understated, perhaps?"

Carlee's smile grew to match Adler's. "No, Sir. It was exactly the right amount of subtle."

"Well then," Adler said, "It would seem you need to put in your notice at the Marshal's Service." He checked his wrist watch and sprang to his feet, dropping his napkin on the table, turning his attention to Lincoln. "You don't have to rush back to the office, but I have a meeting in fifteen minutes, so I'd better scoot."

Adler had already begun walking away from the table. Carlee called after him, "Thank you so much for the opportunity."

Adler hesitated but did not stop walking. "It will be a good thing for everyone involved. I'm sure of it."

She watched Adler leave the restaurant. The door had just closed behind him. She turned to Lincoln and squealed with delight.

"How 'bout dem apples?" Lincoln said.

"Dem are sweet, *sweet* apples," she replied as she came to her feet and walked around the table. She bent and kissed him, allowing her lips to linger and graze across his. "But not anywhere near as sweet as you."

Chapter Eighteen

From the moment Lincoln woke, he had been riddled with dread. He wanted this, and had been wanting it for some time, desiring to get it behind him. Although, he was not prepared for the knot in his gut when this day finally arrived. It came as an unwelcome surprise.

Now, he sat with his attorney on one side of a long conference table as they waited for Jeannine and her attorney to arrive. She was late. So common was her penchant for tardiness, he had figured out long ago to add at least thirty minutes to her preparation time when they still lived together and needed to be somewhere at a specific time. Over the years it had settled into a pattern that worked reasonably well, if being on time to planned events and functions was important. Interestingly, neither he nor his attorney had arranged this meeting. Jeannine's attorney had scheduled it. Lincoln grinned, thinking her counsel was in the process of getting an education into the selfish mind of Jeannine Rosen Bridger.

Today the divorce was to be finalized. Lincoln stayed the course and had not changed his mind. He was intent on seeing it through and still had no plans to contest anything. The only caveat was that he retain one car, his job, and that small apartment he had recently rented in south Austin, not far from where he worked. Jeannine was welcome to everything else. If necessary, he would insist on her taking everything—the house, the furniture, the other two cars in that oversized garage—everything. All he wanted was out of a situation that, over a number of years, had become unsustainable. And he wanted out as fast as possible. The building tension didn't agree with him. He hadn't had indigestion this bad since those greasy, over-spiced enchiladas he had at a restaurant in Santa Fe a couple of years ago. He sure had a case of it now.

As flawed as his marriage had been, his memory had already begun the age-old process of softening memories of bad times while enhancing the good. As he stared at a gaudy abstract painting on the opposite wall of the conference room, trying to get his mind in a neutral place and off his grumbling stomach, snapshots of him and Jeannine in happier times marched through his mind. There were many wonderful memories in the early years, but that was long ago. Still, he smiled when remembering pleasant moments with her. The smile sagged once the reality of what was about to transpire replaced treasured memories. He moaned lightly and rubbed his stomach.

As Aaron Paul, his attorney, scribbled notes on a legal pad. Lincoln wanted only to think happy thoughts. He let Carlee Cayne replace this current unpleasantness. She had been with Adler, Howard and Levy for almost a month and had quickly developed an admirable level of proficiency at her new job. She remembered everything she had been taught and, like the professional he always knew she was, learned how to apply her training with scant additional prompts. There was nothing about Carlee he did not like. She was the perfect package of brains, beauty, and benevolence. Beyond her job assignment, Carlee always asked if she could be of help to others during downtime. Everyone at the agency liked her. Even his resident stalker, Betty Jaworski, had whispered admiration of Carlee in his ear one day. Betty, being whom and what she was, could not resist a shot across his bow, knowing his budding relationship with Carlee. She whispered in his ear for no one else to hear, "But, remember, sugar, even perfection doesn't last forever sometimes." She then winked at him. "And, doll, I am a very patient person." She smiled, nodded, and moved on.

Carlee's attire had swung to clothing that highlighted her femininity. Every new thing she wore would take his breath away all over again. What a vision she was.

Lincoln was jolted from his thoughts, but only after Jeannine and the Rosen family attorney, Nicholas Johnson, had already entered the room. "Good morning," Johnson said to his attorney, Aaron Paul. "I assume you and Mister Bridger are prepared." He reached across the long table and shook Paul's hand. He shook Lincoln's hand while still leaning across the table.

"I believe we have everything in order for an expeditious

proceeding," Paul replied.

Lincoln's courteous smile persisted as he shifted his eyes toward his soon-to-be ex-wife. He nodded. "Good morning," he said, as low-key and courteous as possible. He noticed her eyes. They were puffy and red. She apparently had been crying until shortly before entering the conference room. He was no less sad. It was the end of an era, after all. Nineteen years of marriage cannot be easily, or quickly, set aside. He retained feelings for Jeannine, and always would. But, it was as clear as a cloudless spring day that co-habitation as husband and wife was no longer possible.

Paul and Johnson exchanged pleasantries. As they did, Jeannine held her gaze on Lincoln and whispered, mostly mouthing, the question, "Are you *sure* this is what you want?"

Lincoln's courteous smile transformed into an innocuous expression. Suddenly, Jeannine's simple question held a frightening amount of finality. He hesitated. It was a true force of will to offer a simple affirmative nod. It did not come easily.

Jeannine spoke no more. Her expression was not one of anger or impatience, but of sadness complemented by teary eyes. The proceeding turned into a boiler plate recitation of standard divorce documents that neither he nor Jeannine questioned. They both signed every piece of paper shoved before them. Once it was pronounced complete, Jeannine sprang up and headed for the door in a rush. She slowed and then stopped walking. She looked back a last time at Lincoln, lower lip quivering. She then turned and hurried out of the room.

A shuddering chill consumed him when it suddenly occurred to him this could be the last time he ever saw her. He never considered himself callous. He sincerely hoped Jeannine would suffer no long-lasting detriment, and that she would find true happiness with someone at some point in the future. Her happiness was as important to him as his own. It had simply become impossible to be happy together.

As Lincoln stepped out onto the street of downtown Austin and breathed in the typical smells, diesel fumes and the less intense aroma of impending rain, he checked his wristwatch. It was after four and he was in no mood to go back to the agency this late in the afternoon. He called Carlee's desk. She was still at work.

"Carlee Cayne. May I help you?"

His spirits shot up. "I don't know. Can you?"

There was a pause. "If you're a client, I'm sure I can. If you're a wiseass co-worker...well then, it might be debatable."

"I don't know if I like being called a wiseass. Although, at the moment, it does seem to apply." A moment of silence followed.

Finally, she asked, "Are you okay? Is everything over now?" There was obvious hesitance in her voice.

He drew deeply and sighed. "It's done."

"How are you feeling about it?"

"It's an odd feeling. One minute I smile, the next I swallow a sad lump in my throat. This back-and-forth has been going on since I walked out of the attorney's office about half an hour ago. On the upside, my indigestion seems to be going away."

"I understand. I went through the same thing when my ex walked out on me and Rylee." She paused. "Look, I don't know if my presence would help or hurt. But if you're up for quiet conversation, we can meet at my place and have some Chinese delivered after I get off work."

"Sounds wonderful."

~ * ~

At Carlee's insistence, Lincoln sprawled on the sofa with his legs fully extended and his socked feet crossed at the ankles on the coffee table. His reclined upper torso was surrounded by the over-stuffed faux suede sofa cushion as his head lay upon it. "Are you sure you don't mind my feet on your coffee table?" he called out over his shoulder.

She was in the kitchen behind him, pouring two glasses of wine. She chuckled. "If you saw how Rylee treats that poor little table you would understand how silly that question is. That girl has always taken short-cuts right over the top of it, and then jumping off the other side."

A San Antonio Spurs game was on the television, volume purposely kept low. Lincoln had his eyes trained on it but not watching it. He would not have been able to quote the score if asked. "Speaking of Rylee, where is she?"

"Mom was gracious enough to take her to see one of those Pixar animated movies so you and I might have some alone time."

"Beth sure seems like a wonderful lady."

"She is...and a great mom and grandmother too. She makes it too easy for me to take advantage of her good nature." She came around the sofa and handed Lincoln a glass of wine filled to near the brim.

He held the glass up and looked at the level of fill. He grinned. "I say, Miss Cayne, are you trying to ply me with alcohol?"

She matched his smile. "I want you to relax. If you wish to refer to it that way, then who am I to argue the point?" She sat sideways on the sofa facing him, propping her elbow on the back of the sofa, resting her cheek against her palm. For a couple of seconds, she merely smiled while studying his face. Finally, she held her own glass up. "Cheers."

He raised his glass and clinked hers. "Back at you." He took a drink.

She sipped and then set her glass on the table. "Have you been able to gain clarity on the contentious events you had to endure today?"

"I think so. I'm not as muddle-headed as I was earlier. The divorce was necessary, but it still may take time for the heart and mind to realign. One says I'm doing the right thing. The other asks if I'm sure about that." He lolled his head to the side and gazed into Carlee's eyes. "Thank you for being a friend and understanding my emotional malaise."

Carlee moved closer to Lincoln and retrieved her wine glass from the low table in front of them. She matched his posture, reclining back on the sofa cushion with her feet on the coffee table. She spread her feet and flicked her eyes toward the television between them. "Is the game any good?" she asked, eyes still trained on the television.

Gazing at her profile, "Don't know. Don't care," he replied.

She turned and offered her full attention. "Me neither." She moved in and kissed him lightly on the lips. She slowly pulled back and traced the outline of his face.

He watched her eyes going over and examining every square millimeter. He put his hand behind her neck and pulled her back in. This time the kiss reflected growing intensity. He felt her breathing quicken, as did his.

Suddenly, a series of rapid pops sounded off followed by

simultaneous shattering glass blowing into the apartment. The large window at the end of the sofa had exploded inward. Now a glassless window frame facing the street in front of Carlee's ground-level apartment retained only a few dangling shards of glass and curtains left in tatters.

Lincoln sprang upright, spilling the entire contents of his wine glass on himself. "What the hell...?"

Carlee rolled off the sofa and shouted, "Get down, Linc!"

Apparently, he did not react fast enough to suit her. She grabbed his shirttail and yanked him off his feet to the floor. "Hurry! Lie flat! Watch out for broken glass."

Another volley of automatic gunfire came through, peppering the wall on the opposite side of the room, splintering and shattering picture frames and artwork in a rattling sweep.

"What's going on?" Lincoln said as he lay on his stomach with his hands over his head.

"I don't have a clue." She came up on her hands and knees and pulled her cell phone from her jeans and dropped it next to him. "Call nine-one-one, but stay down."

Lincoln finger-pecked the emergency number. "What is your emergency?" came the reply.

"Some idiot is spraying machine gun fire through the window of this apartment and has two of us pinned down," he said hurriedly and then gave Carlee's address. On the orders of the dispatcher, he did not hang up but laid the phone on the floor and slid it beneath the coffee table.

As he spoke, Carlee turned and crawled toward the bedroom.

More gunfire came through the window like stuttering thunder.

She dropped onto her belly, fully prone. A few bullets penetrated all the way through the front door next to the window.

When the gunfire paused, she continued crawling rapidly into her bedroom.

After less than half a minute, Carlee returned with a pistol from her bedroom closet. She crawled to the window, picking her way carefully over glass shards. She slowly came up to lean back against the wall beneath, and next to, the window. She released the magazine from the handgrip and checked its load then slammed it back into place. She racked the slide and chambered a shell. "Stay right there. Don't move," she demanded.

"I will, as long as you don't do anything foolish."

Carlee had already begun lifting her head slowly over the bottom of the blown-out window frame. "Believe me," she said in monotone, "being foolhardy is not in my plan." She visually swept the parking lot in front of her apartment.

Carlee poked her head above the window stool repeatedly, looking beyond the sill in rapid flicking glances, the sound of an engine roared and tires squealed.

Seeing the source of the vehicle sounds, Carlee sprang to her feet.

A final volley came her direction as the vehicle roared away.

She hurriedly climbed through the glassless window, leveled the pistol and fired three quick shots at the retreating vehicle. She dropped the pistol to her side. "Linc? Quickly, bring me a pencil and paper."

Lincoln searched himself, pulling a restaurant receipt from his shirt pocket and the ballpoint pen next to it. "I've got it." He leapt up and ran to the front door, jerking it open, and running to Carlee's side. Although the sun had finished its daily slide below the horizon, it was still fully light outside.

Carlee snatched the scrap of paper and pen from his extended hand and jotted the license number onto the crumpled receipt. "That was a Nissan Maxima and a rental. I saw the Enterprise sticker on the bumper."

Curious people streamed out of their apartments throughout the complex. The grassy easement bordering the street in front of the stacked and grouped apartments quickly filled with a crowd of chattering people, reminiscent of a gaggle of excited geese, all wondering what had happened.

Lincoln watched the gathering for a moment. Sirens were converging from different directions. He turned his attention back to Carlee. "Well, it's about time they..." He suddenly noticed her face had lost color. Her lips were grayish, jaw slack.

She stared blankly straight ahead and had difficulty balancing on her feet.

"Carlee?"

A spreading red patch on the upper left side of her chest appeared. The ballpoint pen slipped from her fingers and bounced on the asphalt at her feet, followed by the slip of paper, fluttering to the ground. With obvious effort, she turned her face toward him. "Oh Linc..." Her legs buckled.

Lincoln caught her before she hit the surface of the paved parking area, protecting her head.

She was conscious, but barely. "Hold me. Please...just hold me." She lost consciousness.

An Austin police officer approached. Lincoln shouted to him, "Call an ambulance! She's been shot!"

Lincoln had never been inclined to blatant emotional displays. He had no idea how badly Carlee was injured, but the location of the bullet wound in her chest scared the hell out of him. Tears dripped onto her limp body before he realized he was crying.

Chapter Nineteen

Carlee's eyes fluttered open. Sense of time and place did not accompany her awakening mind. The first and only thing she sensed was pain. She heard a voice—the words indecipherable. "Where am I?" she slurred.

"You're in Seton Medical Center," came the same feminine voice, now somewhat clearer and nearer, spoken softly into her ear.

Carlee shifted her head left. A blurry human form stood behind the person speaking to her. She strained to better see. Slowly coming into focus was her old partner, Jimmy Fenn. He replaced the woman who had spoken to her and leaned over her. His face moving closer and not stopping until it was near her own. It was difficult to keep her eyes open. Her eyelids felt heavy. "Jimbo?" she said questioningly, wondering if her eyes or mind might be playing tricks. Forming the two-syllable nickname was difficult. She felt heavily drugged. Maybe she was. She wondered.

Jimmy Fenn scooped her hand up and kissed the back of it. "You're a lucky, lucky girl, Carlee Cayne," he said, keeping his voice down into a soothing range.

She closed her eyes and attempted to swallow. "I don't feel lucky," she said, garbling the words.

"A bullet barely missed your heart, but did take a piece of rib on its way out through your back. Had that bullet been one or two inches lower, it would have...I don't even want to say it aloud."

"Well," came another voice from the other side of the bed, "I will say *my* heart would have been shattered into a thousand tiny pieces."

Carlee shifted her sluggish eyes to see Lincoln. She tried smiling. As she held her hand open, he slid his over the top of her bared palm and squeezed. "Oh, Linc," she muttered.

She noticed Dixie standing a couple of steps away from the bed behind Lincoln. Her eyes were bloodshot. Had she been crying? "I just now took your mom and Rylee down to the cafeteria to get some breakfast," Dixie said. "Neither one of them have eaten anything since they brought you in last night."

"Last night?"

"Yeah. I had to force them to leave long enough to get something to eat."

Carlee blinked lazily. "Thanks, Dix. Let's leave them be until I shake the grogginess." She thought for a second and suddenly wondered, "How long have I been in here?"

"You were unconscious when they brought you into the emergency room from shock, according to the doctor, because you didn't lose much blood, luckily," Lincoln said. "I rode with you in the ambulance. They immediately took you into surgery to repair the damage. You were brought here to ICU about midnight. It's almost ten now."

Carlee nodded. "Could I get some water?"

Dixie snatched a cup and put some crushed ice in it from the bucket near the sink and filled it with water. She returned to bedside, taking Lincoln's position. She put a plastic straw in the cup. "Here ya go, sweetie."

Carlee gagged on the first attempt.

"Take it slow," Dixie said, holding the straw close to Carlee's mouth.

Her throat was dry and unresponsive. She chose to simply coat her tongue with small amounts until the sips went down easier. Drawing a good swallow of the heavenly chilled liquid came slowly, but finally began going down with less inclination to gag. It helped clear her mind somewhat as well. She began to think on the events that resulted in her lying on her back in a hospital and then snapped a look toward Lincoln. "The slip of paper with the license number on it, did you give it to the police?"

He nodded but there was no pleasantness associated with it.

She noticed his odd expression and suddenly became more alert. "What? Why are you looking like that?"

"It would seem," Fenn said, "Rogelio Ortiz is not dead after all."

"I don't understand," Carlee replied.

"We were notified of it several days ago. The man who tried

shooting his way out of the country back into Mexico was one of Rogelio's goons carrying all of Rogelio's identification. Since he carried ID, DNA testing was put on the back burner. Once it was done and compared with the blood sample taken from the top of the fence that night in my backyard, it was proven definitively the man was not Ortiz. The rental car you saw last evening was rented in Del Rio by a woman known to be a consort, one of several we believe, within the Ortiz Cartel. Carlee, I hate to be the one to tell you this, but Rogelio not only made it back into Mexico alive, he apparently has wised up and no longer interested in personally coming after you. It appears he will, though, be content sending hit men, conducting it all from the safety of his lair in Ciudad Acuña."

Carlee closed her eyes and pushed her head back into the pillow. "Crap," she hissed. She opened her eyes on Fenn. "What's our plan, Jimbo?"

"Hey, kiddo, there is no *our plan* in this scenario. You work at an advertising agency and no longer in law enforcement. Remember?"

Carlee lifted her head from the pillow. "If the next thing out of your mouth is I don't have skin in this game, I'm going to stab you with this IV needle," she said, waving her arm unsteadily with the intravenous needle taped to it. Although lucidity was returning, muscle control was slow to follow.

Lincoln put a hand on her shoulder and gently pushed her back down from the opposite side of the bed. "Don't excite yourself," he admonished with a frown. "All Mister Fenn meant, I'm sure, is it's now other people's job to protect you. And, your job is to get well and, of course, lay low until they can get the situation with Ortiz taken care of."

"He's right, Cayne," Fenn quickly added. "You concentrate on healing. We'll go after Ortiz."

"How?" she asked, unable to conceal frustration. "The bastard is sitting smugly across the border, tossing out kill orders. I would bet he's put an open-ended bounty on my head for killing his brother, and probably a big one. The man has deep pockets, you know. There'll be goons from all over the country streaming in here to earn it."

"Don't think about that. Austin police have already arranged a protective detail for you and your family," Fenn said, patting her hand.

"Not only that, the Mexican government has been contacted. They have sent assurances Ortiz will be captured and extradited for his crimes on this side of the border."

"Who do you think you're talking to, Jimbo? I know how that works. Rogelio Ortiz likely has the Acuña police on the payroll and a few high-ranking government officials as well. Even if their government is sincere, it will take weeks, months maybe, for that process to run its course. Mexican officials will sit on it, stick the paperwork at the bottom of a to - do pile in some dirty and overworked precinct headquarters and purposely procrastinate. That'll give Ortiz all the time he needs to have me killed and then plan, at his convenience, for his safety from prosecution in the United States. He will be given plenty of time to get it done. At some point, one of those thugs *will* get through with a kill shot. You can be sure of that."

"Look, Carlee," Lincoln said, "I'm making it my personal mission to be with you twenty-four hours a day until they capture that guy."

Carlee settled. Her concerned frown transformed into a soft smile as she looked at Lincoln. "You are more than a friend to me, which means, there is no way I'll allow you to put yourself in harm's way again over this. For heaven's sake, Linc, you've been too close to my problem twice already. You could easily have been the one lying here with a bullet in you." She reached up and grabbed his shirt and forced him to lean over. She kissed him. "I'm not going to lose you because you want to be a nice guy."

"Don't you see? I don't want to lose you either. But, Carlee—"

"Uh-uh. No *buts*. Whatever you're about to say, don't." Carlee looked past Lincoln to where Dixie had been standing a few minutes before, hoping for her friend's support on the issue. She glanced around and didn't see her. "Where'd Dix go?"

Chapter Twenty

"Fitz? Dixie."

"Glad you called," Fitz replied. "I've been wondering about Carlee. How is she?"

"She has healing to do, but she'll be okay, eventually." She checked her rearview mirror and moved into the passing lane and accelerated around slower moving traffic, heading south on the interstate. "Look, the reason I called is to tell you I have to cancel our training session at the gym tonight. I'm sorry about having to do that."

"I'm sorry about that too. How about—"

"I'll call you later," she blurted abruptly. "I'll be out of town a few days. I don't know for how long. I've taken a leave-of-absence from work. There's something important I have to do. I'm not sure how long it will take."

"Oh? Where are you going?"

She began to speak but then hesitated, uncertain how much she should share. She then remembered how she so detested people who were purposely vague with her and figured partial disclosure would be okay. She certainly did not want to lie to the guy. She cared for him too much. "I have personal business to take care of in Del Rio. I'll tell you about it when I get home."

"Does it have anything to do with that cousin of yours? He's a dangerous man."

No response.

"If confronting the guy is the plan, I'm not going to let you do it alone. That's all there is to it. I'll go with you."

"It seems telling you my destination was a mistake. You're a sweet guy, but don't resort to becoming a dumbass because of me. Look, Fitz, this is my problem to fix. Stay out of it." Dixie abruptly ended the call and tossed her phone onto the passenger side seat. *Rogelio has ruined my brother's life and my relationship with him. I'm not about to let Fitz get involved any deeper than he already is. And, as God is my witness, I won't let Rogelio hurt Carlee ever again!*

Her face screwed down tight. Tears flowed freely. She was alone and no reason to hold back. But, now, it was less about sadness for her best friend. These tears had everything to do with anger swelling to a dangerously explosive level and needed release. Streaking tears were her only recourse, that is, until she arrived and set foot on her cousin's home turf. *Cousin or not, Rogelio, your day of reckoning for your sins is upon you. I'll see to it personally. I have made God witness to this vow.*

~ * ~

Fitz let the phone dangle between fingertips as he considered the odd phone conversation with Dixie. He absently stared out his office window across the lake to the skyline of downtown Austin. *What does she plan on doing? What's on that girl's mind? Whatever it is, I have a strong feeling it's dangerous. If so, it's stupid and careless for her to think she can deal with it alone.*

He punched a single quick dial number on his office phone. It rang once. He began pounding the top of his desk with a soft fist. "Come on, come on. Answer the phone." The third ring was abruptly interrupted. "Linc?"

"Yeah. What's up, Fitz?"

"Where are you?"

"I'm still at Seaton Medical Center with Carlee, Rylee, her mother, and Carlee's ex-partner, Jimmy Fenn. Is everything okay at work?"

"It's not about work. It's about Dixie. Did you know she headed to Del Rio a short while ago?" Lincoln did not respond quickly enough to suit Fitz. "Well?"

"Hold on. I'm going out in the corridor so I can talk freely," he whispered. After a few seconds, Lincoln was back on the line. "Fitz, I have you on speaker. Jimmy Fenn is with me. Repeat what you just told me."

"Dixie is headed for Del Rio. When I asked if it had anything to do with Ortiz, she would not answer the question. Guys, I think she's going to confront him. I don't care if he is part of her extended family. I feel certain the family connection means very little to an amoral ass like him. I'm tellin' ya, that's a recipe for disaster. She's going to get herself hurt...or worse."

"Are you confident that's what she had on her mind?" Fenn blurted.

"The only definitive answer I can give you is that she didn't deny it. But when she said to me it was her problem to deal with, that told me everything I needed to hear to believe she's about to step off into something that will reel out of her control. If she gets in the guy's face, who's to say what that maniac will do? The guy obviously has serious anger and sociopathic issues. I'm going after her and bring her home before she does something stupid," Fitz said.

Fenn blurted, "No, don't," he demanded. "Let me take care of it. I think I may be able to get the local police in Del Rio to stop her before she can cross the border into Acuña. If she sees you coming, she'll only run faster. It's imperative you don't attempt to catch up to her. She was here at the hospital about half an hour ago, so we have time to put out the word to hold her a few hours in Del Rio before she can make it across the border into Mexico. That will give me time to get down there."

"I cannot think of anything harder for me to make a promise on than to hang back and do nothing, but if you believe you can keep Dixie from crossing the border and getting herself hurt, I'll do it," Fitz replied. But even as he agreed to Fenn's demand, his conviction to comply wavered.

~ * ~

Lincoln stood by quietly, not calmly, holding the speaker-activated cell phone for the conversation between his friend, Fitz, and Jimmy Fenn. Lincoln was as eager to jump into the fray as these two guys. He glanced back over his shoulder through the door into Carlee's room, as a sudden second thought struck him. He realized by Carlee's side was where he needed to be, not traipsing off to south Texas on a rescue mission that might turn dangerous for everyone involved if Dixie happened to penetrate the border into Ciudad Acuña, Rogelio Ortiz's criminal playground.

Fenn gave Lincoln a decisive nod to end the call. Lincoln slipped the phone back into the side pocket of his pants.

"Tell Carlee I had to get back to work," Fenn said, "but I'll be back in a couple of days to check on her." Fenn whirled around and hurried away.

Watching Fenn turn the corner down the hall, hurrying toward the elevators, Lincoln felt deflated and helpless. Slowly, he turned and sauntered back into Carlee's room. She was still groggy from postoperative pain medication but alert.

She lolled her head toward him. "Where did Jimbo go?"

He broke eye contact with her and bobbled his head. "Oh, he had to get back to work."

Carlee smiled lazily. "You're a terrible liar. How about you? Are you going to stay a while?"

"I'll be by your side as long as you need me."

Carlee pressed her head deeper into the pillow. "I sure like the sound of that," she replied, hinting continued disbelief.

"I'm telling you the truth. I swear it."

"I want to believe you and, this time, I think you are telling me the truth." Beth Cayne and Rylee stood next to Carlee on the opposite side of the bed. Carlee turned to her mother. "Mom, you have to be exhausted and I see it in Rylee's eyes that she is. Why don't both y'all go on home? I'll be fine. I have Linc to keep me company. You can come back tomorrow."

"Are you sure, Sweetheart?" Beth asked.

"Yeah, Mom, I'm sure."

Rylee leaned over and kissed her mother on the cheek. "Love ya, Mama."

"Love you, too, baby."

"Okay then," Beth said. She looked to Lincoln. "Call me if anything changes. Would you do that for me?"

Lincoln smiled warmly. "Of course."

Beth Cayne and granddaughter left, but reluctantly so. Once out of sight, Lincoln leaned over and asked, "It's my turn. May I kiss you now?"

"Two things: you don't need to ask and you don't need to whisper. Now, kiss me."

Lincoln grazed his lips across hers, savoring the simple feel of them against his own. "Oh, Carlee," he murmured as he pressed their lips together, pulling her lower lip between his before pulling away. He held his face close. "You sure scared me."

"I suppose I might have been scared, too, if I would have been conscious." She grinned. Even though sluggish, the grin glinted sarcasm.

"It sure made me realize how deep my feelings for you have become. It doesn't matter we've only known one another for a short time. I cannot, and do not want to, imagine my life without you in it." He kissed her once more quickly and straightened.

"Nor I you, Lincoln Bridger." She reached, IV tube and fingertip lead in tow, and squeezed his hand.

He returned the cuddling embrace of her hand. "Feel any pain?"

"Are you kidding? With all the meds they're pumping into me, I'm surprised I can feel anything." She snickered lethargically. "But, what I'm feeling for you right now is overriding it." Still squeezing his hand and rubbing circles on the back of it with her thumb, she shook it and then released it. "Truth time. I'm not surprised Dixie and Jimbo had to get back to their lives. It's odd, though, neither said goodbye, just left. Something's going on. I can feel it."

Lincoln did not want to upset her with the truth, but Carlee said it herself, he was a poor liar. He opened his mouth to speak but did not, certain the look on his face was one of abject stupidity.

His expression amused her. "You're trying to think of a lie. Aren't you?"

Lincoln heaved a sigh. "Yeah. I'm afraid the truth will upset you."

Carlee's charmed expression changed. A dour cloud replaced amusement. "Whatever it is, Linc, I can handle it. Not knowing will do more harm. I promise you that."

He clenched his teeth, working his jaw muscles, still reticent.

"Well?" she asked. "Tell me."

He drew an affirming breath and then huffed it away. "Okay. But, you have to promise that your part in all this, your *only* part, will be to get well. That's all. Got it?"

"Here's a quick answer. My wound is not serious and I'll heal fast. Now, back to the point. 'Part in all this' what? Come on, Linc, spit it out."

He sighed. "I would prefer not talking about it while you're down like this, but I suppose you're not about to let it go until I do."

"You've got that right."

"Dixie cut out of here heading for Del Rio a short while ago, presumably to get across the border and confront her cousin on his own turf. It's only a guess, but I believe she aims to do whatever it takes to get him to back off his misplaced anger at you."

Carlee snapped her head off the pillow. "What? She's going after Rogelio Ortiz...alone?" A pain in her upper back drove her right back down. She groaned.

Lincoln placed a hand on her shoulder. "You see? Right there. That's why I didn't want to tell you. You must rest, or, your body will not be able to heal. I don't care how minor you think the injury is. You trust your ex-partner, don't you?"

"Of course I do."

"Then rest easy, don't stress, and let him take care of it. Jimmy said he was going to put the call out to The Department of Public Safety and all local police departments along the way, including Del Rio police, to be on the lookout for her, and then stop and detain her until he can get down there and convince her to cool down and come home."

Carlee swallowed hard, waiting for the sharp pain in her back to ease. Eyes shut tight, she said, "I know Dixie too well. Once her mind is set, there's no way Jimbo will convince her to back off. The girl is fiercely loyal...to a fault. She's good to the bone but stubborn as a freakin' mule."

"Calm down," he said.

Carlee forced her breathing back into a slow, even range. "Well, if she does get herself into a dangerous situation, God help any unarmed person standing in her way. I'm not worried about the unarmed guys getting the better of her in a hand-to-hand situation. I'm terrified of the ones that carry weapons. Unfortunately, that's everyone associated with Ortiz. I am very sure of that." She paused, swallowed, and then muttered, "God, I hope she doesn't get herself shot."

Chapter Twenty-one

Dixie Vega navigated her way through San Antonio. Having grown up there, she knew the city well and how to get around. She exited Interstate 35 onto US-90 West. Only a couple more hours and she would be in Del Rio. Her jaws ached from clenched determination. The car she drove was nothing fancy but it suited her—an older model, high-mileage Toyota. Although, in the back of her mind, she worried about her beloved little car. It was long overdue for much needed maintenance. Nevertheless, she had difficulty holding her speed within legal limits, wanting to get across the border into Acuña, find Rogelio and, hopefully, convince him to stop going after Carlee Cayne, certain a face-to-face appeal to her cousin was the only way. She maintained a level of confidence she could succeed.

She wondered if Rogelio remained in the same neighborhood she remembered as a child. It was in a northwestern section of Acuña, near a bodega he and his crew likely kept in business singlehandedly. Her last visit had been over fifteen years ago, having gone there when she was thirteen before her mother died, before Rogelio decided the drug trade was a good way to make a living and before Manuel thought armed robbery was low-risk fast cash. Even though it had been years, she was confident she could find her way there.

Dixie passed a sign that indicated only four miles until she reached Bracketville. A fast approaching vehicle caught her eye in the rearview mirror. It was a Department of Public Safety Trooper, lights flashing, closing in behind her. *What the...?* She glanced at her speedometer. It registered just over eighty-five miles per hour. "Damn it," she muttered, realizing she had no one to blame but herself, having become too caught up in making it to the border quickly. Take the citation and move on. It was her only option. Silently, she vowed to acquiesce to whatever the officer would say to expedite the process and get back on the highway. Dixie didn't want anything to alter commitment to what she had to do. She slowed and veered off the blacktop, crunching gravel beneath the tires as she rolled to a stop.

When the officer got out of his car and approached, she fished through her purse, retrieving her driver's license and proof-of-insurance card. She let down her window. The officer came to a halt one step behind her window. She had to look back over her shoulder to see him. "Sorry. Didn't realize how fast I was going until I saw you behind me." She handed him the two pieces of information he would have asked for anyhow.

"Yes, ma'am. I clocked you at eighty-seven. The speed limit through here is only sixty-five," the officer intoned, as if this was not his first stop of the day and simply another day at the office, so to speak. The officer took her license and insurance card. He scanned them quickly and pulled a citation book from his hip pocket, flipping it open.

Dixie watched him in the rearview mirror walking to the rear of her car to write down the license number. He began jotting it down, but suddenly seemed distracted and dropped the citation booklet to his side and walked back to his cruiser, presumably to check something on the dash-mounted computer. She continued watching. He lifted a microphone from its hold and looked to be having a brief conversation with someone. After mere seconds, he got out of his car and walked back to hers. "Ma'am, we have had a request from the US Marshals office in Austin to hold you for return transport."

"Wait a second. You have no legal right to detain me. I have things to do and places to be."

"Actually, ma'am, I do have a legal right to detain you. Your tires are dangerously worn and your brake lights are faulty. You are a danger to yourself and other motorists. I can call a truck to tow you to a tire store in Bracketville if you like?"

Dixie stared at the officer, mouth agape. "I don't understand. I've never heard of anything like this. Besides, I can't afford new tires *and* a speeding citation."

"I can remedy one side of that equation," the officer replied, now appearing less businesslike—even pleasant. "I'll let you off with a warning on the speed violation. But, seriously, ma'am, you do need new tires rather badly."

"Uh...okay...I guess," Dixie stammered. "Can you at least tell me who put out the request for me to be held? Was it Jimmy Fenn?"

The officer did not attempt to respond. "Sit tight," he said, "I'll call a tow truck. I'll wait with you from my cruiser." He sauntered back to his car at a leisurely pace.

Her phone, lying on the passenger seat sounded off. She picked it up and saw Fitz was calling. She began to answer it. It then occurred to her he would try to talk her out of following through on her plan and really did not want to debate it further with him. She punched the icon, sending it to voicemail and tossed the phone back onto the seat next to her.

Listening to the radio, she became impatient after twenty minutes. There was no tow truck in sight. She slipped into a pattern of checking her wristwatch then her rearview mirror at the DPS officer sitting in his car. He appeared calm. That, itself, was unsettling. Upon second thought, the man probably sat in his car for several hours every day as part of his job and thought nothing of it. She wondered how law enforcement people did it— waiting, sometimes hours, and then moving swiftly toward danger. It certainly was not a lifestyle that appealed to her. If she was to be involved in a dangerous situation, she wanted to be the instigator of it, not a minuteman go-between mediator or, in her case, a minutewoman.

Another fifteen minutes went by. Dixie fidgeted. Whether it was waiting for a deputy marshal or a tow truck did not matter. It was sitting and doing nothing that was maddening. She made up her mind to walk back and ask the trooper if he might check and find out when that tow truck would be arriving. She reached for the door handle. Before she could open it, another vehicle slowed and pulled off the highway in front of her and parked. It was a plain looking four-door sedan and unremarkable in every way except one—it had a government license plate.

Carlee's ex-partner, Jimmy Fenn, exited the vehicle and approached. She was quick to judge. *Damn it! I was right. Fitz, you just couldn't keep your mouth shut. Could you?* She let her window down. "Why are you here?"

"I want to talk to you before you go another mile south," he replied. "Wait here." He walked back to the DPS Trooper's car, said a few words, tapped the top of the car, and the officer pulled onto the highway and drove away. Fenn offered a friendly wave as the car receded at a leisurely speed down the highway. He returned and was getting into the passenger side of Dixie's little car.

Before his butt touched the seat, she stated flatly, "You planned this with that DPS guy, didn't you?"

"He was helpful. Yes."

She pursed her lips and stared straight down the highway, refusing to look at Fenn. "Okay. You wanted to talk. So, talk."

"Do you realize you're about to put yourself in a situation that might get you killed and still would not prevent Ortiz from going after Carlee?"

"I have to take the chance. He's family. I think I can get through to him and stop him from pursuing this vindictive binge he's on."

"What could you possibly say to him that would make it happen?"

"Look, I don't agree at all with his lifestyle, the drugs, the violence, or anything related. But I think I can convince him going after Carlee will bring an abrupt halt to everything he's come to enjoy. The money, the power he wields in Acuña, and all the trappings of both. I think his anger and arrogance has overridden good sense, unable or unwilling to see he's jeopardizing everything he has built down there."

"Point made. Please allow me to counter. Can you honestly trust the man to see you as family? He will know *exactly* why you're there. I think men with definite sociopathic tendencies, possibly psychopathic as well, like Rogelio, see nothing but winning and losing. I do not think for a second the killing of Manuel Ortiz angered him because the guy was his *brother*."

"You believe that? Seriously? You don't think he has retained even a smidgen of family love and loyalty?"

Fenn pursed his lips, presenting a quick negative head shake. "Here's what I do believe, Miss Vega. Bear with me on this. Rogelio lost a reliable pipeline for his drug trade north of the border, and he's not going to let it go without making an example of what happens to people who interfere with his business, not his *family,* his *business.* He uses people and usually at their peril. It has nothing to do with loyalty toward his deceased brother. He was in the process of doing the same thing with *your* brother, Daniel. I'm sorry I need to say this, Miss Vega, but it would not surprise me in the slightest if Rogelio shoots you, or has you shot by a paid assassin, once he learns why you're looking for him. Once he's done it, he would likely turn his back on your bloodied corpse and think no more of it than he would washing his hands after taking a leak. I know this sounds harsh and I'm sorry to put it in such brutally ephemeral terms, but I have to make you understand the true danger to *you* in the situation you plan on instigating."

Dixie slumped deeper and deeper as Jimmy Fenn laid out a plausible scenario she could not debate. When he finished talking, she slowly lifted her head and faced him. "Are you saying that the only way to stop the man is to kill him?"

Fenn shrugged his shoulders apologetically and nodded. "Yes. Unfortunately, I think that's right, unless he thinks of a personal reason to back off, but that's not likely. Of course, I don't need to investigate it to believe, and quite firmly so, he has the police in Acuña on his payroll. So, even if you do decide to follow through, you would never make it back across the border alive, whether you got to him for a face-to-face or not."

An overpowering sense of impotence dropped a negative curtain over her motivation to complete the mission. "Then what do I do, Fenn?" Tears blurred her view of the man. Her lip quivered. "What the hell do I do? I can't sit and wait for him to murder my best friend, for Christ's sake. He's tried twice already and both times has come close. If left unchecked, there's no lingering doubt in my mind that my best friend, my sister by choice, will end up dead at Rogelio's hand. I can't emphasize enough that Carlee is so much more than a friend. I couldn't ask for a better sister and confidante. I won't lose her, damn it!"

Fenn reached and put a hand on her arm. "Calm down. What you're saying is exactly the reason I wanted to talk to you before you could get across the border. Your place is by Carlee's side as her protector. You certainly have the skills for it and the intense desire to keep her safe. Go back. Be her guardian. You can't be that for her if you're dead, no matter how noble the intention."

For several long, quiet seconds, Dixie stared beyond Fenn out the window at the rural landscape and thought about what he had said. Her eyes followed a large jackrabbit as it churned dust, racing across an open plowed field in response to some unseen predator. Finally, she wiped away accumulated tears and nodded. "I suppose you're right."

Tension between them eased. Fenn smiled and remained quiet for a moment. Finally, "Now, I'll follow you into Bracketville, find a tire store, and help you get new tires. Heck, I might even spring for the cost of repair on that faulty tail light," he said. "That, of course, would be my gift to you."

"That's terribly nice of you, but I couldn't let you do that." She then frowned. "Do I really need tires? Wasn't that just a ploy to get me to sit calmly and give you time to get here?"

"Yes...and yes. By the looks of those slick tires, you might not have made it into Mexico anyhow. What could you have accomplished laid up in a hospital with broken bones from a car accident?"

Dixie rolled her eyes, hinting a smile.

"You see?" Fenn added. "There is more than one reason it was a bad idea to go down there."

Chapter Twenty-two

Carlee sat on the edge of the hospital bed, legs crossed at the ankles, swinging them like a school girl sitting on a fence. It was impossible to have the same thoughts and feelings as a happy-go-lucky child though. Such carefree days were another lifetime, many years in her past. Her thoughts were of a very adult frame. She plotted. Earlier in the day, she shed the hospital gown in favor of black sweat bottoms, an oversized gray sweat shirt, and her favorite sneakers with the help of a nurse. Almost three days of confinement in a hospital room, mostly lying in bed, had become increasingly difficult. Doing nothing was not her style and never would be. Boredom eroded her attitude at an alarming rate. She had memorized every brush stroke of the cheap landscape prints screwed to the walls. Even the new magazines left for her had been handled to the appearance of years, not days, old. Plus, she knew every tile on the ceiling intimately. Having picked out shapes in the tile patterns reminding her of people and animals. She became so familiar with their locations on the ceiling she had given them all names.

It was late afternoon. Welcome rays of sunshine streamed through the westerly facing window at a severe angle, the only window in this hospital room, spotlighting a jar of cotton balls on a counter across the room. She waited for the doctor, hoping to be released. Pain in her upper back from the repaired rib bone remained an issue, but hydrocodone did a nice job of dulling it to a manageable level. Interestingly, it also calmed anxiety so she was capable of piecing together a complex plan.

She wanted to be home with Rylee. Her daughter could help with things she still had trouble doing while her arm remained in a restrictive sling and harness, immobilizing the arm entirely across her chest, preventing rolling of the shoulders, intended to protect that rib. Thank God for her mother, Beth, at times like this.

Carlee would have been severely hampered without her mother's help with Rylee over the years. Each time she thought about how wonderful her mother had been since Rylee was born deepened her love further. And, each time, she thought love for her mother could not become any more intense, it did.

She glanced at her wristwatch. It was four o'clock. She waited for Lincoln, glancing often toward the door. His presence was eagerly sought and appreciated, always. He had promised to be there when the doctor came in to talk to her. She depended on him, maybe too much. Was she in love with the guy? It certainly seemed as though her need for his presence went beyond dependency. Could it be she wanted him by her side for its own sake? That was probably the answer, more want than need. She smiled and hugged herself on that thought. Lincoln made her feel happy, protected and, yes, loved.

"Good afternoon, Miss Cayne," came the familiar voice from the direction of the door.

Carlee snapped from ponderous thought and looked up to see her doctor. "Oh, hi, Doctor Pendergrass."

"How are you feeling?"

"Bored. Very, very bored." She chuckled mirthlessly.

"That's good."

"How so?"

"It shows that, beyond the dulling effect of medication, you're energetic enough to become bored. That, unto itself, is an excellent sign. Which brings me to the point. I think we can discharge you today, *if* you have help getting home and then around the house for the next week or so. You don't need to be jostling that rib. We need to keep that arm and shoulder immobilized for at least one more week and then get you into physical therapy for a couple more weeks after that."

"My mother picked up my daughter from school and took her home to fix her dinner and help her with homework. God love her. As far as my welfare is concerned, I have a friend coming straight here from work. I expect to see him walking through that door any minute. So, yeah, I think I can cover that concern."

"Excellent," Doctor Pendergrass said as he walked to a computer screen on a swing arm extending out from the wall. "I'll get the discharge going." The doctor spent a few minutes entering information.

Carlee slid off the bed and sauntered to the window. The sun bathed her in radiant warmth. It felt nice. A small piece of the outside world she hadn't realized she would miss, until she became trapped in a hospital room for a few days. Forced confinement was all it took to take stock, develop a renewed appreciation for the smaller things in life, like the simple freedom of the outdoors. She examined everything within view. Her mind shifted from the hospital to resuming life out there, and her plan-becoming, now in the process of being pieced together.

"I'll be back before you leave, Miss Cayne," the doctor said, as he headed toward the door.

Without looking away from the view beyond the window, "Thank you, Doctor," Carlee monotoned. She wondered how safe she and her family would be from now on. The prospects were not good. Nothing will have changed in that regard. As long as Ortiz sat on his cocaine-financed throne, the threat would continue to exist. He was likely biding his time until another opportunity presented itself to send someone after her. In fact, it was now obvious beyond debate that he considered those in his employ as dispensable and, over time, would pay thugs whatever it took and would send as many as necessary to get the job done. And that job would be her murder and, possibly, her family as well. She wondered if he would be foolhardy enough to try again himself. If so, what would she have to do to lure him north across the border to level the field?

While Rogelio Ortiz lived, the threat would certainly remain alive. It would be virtually impossible to neutralize him on his turf in Acuña without a small army. She tipped her head, raking her upper teeth over her lower lip, thinking. Possibilities, somewhat disconnected, emerged. There were two things she did know definitively. She had to go on offense or the problem would never go away, and that Rogelio Ortiz was arrogant and vengeful, a textbook sociopath in every sense of the word. She had to figure a way to play that inflated opinion of himself, to provoke him to react impulsively, in a way that would not be in his best interest but would definitely be to her advantage. After ten minutes of uninterrupted thinking, she had mapped out the basis for a plan.

Suddenly, she felt the gentle pressure of a hand on her shoulder. She spun clumsily, expecting to see Lincoln. Instead, she dropped her eyes about six inches into the face of Dixie Vega. "Dix. You came back."

Dixie nodded, but the disgust on her face was clear enough. "I wasn't given a choice. I didn't even make it to Bracketville, thanks to your friend, Jimmy Fenn. But, hey, on the upside I have a new set of tires."

Carlee pulled her into an embrace with her one free arm. "Oh, girl, it's a good thing he did. I may never have seen you again if he hadn't."

"If I can't confront Rogelio and appeal to him to leave you alone, then what? He'll keep sending goons up here to try and take you out. I cannot let that happen."

"I think I have a plan coming together that might anger him enough to try it again personally. I think I may have a plan to get *him* up here, not just his goons. It's the head of the snake that has to be dealt with."

Dixie frowned. "I don't see how. Rogelio is too smart to get that close to being captured or killed again."

"Yeah, he is smart. But I think there is a way we can play that over-the-top arrogance of his, manipulate it in such a way as to supersede intelligence, and make him react without considering consequences closely enough. To your way of thinking, what do you believe would be the *one thing* Rogelio would not allow under any circumstances?"

Dixie bounced a shrug. "Someone messing with his drug business, I suppose."

"Exactly. What if a rival cartel was looking to move in on his territory there in Acuña and he should find out about it?"

"He would puff up like a toad and probably go to war to prevent it. But, Carlee, how does that entice him back into Central Texas?"

"This is where you can help. How would you like to become a provocateur?"

"I know what the word means, but what is it I can do to provoke him?"

"Here's what I'm thinking. The top of Rogelio's head might blow off if he got wind *you*, his own blood, had become so angry for what he had done to me you contacted a hungry and still-forming cartel in Columbia or Costa Rica—one he has never heard of. We'll make up a family name for it."

"To what end."

"To move in and take over the Ortiz drug empire right there where he lives, his base of operation. If you can make him believe *you* are the one instigating it, working against him, he would come after both of us and it would be personal on both counts. Would you have a problem joining me as bait?"

"Of course not, and I think you're right. That would piss him off beyond good sense," Dixie said and then scooped up Carlee's hand and squeezed it. "You do realize, don't you, if we do this, he would not stop until he's dead...or we are?"

"I know," Carlee replied. "But, unless you can think of another way, it's the only thing that will bring it to an end. And, as much as I hate to admit it, when I say 'bring to an end' I mean kill. Could you handle it, if that happens?"

Dixie quietly thought about the idea while staring into Carlee's eyes, but only for a second. She began nodding, slowly at first. "Yes. I am thoroughly convinced that's the only way this thing will end."

"You in?"

"All in," Dixie replied. "But, before we dive off into this, you have a lot more healing to do to be back at a hundred percent."

"While I'm working my way back to health, you have to promise not to share this with anyone, not Fitz and certainly not Linc. They would only be in the way. Their intentions would be noble but it would endanger them both. It would also be a problem for us, trying to keep them safe while this goes down. I'm confident you and I can handle the situation, as long as we are prepared. I'll have your back and you'll have mine. Above all, unlike those other times, we *will* be ready for whatever comes out of the gates at us."

Dixie's eyes drifted to the skyline beyond the hospital room window. "I haven't had the nerve to tell Fitz yet, but lately, I have begun fantasizing him and me as a couple." She reconnected with Carlee. "I agree wholeheartedly. The guys should not know about this. I want Fitz to stay healthy. I think I may want him around a while longer." She wrinkled her nose and added, "Maybe a long while."

Carlee returned to the bed and sat on its edge. "All I have to do is see the sparkle in Rylee's eyes when Linc is with her, or just when I mention his name to her, for that matter. That girl gets giddy when she's around him. So, I know exactly what you mean, Dix. I want Linc to stay in our lives."

Dixie raised an eyebrow. "Are you saying it would *only* be for Rylee's sake?"

Carlee smiled and then smiled bigger. "Oh no, not at all. The three of us just...fit. That man is good and good-lookin' to the bone. I want Linc for me. Rylee liking him is just a happy bonus."

"I'd say those are two very good reasons not to tell them about the plan."

Carlee's winsome smile melted away. "I haven't mentioned it, but I guess you got the inference that I don't plan on involving law enforcement. If I told Fenn, he'd take it over and shut me out of it," She fingered air quotes and rolled her eyes, *for my own good*, of course, because I'm no longer a deputy marshal and, quite literally, at the center of personal involvement."

"I know what you mean. He did it to me a few hours ago."

"Well, on that count, I'm glad he did. Still, I can't let Fenn do that. The information would pass through too many hands. I'm convinced Rogelio would find out and not take the bait."

"He does have a lot of connections in Central Texas, probably in law enforcement as well." Dixie paused and then added, "You may be right."

"I know you don't like guns, Dix, but over the next couple of weeks, you and I will spend ample time at the range. There is no choice, you must become familiar with my spare Glock. Would you have a problem with that?"

"Well...yeah," she said, and then sighed. "But necessary I suppose."

"I realize you're a capable and dangerous fighting machine in close quarters, but Rogelio and his thugs favor automatic firearms. You might not have a chance to get close enough to kick ass even though I know you could and would."

"You made your point. I'll learn to shoot," she replied, clearly resigned to the inevitable.

Carlee's smile began returning. "You truly are a sister to me."

"And you are the only family I need, *Hermana*." Dixie sat on the bed next to her and embraced her.

"Hey, I want in on this," came Lincoln's voice from behind them.

Carlee looked over her shoulder toward the door. "Then get over here and get some."

He came around the bed and patted Dixie on the shoulder. "Hey, Dix."

She grinned up at him. "Hey, Linc."

He leaned over and kissed Carlee on the cheek.

She placed her free hand on the side of his face and kissed him on the lips. "I want out of this place. Would you take me home?" She kissed him again. "And, for God's sake, *please*, don't make me beg."

He grinned. "But, you're so cute when you beg." He paused. "Aw heck, what am I saying? You're cute no matter what you do or say. Let's get your things and get out of here."

Chapter Twenty-three

Lincoln busied his hands with paperwork at his desk at the advertising agency. As he shuffled stacks of client folders around and made notes in each, his mind was across town and on last evening at Carlee's apartment. Rylee had clung to him as if he were her best friend in all the world. She talked on and on about things of great importance to her. He had not minded at all. He enjoyed it. Each time he had the chance to watch Carlee it was with warm affection, but it went far beyond simple fondness. He was becoming convinced he was falling in love with her. How could he not? There was an obvious mutual attraction, a magnetism invariably pulling them together whenever near to one another. It was clear she felt it as well. But, all these good feelings came tinged with concern. When dwelling on that immobilized arm across her chest, it was a constant stark reminder of the danger she was in and there was no reason to believe it would stop. He did not consider himself a coward, but he wondered about his own safety if he pursued a more committed relationship with her. The phone on his desk rang. He snatched it from its cradle. "Lincoln Bridger."

There was a second of silence. "Linc...it's Jeannine."

"Is everything okay?"

"No. Nothing is okay."

The tone of her voice alarmed him. He rattled, "Are Saul and Lidia all right?"

"It has nothing to do with my parents." Another silence ensued. "Lincoln, would you meet me for lunch?"

He had to think a moment about that question. "I don't know if that's such a good idea. But, hey, if you need help with something, tell me what the problem is and I'll try to lend whatever support I can."

"I do need help. But I need to tell you the problem face-to-face."

Lincoln felt cornered. He didn't want to brush her off if she truly had a problem he might be able to help with. A conversation over lunch, especially so soon after a finalized divorce just did not seem appropriate. Not to mention suspicious to Carlee if she should find out.

"Lincoln? You still there?"

"Yeah. Just thinking. Okay, I'll meet you at the sandwich shop on the corner of this block at one o'clock."

"Thanks, Linc. See you there." She ended the call.

Lincoln hung the phone up slowly. He wondered what she would have to talk about. He also wondered if her strained voice meant she was crying.

~ * ~

Lincoln walked from his office building to the end of the same block. It was a small sandwich shop on the corner, the last business in a small four-business strip center. It appeared most of the lunch crowd had thinned out by one o'clock. He stepped through the door of Sandy's Soup and Sandwich Shop. He saw Jeannine sitting alone at a table for two butted against the window wall at the front with a northward view of the busy street and the lake beyond, where kayakers were paddling in the calm water.

There was something about Jeannine's appearance that captured his attention immediately. It wasn't what she wore. He had seen that gray pin-stripe pantsuit many times. Nor was it her hairstyle. She had worn her auburn hair in that wedge cut for several years. As he approached the table, his step stuttered slightly when he realized it was none of those things. It was a striking look of maturity. She had the hinted appearance of it the day the divorce was finalized. Now, it went beyond the expression on her face. Instead, it was an exuded embodiment he had never seen, and certainly never when they were married. It included how she sat, erect with one leg draped over the other, and how she smiled when she saw him come through the door. It was diametrically opposite the childish frowning face filled with bad attitude and constant closed body language that had come to define her in the latter years of their marriage.

"Hi. How have you been?" he asked as he pulled out the chair opposite her and sat.

"Struggling somewhat. How about you?"

"The job is fine." He smiled and added, "Of course, I'm still attempting to decorate that little apartment I rented. I really don't have an eye for that sort of thing like you do." As he spoke, an approaching waitress caught his eye.

"Do you folks know what you want?" the pretty young waitress asked, eyes shifting back and forth between them with a beaming smile.

Lincoln looked to Jeannine. "You still into turkey and Provolone with lettuce and tomato on sour dough with mayo?"

Jeannine's eyes sparkled. "Yes. And thanks for remembering."

"There are many things about you that I will remember for years to come." Lincoln turned his attention back to the waitress. "Then that's what the lady will have. You can bring me a Reuben. Add a Coke for me and a Sprite for her, plus a couple of bags of potato chips. That should be plenty."

The waitress scurried off, still writing on her order pad.

"Tell me about your problem," he asked. "Is it something I can help with?"

"You're the *only* one that can help me with it."

Lincoln frowned and reared his head. "I don't understand. What is it?"

An awkward silence thickened the air between them. "I'm still in love with you, Linc."

He held up a defensive palm. "Whoa. I can't—"

"Please, let me finish. I know I messed things up by that stupid stunt I pulled. But, Linc, I swear that's all it was...a stupid, regrettable stunt. The idiot in me came out and took over." She paused and drew a breath of courage and sighed long. "Linc, I wanted this opportunity to ask...no, not ask, but *beg* you to give me another chance." She drew a breath. "Do you have any feelings left for me?"

"Of course, I still love you. I always will," he replied. "It's just that..." Lincoln suddenly realized he just told his ex-wife he still loved her. That would surely crack the door of possibility in Jeannine's mind. He let it slip before he realized how difficult it would make the rest of this conversation. He certainly could not reel the words back in. They were out there between them and would stay there, regardless how he might attempt to explain it away. His lips attempted forming words to complete the sentence. He could think of no way to say what needed to be said without breaking Jeannine's heart. He suddenly could not remember where he was going with it when it tumbled unexpectedly out of his mouth.

"I'm sorry for putting you on the spot like this, but I could not think of a gentler way to ease into it. So, I decided to dive in and say it. Please forgive my abruptness," she said.

Lincoln gave up trying to respond and stared at Jeannine for a moment. He had difficulty believing this was the same woman he had finalized a divorce with mere weeks ago. That air of maturity had now manifest in her overall demeanor. It was a great look on her. He wanted to mention it, to compliment her, but he was terrified, scared of his own ability to objectively step away from his feelings and where that might lead, if the conversation continued down this trail. And, he knew well, the path led nowhere other than to that, so-called, slippery slope. He saw Jeannine was becoming anxious by his lack of response. She fidgeted.

Jeannine nervously rubbed the heels of her hands together below laced fingers. "Speaking of my parents..." She bounced a nervous smile. "...I thought they were going to disown me when you left." She snickered, but it was forced.

"I didn't mean for you to be put in an uncomfortable situation with them. For that, I apologize," he replied. "I simply wanted them to know directly from me how special they were and would always be. That's the reason I went over there that day."

"I know you have deep admiration for them and they have told me on numerous occasions in the past few weeks how much they love you. For that reason, I have not shared with them that I planned this talk with you. I don't know how they would have taken it. So, I didn't want them to find out. Still don't. I have a feeling they would fill with anticipation that might turn out unrequited. Although, I hope that's not the case and will have good news for them soon."

Lincoln knew he should leave with a pleasant but firm good bye. He suddenly could not get in touch with objectivity. Every happy moment of their long marriage flashed through an abruptly enhanced memory. He stared dumbly at Jeannine and the strangest thought weaseled in, shoving better judgment aside. *Is it possible she and I could make it work if given a second chance?*

The approach of the waitress interrupted the monumental awkwardness of the moment. "Here ya go, folks." She set the sandwiches in front of them, along with drinks and chips.

Jeannine calmly smiled up at the girl. "I hate to do this to you, but would you mind boxing my order to take out?"

"I don't mind at all. I absolutely will," the girl replied with a beaming smile. The girl returned the sandwich, drink, and chips to the tray. "I'll be right back." She hurried away.

The smile she had for the waitress remained fixed on her face as she returned her attention to Lincoln. "I know I dropped a bomb in your lap and I don't want you feeling any more uncomfortable than I know you are at this very moment." She pushed her chair back and rose as the waitress returned with a sack. Jeannine handed the girl a twenty and a five. "Keep the change."

"Thank you so much," the girl replied, clearly filled with gratitude. She moved on to other customers.

"Linc, before I go, I'm compelled by my heart to repeat it. I love you—always have, always will. There will be no such thing as replacing you. I realize I fouled things up badly. That said, I will not bother you again. Just know if you decide I might be worth one more chance, I'll be waiting. It doesn't matter if it's a day or a year. I *will* be waiting." She put two fingers to her lips and gently blew a kiss. She walked away and out the door. As she walked by the full-view window next to his table she, again, kissed her two fingers and pressed them to the glass next to where he sat.

Lincoln was flabbergasted and speechless. His head was a jumble, a tightly tangled romantic mess. No longer were his thoughts solely about Carlee Cayne.

Chapter Twenty-four

Carlee grew impatient, nearing the end of the third week following her near-fatal encounter with Rogelio Ortiz's hired thugs. She was bored with her mundane job at the advertising agency. Boredom escalated in direct proportion to returning strength from the healing bullet wound. Knowing what she had to do made her antsy to get on with it, and soon. It also made her new job feel all the more confining.

Professional physical therapy had ended. Self-motivation and purpose drove her to keep it up on her own at Power House Fitness, in fact, stepping up the pace, placing increased physical demands upon her body, going beyond self-motivation to an all-encompassing sense of self-preservation. She needed to be in peak physical and mental condition to handle whatever may come at her in the coming weeks. She refreshed her skills in martial arts, especially the more offensive discipline of Krav Maga. Carlee pushed herself toward a self-mandated deadline to affect a definitive solution to her difficult situation. A problem that would keep her looking over her shoulder long into the future if she did not follow through with her plan to end it—the sooner the better. Now, it was time.

The indoor pistol range that she frequented as a deputy marshal had only one other shooting lane occupied when she and Dixie arrived for a lunchtime round of practice. Carlee was proud of her friend. Dixie had attained an admirable level of mastery in the use of the back-up Glock Carlee had never needed to use while still with the Marshals Service, but kept it holstered and encased in a lockbox in her closet at home in the event a need for it ever arose. Eight practice sessions in eighteen days and Dixie rarely put a bullet outside a four-inch circle at forty feet with careful aim. Even rapid-firing multiple times at twenty-five feet, she was a deadly shot. When they began, Dixie Vega had never touched a gun, much less fired one. She was so beautiful and multi-talented, with a definite flair for an unwavering commitment to friendship. She was a grand master of that art.

Dixie stepped up to the waist-high counter at the head of one of the lanes partitioned in a row of shooting bays. She removed the range-supplied hearing protectors from a hook on the side of the partition. The large room had a cave-like feel, complete with musty smell laced with the lingering tang of burnt gunpowder. The walls and low ceiling were reinforced concrete. Each bay had paper targets suspended from clips attached to a track that could extend to over fifty-feet, if desired. Setting a box of shells on the counter, Dixie pulled the semi-automatic pistol from the holster in her hand. She glanced over her shoulder to Carlee, standing behind her and asked, "What did Linc say when you told him you thought the advertising job was boring?"

"I haven't, and I don't plan on telling him," Carlee replied abruptly. She placed a hand on Dixie's shoulder, adding, "And, please, don't tell him I shared that with you."

Dixie set the gun on the counter and turned to face her friend. "I thought you told me he was worried about it before you agreed to work there."

"He *was* worried about it. But, please, don't say anything to him. That's a can of worms I would prefer left in the can a while longer."

"Okay. I promise. But don't you think he should know you're considering bailing on it?"

Carlee sighed. "Linc is a gem of a guy. He went far out of his way to get me a safe job for the sake of Rylee, Mom, and myself. I don't have the heart to tell him, not yet anyhow. God help me, since you and I have been coming to the pistol range and planning the operation, I've felt exhilaration, despite the danger. I should not be feeling this way if I didn't love and miss being a deputy marshal." She stepped over to the next lane. "I have a feeling if my former supervisor at the Service, George Turner, had not been such a problem, I would have stayed at that job. Danger be damned. Still, I feel selfish for such thoughts because of Rylee and Mom. I switched jobs for them, after all."

Dixie followed. "It could be your head is a little messed up by all this Rogelio stuff. Maybe you'll feel differently once the current threat is taken care of, once and for all time."

"I'd like to think so, but now, I don't believe I will ever truly enjoy the advertising business, at least, from the perspective of a media buyer. I've concluded, as long as I'm there, I'll only be enduring the job, certainly not enjoying it." She paused and smiled. "The only upside to it is the proximity to Linc. That's pretty darn cool." Her smile drooped. "Although, before that last attack, I was wondering how much longer I could tolerate that office-bound, and sometimes mind-numbing, position. Monotony is my nemesis. I suppose I'm more of an adrenalin junkie than I realized."

Carlee pulled one of the loaded magazines from her jacket pocket and clipped it into place in the pistol handgrip and then chambered a cartridge. "You're right though. I should share my feelings with Linc, and I will, just not right away." She pulled the ear protecting headset up over her ears, flipped the hinged shelf in front of her up and out of the way, aimed the pistol, and fired a rapid burst of three shots at the paper target and pulled the narrow shelf back down into place in front of her. She placed the gun on it and pressed the retrieve button. The target whizzed and clattered on its track, coming in for a closer look at the pattern effected on the human torso shaped target. All three shots formed a tight triangle in the circle positioned where the heart would be. She pulled the ear protectors off. "Dix, I know you get tired of hearing me ask this, but I need to constantly know where your head is at on this thing I've gotten you into."

Dixie did not reply. She replaced her ear protectors and stepped back around the partition to her own shooting lane and picked up the Glock 27, 40 caliber pistol. She shoved the little hinged shelf up and out of the way, jacked a shell into the chamber, and emptied the nine-shot firearm through the paper target, every bullet striking within the circle. She pointed at the target. "That's Rogelio Ortiz. Does that answer your question?"

Carlee drew a breath, exhaling slowly. "I think we're ready."

Chapter Twenty-five

Lincoln stopped at Fitz's open office door. He appeared preoccupied, leaning back in his chair, hands on his chest, fingers laced together, and twiddling his thumbs. He stared, but clearly not looking at anything. It did not take an analytical mind to see his friend was thinking about something.

"Got a minute?" Lincoln asked.

Startled, Fitz abruptly leaned away from the backrest, letting the spring action of the chair throw him forward. He dropped his elbows onto the desk. "Sure. Come on in."

"Have you noticed how aloof Carlee has been acting the last few days? Or, have I become so possessive of her that it appears that way only to me?" Lincoln asked.

"As a matter of fact, I have noticed. I don't think it's your imagination."

Lincoln sat heavily on the chair fronting and facing Fitz's desk. "Every time I try to start a conversation with her, she gets fidgety, cutting it short, and moving on. She offers fast choppy responses to anything I say and then excuses herself with any one of a number of different reasons why she must hurry off. I can see impatience in her eyes. She can't seem to get away from me fast enough. It's odd. I hope I haven't done or said something to make her angry with me. I fear if I have, she's too nice to let me know. Maybe I should come right out and ask if she's mad at me for some reason."

"It's interesting you're sharing this with me at this particular time," Fitz said.

"Why?"

"I just got off the phone with Dix a bit ago. She told me she needed for us to take a break for a while. I thought she was joking—that sarcastic nature of hers, you know. But, hey, she was dead serious, nary a snicker. Why would she put a relationship on hiatus, even though the, so-called, relationship is still in an embryonic stage? I've only known her a few weeks, for Christ's sake. What's up with that?" Fitz frowned. "What the hell is going on with those girls, Linc?"

"Not a clue." He rose and headed for the door. "But, whatever it is, they must be sharing it. I'm going to find out right now." When he stepped out of Fitz's office, he saw Carlee walking fast. They locked eyes. She hesitated for half a beat and then hurried through the front lobby and out the door. The sight stopped him cold. "What the hell?" he mumbled.

"What's wrong with Carlee?" Stuart Adler called out as he approached Lincoln standing in the corridor.

"I have no idea. Why? Did something happen?"

Adler shrugged his shoulders. "Not sure. She came into my office and announced to me that she was taking a leave-of-absence for an indefinite period. She made it clear it was going to happen whether I approved it or not. Although, she *was* polite about it." He scratched the side of his head and frowned. "Damnedest thing I ever saw." He, again, bounced a shoulder shrug. "She then apologized for the abruptness and said she'd understand if she lost her job over it."

Fitz sprang out of his chair and joined the pair outside his office in the corridor.

"I saw seriousness on her face, maybe worry. I couldn't tell for sure," Adler added. "Nonetheless, I told her to go ahead and take care of whatever business it was that concerned her so. She thanked me and left. Linc, if she's gone for over a couple of days, I won't have any choice but to terminate her employment."

"And rightfully so," Lincoln mumbled, staring at the front exit Carlee had passed through seconds before.

"Sorry, Linc, but we have a business to run," Adler said. He patted Lincoln on the shoulder and headed back toward his office.

What's going on, Carlee? Suddenly a flash image of yesterday's surprising luncheon with Jeannine crossed Lincoln's mind. *I wonder if Carlee, somehow, found out about it. Maybe that's the problem. Could Carlee possibly be thinking that I'm subverting my relationship with her—*

dating Jeannine and her at the same time?

~ * ~

Carlee rapped hard on Dixie's apartment door. Her friend opened it before her fist had unfurled. "Did you have any problems taking off from work at the fitness center?" Carlee asked.

"They were peeved at the suddenness. But, I'm not worried. It's fixable. How about you?"

"I'm thinking my position at the advertising agency might not be fixable. I had to get out of there fast, before Linc could confront me. I'm sure he would have. In fact, I think he was about to when I walked out of there a while ago." Carlee felt a guilt riddled stab of pain in her heart. "I don't think I could have lied to him if I gave him the chance to ask about my abrupt departure. If he knew, it would complicate things immeasurably for you and me."

Dixie held up her cell phone and waggled it toward Carlee. "Are you ready for me to make the call and get this thing underway?"

"Yeah. It's time to shove this snowball off the mountain and see just how big it gets." Carlee had been in Dixie's apartment on many occasions but due to a heightened sense of awareness on this day, it was the first time she noticed how spartanly furnished it was. Carlee had always known her friend to be modest, but she had not noticed how humility was also evident in her choice of home decoration—more precisely, the lack of it. There were no pictures or paintings on the walls, very little bric-a-brac atop flat surfaces. Virtually everything within her field of vision had some utilitarian function. It was Dixie's modesty of dress and lifestyle that drew Carlee to her in the beginning of their friendship. There wasn't anything at all pretentious about her sister-by-choice.

Dixie dialed the number and one of Rogelio's henchmen answered, "*Si?*"

"*Necesito hablar con Rogelio. Dile que es su primo, Ramona Vega.*"

"*Espera un minuto,*" came the disembodied reply.

When the line went silent, Dixie actuated the speaker on the phone so Carlee could hear the conversation. Rogelio came on the line speaking English, "How is my Little Mona?" he asked in heavily accented and buttery tone.

"I go by the name Dixie now," she replied, in purposely hate-filled tone.

"Ah, yes. I had forgotten that Daniel was referring to you as Dixie. What is it I can do for you, *Primo*?"

"I'll be blunt—"

"It seems I may have already detected that bluntness," he interrupted."

"I have taken great offense to your selfish attempts on Carlee Cayne's life. I am boiling angry about it."

"What is she to you?" The surprise in his voice sounded genuine.

"She is my best friend and more family to me than anyone else in this world. And that includes you and my own brother." Dixie glanced at Carlee, adding, "She is my *hermana*, sister by choice, not birth."

Carlee was awash with emotion to hear Dixie say it. She dropped her head and fought an urge to cry. But success in that regard was fleeting. She turned and stepped toward a window with a desultory shuffle. She must focus on something else as an emotion-filled tear gathered and dribbled from her lash.

"Rogelio," Dixie continued, "I have no choice but to tell you, your actions against her have driven a stake directly through the heart of whatever family loyalties I have felt toward you."

"*Primo Dulce*, it pains me to hear you say that," he replied, continuing in a smooth arrogant tone. "Now, you have left *me* no choice but to warn *you*, and I'll do it this one time only. Do not interfere with my business and what I must do. Your *new family* must pay for the death of Manuel. I have sworn it."

"I figured as much when I dialed your number. Now, I feel justified in what I have already done."

"And, what is that?"

"Do you know of the Alvarez Family in Costa Rica?"

"I've never heard of them."

"Here is some insight for you, *Primo*. They have quite the family business in San José. I have been in contact with them and I encouraged a plan the Alvarez family has set in motion. In fact, they are more eager than me to get it underway. You see, Rogelio, they are in the same business as you and are zealously preparing to take over your established business in Acuña. I assured them it would not be a difficult thing to do."

Rogelio's evenness vanished. "You little bitch! I'll heap your dead, bleeding body right on top of Cayne's," he growled.

"No, you won't," Dixie replied, now using the same arrogantly smooth tone Rogelio abandoned. "In a couple of days, you'll have your hands full covering your criminally insane ass against a very aggressive Costa Rican family."

"You think so, huh? If they try it. They will die!" he shouted. "All of them! Men, women, and children! I'll eliminate the whole goddamn Alvarez family from the face of the earth!"

"Oh, by the way, I forgot to mention the Alvarez Cartel has the entire Costa Rican government in their pockets, not a few lazy overweight Mexican cops in Acuña. You know, like the ones you bought. It will be impossible to pay your local police enough to fight the army that the Alvarez's can summon, and probably will. Your pathetic little band of Keystone Cops will be like rats abandoning a sinking ship, and you are the ship. You hear that, Rogelio...like rats."

A sudden sharp noise blasted from the small speaker of Dixie's cell phone followed by a grinding sound and then nothing. "Rogelio?"

Carlee turned away from the window to face her friend. "I think he tossed the phone on the floor and stomped it. Well, that conversation has certainly been punctuated in an interesting way. You handled yourself magnificently, Dix. Slipping in that tidbit about him having a couple days before a drug war explodes around him was genius. That lets him know how little time he has to act against us. We now have a timeframe to reference and work within."

"Whew!" Dixie drew a breath and blew it out through rounded lips. "I was scared out of my mind the whole time."

"You were? I didn't detect fear at all. What I heard was a brave soul giving a ruthless criminal an ultimatum in a very clear, concise way. It worked better than I hoped. Now, we must work fast. He's probably making arrangements to come to Austin as we speak."

"True. I'll go see Daniel in federal lockup and visit with him and then let the location of that old farm house you rented slip out. I hate to do it to him, but it's obvious he'll be the pipeline of information Rogelio will seek first. I have no choice but to use him. I better get down there and get it done."

Carlee nodded affirmation of each point Dixie made and then added her own piece of the plan. "When you're finished, I'll meet you at the old house in the country and then...we wait."

Chapter Twenty-six

At straight up five o'clock, Lincoln left the ad agency muddle-headed and confused over Carlee's evasive behavior. He realized he was probably over-sensitive and reading too much into her strange behavior and, possibly, for no good reason. Maybe it was a personal problem she grappled with that did not concern him. If so, why would she feel she couldn't share it with him? He thought he had proven himself to be a trustworthy confidant and sounding board for such things. Upsides to her avoidance of him were few. Not knowing the reason why she behaved as she did troubled him. Each new unanswered question crossing his mind deepened that concern.

On his way to the parking garage, he attempted calling her one more time, but, like the eleven previous attempts since she hurried out of the agency earlier, it went straight to voice-mail. When he called Beth Cayne, Carlee's mother, she told him Carlee had asked her to watch Rylee for a few days because she had a couple of out-of-town job interviews lined up. That provided Lincoln with a possible answer. Could it be she did not want to tell him she hated the job until she had secured another one? Surely, that couldn't be the problem. He suspected from the beginning she might not enjoy such a confining job. He questioned her at the time about that very subject. She would have trusted him with the information if it were true. He felt certain of that. Nothing added up. Fitz discovered Dixie had suddenly walked away from her job at the gym today as well. What did Carlee's out-of-town job interviews have to do with Dixie's sudden departure from work the same day? Coincidence? *This is too crazy. What the hell are they up to?*

The only course of action for Lincoln was to follow-through on his evening routine and go to Power House Fitness Center. He wasn't going back to his tiny apartment and watch television all evening, not without

Carlee. Besides, maybe a sweat-popping workout would clear his mind.

As summer fast approached, it was becoming more obvious by the day that the season was shaping up to be a hot one. The air was stale and overly warm in the labyrinthine parking garage in the building where the ad agency was located. He did not dawdle on his way to his assigned parking space and his BMW.

As he pulled into the Power House parking lot, he saw a familiar late-model white Land Rover parked. Rolling slowly by the familiar vehicle, he saw Jeannine sitting behind the wheel. He pulled into the unoccupied space next to her and parked. He got out of his car and walked around her SUV to the driver's side. "What are you doing here? I would have thought if you wanted to exercise, you'd do it at the facility in the country club."

She smiled up at him through the open window. "Well, the club is closer to home, for sure. But, if this is where I can find you after work, I may join here. Would that be so horrible?"

Suddenly, Lincoln could not maintain eye contact with his ex-wife and stammered, "Uh, no. Not at all." He flipped a quick gesture to the front door. "This is a fine facility."

She smiled and then chuckled. "Linc, I was joking. I'm here to see you, no other reason. I thought I might find you here. And here you are. Are you fully committed to going in there this evening? I'd love it if you would join me for an early dinner. I'll buy. That is, if I can talk you out of your gym time."

He simply stared at her through the open window of her Land Rover, unable to give her a quick response. His mind raced with potential answers and thoughts about where an evening with Jeannine might—no, not might—but most assuredly would end. The abrupt absence of Carlee Cayne left a chasm of uncertainty in his near future. He wondered if he and Carlee could be considered a committed couple. He had begun to think so, but now...? Was there even a relationship to salvage? Or, was the "couple" thing just a product of his own imagining? Maybe Carlee believed it to be a temporary fling and let it go, never thinking twice about it and never thinking of it any other way. A more troubling thought: she had played him for the agency job which she now apparently wanted out of. If so, it would mean he was no longer of value to her.

His ability to think objectively took a giant step backward. And now, he must deal with this invitation from Jeannine. It suddenly seemed clear. Jeannine was here and wanted his company. Carlee was not. He smiled at his ex-wife. "Sure. Why not? I can work out anytime. An early dinner it is."

~ * ~

Carlee pulled out onto the street fronting Dixie Vega's apartment complex en route to the old country house she had rented a couple of days ago. It was somewhat remote on a farm about five miles east of Austin, specifically chosen for that reason. The house was located in the middle of a two-hundred-acre farm, substantially distant from the highway and other houses. She did not want anyone inadvertently catching a stray bullet from the barrage she was certain would erupt. Looking out for the safety of others was not a distraction she needed. Her focus must remain firmly fixed on her quarry and, of course, watching Dixie's back.

She glanced to the back seat, taking quick inventory. She had packed a bag for a three day stay. She was now certain it would not be needed for more than two, if that long. Depending on how angry Dixie had made her cousin, it might come down in less than twenty-four hours. She had surreptitiously taken her deceased father's guns from the closet at her mother's house—a Remington 1100 semi-automatic twelve-gauge shotgun, an unadorned Remington six-millimeter bolt action deer rifle and a short semi-automatic twenty-two magnum carbine. She had purchased two over-sized magazines made specifically for that model, both loaded and ready.

Her cell phone rang. At first, she ignored it, thinking Lincoln was trying again. It pained her to snub him like this. He was such a great guy. She refused to get him in the middle of her dangerous problem again. He had almost gotten killed twice because of her. There would be no repeat, if she could help it.

The phone rang again. She picked it up and checked the display. It wasn't Lincoln this time but ex-partner, Jimmy Fenn. She couldn't talk to him either. She tossed the phone onto the passenger side seat and let it keep ringing. If involved, he would try to arrest Ortiz to stand trial. There could be no other outcome than to put him down, eliminating her problem permanently. Fact is, Rogelio Ortiz could run his operation from inside a prison. Kill orders would continue to be issued on her, her friends, and her family from behind prison bars. It would not be convenient for him, but he could, and probably would, continue his operation from inside prison walls. She and her family would be no safer if he should be incarcerated.

The ringtone of her cell phone finally stopped.

After several seconds, the text alert on the phone went off. Carlee picked it up. It was Fenn again. The message on the display read: Ortiz and six men. Private jet heading north. DEA confirmed. Protective detail? Call me.

"Shit," she hissed. That answered her question. Dixie had angered Ortiz beyond expectation. Carlee did not anticipate dealing with seven of them, or this soon. It now seemed likely that hell would be unleashed before this day ended. The rapid response by Ortiz made it clear, he planned on taking care of this situation with her personally once and for all, and quickly. It also meant he must have believed Dixie's story about the rival cartel coming after his business. He had to get this done definitively and get back to protect his organization. So much for packing a bag for a night or two. She figured it would be Rogelio and a couple of guys for backup like before, but not seven, for Christ's sake. With that amount of firepower, she saw his determination to end her, Dixie, and this problem today and be done with it. On this issue, she and Ortiz were in perfect agreement. It was going to end, one way or another. Like the old saying goes, three's a charm. He would not go back to Mexico, leaving her alive, a third time.

She rolled to a stop at a cross street. The light had just turned red. A white Land Rover began accelerating through the intersection. Carlee's eyes locked onto the passenger on the near side of the vehicle. It was Lincoln. Who was the woman driving? Was it Jeannine? She had never seen his ex-wife, but it suddenly occurred to her Jeannine had gotten two vehicles in the divorce, one of which was a Land Rover. Plus, the woman matched Lincoln's description of Jeannine, a brunette with a wedge-cut hairstyle. Carlee swallowed hard, realizing how beautiful the woman was.

Carlee had always envisioned a tantrum-throwing woman with the bad attitude of a teenager and a never-ending scowl or, perhaps, a spoiled pouty frown. The woman driving that vehicle appeared to be a mature sophisticate.

"Damn it," she muttered and then slouched, turning her face to the side, hoping he did not see her or recognize the car. She need not worry. His attention was solely on the woman behind the wheel. That was more bothersome than being seen. *Oh, Linc. I hope I haven't destroyed my chance with you.* Once the white SUV passed, Carlee looked both ways and ran the red light. At the same time, she snatched her cell phone from the dashboard and hit Dixie's quick dial number.

"Hello," came the reply.

"How did it go with Daniel?" Carlee asked.

"I saw it in the goofball's eyes when I told him the location of your safe house in the country. I did not tell him that I would be out there too. Just in case it might cause him to hesitate with the information."

"Believe it or not, I think he has already passed the information to Rogelio," Carlee said.

"Seriously? That fast? How could you know?"

"I received a text from Fenn. DEA, probably from informants in Del Rio, told him Rogelio and six men boarded a private jet and took off heading north. They all carried single pieces of luggage, identical cases. What does that tell you?"

"Not sure. What?"

"I believe those cases were gun cases. They only carried weapons, fully automatic weapons, no doubt. Why else would Ortiz take a chance with American authorities by coming this way, if not to settle his score with me? Dix, it appears what you told him was successful far beyond my expectations. You have royally pissed off your cousin."

"Damn, girl. I'd better get out there and join you pronto."

"That's why I called. See you in a few." Carlee ended the call and tossed the phone onto the passenger seat. She resisted an urge to speed. If she should get stopped, it would lengthen her travel time. She needed every advantage. Nothing should be left to chance, if possible. After a few minutes, houses and businesses thinned as she left the eastern city limits of

Austin. The countryside transitioned to rolling hills and farm land with occasional fenced acreages for cattle, sheep, or goat operations. Finally, on the right about a quarter mile ahead, her destination appeared beyond the hill she had just topped. As she approached, she gave the chosen location another critical assessment. Tactically, everything had to be perfect. There would be no unnecessary risk taking. It would be dangerous enough. Nothing could be assumed. Even the smallest details must be thought through. It was paramount she think through how to handle an assault—and not just once. The plan had to be deeply ingrained and executed with precision, without thought of what to do or where to go next. One advantage would be Rogelio will think he has the advantage of surprise. He and his crew only knew it was a supposedly secret safe house. He couldn't know she would be expecting them and on the lookout. Whatever benefit that would provide would be short-lived. She must remember it as the first and most important strategic detail.

As she slowed and eased toward the long driveway up to the old farm house, she surveyed everything for potential use. She turned off the highway onto the long straight graveled drive, sloping gently upward for about two-hundred yards, ending in front of the old house. The approach was lined with poplar trees next to deep cut ditches on both sides. Beyond the rows of trees lay a working farm, lush with waist-high green wheat. The heads were full of weighty grain and drooping. Light wind worried the wheat into gentle waves.

Gravel crunching beneath her tires, Carlee rolled to a stop near a low white picket fence surrounding the front yard of the old and poorly cared for house. Other than the two rows of poplar trees, the only other trees were in the yard around the house and one sprawling oak tree just beyond the low picket fence fronting the yard. The remainder of the farm had been denuded for crops.

She got out of the car and looked back toward the highway. There was an excellent view of it, as well as the approach to the house. It would be easy to see anyone coming. No one could drive or walk up to the house unnoticed, unless she and Dixie simply were not looking. And that notion was absurd.

As she stood next to the car, premeditating options, she saw Dixie's older model Toyota turn onto the driveway and speed toward the house, dust boiling from beneath it. Carlee began walking toward her. As soon as her friend stopped and got out, Carlee said, "Okay, Dix, here's what I'm thinking..." She pointed to the wheat field that ended about fifty feet from where they stood. "...A view of the house and yard are unobstructed from the near edge of that wheat patch. I can lie flat with a scoped six-millimeter deer rifle. The wheat is tall enough to provide excellent cover. When they drive up here and get out of their vehicles, I think I can reduce their numbers by two, maybe three. The rifle only has a three-bullet magazine in the clip and I'll have one chambered. It's a sport rifle and never meant for anything like this. Plus, it's bolt action. That'll slow me down. I'm confident I can hit two before they take cover, possibly three. But that would be a stretch."

"What about me?" Dixie asked.

"I'm thinking you need to be inside the house. If we're both outside, they'll have the advantage of superior firepower. If forced to enter the house, they will be forced into close quarters. That should swing a tactical advantage to you, making it better for you to engage them with your very special skills. Unless you have no other choice, hold your fire. Don't waste ammunition, if at all possible."

Dixie pulled a switchblade knife from her jeans. "I brought this. I thought it might come in handy." She flicked it open to reveal a highly polished five-inch blade. "It's the only thing of my father's I have. I keep it in my bedside table for protection. I've never had to use it, but I can stick it in a tree from about twenty paces."

"Whew. That's impressive. Glad you have it. You might need it." Carlee put a contemplative finger to her lips. "Let me see. Where was I? Oh, yeah. By the time I take the second rifle shot, they'll have my position located and return fire, most likely with fully automatic weapons. At that point, a leap of faith will be called for. I won't have a choice but to abandon the rifle, pull my Glock and run like hell for that big oak tree over there outside the yard fence where I will have stashed a magnum 22-cal semi-auto carbine with a fully loaded banana shaped magazine clipped in and ready for action. When I leap up from the wheat patch and begin running toward the tree, I need you to begin firing, not a second before, to split their attention and give me cover fire. Once I make it to the safety of the tree, I'll grab that little carbine and spray bullets as fast as I can pull the trigger while you're firing from inside the house. We'll have the advantage of a crossfire, but only for a few seconds. That will be our next best chance to put a couple of them down. During this confusion and, hopefully, before the second magazine on the twenty-two is empty, I'll break from cover and run for that window at the end of the house. I'll have it open beforehand with the screen removed so I can dive through quickly. The shotgun will be leaned against the wall, waiting for me just inside next to the window."

Before Carlee had finished laying out her plan, she began walking through the low picket gate of the front yard toward the double front doors of the old house. The structure appeared solid enough and livable, if that had been the plan, but it was clearly well past its prime. Shiplap siding was covered in multiple coats of blistered and peeling white paint. The windows were of wood and in the old style—tall and reaching low. A style meant to catch breezes in the summer, pre-dating the advent of air conditioning. Not ideal for protection from flying bullets. The front doors were ill-fitting and, clearly, neither door lock functioned. Instead, metal straps had been installed to accommodate padlocks, for which Carlee had been given a key. She removed the padlock on the right door and walked through as it creaked open without a push assist.

Dixie followed her through and stopped just inside. She dropped her hands onto her hips and looked around. "It needs TLC but, otherwise, it appears in okay shape."

"Uh-huh," Carlee replied. "This place was built in the shotgun style. Each room leads into the next with no hallways, split down the middle by a wall—bathroom and bedrooms on the left—living, dining, and kitchen on the right and, of course, separate front doors for each side." She spun around to check out the view of the only approach to the front of the house. "This is where you should be when they show up."

Carlee felt a sudden tingle of fear. She rounded on Dixie and grabbed her by the shoulders, pulling her friend into a tight embrace. "And, for God's sake *do not*, for any reason and at any time, stand in front of those tall windows. If you do, you might as well put a red bull's-eye on your chest. In fact, don't be standing at any time. Stay down and try not to be seen. Lying flat on the floor most of the time would be best."

Dixie gently broke Carlee's desperate embrace and pushed her back. "*Hermana*," she pleaded, "please concentrate on the plan, not my safety. I'll be fine, as long as I know you are."

Carlee's building anxiety eased. Her eyes glossed. "I can't tell you how difficult this would be if I didn't have your support. I'm not talking just about extra fighting hands. The fact you are here is an undeserved gift of kindness." She pulled Dixie into another tight embrace, hugging her and growling affectionately.

She backed away and checked her wristwatch—almost six o'clock. This time of year, the sun would be going down in a couple of hours and dark a half-hour later. She could not be sure when Rogelio left his lair in Acuña, but she must assume he was already in the air when Jimmy Fenn texted her. The flight and then securing rental cars would take a couple of hours at the most. Aided by GPS, it would take mere minutes to drive from Austin out to this farm. By necessity, plotting and planning came to an end. She and Dixie were running out of time. Now, they must execute the plan flawlessly, or suffer irreversible, and eternal, consequences.

Chapter Twenty-seven

It was a beautiful early evening in Austin. Jeannine Bridger drove purposely slow from the parking lot at Power House Fitness Center to the Four Seasons Hotel that backs up to Lady Bird Lake. She stole glances to the passenger side. *What are you thinking, Linc?* Jeannine knew where she wanted this evening to lead and how it should end but, at this point, she had to be satisfied with keeping faith it would end as she hoped it would. "Is Trio Restaurant in the Four Seasons okay with you?"

"Absolutely," he replied, looking straight ahead, face unreadable. "It's one of the best restaurants in Austin." He finally looked her direction, but it was only a flicking glance. "I take my better clients to the Trio," he added, his tone apprehensive.

The glance her direction was nice, and a good beginning, but she sought something longer. A lingering gaze with a story to tell, lacking apprehension and hesitance. *Look at me, Linc. I must know where your head is on this. I have to know.* Her eyes split time between the street ahead and sideways at Lincoln. *Better yet, where your heart is when it comes to me. Please, look at me. Whatever is on your mind, I'm positive I'll read it in your eyes.*

"How about you?" he asked. "Have you been going to Trio lately?" The blurted question filled the gap in an awkwardly lengthening silence.

"A couple of times in the past few weeks, but as a rule, no. It's not a regular destination for me. I tend to stay on the north side of town. I hardly ever have reason to drive to the south side..." She glanced and smiled at him. "...until recently, of course." On that comment, Jeannine noticed Lincoln fidget. Was that a sheepish look racing across his face? It almost seemed for the briefest moment he might have been unnerved by her comment, like a high school freshman on his first date.

"I suppose you've noticed I haven't taken the initiative to change my name from Bridger back to Rosen. Are you okay with that?" she asked, craning her head around, still attempting to get a better read on his face.

He bounced a shoulder shrug. "I guess so. But why haven't you? I thought it would have been top priority after finalizing the divorce."

She continued smiling but shifted her gaze back to the street and traffic ahead. "Then you still are not fully understanding where my heart is and, frankly, always has been. I was just too stupid to realize it until everything changed." Jeannine felt a small chill settle in the air between them. She glanced his way. *Sorry, Linc. I had to get it out there, better sooner than later.*

Nothing more was said until they entered the restaurant and Lincoln told the maître d'hôtel, "Table for two. Outside on the patio, if one is available."

"Of course. This way," replied the young man in a crisp, friendly manner.

As she and Lincoln followed his lead, Lincoln turned to her. "Is the patio okay with you?"

"Perfect."

"Are you sure it's not too warm to dine outside?" he added.

"It's beautiful back there with good shade from those stately o ak trees and a nice view of the lake. I would have suggested it, if you hadn't."

The young man seated them at the requested table for two. The small linen draped table set against a low ornately cast concrete rail, of equal height to the table, with a beautiful view of Lady Bird Lake. Jeannine looked across the gently rippling water to the office building housing Adler, Howard and Levy where Lincoln worked. "I may not get to this side of town often, but it is a nice view from here. It's quite romantic. Look how the setting sun plays on the water. Gorgeous."

Lincoln faced the setting sun at Jeannine's back, which was now merely an orange bump on the western horizon. Trees provided an attractive dappling of swaying light over the patio. Jeannine looked back at what he saw. "I think you may have the prettier view. That sunset is magnificent...and romantic."

Lincoln hinted a smile. "It really is."

Jeannine saw he remained uncomfortable. That was plain enough by the briefest of answers to her questions and continued reluctance to take the lead in conversing. *How can I make you accepting of me again? How can I ease your mind and rekindle desire for me that I know is still inside you? Or, at least, I hope so.* "I understand your friend, Miss Cayne, is now working with you at the agency. Is it working out for her?"

"Honestly, I'm not sure," he replied. It was a subtle expression change, but she noticed what may have been hinted shock, or maybe sadness, by her question.

"Oh?" Her surprise by the tone of his response segued into an easy smile remarkably quick, but it was a contrived mask. She felt her hopes dim when she steered the conversation to Carlee Cayne. The read she so fervently sought, she now had, and didn't like. She sighed, thinking it best to simply let him talk about the woman and worry about bending him to another topic later. After all, she was working hard at leaving selfishness in the past. This may be one more way to do it. Not only that, she was the one asking the question. So, the burden was on her to see it through. Maybe if she put his feelings first and remained pleasant about whatever he chose to discuss, he'd notice and like her more for it. Think of him first and what he wants. It seemed to be the best direction to steer the conversation, for now. "Want to talk about it?" she asked.

"Well, Carlee learned the job quickly and took on more than necessary, endearing herself to every employee at the agency. She's a hard worker and never complains, but I think the job bores her."

A young waitress stopped at the table and opened a menu for Jeannine and handed it to her. She followed suit for Lincoln. "While you decide, how about something to drink, wine or something from the bar, perhaps?"

"You still a pinot noir fan?" he asked Jeannine.

Her smile broadened upon hearing he remembered that detail without hesitation. "I am," she replied.

"A glass for the lady and one for me as well. Whatever the house suggests will be fine."

"I'll be back with your wine and take your orders shortly," the waitress said as she turned to walk away but then stopped and turned back. "By the way, you two make a beautiful couple." She grinned big and glided away across the patio.

Jeannine leaned across the table shielding her mouth with a flat hand and whispered, "That girl has just earned a huge tip." She chuckled. "And I don't really care how good her service is."

Lincoln seemed to slip back into that uncertain mode. He smiled at her humor, but it was fleeting like most of his pleasant expressions since picking him up late this afternoon, except for when he spoke of Carlee Cayne. "Do you think Miss Cayne misses the badge and a pistol strapped to her waist?"

"Yeah. I think that's a reasonable assumption."

The look on his face now was most troublesome—thoughtful sadness, as if there was more between that woman and Lincoln than she figured. He may be sensing the Cayne woman was slipping away. This sent a shiver of panic through Jeannine. Was she about to lose control of the evening? She had to turn him. Encouraging him to talk about the woman may have been a mistake. She saw his mind and possibly his heart were skidding into an irretrievable rut. Then she remembered how much Lincoln admired her father, Saul.

"Did you know that the very day we were at the attorney's office, my father told me he wanted me to go to work at our shoe store in the mall?" she asked.

"No, I wasn't aware of that."

"My father refused to allow me to sulk. So, he thought the best way to prevent it was to keep me busy. As it turns out, I really enjoy the job. Maybe someday he'll let me manage it."

"I think that's great," he replied. "That's Saul's way of demonstrating how much he loves you. He's a good man...the best, actually."

Jeannine breathed a sigh of relief when she noticed Lincoln returning to her side of the fence in this conversation and away from that Cayne woman. "I used to get so angry at him, but it was juvenile of me." Her eyes drifted to the shimmering gold and orange reflections across the rippling lake. She added, muttering, "So damned juvenile."

Lincoln tipped his head to the side. "You do seem different now. There is a serenity about you I don't remember ever noticing before." He finally offered what she wanted, a warm smile that lingered. "It's a wonderful look on you, Jeannine. I'm very proud of you," he added.

The remainder of the evening became increasingly relaxed with each glass of wine consumed along with wonderful food. Night descended. Orange and gold ripples on the lake had turned silver and blue. Jeannine scarcely noticed. Her eyes remained on her handsome ex-husband across the table. Lincoln seemed to be enjoying an exchange of ideas on a variety of subjects, even leading the conversation now. Fortunately, he spoke of Carlee Cayne no more.

Chapter Twenty-eight

Dixie stood facing Carlee. Vehicles of various sorts were easily visible passing by on the highway at the end of the gently descending driveway, some two-hundred yards from the house. Suddenly, Dixie glimpsed something different about two of those vehicles. The glance over Carlee's shoulder through the front window of the old farm house turned into a focused examination. The bottom of the dusty and cobweb-laced window extended down to about a foot above the floor, and upward to within two feet of a nine-foot ceiling. Dixie saw two vehicles had topped the hill about a half mile up the highway, now only seconds away from cutoff onto the Poplar-lined lane to the house. Any other time such a sight would be of no special interest, but what she saw deserved closer inspection. She stepped around Carlee to a position nearer the window.

"What is it, Dix?"

"Two dark colored SUVs topped the hill driving very near to one another. The vehicles are identical, shiny and black. Rentals, I'd say. It looks like it's about to hit the fan."

Carlee stepped in behind her and gazed out the window as well. Dixie heard her draw a deep breath and huffing it away, filling the air with sudden nervous energy. She grabbed Dixie by the shoulder and spun the shorter woman around to face her. "Don't forget what I told you. Stay away from the windows and down low at all times, preferably lying flat on the floor. Make as small a target as possible. Don't give them a clear view of you at any time. I don't know what kind of weapons they'll have, but don't depend on these old walls to be stout enough to stop bullets either."

Dixie nodded.

Carlee gazed into Dixie's eyes becoming clearly emotional. She jerked Dixie into a tight embrace. "Okay, sister. It's time. Let's get this done. Be safe."

Dixie replied by patting Carlee on the back. "You, too, *Hermana*." She then backed away. As she was taught, Dixie pulled the loaner Glock from its holster, popped the magazine from the handgrip, checked it, clipped it back into place with a resounding click, and pulled the barrel slide back to chamber a shell.

Carlee mimicked the ritual, reholstered her Glock, and hurried out the door.

Dixie moved to the window and watched Carlee sprint across the front yard, through the gate of the low picket fence, on out to the edge of the wheat field. Carlee went far enough into the wheat patch to locate where the stand of grassy plants was sufficiently thick and tall enough to provide adequate camouflage. She dropped to her knees then onto her belly, lying prone where a scoped six-millimeter rifle lay. Even from Dixie's slightly higher vantage point, she saw Carlee was well-concealed once she was down flat on her stomach. Dense wheat stalks with heavy drooping heads concealed her well. The breeze brushing the tops of the stalks made extraneous movements difficult to detect at a glance. Dixie figured it was as good as it was going to be under the circumstances.

The two SUVs turned onto the driveway. *Of course, they're Escalades. Rogelio would rent nothing less. Sure, it's only a quick trip to commit murder. Why not do it in style? The arrogance of that man knows no bounds. He's such an ass.* She backed up to the wall next to the window and slid down to sit, knees raised. She noticed a thin stream of daylight shining over her shoulder onto the point of her knees. She lay over on her side and turned to face the wall. The light streamed through a vertical crack. A short length of the window molding had been broken away near the bottom, leaving a space between the ill-fitting window frame and the adjacent framework of the wall. She peered through it. It offered a reasonable one-eyed view of the area directly in front of the house beyond the three-foot white picket fence where the SUVs would surely stop.

Suddenly, she heard gravel grinding beneath tires. She, again, put an eye to the makeshift peephole to the front yard. The glistening Escalade was navy blue, not black. It filled the space beyond the crack she peered through. The other Escalade must have been right behind the lead vehicle, but she could only see straight ahead. She ducked lower and pushed her head slowly left to get a better view through the bottom corner of the old-style window. A cobweb undulated over the grimy window pane, the odor of dust pronounced where she lay. She was right. The other SUV was parked, almost bumper-to-bumper behind the one in front.

Rogelio was the first one out of the lead vehicle. He walked slowly and stopped, looking over the hood toward the house, surveying the area. He was cautious, showing little of himself, keeping the vehicle between his body and the house.

Having not seen him in over a decade, the view repulsed her. The man's ego and arrogance were a disgusting spectacle with every move. His hair was neatly cut and combed back. A beard, razor-trimmed pencil-thin, extended down both cheeks and around his mouth to connect with a moustache of equal width and trim. He looked as though he just stepped from under the barber's razor. Even his fingernails sparkled in the severely angled light from the setting sun—fresh manicure on display. He wore a black suit, white shirt, and red tie with black shoes so highly polished, they could have been patent leather. His over-the-top narcissism was in full bloom.

I bet he came up here thinking this would all be over quickly—no muss no fuss, and then off to dinner at a fancy restaurant back in Mexico. Well, primo, get ready to have that fine-looking suit get dirty.

There are no outbuildings. That's probably why the bastard has such a smug grin spreading over his face. Nowhere to hide, or so he thinks. She recognized in his expression, he figured all he and his henchmen had to do would be to flush Carlee and her out of the house, cut them to shreds with those automatic weapons, and then be off to the airport to jet back to Mexico, all in a matter of minutes. That self-satisfied look on his face could mean only one thing. In his mind, this was going to be a turkey shoot. Dixie was certain that's what he thought. *Yeah, you just keep on thinking that, primo. Carlee and I will take every advantage you have to offer. This operation will not be as high and tight as you're imagining it will be.*

Rogelio's blatantly obvious bourgeoning confidence prompted him to saunter around the front of the Escalade to the house side of his vehicle. The six other men met up with him. Dixie recognized none of them, but she sure recognized those fully automatic weapons they carried. She was suddenly supremely angered as the men took steps toward the house. "Rogelio!" she shouted and glanced out the bottom corner of the window.

The row of men all stopped at the same time, readying weapons into firing position.

"Go back to Mexico and never come back! This is the only warning you deserve for what you have done to my friends and family!"

He laughed, boldly derisive. "Ah, sweet little Mona, I admire your misguided optimism. Now, I must turn the warning on you." His voice suddenly shot into a louder, more forceful range. "You have made a huge mistake by siding with that woman," he shouted. "I owe you nothing!" His shout crescendoed higher and angrier. "Nothing! You hear me? You betrayed me!" Rogelio paused. He then softened his tone. "But...if you send out Carlee Cayne, I will let you live and you can get back to your little life. How about that for a generous offer?"

"You have made a life of lying. The truth you do speak is twisted to your advantage. No, Rogelio, I did not betray you and I certainly do not believe you. *You* betrayed Daniel, and your own brother Manuel. You fed them lies to make yourself wealthy at their expense. If you need to kill someone to feel better about your inadequacies, put that gun to your own head. The only reason you are here is to divert attention from your failures, to blame others. Now...it's your turn to hear me. So, hear this, Rogelio. You are a pervert!" She snuck another glance and saw anger distort his features on a deepening rubicund face, veins swelling tightly on his temples and across his forehead. The man was headed for an explosive temper tantrum. It came quickly.

"*Pinche Puta*! He shrieked as he raised the automatic assault rifle.

Dixie did not wait to see what came next. She stuck the muzzle of her Glock against the lower right window pane and pulled the trigger, shattering the glass. She hoped to hit Rogelio but it was the guy standing next to him that spun away and fell. He was injured but crawling. All but the injured man took cover the other side of the two shiny vehicles.

The ring of her own pistol shot had not faded when six machine guns answered with a staccato spray of bullets into and through the window, blowing splinters and glass to the interior of the house. All guns clearly aiming for the general vicinity of where her voice had come from.

She covered her head and hunkered lower.

Spraying splinters and glass forced Dixie to fall over to lie flat on the dusty and debris littered floor, as Carlee had advised earlier. She wriggled on her belly quickly to a new position down the front wall, away from the window.

As bullets created a deafening cacophony of noise, the sound of a single, but obviously large caliber, bullet was fired, sounding more like a small canon than a handgun. Carlee had taken her first shot with that six-millimeter deer rifle. A howl of pain immediately followed the shot.

One down and one injured.

Automatic weapons fire ceased. The men had to have been confused momentarily.

Dixie peered through a bullet hole and saw a fortuitous, but unintended, advantage that taking the first shot from within the house created for Carlee. All the men had taken cover on the opposite side of the two Escalades. But, in doing so, exposed themselves like figures in a shooting gallery to Carlee's rifle.

Another large caliber shot rang out.

One of the men leaning over the hood of the lead Escalade dropped out of sight.

Two down and one injured.

Dixie saw Rogelio and three men come back around the SUVs, now giving Dixie an unobstructed shot.

She quickly snaked her way back to the window and took advantage with three quick shots toward Rogelio which she instantly regretted, missing them all. She would have had a better chance at hitting one of the others. Hate clouded her judgment. "Damn it," she hissed. She retreated down the wall away from the window as she once again took fire—a lot of fire.

Then came an erratic barrage of pistol shots, two and three at a time. The plan. Carlee was making her break to the big oak tree out front.

Once again, the automatic fire hesitated, but only for a fractional second as they turned the guns on Carlee.

Dixie hurried back to the window to see Carlee take a bullet in the upper part of her left leg, twirling her to the ground. Her friend seemed to ignore the pain and rolled to face the men, firing her Glock twice. The look on Carlee's face was not one of pain, or of fear. It was the grit of determination.

Three down and one injured, but now, the remaining three men were advancing on Carlee.

Caution be damned. Dixie darted to the front door and jerked it open. This time she took the better shot, hitting the one nearest to her. It appeared to be a clean heart shot. He crumpled to the ground.

Four down and one injured. Only Rogelio and one other remained upright. The one remaining hired gun whipped around and returned fire at Dixie. She pointed her pistol and pulled the trigger. It clicked impotently.

The man grinned wickedly and advanced on Dixie.

Dixie hesitated long enough to see that Rogelio stalked Carlee. Carlee tossed her empty pistol aside and sprang to her feet, quickly but clumsily. In a loping limp, she dove behind the big oak tree and reappeared holding the short barreled .22 magnum semi-automatic carbine, firing it as fast as she could pull the trigger.

Dixie had no choice but to let Carlee defend herself, hoping her sister-by-choice could make it to that open bedroom window at the end of the house as planned. Dixie spun around, preparing to run back inside the house. The armed man kept coming. It was clear by his slowing walk and the expression that he thought it was all but over. The only weapons Dixie had left were a switchblade knife in her jeans pocket, her wits, and her talents.

She heard Carlee and Rogelio exchanging gunfire outside. She only had time to think, *Please God, take care of Carlee.* Just as she began to run for the relative safety of the house's interior, the man fired, sweeping bullets across her. One ripped through her left forearm and another struck the fleshiest part of her upper right deltoid muscle. She yelped but kept running, making it through the door to the interior of the house.

Once inside, she realized her left hand had been rendered useless by the bullet through her forearm. The pain at the site of the wound was excruciating. The hand was numb. Her fingers refused to respond. She had no grip. Although a bullet tore through her upper shoulder, that wound was painful but barely beneath the skin. She had use of her right arm and hand.

She glanced back. The man had not come into view yet, but she heard the creak of weathered and warped decking boards on the front porch.

She sprinted into the central room on the right side of the old shotgun style house and made a quick left turn through a doorway into a tiny vestibule. Its sole purpose was to link two bedrooms—right and left—and a bathroom straight ahead. She squatted and sat on her heels, her back against a short vestibule wall created by the crook between the bedroom door and the dining room door.

From that squat position, she leaned back tighter against the narrow wall partition, waiting, listening. Without so much as an eye blink, she stared at a point about halfway up the open doorway to the dining room in front and to the right of where she crouched, waiting to see the muzzle of an automatic assault rifle appear. She figured if she grabbed the barrel and disarmed him, she might be able to engage him physically.

Suddenly, Dixie heard the crackle of breaking glass shards the other side of the wall she squatted behind. She flexed and tightened every muscle in her body, staring with laser intensity at the open doorway just ahead and to her right. After a couple of seconds, the muscles in her legs began to burn. *Come on! Come on! Come on!*

Unexpectedly, the first thing she saw was the point of his right shoe, not the muzzle of the gun higher up. He was moving in extreme slow motion, stalking speed. Her eyes flicked up then down repeatedly. Was he holding the rifle down to his side?

He took another step and his left leg was now in full view.

Change of plan. She slowly turned sideways and leaned away. Then, with the speed of a striking cobra from that squat position, she shot out her right foot striking the outside of his left knee with her booted heel collapsing the joint inward.

The man howled and slung the rifle up from his side while depressing the trigger at the same time.

Bullets ripped across the wall over her head as he attempted to swing the muzzle around and down at Dixie.

But he was already falling sideways in her direction.

With all the power she could muster from her five-foot-five-inch frame, she sprang from her tightly coiled posture upward as he fell toward her. She used his collapsing momentum and her upward thrust to drive the space between her thumb and forefinger on a tightly flexed open palm into his throat with devastating force before he had gained enough control to aim that gun.

Dixie felt the hyoid bone snap and, as the thrust continued, on the follow-through, the vertebrae protecting the brain stem separated, as did the brain stem itself. He was dead before she could retract her hand from his throat.

Breathing hard, she stared down at what she had done. It was nauseating, even though she had no choice. If she had not taken it to this extreme, the guy would have killed her. After all, it was what they had traveled so far to do. She had employed a deadly move practiced on numerous occasions but thought would never be needed.

Five down and one injured. Only Rogelio remained as a true threat.

Suddenly, she heard noise coming from the bedroom next to where she stood. *I must help Carlee. She's struggling to get through the window.*

Dixie took two quick steps through the door of the bedroom and saw Carlee crawling over the window sill onto the rotting window stool, fighting to get her injured leg inside the bedroom as quickly as possible. She walked on her hands, dragging her body over the bottom of the open window. The window was at the opposite corner of the bedroom from where Dixie stood.

Dixie's view shifted upward to see Rogelio conceitedly watching her struggle, clearly enjoying her suffering. *What a monumental ass!* She reached into the hip pocket of her jeans.

~ * ~

Even as she struggled to pull herself inside to safety, Carlee could not understand why Rogelio had not already shot and killed her. He could have, anytime within the past few seconds when her .22 carbine had run out of bullets and she had no time to eject the empty magazine and replace it with the pre-loaded one.

She had to know, to look, and see why he had not ended her yet. She twisted her head around to see back over her shoulder even before her feet had cleared the window stool to the flat of the floor on the inside. His attention was entirely on her and seemed to enjoy what he saw. He stood only a couple of feet behind her. He could literally touch her with the muzzle of that automatic assault rifle if he chose to. She closed her eyes, clenching them tightly shut. "It's all you, Ortiz. Get it over with," she said.

"God damn it!" he abruptly shouted.

Carlee opened her eyes to see a switchblade knife embedded to its ruby-colored handle in the upper right side of his chest.

Rogelio fired over her head.

She saw Dixie hit with a spray of bullets, slamming her into the wall behind her.

Carlee quickly pulled her injured leg over the bottom of the window and grabbed the 12-gauge shotgun leaning against the wall. She rolled over onto her back and with a deafening blast, hit Rogelio in the gut, violently blowing him away from the window before he could get the muzzle of his gun lowered.

She lay unmoving for a couple of seconds.

All went quiet—ear-ringing silence.

She slowly raised up to look out the open window. Rogelio was not moving. She was convinced he would never be moving again. It crossed her mind how strangely coincidental it was that Rogelio and his brother Manuel had met their end by the same means and by the same person. The only difference? The brand and style of shotgun.

Carlee turned her attention to Dixie, who still stood, backed up to the wall behind her.

"We...did it...*Hermana*," Dixie said, struggling to stay on her feet. She wobbled. Her knees folded and she slowly slid down the wall. Two pronounced blood streaks appeared on the wall behind her. Her legs fell flat and splayed as her buttocks touched the floor. Her hands lay palms-up and limp at her sides. Her jaw slowly went slack. Her eyes fluttered shut as she fell sideways.

"Dixie!" Carlee shrieked.

The wail of approaching sirens became audible in the distance.

Chapter Twenty-nine

What the hell are you doing, Linc? Lincoln Bridger's mind was whirling in overdrive, as Jeannine steered onto the circular driveway fronting the two-story house they had shared as a married couple for more than fifteen years. *I should have had her take me to my car and gone back to my apartment. I didn't think this through. I'm stranded across town, moving head-long into what might be the biggest mistake of my life.*

Once out of the Land Rover and walking toward the house, Jeannine hurried around the vehicle so they could walk abreast. She reached for and held his hand. She looked sideways at him. "Do you mind?" she asked, waggling his hand.

He offered only a quick negative shake of the head.

"Are you okay?" she asked.

He glanced quizzically toward her.

"I mean being inside this house again," she added.

He nodded and offered a faint smile. "I'm okay with it," he replied.

The bravado in his reply was for her benefit. The truth was, he was not confident at all. Quite the opposite, actually. He was intimidated, but not by Jeannine or this house. His own rumbling desire tingled. That's what was unnerving. His growing inability to control a physical craving for Jeannine. Such intense longing had not existed since their college days and the early years of their marriage. He had many opportunities this evening to cut it short but continued to allow Jeannine to guide the entire evening. Now, here they stood on the front porch of the house, a firm reminder of a lengthy marriage that had failed. That was the hell of it, and the source of his fear. Why was he allowing it to happen?

As she searched her purse for the keys, Lincoln studied her profile. How could this woman be so familiar, yet nothing like the woman he divorced? It wasn't simply that. She only faintly resembled the woman he met all those years ago on the University of Texas campus. The woman who eventually became his wife. Jeannine had transformed, like a butterfly from a chrysalis, into a totally different woman from either of those other two personas. It was perplexing, but not in a disagreeable way.

The tightness of indecision began to relax away. Still, a little voice in his head continued murmuring the word "mistake." The whole evening was a mistake. He seemed to float without control of his own body toward the *coup de grâce.*

"Ah. There it is," she said, retrieving the front door key from the bottom of her purse.

"Allow me," Lincoln said. He gently took the key from her and unlocked the door.

Once inside, Jeannine dropped her purse on an intricately detailed gilded Bombay sidebar chest of drawers beneath an equally ornate gilded mirror next to the front door. "Can I fix you something to drink?" she asked.

"I'd better not drink anymore tonight. I'm still enjoying the glow from the pinot noir. Was it three or four glasses I had?"

She draped her arms over his shoulders and smiled. "Who cares?" she whispered and then kissed him lightly on the lips. She stared into his eyes. "Please, Linc, tell me now if this...any of this bothers you, because...I want it. I'm still not sure where, exactly, your head and heart are."

Once again, Jeannine had thrown the door wide open for him to walk away if he was of a mind to do so. *"Bother" me? Hell yeah, it bothers me. I should walk away right now and break this off before it goes any farther.* Still floating along, as if his mind and body were separate entities, what came from his mouth surprised even him. "How about we go upstairs to the bedroom and talk about it there?"

Jeannine said nothing but did offer an enhanced smile. She took his hand and led him up the stairs.

As he followed and watched her ascend, it crossed his mind that if this was truly who she had become, then a renewed relationship might work. He lifted her hand that held his and kissed the back of it.

Chapter Thirty

A mournful symphony of sirens grew louder as a bevy of law enforcement vehicles raced up the long graveled driveway to the old farm house, chalky dust boiling from beneath the caravan of vehicles. The sound should have been a comfort to Carlee, but it was stuck at the periphery of awareness. Her focus and all attention were on her injured friend. The sight of Dixie collapsed and unconscious scared the hell out of her. She tossed the twelve-gauge shotgun onto the floor and struggled through her own pain of having caught a bullet through her leg. It was of little consequence at the moment. She had to get across the room to check on her friend. It looked bad, really bad. Dixie's shirt was saturated with blood. She was losing a shocking amount. The bleeding must be stanched quickly.

Instead of trying to stand, Carlee realized she could crawl faster than stand and limp across the unfurnished bedroom. Using her unaffected leg, she pushed with it while pulling herself along with both arms, to where Dixie had keeled over onto her side unconscious. She slid a dirty hand beneath Dixie's head and lifted it onto her lap. With her free hand, she pressed the site of the abdominal wound firmly. The sight of her friend like this sickened her. She began to cry and pulled Dixie's limp head to her breast. Carlee still drew air deep into her lungs from the physically draining shootout with Ortiz and his thugs, but was now mixed with shuddering sobs. She put two fingers to Dixie's neck. She searched frantically. A pulse was difficult to locate. It was so weak when she found it that she wondered if it might be her own heartbeat in her fingertips she felt. "What have I done?" Carlee leaned her head back against the wall and looked to the ceiling. She cried harder yet.

After a few seconds, she heard law enforcement officials filing into the house in tight formation, systematically clearing it of any continued threats. Carlee shouted, "Back here. Hurry."

First through the bedroom door was a young deputy sheriff, pistol drawn and held high.

"There is no more threat," Carlee told him. "There might still be one of seven alive out front, but that's all," she added hurriedly. "The bigger problem is getting medical attention for this woman."

The young deputy stared dumbly at Dixie's blood soaked upper torso.

"Damn it, deputy! Make the call!"

No sooner had the shouted demand left her lips than her old partner Jimmy Fenn appeared standing outside the bedroom, framed by the open window she had come through only minutes before. "Ambulances have already been called," Fenn told her. "Help will be here soon." He looked around the corner of the house and quickly added, "An ambulance is coming up the driveway now."

Carlee heard the siren and let her head fall back against the wall, relieved by Fenn's encouraging words and take-charge attitude. She took a ragged breath. "Thanks, Jimmy."

"How is she?" Fenn asked.

"Her pulse is weak and her heart is beating fast. One of the bullets caught her squarely in the gut. I'm really scared." Carlee's face screwed down tight as fresh tears spilled out and down her cheeks.

"We need to get you help too. Your own injuries may be worse than you think."

"Don't worry about me. I took a through-and-through in my right quadricep. It clearly missed the femoral artery and the bone. I'll be fine," Carlee told him without taking her eyes from Dixie, continuing to stroke her friend's hair. Dixie looked so young and so helpless. But Carlee knew better. This little *Latina* had the roaring heart of a lioness. "It's this little girl we need to be worrying about," she muttered, thumbing a smudge from Dixie's chin.

Fenn threw a leg over the windowsill and climbed inside the bedroom. He squatted next to Carlee. "You and Dix took a huge chance, but you apparently pulled it off."

When he said that, it was the first time to cross Carlee's mind law enforcement arrived unusually quick. "How did y'all know to come out here?"

"A neighbor a mile up the road called the sheriff's office and reported that it sounded like a war had erupted at the old Miller place. I heard county dispatch on my radio and didn't think much of it until mention was made of fully automatic weapons fire. Carlee, the only automatic weapons fire in the past six weeks in this area has been aimed at you. Since I already knew he was coming to try again, it was no stretch to realize Rogelio Ortiz had found you. I simply followed the responders out here. Here's my question to you. How the heck did the showdown wind up all the way out here?"

Carlee remained silent, not wanting to get into details yet. Her friend may be dying and her leg throbbed. Fortunately, it proved unnecessary. Two emergency medical technicians came through the bedroom door carrying equipment and a stretcher. "Give us room to work," one of the men ordered, forcing Fenn to stand and back away.

"Fenn, you deserve answers and I'm obligated to tell all...and I will. But please, let's table this conversation until I make sure Dix is going to be okay. I can't give you my full attention, not yet."

"Fair enough," he replied. "I'll meet you at the hospital."

Chapter Thirty-one

Lincoln sat on the patio at the rear of the house he and Jeannine had shared during their marriage. He gently rocked in a heavily padded, metal rocking chair next to a round, glass-top table and sipped from a large mug of strong, black coffee. The rising sun was at a severe angle to his left, casting long shadows but getting shorter fast. His eyes followed a squirrel chasing another through the branches of a massive and old live-oak tree. It was a native tree left undisturbed when the house was built. His gaze shifted to a blue jay dive-bombing the neighbor's Siamese cat. The feline ran to get away from the pesky bird through the backyard. But it was not the two fuzzy-tailed rodents or the cat's dilemma with a feisty jay on his mind. His head was a jumble of questions coming into his head faster than answers could be applied to any of them. This tornadic whirl of thoughts all concerned Jeannine and Carlee—intertwined, and since last night, inseparable. He didn't know what to do, which way to go, incomprehensibly terrified that no matter which path he chose would be the wrong one. He glanced back over his shoulder at the house. He wondered if coming home to this place every day could work as well as it once did long ago. Or, should it be left in the past, where he so carefully placed it only a few short weeks ago? He saw Jeannine holding a steaming cup and still in her robe, coming through the French doors out onto the patio.

He smiled. "Good morning."

"Hey, Linc," she cooed. "Seeing you sitting out here made my heart soar."

"Oh?"

"I was sort of expecting you to be gone when I got out of bed."

"I wouldn't do that to you. I *couldn't* do that to you."

"Thank you. That simple assurance means the world to me," she murmured.

He continued to be awed by the amazing change Jeannine had gone through. Or, at least appeared to have gone through. There remained lingering concern it was a well-choreographed dance she indulged in. If so, she danced it to perfection. She was not at all the same woman he divorced. Gazing silently into her eyes, one of those questions spun out earlier did have an answer coming together. *I think she and I just might be able to make it work this time. If what I see in her is the truth.*

His cell phone, lying on the table, sounded his ringtone. He picked it up and saw Fitz's name. He hit talk. "Mornin', Fitz. What's up?"

"Where were you last night? I dropped by your apartment to see if you wanted to go get a beer or something and you were nowhere around."

Lincoln grinned and winked at Jeannine. "You should have called first," he told Fitz. "I could have saved you a trip over there. I was with Jeannine. Still am."

Fitz said nothing.

"Fitz? Are you still there?"

"Okay," Fitz drawled. "I guess we can talk about *that* later."

"Why did you call?"

"Oh yeah. I meant to ask if you wanted to meet me for breakfast before going in to work."

"Sounds good, but I think I'll make breakfast here and hang out with Jeannine a while longer."

"Okay. Then I'll see you at the agency in a couple of hours."

~ * ~

Whoa. This is big, Fitz thought. *Linc and Jeannine...back together. Seriously?* He left his apartment, shaking his head, on the verge of disbelieving what Linc had said, thinking it might have been a joke he failed to grasp. He grinned and then chuckled. *Heck, maybe they are that rare couple I've heard tell of that divorce actually brought them closer together. How weird is that?*

He unlocked his car door and slid in beneath the steering wheel and started it. Preparing to back out of his assigned parking space, he dropped it into reverse. Before he began to roll, his phone rang. He shoved the gear selector back into the park position and answered it. "Hello."

"Fitz?"

"Yeah. This is Fitz."

"Carlee Cayne."

"Hey, Carlee. I'm surprised to get a call from you, especially at seven in the morning."

"Fitz, Dixie has been asking for you."

"Why? What's going on?"

"There's no way to sugar-coat this. She and I were involved in a shootout with that Mexican drug cartel late yesterday afternoon..."

Fitz's heart pounded in his ears. Carlee's comment hit him like a hammer.

"...Dixie and I were both shot. But, Fitz, she caught the worst of it."

Terror seized him as the awful news filled his mind with worst-case scenarios. "Carlee, are you saying that she...that Dixie is—"

"No, no. Don't even say the word. Dixie was immediately taken to surgery when we came into Seaton Medical Center last evening. Doctors repaired a perforated colon. The bullet entered at such an angle, it contaminated a large area. The doctors are worried about peritonitis getting out of control. They'll be treating her with a steady drip of strong antibiotics and pain meds for several days. It will be a day or two before doctors know anything certain though."

"Oh, my God. I thought you were going to tell me that the worst had happened."

"As soon as Dix came out from under anesthesia, she muttered your name, wanting to know if you had been notified. She's very groggy and has been tagged critical, but you know Dix. She's a fighter."

Fitz detected in Carlee's strained voice a clear lack of confidence about Dixie's ability to recover. It must be much more serious than her words indicated.

Carlee continued, "So, when I heard the name Fitz as the first thing from her mouth when she woke, I knew it was coming straight from the heart, not her head."

"I'm already in my car. I'll be there in ten minutes or less."

~ * ~

After getting directions to the critical care unit from the lady at the front desk of the hospital, Fitz walked so fast he occasionally broke into a trot down the halls.

Once there, he lied to the nurse, telling her he was family to get information without the need of discussion or, more likely, an argument over being allowed into the critical care area to see Dixie at all. It occurred to him that to say Dixie was family may have been an untruth but, somehow, he did not see it as an out and out lie. He considered it a possible future truth. Besides, after Carlee's call, and becoming instantly terrified Dixie might have been killed, he now seriously considered the notion of making her family. She had to be okay. That's all there was to it.

As he approached Dixie's room in CCU, another nurse intercepted him. "According to the information given to me, you are Benjamin Vega. Is that right?"

"That's right."

"And you're a relative of Miss Vega?"

"Of course."

"How come Ms. Vega and Ms. Cayne have been calling you Fitz?"

He rolled his eyes. "Okay, okay. My name is Ben Fitzsimmons." He was nervous about being barred from the room and his weak smile reflected that. "I believe, someday, Dixie may become family...no, not *may*, but most certainly will become family."

Although his response caused the nurse to match his smile, she replied, "I'm sorry, Mister Fitzsimmons. After that most romantic comment, it pains me, but I must tell you, only immediate family is allowed in. Hospital policy."

Fitz craned his neck to see around the edge of a curtain covering an observation window into Dixie's room. He saw Carlee in a wheel chair with her left leg elevated and extended. She was parked next to Dixie's bed. "How come Carlee gets to be in there?"

"Miss Vega identified her as her sister."

Fitz snickered. "Sister? In that case I'm a brother to them both."

Carlee appeared, holding the curtain back from her seated position in the wheel chair. Her muffled voice penetrated the window. "It's okay. He's family too. Let him come in," she said to the nurse.

"All right," the nurse replied hesitatingly. She turned back to Fitz, examining his face, and then glancing to the two women inside the room. "I don't think I've ever seen three members of the same family look so different in my life."

Fitz's grin grew to Cheshire cat proportion. "It takes more than blood to be family," he replied with an air of sarcasm on his way through the door. He then looked to Carlee. "Thanks for the assist."

She nodded and smiled.

"How's our girl?" he asked.

"Ask her yourself. She hasn't been from under anesthesia for long and she's on heavy pain meds, but at least she's awake."

Without opening her eyes, Dixie rolled her hand over and opened it, splaying her fingers wide, and, with slowly curling fingertips, she silently beckoned him over. "Fitz. You came," she said, slurring every word.

"How're ya feelin', Dix?" he asked as he slid his hand into hers.

"No pain." She swallowed. "Good drugs. *Really* good drugs," she replied, but only with much effort. Lifting her eyebrows first, as an assist, she forced her eyes open. Heavily veined, they floated in liquid pools, unfocused. "Gonna stay a while?"

Fitz put his other hand in play and sandwiched her hand between his palms. It wasn't difficult to read her simple question as an urgent plea. Aside from Carlee, Dixie had no one else. A sudden burst of emotion overwhelmed him. "Oh, Dixie. When I told you I wanted to be your friend, it was more than a throw-away line. I meant it, deeply and sincerely. There is no place else on this little blue planet of ours I'd rather be."

Dixie nodded lazily. "Sorry. Can't stay awake," she whispered, voice trailing.

Fitz lifted her hand and kissed it. "Rest, dear friend. You can sleep, knowing I'll be here when you wake."

She forced a smile that wilted away, as her breathing quickly established a sleeping rhythm.

Fitz backed away and walked around her bed and sat in a chair next to Carlee's wheelchair. "Truly, is she going to be okay, you think?"

Carlee pursed her lips and shrugged her shoulders. "I hope so," she said. "It hinges on keeping an infection from establishing. I'm terribly afraid if infection does set in, it might take her from us before the doctors can do anything about it. That's my honest opinion and ultimate fear." Carlee looked at Dixie with a loving smile. "So, she'll be here in critical care for...well, until something changes, for better or for worse."

No words were exchanged for a few seconds. She sighed and turned to Fitz. "I had better call Linc and apologize for being so distant lately. I treated him badly. I simply did not want to get him involved in my dangerous problems again. He put his life in jeopardy twice, simply by standing too close to me. Three may have been too many. I would not have been able to live with myself if anything bad would have happened to him. I have one friend lying there because of me. That's one too many. If you don't think I'm abandoning you, I'm going back to my room and call Linc. They don't allow cell phones in this critical care wing."

"Uh...there's something I think you may need to know, something I just found out myself about half an hour ago."

"Can it wait until after I call Linc?"

"Well...you see...uh..."

"Whatever it is, surely it can't be that confounding."

"Honestly, Carlee, I'm afraid that is *exactly* what it will be."

Frustration showing, she wheeled her chair around to face him straight on, dropping her hands onto the hospital gown covering her lap. "Just get it said. I'll be the judge of that."

Fitz was conflicted, uncertain whether to share what he knew or not, but he had opened his mouth and it was too late to back up now. His neck muscles tightened as his head torqued to the side, fearful. "Okay. Here goes. I called Linc earlier to see if he wanted to join me for breakfast before going in to the agency. He went over to Jeannine's house last night and stayed. That's why I was hesitant tell you. He might not have wanted me to, but I felt you needed to know."

Carlee's color drained, facial expression sagging.

Her changing appearance made Fitz cringe. "I hope I did the right thing," he added.

In an odd monotone, "It's okay, Fitz. Whatever happens between Linc and his ex is my fault and, now, none of my business. I pushed him away and couldn't tell him why. Now, I've lost him and must learn to live with it," she said. She fell silent, slowly drawing her eyes up and away from her lap to connect with his. "I won't call him. I don't want to interfere." She turned and slowly began wheeling her way out of the room. "I have to be alone for a while though. Sorry." Her lower lip quivered as she plainly fought back tears.

Fitz wanted to stop her, to say something encouraging, but everything crossing his mind would only deepen the muck she was sinking into. He stepped out of the room and watched her roll herself along, head hanging low, probably to prevent those she passed in the hall from seeing her cry. Even from behind, her body language told the tale of a woman whose heart had just been shattered. *God, I'm so sorry, Carlee. You're a gem, a real gem that doesn't deserve this...or any of the shit life has thrown at you lately.*

Chapter Thirty-two

Lincoln stood in front of the bathroom mirror combing his hair as Jeannine's reflection appeared standing in the doorway behind him. "Sorry to be rushing, but I need to quickly get back to my apartment before going in to the agency," he told her. "I can't go to work two days in a row with the same clothes on." He grinned mischievously. "I shouldn't need to tell you how that would look."

Jeannine leaned her head against the door jamb. "I think it would look just right. That, of course, is a personal opinion, mind you." Her head suddenly snapped straight. "Hey, I have an idea. Why don't you play hooky from work today? Let's spend the day, the whole day, playing and getting to know one another all over again."

Lincoln stared at her in the mirror, tilting his head thoughtfully.

"I know, I know. It sounds a little irresponsible. But, hey, the way I see it, you and I are worth it."

Lincoln's fingers that had been hurriedly buttoning his shirt fell down to his sides, leaving the job partially done. *That's not a bad idea, not bad at all. I've already met my business goals for the month at the agency.* He gazed at Jeannine's reflection in the mirror a moment longer. "Ya know, I sort of like that idea."

"Sort of?"

He chuckled. "Sorry. I *really* like that idea," he clarified. "Better?"

Jeannine squealed, bounced on her toes, and clapped her hands. "How about we take in an early matinee and see that new action flick. I hear it's a great movie."

He slowly turned to see her without the aid of a mirrored reflection. "You would go to a movie with me?"

She glided two steps and closed the gap between them, stopping when her nose touched his. "No. I won't go to a movie with you. But, I'll

229

take you to a movie and hold your hand while we devour a decadently large bucket of popcorn. And then, we'll go see every new movie release the day they hit theatres for the rest of our lives, if that's what you want, honey." She pressed her lips to his, gently caressing. She slowly reared her head back to gaze into his eyes. She put her arms around his waist and pulled him in to full body contact, again pressing her lips to his. This time, she gently bit his lower lip, breathing heavily into his mouth. "But first, dear Linc, let me show you just how much I love the idea of a full day with you," she said, already guiding him back to the bed, unmade from the night before.

~ * ~

Fitz sauntered down the hospital corridor toward Dixie's room in the critical care unit of Seaton Medical Center. He saw one of the CCU nurses make a bee-line toward him.

"Mister Fitzsimmons, Miss Vega woke a few minutes ago and asked for you," the young pony-tailed blonde in scrubs announced.

Fitz gave the young nurse an appreciative touch on the arm. "Thank you," he replied and stepped up his pace toward Dixie's room. He rounded through the door into the room and saw that Dixie faced the door and seemed slightly more alert than she did a couple of hours ago when he had first arrived.

She offered a lazy smile. "Hey."

"Hey to you too." He stopped next to her bed and smoothed away errant strands of hair that had escaped Dixie's signature French braid. "You are so beautiful. I never tire of looking into those gorgeous brown eyes of yours or examining that magnificent face."

Her smile broadened. "You are such a liar," she replied slowly, each word labored. "I know how I feel. Therefore, I don't need a mirror to know what I must look like. Thanks for saying it though." She licked her lips and swallowed. "Where's Carlee? Is she okay?"

Fitz was conflicted whether to tell her the truth of the situation about Lincoln's apparent re-connection with his ex-wife. To share anything of a heart-breaking nature about her best friend would only make her feel worse.

Dixie did not deserve to share that heartache, on top of everything else she had done for Carlee. The hesitation was brief. He quickly concluded, Dixie had given enough of her heart and soul to Carlee's problems, at least for a while. "When you nodded off again, Carlee thought it was a good time to go back to her room and rest. She may be asleep. Don't worry about her injuries. She'll heal a lot faster than you. So, just rest. Okay?"

Dixie offered an affirming nod. "Good. She's been through so much. She deserves a calm mind, free from worry."

As good-hearted as the comment was, it irritated Fitz she continued to burden herself with Carlee's problems. "And you haven't?" he replied with an edge.

Dixie took his hand in hers and squeezed it. "Don't forget, dear friend, all her problems were caused by my, so-called, family. I'm thankful she allowed me to help her put the problem away, permanently."

He sighed and nodded, not wanting to address that concern anymore. It was now history and should be left there and never looked upon again. In a low even tone, "I understand what you're saying, but it had nothing to do with you personally. Whatever you felt you owed, has been paid many times over in loyalty and, most certainly, in the pain you're forced to endure right now," he said. He leaned over and kissed her on the forehead.

Dixie closed her eyes and fetched a deep breath. She opened her eyes and gazed into his. "You grow more special to me by the day. Have I told you lately how much that is?"

"No, but you don't have to. We've agreed to be friends only. I respect that wish. So, all I want is to be the best—"

"Shut up," she said sluggishly.

"Uh...okay."

"What would you think of being more than just friends?" she asked. "Ya think something like that would have a chance?"

The smile that replaced the questioning look on his face was so wide it disappeared into his cheeks.

~ * ~

Carlee considered asking the nurse to help her back into bed. Thinking better of it, she attempted mustering defiance against helplessness. *No, I won't ask for help. I won't. I'll stand on my own. Whatever pain I have to endure, I created this situation for myself. I refuse to bother anyone else with my problems.* She locked the brakes on her wheelchair and, with both hands, lifted her extended injured leg off the horizontal support onto the floor. It throbbed, but not as much as she thought it might. She positioned her hands on the mobile chair's armrests and, with the additional assist, managed to come out of the chair and stand. Unmoving, she tested her weight on the injured leg and discovered the weakness and pain she feared were less than anticipated. Placing a hand on the bed at its foot, she took an exploratory step toward the head of the bed, and then another. She turned and sat on the bed's edge. *Little things like this prove it. I can get by on my own. I don't need Lincoln Bridger.* She gingerly rotated her body and lay back on the inclined bed. *As long as I have Rylee, Mom, and a great friend like Dixie, I don't need a man to prop me up.*

Regardless where she attempted to steer her thoughts, tears continued flowing uncontrollably. With every endeavor to banish Lincoln from her head, contrived belligerence failed. The heart ruled. A montage of treasured snippets paraded through her thoughts. That first night in the hotel bar with him, sitting on the curb next to him after the harrowing experience in the hotel parking lot, watching how kindly he had treated Rylee, how quickly her mother, Beth, had accepted him, and how much Rylee and her mother adored him. There would be no forgetting of those moments. Memories were deeply etched. They would be part of her for the rest of her life, as would the image of Lincoln himself, having grown cherished. She drew a ragged breath and whimpered. *Damn it! How could I have allowed myself to fall so completely in love in such a short time?* With clenched fists, she softly hammered the mattress on both sides of her body.

The process of mourning a lost love had begun. It didn't matter how deeply she had fallen. Life would go on. She must learn to cope. Movement from the direction of the door caught her eye. Her mother and sweet baby, Rylee, were coming into the room.

Rylee sat on the edge of the bed. "Hi, Mama."

"Hi, baby," Carlee replied and pulled the child's head to her lips and kissed her forehead.

"I sure am glad all that Mexican cartel mess is over and done with," Beth Cayne said. "Now, you can get on with your life in peace. I'm so grateful I don't have to worry about you any longer...well, not as much." She smiled as only a mother could at her child.

"Getting on with my life in peace sounds like a great plan." She quickly swept tears from her cheeks.

"Are you in pain, dear?"

"Oh no, just emotional over everything that has happened the past few weeks. I guess I'm crashing, finally coming down from an adrenaline roller coaster ride." She tried unsuccessfully to smile. "Let's just call these girlie tears. I'm fine."

Beth sat next to Rylee on the bed. "Have you had a chance to check on Dixie this morning?"

"I just returned from there. If they can keep infection out of her abdomen, she should heal. But, it's still a touchy situation. She's very weak. Not good, but, according to the doctor, expected. They have to monitor her closely. It's all they can do, for now."

"How about Linc?" Beth asked. "Have you, or anyone, called to let him know it's all over now?"

All over? Carlee did not respond. Her mother had no way of knowing how true that was. It was indeed all over. Fresh tears shined her eyes.

Chapter Thirty-three

Fitz stepped through the door into the lobby of Adler, Levy and Howard and checked his wristwatch—only a half-hour late. Which, unto itself, was amazing considering all that had transpired earlier, taking his mind entirely off his career for a time.

He had planned to sit with Dixie all day but, at her insistence, he came on to work. She had told him, "As long as they have me on a constant drip of pain meds and antibiotics, I'll probably sleep most of the day. So, please go on to work." She then reached for his shirt front, pulled him close, and kissed him. She refused to release her hold on him. "Of course, I do expect you back here this evening. Ya got that, buddy?" She smiled sleepily. "Speaking of sleep, I won't be able to hold my eyes open much longer. I'm so very weak. Go do your thing...and I'll...do mine." She smiled, closed her eyes, and drifted off to sleep in scant seconds.

Fitz could not argue with the logic. Although, sitting for hours staring at her beautiful sleeping face did not seem like it would be wasting a day. Rather, it would have been the perfect day. Still, he began to think about projects left dangling at the agency the day before and calls he had promised to make today. He sighed and kissed Dixie lightly on the lips. "Okay then," he had whispered, "you win. I'll see you sometime after five." He kissed her again and left her to rest and heal.

Fitz stopped in the agency's lobby. "I didn't see Linc's car in the parking garage. Did he come in this morning?" he asked Pamela Hernandez, the pretty and young brunette receptionist.

"Sorry, Fitz, no. He called in a few minutes before nine and said he was not coming in today."

Fitz frowned. "Did he say why?"

"No. He only said that he was taking a personal day and would be back at work tomorrow but to go ahead and send all work related calls to his cell phone. So, if you need him, I guess you can call him."

"Thanks. I think I know what he's doing. I won't bother him unless I have a work-related problem." He walked on toward his office, thinking, *I won't interrupt his day, if he's spending it re-connecting with Jeannine. I'm sure that's what he's doing. I wonder if he would be going down that road if he knew why Carlee worked so hard at avoiding him. I've got to have a heart-to-heart conversation with the boy very soon.*

Before he could turn the corner into his office, managing partner, Stuart Adler, called to him from down the corridor between offices. "Fitz?"

"Yeah, boss."

"Have any idea why Linc needed a personal day? Nothing bad I hope."

"I don't think so. If I had to guess, I'd say that his love life is in a tizzy and it all revolves around that."

"I'm sure glad he had his monthly revenue goal made early. When he has been at work the past week or so, his mind was always somewhere else."

"I know, boss," he replied, and then murmured, "Believe me. I know."

"What about Carlee? Does Linc's behavior of late have anything to do with her?"

Fitz didn't know how to answer the question without betraying an implied confidence. So, he simply rolled out his lower lip and nodded agreeably.

"Ah. So, can I assume Carlee's sudden and unexpected absence is tied in there somewhere?"

"Well...sort of. Did you hear about that shootout east of town yesterday?"

"I heard snippets about it, not the whole story. Why?"

"That was Carlee and her friend, my girlfriend, Dixie Vega that went up against seven heavily armed Mexican drug cartel guys with no help and took them all out."

"Good Lord! Really?"

"Dangerously impressive, right?"

"Are they okay?"

"It sure could have been a lot worse. Dixie took three bullets. The worst was in her abdomen, tearing a large perforation in her colon. Carlee took one to her leg. Dixie's in very poor condition, but the doctors seem to have her stabilized, for now. Carlee will be fine. Her bullet wound was in the leg and minor in comparison. The reprisal against Carlee is over. She and her family are safe now."

"Linc didn't get involved with that, did he?"

"Well, ya see, that's the other side of this story. No, he was not involved with the shooting part. In fact, he didn't know anything about it. It's possible he's still unaware of what happened."

~ * ~

"Miss Cayne, your dinner will be brought up shortly," the nurse told her.

Carlee rolled her head toward the kindly aging health care professional and offered an insincere smile. "Thank you," she monotoned, and then turned back to her Mom and Rylee. "Why don't y'all go on down to the cafeteria and get something to eat?"

Beth Cayne looked to ten-year-old Rylee and asked, "What do you think, kiddo? You hungry?"

Rylee nodded enthusiastically. "A hamburger sure sounds good."

Beth chuckled. "Does that answer your question, dear?"

Carlee nodded and watched them leave the room. They had only been out of sight a matter of seconds when her ex-partner, Jimmy Fenn, came through the door. "Hey, Carlee. Doin' okay?"

"Physically, yeah. My problem now is how to arrange the rest of my life. That doesn't seem to be going so well." She paused, thinking about what a good friend Fenn was. "Get over here and give me a hug, Jimbo. I really need one."

Fenn sat next to her and scooped her up into his arms, pulling her to a sitting position on the bed and embracing her. He growled affectionately and squeezed. As he backed away, "Is there anything I can do to make it better, to help you have a better day, and, maybe, a better life?"

"You just did. No matter what happens in my life, I insist you always remain part of it. It would destroy me if I ever lost track of you. "

"Same here, my friend, same here," he said and then paused while examining her face. "Judging by the red, puffy eyes you've been dealing with a bit of sadness today. Is that a fair assessment?"

"Not only fair but spot on. And it has been more than a 'bit of sadness.' More like devastating."

"Care to share?"

Carlee's lip quivered as new tears glossed her blood-shot eyes. "I tried to do the right thing, Jimbo, and it blew up in my face. I didn't want Linc involved in my war with Rogelio Ortiz. I love him too much to take a chance he might get hurt on account of me and my problems. When I began formulating a plan to lure Ortiz out of Mexico, I became aloof and distant, never explaining to him why, because I knew if he asked I wouldn't be able to lie to him and he would get involved whether I wanted him to or not. It's not difficult to guess his take away on my actions. He assumed I was done with him and wanted nothing else to do with him. " She snuffled, drawing a fast finger across her nose as her face tightened. She tried unsuccessfully to ward off another crying jag. "I saw him with his ex-wife. Jimmy, I think he went back to her." Carlee covered her tightening face with both hands and she cried.

Fenn pulled her back into an embrace. "It'll be okay. Give it some time. For now, just breathe. Things have a way of working out, whether Lincoln Bridger is part of your life or not. Wait and see," he whispered into her ear.

Carlee did not share his optimism. "I love him so much, and I handled the situation so wrong. I can't break free. I can't let go." She patted her chest over her heart. "He's locked in here and he's not coming out. What do I do? What the hell do I do?"

Fenn leaned back in and kissed her forehead. "No one is expecting you to let it go, not this soon. And, you certainly shouldn't be expecting it of yourself. Allow the passage of time to do the heavy lifting for you. Linc will see the truth eventually."

"Patience will not fix it," she said, voice strained to prevent squealing. "He's already back with his ex-wife." She sobbed.

He frowned. "That was sure a quick turn-around. I wonder what precipitated it."

Carlee shrugged her shoulders. "I don't know." She had no idea how or why Lincoln and Jeannine had reunited so quickly. If it was in process before her planned aloofness had begun or if her actions sent him reeling back to her, causing him to explore the possibility of repairing his relationship with his ex-wife. Either way, she felt responsible as the nexus for the outcome. She lost him. There was nothing she could do about it now. Furthermore, she didn't believe she had a right to go after him or interfere in any way. It was her fault. That's all there was to it.

Fenn's ringtone on his cell phone sounded off. He pulled it from his jeans pocket.

She noticed the display. It indicated that supervising director, Deputy George Turner, was calling.

"Sorry. I'd better take this," he said.

With a fast but shaky hand, she swept tears from her face. "I know you do."

After a brief conversation, he ended the call. "Carlee, I'm sorry for leaving you like this, but Turner wants me to serve a subpoena within the hour."

She smiled, despite the tears. "Go on. Get out of here. You have a job to do. No one knows that better than me. They'll bring dinner in shortly and then Mom and Rylee will be back up here soon afterward. I'll be fine."

Fenn hurried over and pressed his cheek to hers. "I'll be back to see you tomorrow."

She kissed his cheek. "You'd better."

Now on a mission, Fenn rushed out the door.

Carlee maintained the smile as long as he was in sight, but it then sagged away fitfully. As much as she loved Jimmy Fenn, being alone was what she desired most at the moment. She rolled her head away from the door, away from a world of people going about their busy day. No distractions. All she wanted was to be alone with her melancholy.

Chapter Thirty-four

On his way through the front door of Seaton Medical Center, Fitz wondered about Stuart Adler's concern over Lincoln's distracted behavior the past couple of weeks. Fitz had agreed with his boss and, at the time, equally concerned for his friend. But a mere five minutes after that conversation with Adler, Dixie entered his thoughts and stayed there the remainder of the work day. Lincoln Bridger could not claim sole possession of distracted behavior. Fitz had only managed to accomplish the bare minimum at work. Dixie's question before he walked out of her hospital room on his way to the agency earlier in the day left him with a mix of fantasies and concerns. She had asked, "Would you want to be more than just friends?" It was a simple question but loaded with a lifetime of possibilities. *I wonder if that was the pain meds talking.* He thought about that, and had been thinking about it, a lot. It seemed to be a rational concern. That her words were fueled by a drug-induced overly relaxed mind. He wanted to believe her question about taking the next step was genuine, desiring a thoughtful exploration of a deeper relationship. The notion intrigued him, and scared him at the same time.

As he walked past a glass encased bulletin board in the hospital corridor, he caught sight of his reflection in the glass. He hesitated long enough to run fingers through his board-straight and wiry sandy brown hair, hoping for a slightly better arrangement. But his hair only knew how to do one thing, hang in his face. Twice he pushed it back, only to watch it spring back to its original unkempt position. So, he did the next best thing. He tugged on his loosened tie so it hung straighter. He shrugged off the inadequate grooming effort and kept walking toward Dixie's room. His mind remained awash with all things concerning Ramona Louise Vega, his sweet Dixie.

As he crossed the threshold into her room in CCU, he saw the head of her bed had been elevated. Although clearly sluggish from whatever all that stuff was flowing into her through the intravenous drip, she app eared to be more alert. "Hey, Dix."

She smiled. "Hey, Fitz."

"Feelin' okay?"

"Flyin' high. No pain. But I'm weak as a kitten. Can't shake the cobwebs from my head. The doctor says it's less about the drugs and more about my body in a battle with itself over the infection. He said the antibiotics are working, just not fast enough. The narcotic pain meds have to be a big part of my problems with seeing and talking right." She had to over-enunciate every word to keep from slurring her speech.

"Maybe I need to stick that needle in my arm for a while? We could fly together. I can't think of anyone on the face of this old earth I would rather soar among the clouds with," he said, using a flattened palm to make an exaggerated flying gesture.

She snickered lazily. "Shut up and come sit beside me." As he was sitting, she added, "I'm glad you saw fit to come back after work."

With a look of mock indignation, "Hey, I promised I would. So, I did."

"That's one thing I really like about you. You keep your word." She covered his hand with hers. "But...it's not the only thing." She pressed her head deeper into the pillow, offering an alluring, albeit drugged, gaze at his face. Her eyes floated in liquid pools, leaving the impression eye movement was almost independent, one from the other.

"I...uh..." He was embarrassed and did not know how to respond to such a compliment.

Even weakened as she was, it was clear Dixie realized his uneasiness with her comment and changed the subject. "Have you seen Carlee or Linc this afternoon?"

"I haven't seen Linc all day. He didn't come in to work today. And, I haven't seen Carlee since we were all together in your room this morning."

"I sort of expected Carlee to come back up this afternoon, but she hasn't. What about Linc? Is he sick?"

"There's something I need to tell you about those two," he replied but then paused. *I shouldn't be saying anything...I shouldn't be saying anything.* The thought looped through his mind repeatedly. But he couldn't just sit like a loose-lipped dolt and stare at her. He had to say something. Going against his own better judgment, he decided to try and explain it. He wanted to say it in such a way it wouldn't upset Dixie. He pressed his lips together thoughtfully. *Oh, for God's sake, man. Get it said!* He blurted in a stream, "Linc has been seeing his ex-wife. He believes Carlee was avoiding him because she was trying to break it off with him, but would not admit it to him."

"Oh, my God. That's not true at all."

He placed a hand on her shoulder. "Now, don't go getting upset." He gently squeezed and then patted her shoulder. "He had no reason to believe otherwise. All he could see was Carlee dodging him and quite obviously so."

"Yeah, but—"

"I know. She was doing it to protect him. Carlee explained it to me this morning."

"Fitz, you...we have to tell him. He has to know."

He torqued his head around. "Well, you see, that's where I'm conflicted. If he's trying to repair his relationship with Jeannine, is it my place to throw a wrench in those gears at this point?"

She lifted her head off the pillow and pointed at him with a wandering finger, still too drug-addled and weak to hold it steady, "You listen to me, Bucko. I disagree with every word of your concern. We *should* toss that wrench in those gears—the sooner the better. Carlee is my best friend in this whole stupid world and she should have a fighting chance, which she is being denied."

"I'm not denying her anything. She's the one who refused to call him this morning when I explained it to her. She figured it was her fault she lost him and didn't want to interfere. She asked that I not interfere either. I'm simply doing what she asked me to do...or not do, as the case may be."

"That's crap."

Fitz reared his head, surprised.

"Yes, I cuss sometimes," she said. "Get used to it."

His eyebrows shot up. "Okie dokie."

Dixie grabbed his tie and pulled his face closer to hers. "You and me, Fitz, we're gonna fix this."

He grinned and bounced a shoulder shrug. "Is right now soon enough?"

~ * ~

"Renting a houseboat for the afternoon and night was a wonderful idea, Linc," Jeannine said. She squeezed a small amount of tan lotion onto her palm and spread it over her bare midriff.

Sitting side by side on chaise lounge chairs, looking across the breeze fretted water, Lincoln sat with his bare legs crossed at the ankles. He rolled his head sideways toward her. "After all those early spring rains, Lake Travis is looking good. We can float around on the lake and shut out the world for a short while. It's nice out here, really nice." With every tick of the clock, Lincoln was becoming increasingly comfortable with the possibility of renewing a relationship with Jeannine.

"Yeah. It is nice," she replied.

"A beautiful day for a mini-vacation."

Extending her arms over her head, Jeannine stretched her bikini-clad body and then with feline grace rolled onto her side to fully face him. "It's wonderful. No parents, no children, no nosy friends...just the two of us," she murmured.

Lincoln continued smiling, but the luster melted away. Her comment plucked a nerve. The no parents and the no nosy friends thing was fine, but to throw children into the mix was bothersome. He wanted children, always did. They both had parents and they both had friends but they had no children. Was it a subtle way to say she never wanted them? It was a hint of selfishness, reminiscent of the woman he had divorced, not the one he was hopefully believing that she had transformed into. He attempted holding onto a pleasant appearing face, but abruptly became unable to maintain eye contact, rolling his head back to stare at the puffy cumulus clouds set in a crystalline blue sky.

Jeannine was likely unaware she had said anything wrong, simply expounding on his mood and feelings, using her own means of expression. The problem was, the comment was evocative of her unattractive side, the self-centered and childish woman he left. She didn't want children because she had never grown up herself, desiring all attention remain directed toward her. It now, and quite suddenly so, seemed that his fear of her playing a well-rehearsed role may have been spot-on after all. The notion was now moving beyond simple guesswork. She may not have changed at all. She could be manipulating him. It was a scarily plausible scenario. If so, he had fallen for the ruse.

Lincoln's ringtone on his cell phone sounded. He retrieved it from the side pocket of his swim trunks. He saw Fitz's name on the display. He turned to Jeannine. "Sorry, but I told the agency to call me with work emergencies since I gave them such short notice about taking this day off." He turned and stood. "I'd better take this." He walked the narrow path between the rail and the cabin to the opposite side of the house boat as the craft gently rocked. While walking, he answered the phone. "Yeah, Fitz. What's up?"

~ * ~

Fitz explained to Lincoln the situation with Carlee and why she had avoided him recently. He went at it several times, using different ways of getting it across to his friend. During the one-sided conversation, Fitz pumped Lincoln to ask questions he might have and if he understood everything said. Lincoln remained irksomely quiet with only short abrupt responses. By his reactions, or lack thereof, Fitz read as anger and chose to take it no further or risk his own friendship. "Okay then," Fitz said after a long pause. "Will I see you at work tomorrow?"

"Yeah, I'll be there," Linc replied, again rather abruptly. He ended the call.

Fitz, standing next to Dixie's hospital bed, stared at his phone, confused by the conversation.

"Well?" Dixie asked. "Did you get through to him?" Her speech was slow and labored.

"I...I honestly don't know. Linc sounded irritated I called him."

Dixie suddenly appeared more alert. "Irritated? Really?"

"Can't say for sure. If it wasn't annoyance then it was the most cryptic conversation I've ever had with him."

Dixie lay back, moving her head around, searching for comfort on the pillow. She grimaced, as if struck by a sharp pain. "Damn," she muttered. "We missed our chance. It's too late. He really is back with his ex-wife." Her voice softened and weakened further. Her face tightened again.

Fitz sat on the bed next to her. "Are you in pain?"

"A little."

"I'm sorry," he said. "I know how much you wanted it to work out for Carlee's sake."

She gazed into his eyes and offered a wan smile. "It's okay, Fitz. You did all you could do." Her eyes fluttered and closed. She repeated in a voice low enough as to be almost unintelligible, "...all you could do."

Fitz thought she had drifted off to sleep, but he noticed the rise and fall of her chest stopped. He sprang to his feet, alarmed.

He spun toward the door to go get help but hadn't taken a single step before the relentless beep of the heart monitor changed from a rhythmic chirp to a steady tone. By the time he raced into the corridor, a cadre of medical professionals were already running toward him.

Fitz turned to follow them back into Dixie's room. A nurse grabbed his arm. "I'm sorry but you'll have to wait out here."

"But—"

"Sorry, sir. It has to be this way. We have to work quickly with no distractions." The nurse released his arm and raced into the room, closing the door behind her.

Fitz stepped laterally and watched through the observation window. There were so many doctors and nurses standing around Dixie, he couldn't see her, and kept angling for a better line of sight with no luck. *Don't you die on me, girl. Don't you dare die on me.*

The small hairs rose on the back of his neck as a chilled breath of air touched him, but there was no breeze.

~ * ~

Carlee lay on her side, facing away from the closed door of her hospital room. Deep sadness refused to relinquish its crushing grip on her.

"Here's your dinner, dear," came a voice from behind her.

Carlee glanced back to see the elderly nurse coming through the door holding a tray. "Thank you. Would you mind just leaving it? I'll get to it later. I'm not hungry right now."

"Is everything okay, dear? Is there something I can do for you?"

Carlee glanced back again, this time offering the best smile she could. She read it on the nurse's face. The woman, who appeared just past middle-age, had detected something might be amiss. "Physically I'm fine. I have a few personal matters that are weighing on me."

"I don't mind sitting with you a while if you need someone to talk to," the nurse said, stepping closer to bedside.

"You're sweet to offer, but...no. It's something I must come to terms with on my own, in my own time."

"Okay," the little lady in floral scrubs drawled. "If you change your mind, hit the call button."

Carlee nodded as the nurse left the room. She pounded her pillow into a more comfortable shape and resumed the position—on her side, facing away from the door.

The room phone rang.

"What now?" she hissed. But, it crossed her mind that it might be Lincoln. She yanked the phone off the hook and hurriedly said, "Hello."

"Carlee?"

"Speaking."

"Stuart Adler here."

Carlee's enthusiasm vanished like a wisp of smoke in a strong wind.

"I heard what happened yesterday. How are you doing?"

"I'm fine, Mister Adler. I apologize for having been so secretive with you."

"Don't worry about it in the slightest. Fitz explained it to me. Your job is secure and I'm in no way upset. With this call, I simply wanted you to know you can take as much time as you need. Your job at the agency will be waiting for you."

"Thank you so much for understanding," she replied. She wanted to sound enthusiastic but it came out flat.

"I'll let you rest now. I just wanted to find out how you were doing and, of course, to let you know your job with the agency is secure."

"I appreciate you so much. You're a good man and a great boss."

After exchanging a few more pleasantries, she hung up. As nice as Adler was, she remained uncertain about her future with the agency. She thought of her job as tedious and those thoughts made her feel awful, considering what a nice guy Stuart Adler was and everything Lincoln went through to get her the job. She realized how she felt about her position at the advertising agency was selfish and unfair to people she cared deeply for, especially her daughter and her mother.

She heard sounds in the corridor become more prominent as the door to her room opened yet again, assuming it was the elderly nurse. This time, she did not even turn her head to look. "Honestly, I appreciate your offer to talk, but I really want to be left alone right now."

"Fine," said a male voice. "But, as long as you're not talking, you should eat."

Carlee snapped her head around. "Linc..."

"Mind if I sit and watch you not talk for a while?" He smiled.

Her lip quivered as emotion swarmed her. Tears exploded. She sobbed and, with fully extended arms, clawed at the air with both hands for him to come closer.

Linc clearly needed no additional encouragement and leaned into her open arms, pulling her into a tight hug.

She clutched double fists full of the back of his shirt and held on desperately. She muttered repeatedly, "You came. You came."

"And here is where I belong," he whispered.

"I don't care what you have to tell me, I'm not letting you go," she said, still sobbing.

"You don't have to," he breathed into her ear. "In fact, I won't let you go...ever."

Beth and Rylee came back into the room. Rylee saw Lincoln and brightened. "Mister Bridger," she said and ran the last two steps to him.

Carlee reluctantly allowed Linc to disengage from her embrace.

"I want a hug, too," the youngster said, as she stepped into Lincoln's open arms and pressed her head onto his chest and wrapped her arms around his waist.

Beth came alongside Lincoln and placed a hand on his shoulder. "It looks like Rylee and I may have interrupted a moment."

Carlee chuckled through her tears. "Oh, Mom, you have no idea how true that is."

"If we had to be interrupted," Lincoln said to Rylee, pushing the child's head back with hands on both her cheeks to look into her eyes, "I can't think of anyone I would rather be interrupted by than you."

"I thought I had lost you," Carlee said.

"Someday I'll tell you the whole story. For now, all I need to tell you and all you need to hear is...I love you, Carlee Cayne."

Epilogue

Seven Years Later

"Rylee is a treasure," Lincoln says, as he wallows a toothbrush around in his mouth.

Carlee steps inside the bathroom with him. "I know that. But...how, exactly, do you mean it?"

Toothbrush dangling in his mouth, he turns his head slightly to better see the side of his head in the mirror and fingers his graying sideburns that seem to be a little whiter every day. He pulls the toothbrush from his mouth and expels foamy paste into the sink. "Well, the way I see it, Rylee'll be graduating from high school in May, yet she always makes time for Anna. I remember when I was seventeen. I was extremely selfish with my time, but, God love her, not Rylee. Even when on her way out the door to meet friends, she'll always ask Anna if she would like to tag along. That is so rare for a teenager. She's a precious jewel in your crown, Missus Bridger."

"Your crown, too, Mister Bridger." Carlee steps in closer and thumbs a dribble of toothpaste from his chin. "You are largely responsible for her attitude in that regard, you know. You always made time for Rylee, from the very first time you two were in the same room together. And, you still do. You treated her gently and with respect. *That*, my sweet Linc, is quite rare for an adult male. Now, rinse so I can kiss you."

Lincoln hurriedly draws a cupped palm of water, fills his mouth, rinses, spits, and towels off his mouth. He pulls Carlee into full body contact and kisses her softly, allowing it to linger. "I'd love to spend the day seeing where this might lead, but you and I both have very busy schedules today."

She sighs. "You're right. Let's put a hiatus on this for now. But, this evening, let's pick it back up from this point and *then* see what happens."

He raises one eyebrow, dips his head, and smiles, strongly hinting lust. "No matter how this day may turn out, I'd say the evening hours will be the best part of it." Before releasing his hold on her, he takes a moment to admire her. The years since he met her have been very kind to her. She is still as beautiful as ever. Her hair has grown long, to the center of her back. She lightened the color to a dusty blonde about a year ago and maintains it. The length, color, and style almost perfectly match Rylee's. Carlee and their older daughter could almost pass for twins, most assuredly sisters.

Carlee pushes away and playfully slaps him on the chest. "Okay, we had better stop before this gets out of hand and we end up locking the bedroom door, and being late, possibly extremely late, to meet the day."

Feigning disgust, "Okay," he drawls, following her out of the bathroom through the bedroom. "Let's see if the girls have finished their cereal yet."

At the end of the hall toward the front of the house, they round into the kitchen to see Rylee and six-year-old Anna sitting on stools at the bar separating kitchen from dining and den. Rylee has finished her bowl of cereal and is coaxing Anna to hurry with hers.

"Rylee, you had your first full day with your new car yesterday," Lincoln says. "What do you think? Gonna like it?"

"Oh, Dad," she says coming off the stool, wrapping him in a tight hug. "It's wonderful. It will be exactly what I'll be needing when I go to college next year."

Lincoln notices Carlee's expression has turned bland. "What's the matter, hon? Don't you like Rylee's new car?"

Clearly shaken from a thought, she pops a smile. "Of course I do. I love it. It crossed my mind Dixie used to have a much older version of that same brand and model. I was thinking about it. That's all. It seems like a lifetime ago."

Lincoln nods. "I remember that car well. It was a much different life at the time for both of us." He turns back to Rylee and claps his hands once. "Okay, kiddo, time to get this day underway. Do you mind taking your little sister to school this morning? Your mom and I need to scoot. I promised your mother I would help christen her new office before going on to the agency. She and I need to leave now so I won't be late getting to work."

"Not a problem." She turns her attention to Anna. "Wipe the milk off your mouth and let's go. I can't be late either, not this morning. I have a biology quiz first period and I sure can't afford to miss, or even be late, for that one."

"Okay, okay. I'm hurrying." Anna scoops up a final spoonful and shoves it into her mouth. She then swipes a forearm across her mouth."

"Good grief," Rylee says, "use a napkin, for Pete's sake."

Anna's cheeks redden as she glances at her mom and dad, both nodding agreement with her older sister. "Rylee is right, Punkin," Lincoln tells her. "There's always time for good manners."

The youngster snatches a napkin from the holder on the bar and touches up the forearm job and then wipes the trickle of milk from her arm. She drops off the tall stool to her feet. "Okay. I'm ready. Let's go," she announces.

Rylee puts a guiding hand on her little sister's back toward the front door of their home, in the event Anna suddenly thinks of something she needs to do or somewhere else to go. Time has suddenly become a rapidly shrinking commodity for the whole family. Rylee is making sure that she and her little sister both make a fast bee-line to her new car parked out front. "Y'all have a good day," she tells her parents over her shoulder as she opens the car door. She hesitates, gazing back over the top of her car to her mother and father standing in the open doorway. "And, Mom, congratulations on your new office."

"Thanks, sweetheart. See you early this evening," Carlee says as Rylee drops into the driver's seat. Carlee shouts an afterthought, "And good luck to you on that biology quiz this morning." Rylee and Anna offer vigorous waves as the shiny silver Toyota Corolla speeds away down the street.

"I think I'll grab my purse and follow the girls right on out the door and go to work," Carlee says. She follows with a sly half-grin. "Frankly, I don't trust you and me alone together."

"You got that right." He laughs.

"You *are* still planning to stop by for a few minutes before going on to the agency, right?"

"Of course. I wouldn't miss the beginning of your first full day behind a brand new desk in a brand new office. I'll be right behind you."

"In that case, I'll see you in a few minutes." She gives him a final peck on the lips and heads for her own car.

~ * ~

Lincoln closes and locks the front door of their home behind him. The home sets in an upscale neighborhood near Barton Springs in south Austin, a beautiful place overlooking one of the most scenic areas of the city, no finer location anywhere to raise a family and grow old with the love of his life. When Stuart Adler retired three years ago, Lincoln was offered a partnership which he gleefully accepted, along with managerial duties. The position of managing partner afforded his family the opportunity of a better lifestyle. He hoped he was as good of a boss as Stuart Adler had been. Every day began with aspirations of doing as well as his former boss had done. The company is now known in the advertising world by the name AHL&B Advertising of Austin—the "B" for Bridger. Over the past few years, the agency has opened offices in Houston and San Antonio. The Austin location remains the flagship.

Another great thing, the location of their home happens to be a mere five-minute drive to work every morning. Since Carlee's new office is literally a stone's throw from the agency, her trip to work is only scant seconds less than his. It happens to be next door to his favorite sandwich shop in the same small strip center on the same block as the agency, Sandy's Soup and Sandwich Shop. No doubt, they will share lunch frequently in the months and years to come.

Lincoln leisurely drives away from their home, in no rush. Minutes later, he steers into the parking area fronting the four-business strip center, one of them is Carlee's new office. It had been a small State Farm Insurance office in a previous incarnation. It isn't large but quite efficient, with space enough to add a secretary/researcher at a still-vacant desk, fronting two small side-by-side offices at the rear of the storefront business.

He stops and takes a moment to admire the facility. He sees Carlee through the glass door already at her new desk in one of the offices with her head down, going over paperwork. He steps inside.

"What do you think of the place?" she asks as he surveys all that has changed since they leased it. At that time, it was vacant. Now, it was nicely decorated, while still maintaining all-important functionality.

Nodding his approval, he turns a full circle, taking in everything within view one more time, admiring what Carlee has done with the place. "I am so proud of this business venture. Maintaining your contacts in law enforcement has really paid off."

"I couldn't have done it as quickly, maybe not at all, without Jimmy Fenn's ongoing support. He has pushed a lot of business this way."

"Regardless *how* it began, it doesn't change the fact you are an excellent private investigator. You deserve success." He grins. "Beats the heck out of crunching numbers at the agency all day. Right?"

Carlee snickers. "If it hadn't been for your daily presence, I would not have lasted at that agency job the entire eighteen months. That was the longest eighteen months of my life. But it all worked out and, frankly, if it had not been for that job, I might still be with the US Marshals Service. Although, I missed the freedom the job afforded me, I sure did not, and still don't, miss the job itself."

Lincoln points to a framed photograph hanging on the wall behind her desk. "That's a nice touch. Where did you find it?"

Carlee looks back over her shoulder at an eight-by-ten action photograph of Dixie Vega training her during a martial arts session at the gym some years ago. "I found it when I was cleaning out the bedroom home office, getting ready to move into this one. It was taken by Bobby Dunwoody, the manager of Power House Fitness Center, way back, when he was a new hire. I had it enlarged and framed. You're right. It is a good picture. Do you think where I have it hanging, over my desk, is a good place for it?"

"I absolutely do," he replies, fondly remembering the early days when he first saw a heavily perspiring Carlee Cayne putting martial art moves on the torso of a practice dummy.

~ * ~

Fitz chews on the inside of his cheek in a contemplative frame of mind. He slouches heavily sideways against the car door as he drives, not paying as much attention as he should to the morning traffic. His mind wanders. He promised Linc and Carlee to be on hand for the first morning of business at the new location of the private investigation office. It's not the place he wants to be, but it should work well enough, being around friends and all.

He drifts across the center line of the tree-lined street, eliciting a prolonged horn blast from an approaching garbage truck. He jerk s his body to a better driving posture and swerves hard back into his own lane. "Yeah, yeah. You're mad. So what?" he mumbles to himself. But, after a moment of serious reflection, he figures he better keep his mind in the moment or he would end up like that squirrel he just passed—road kill. That's exactly what would happen if something as large and heavy as that garbage truck should collide with him.

As he comes to a stop in a parking slot at the strip center, he sees Lincoln and Carlee through the large front window, facing one another, carrying on a conversation. Fitz heaves a ragged sigh, uneasy about everything on his mind.

"Fitz," Lincoln calls out to him as he comes through the door. Lincoln spreads his arms wide in a welcoming gesture. "What do you think, my friend? Will this place work?"

Fitz draws a big breath and exhales through rounded lips. Wide-eyed, he nods. "Sure. I guess so."

"Come on, buddy, don't be nervous," Lincoln quickly adds. "Man, it's time to dive in. The water is not as chill as you're thinking it might be. Besides, there is no better time than *right now* to get it done."

"I'll take your word for that," Fitz replies.

"You don't understand," Carlee says, snickering. "The time is *right...now.*"

"Huh?" He frowns quizzically.

Carlee shakes her head and grins. "Don't give me that lost puppy dog face. Turn around and look," she adds, stepping laterally toward Linc, putting her arm around his waist.

Why is Carlee looking at me like I'm an idiot? He turns toward the door and there she stands, having quietly entered. His eyes pop large, as it all suddenly becomes quite clear what Carlee meant. *Oh. Because I am an idiot.* He swallows hard, giving himself time to build confidence. During this moment of courage building, admiration, and love for this woman could be no greater than at this very instant.

Dixie Vega stands with a clear expression of wonder on her face. Beautiful. He thinks back to that day in the hospital seven years ago when he almost lost her forever. Today, beauty and health fully restored, she is a vision. Her glossy black hair is short, quite short and spiky at the crown with a long sweeping bang frequently hanging across one eye. She is not as muscular as she was in her younger years, but lean and lovely.

Fitz sinks to one knee, swallows his fear, and begins, "Ramona Louise Vega, who I love more deeply every day," he says, voice quaking. "I have a question for you that is long overdue. Dixie, will you marry me?

Clearly in shock, Dixie stands frozen, lips parted, tears filling her eyes. The eyelids can hold no more and those tears track, zigzagging down her cheeks. She slowly approaches Fitz and lowers herself onto both knees to his level and whispers, "You know I will." She kisses him and then sits back on her heels. "Took you long enough to get around to it," she says with a giggle while swiping streaming tears from her face.

Fitz bounces a shoulder shrug. "I'm a man of my word. I promised you long ago we would take it slow and really get to know one another, becoming the best of friends first. And, Dixie, you are my best friend in this whole world. But, seven years is long enough, and I think...well, I'm hoping you know me well enough, too, by now."

"If there is something I haven't learned about you yet, we now have a lifetime to explore it together." Dixie looks up at Lincoln and Carlee standing side by side. "Y'all knew this was going to happen this morning, didn't you?"

"Yeah, sweetie, we did," Carlee says. Her eyes glisten with happy tears of her own. "Now, you and I have a wedding to plan."

Fitz stands and helps Dixie to her feet. Fitz shakes Lincoln's hand

and Carlee pulls Dixie into a tight hug. As the girls part, Carlee says, "I called a sign painter yesterday afternoon. Before the day is out today, there will be a professionally painted sign across the front window that will read: Cayne and Vega Private Investigations. I was going to call it Bridger and Vega, but Lincoln wanted it to be all ours and thought Cayne and Vega sounded better anyhow. So, Cayne and Vega it is. What did Power House Fitness say when you told them you were quitting and coming to work here?"

"Bobby, the manager, is having a hard time with it. He got quite emotional about it, actually. We've worked side by side for over eight years. I'll miss seeing him on a daily basis, too, but, for heaven's sake, the fitness center is just across the lake. It's not like I'm leaving Austin. I told him I would still freelance train and help out occasionally. So, he came to accept it." Dixie again hugs Carlee and then turns and puts her head on Fitz's chest. "It's a brand new day...for all of us."

~ * ~

"Boy oh boy, this was quite a day, Carlee," Lincoln says, stroking the top of Anna's head lying in his lap.

Carlee sits at the other end of the sofa facing him with one leg tucked beneath her. She stares at him for a moment. "Early on, when we met, did you ever imagine life would bring us to this point?"

"Believe it or not, that first night at the gym when I saw you doing serious damage to a practice dummy, an image like this moment, popped into my head."

Carlee smiles warmly, continuing to gaze into his eyes.

Lincoln sees and feels the love flow between them.

"Why don't you put Anna to bed and tell her a story," Carlee says. "Rylee should be home any minute. I'll wait up for her and then meet you in *our* bedroom."

He winks at her. "That sounds like an excellent plan." He looks down at six-year-old Anna. "Come on, Punkin. Let's get you to bed."

"Okay," the girl replies. Her movements are sluggish and sleepy, but she makes it to her bedroom with no help and puts her pajamas on.

Lincoln pulls the bedspread down and the youngster climbs onto the bed. He then covers her and tucks her in.

She yawns. "Don't forget, Daddy, Mama promised you'd tell me a story."

"How about a true love story?"

"Sure," she replies with sleepy enthusiasm. "That sounds great. Tell me," she says, and then yawns. Her eyes flutter closed.

"Before you were born there was a man. And, there was a woman who magically appeared before him, once upon an Austin night..."

Life is simply a loosely structured sentence. All lives begin capitalized and end punctuated. Before everything between has been filled in, ask yourself, "What mark shall end mine?"

-Daniel Lance Wright

About the Author

A lifelong Texan, Daniel Lance Wright is a freelance fiction writer and novelist born in Lubbock, Texas now residing in Clifton, Texas. He lives with Rickie, wife of forty-seven years, and the proud father of two and grandfather of four.

Having spent the first nineteen years of his life on a cotton farm on the South Plains of Texas and the next thirty-two in the television industry, he has seen the world from two distinctly different angles.

Daniel has received recognition for writing skills from The Oklahoma Writers Federation in 2005, 2006, 2010, and 2011, Art Affair in 2008, Frontiers in Writing in 2004, Canis Latran of Weatherford College in 2011, and from The Indie Excellence Book Awards in 2013.

Beware the Bones

Forty-three-year-old archaeologist, Jasmine Chandler, is decimated by an abruptly failed marriage and throws herself obsessively into her work. Meanwhile, several hundred miles away on the California coast, retired oncologist, Lowell Strudemeyer, struggles against his own demons by drinking and surfing with an apparent death wish. With he lp from her friend, Barbara Sullivan, their worlds collide over an ancient burial site and it takes a little magic for these two people, Sweetpea and The Strude, to confess their obvious attraction.

Chapter One
Uncle Lowell's Letter

Today

"I wish Aunt Jasmine could have been here," said Cindy Wayne to her elderly mother.

"Me too, Sweetheart, but you know she can't." Beverly Wayne reached across and placed a hand on Cindy's forearm. She smiled at her forty-two-year-old daughter. "The chance that Jasmine can remain lucid long enough to hear your uncle Lowell's last will read is not possible, I'm afraid. Mentally, she's slipped too far since your Uncle Lowell died."

"Oh, I understand that. It's just that I never had a chance to know either one of them."

Attorney, Phil Dobbins, the only lawyer in Arroyo Vista,

California, had been nodding agreement, finally adding, "She's right, Cindy. But, before Lowell passed away and while Jasmine was in a better state of mind, they agreed it was important you be part of these proceedings because you are specifically included in the will."

Cindy suddenly bolted to an upright posture. "I am?"

"Uh-huh, you sure are." Dobbins leaned back in the overstuffed chair behind his glossy cherry wood desk. The leather squawked as he reclined toward a floor-to-ceiling book shelf loaded with volume sets of law books.

"I'm curious, too," Beverly said.

"It shouldn't come as a real shock to either of you, since Jasmine had no family and you, Beverly, are the widowed wife of Lowell's only brother. That leaves you, Cindy, as the only blood relative."

"Well, maybe not a 'real shock', but I'm somewhat surprised because my husband was never close to his brother," Beverly countered. "I would've thought he'd left everything to others he knew better."

Cindy pushed out her lower lip and shrugged her shoulders. "I suppose it makes sense. We are his only family after all. Still, I'm grateful just to be remembered."

Phil came back to an upright position and dropped his arms to the desktop on either side of the document titled: Last Will and Testament of Lowell Wayne. "Then let's get that curiosity satisfied, shall we? I'll read the will."

Cindy and her mother settled back and relaxed, ready for whatever information might be revealed.

Attorney Phil Dobbins tore a paper seal on the bound document and began to read, "'Being of sound mind and body, I, Lowell James Wayne, declare this to be my last will and testament...'" Dobbins read uninterrupted for almost ten minutes. Provisions were made for Jasmine's livelihood and care for the remainder of her life and an archaeology endowment was to be given to the University of Southern California in the name of a Professor Barbara Shandlin posthumously.

And, then, Mister Dobbins came to the part of Lowell's wishes that concerned his deceased brother's family, Beverly and her daughter Cindy. Beverly inherited Lowell and Jasmine's home located on the beach along the coast highway south of Arroyo Vista. She would be free to sell it or live in it, her choice.

Finally, Dobbins paused, looked to Cindy and said, "And, now, for the part you were so curious about." He, again, began to read, "...And to my only niece, Cynthia Ann Wayne, and my only living blood relative, I leave sole ownership of my novel, Beware the Bones. She will be entitled to all royalties from the date of my death into perpetuity."

Hesitatingly, "Uh, okay, that's nice...I guess," Cindy said.

Dobbins clearly saw her lack of understanding or appreciation of what it was she now owned. He smiled and pulled an envelope from beneath the document he'd been reading from. "It's not my place to tell you *why* Lowell thought it so important you own the book and all rights to it, although I'm fully aware of what he believed. If I attempted to explain it, then that might infer I believe it. I can't say that I do."

"You make it sound like something incredible."

"Personally, I think it is. It pushes my ability to suspend disbelief a bit too far," he said.

Mother and daughter looked at one another, then Beverly asked, "What, exactly, are you trying to tell us?"

"This might answer that question." Dobbins slid the envelope toward Cindy. "It's your turn to read. This is a personal letter dictated to my secretary by Lowell over a year ago and was meant for your eyes, Cindy. There are no restrictions on sharing it with your mother, or anyone else for that matter, but you might opt to keep it from people outside the family after you've read it. That will be entirely your decision."

Cindy snatched the envelope from the desk. "I've got to know why Uncle Lowell thought a fictional story was so important for me to own." She added, mumbling, "Although I'm sure I'll enjoy those royalty checks."

Beverly snickered.

Cindy began to read aloud.

"'My dearest Cynthia, twenty-two years ago something happened to Jasmine that involved her friend Barbara Shandlin and me. As of this writing, I still wonder on occasion if I didn't dream it all. You may find it ridiculously absurd but, God as my witness, much of what you'll read is true. As traumatic as it was and crazy as it sounds, life actually improved following the ordeal. It ended my self-destructive ways and gave me Jasmine as the love of my new life.

'At that time, it was an undeserved blessing that I made it to my sixty-first year, considering the over-indulgence and self-abuse. One huge difference in me, coming out of the experience, was that I no longer claimed to be a skeptic, about anything. My mind had been opened to a new world of possibilities. Life as a doctor taught me pragmatism, believing only what could be proven. I was to learn that there are things in the heavens and upon earth that defy rationality, yet exist.

'I was compelled to chronicle the events in print but as I finished the draft, I came to realize no one would believe such a fantastic account. Furthermore, my sanity would have been questioned. That was certainly not something I wanted shadowing me the rest of my life. I didn't want to confine the truth to whispers either. I believed it was something that should have been shouted loud and proud. Yet, I could not. I had no desire to become an attraction for psychiatrists as an example of the classically insane or, at least, delusional. I felt trapped.

'So, why do it? It was a compulsion that could not be denied. It drew me to the word processor keyboard day after day until I'd written it. But then what? Put it away in a drawer someplace? I couldn't see that happening. That's when it occurred to me I could fictionalize it and make a novel of it. That way I could make it as public as I wanted with no repercussions, maybe even get it published, which I eventually did. I used a safe plot device to get the story out which, of course, is true.

'It was wonderfully cathartic. When Beware the Bones was finished and published, I had gained clarity. Until that time, I didn't know what to believe. Now I do. I believe it with all my heart.

'Although sounding somewhat grim at times, there is a bigger story within Beware the Bones, one of love and how it always seems to find a way. This I tested in the most severe way imaginable and concluded I have myself as empirical evidence of such truth. I'll take it a step further and say no one anywhere has ever taken this route to romance and marriage. I feel safe in making it a definitive statement of fact.

'Next to my desk at home, alone on an eye-level shelf of an *étagére* against the wall sets an ancient skull in a place of prominence. It deserved respect. To this day, the cranial remains are displayed like a trophy under a glass dome resting upon a circle of black-on-white marble. A small golden plate on the base is inscribed with "Protecting Xi (shee)."

'It was the skull of a man I came to know, in a round-about way, even beyond the initial encounter and for years to come after Jasmine and I were married. I spoke to it often, calling it by the name I'd given it, Jag. Jag is short for jaguar. Within the plot of Beware the Bones, the reason for the name will be made clear to you.

'Before I knew Jag, I would have considered communicating with a man, dead for thousands of years, the ridiculous ramblings of an idolatrous pagan whose cheese had slipped off his cracker. There was a time I also considered my prospects for marrying again nil.

'I stared often into the empty eye sockets of the skull, trying to visualize the man it once had been, even to the point of carrying on one-sided conversations with the remains. Once, I remember saying, "I don't know how you did it, Jag, but if it weren't for you, old friend, I would definitely not be married and most certainly would be well on my way to cirrhosis of the liver." The bony orb, in time, became my strength to prevent a relapse to dim-witted ways. Deep in my own bones, I damn well knew Jag was never far from Jasmine or me.

'Please, dear Cynthia, even if you cannot believe Beware the Bones after you've read it, then by all means, enjoy the royalties. This is my legacy I leave to you. Most sincerely, and with love, Uncle Lowell.'"

Cindy slowly returned the letter to the desktop. "I'm still confused. The letter doesn't explain much, other than something really odd happened to them."

Attorney Phil Dobbins opened the desk drawer to his right and retrieved a book. He laid it on the table, shoving it sliding across the desk to Cindy. "Read the book."

"Beware the Bones?"

"Yep."

"Do you think answers are in it?" Beverly asked.

"Answers, yes. The truth of it I'll leave for you to determine."

Cindy lifted the book, pulled it near and opened the fresh-from-the-printer copy of her Uncle Lowell's one and only novel. She looked to her mother. "Well, I know what I'll be doing in my spare time next week. This ought to be fun."

FOR THE FULL INVENTORY
OF QUALITY BOOKS:
http://www.roguephoenixpress.com

Rogue Phoenix Press
Representing Excellence in Publishing

Quality trade paperbacks and downloads
in multiple formats,
in genres ranging from historical to contemporary romance, mystery
and science fiction.
Visit the website then bookmark it.
We add new titles each month!

www.ingramcontent.com/pod-product-compliance
Lightning Source LLC
Chambersburg PA
CBHW051424170626
46809CB00006B/2304